CONTENTS

Dear Reader,

Those of you who read my books know that these days I write contemporary romantic thrillers as Jayne Ann Krentz, historical romantic suspense as Amanda Quick and futuristics as Jayne Castle. At the start of my career, however, I wrote classic battle-of-the-sexes-style romance using both my Krentz name and the pen name Stephanie James. This volume contains two stories from that time.

I want to take this opportunity to thank all of you—new readers as well as those who have been with me from the start. I appreciate your interest in my books.

Sincerely,

Jayne Ann Krentz

CORPORATE AFFAIR

CHAPTER ONE

IT WAS THE sound of his voice that first caught at her attention, tugged at her awareness. A deep, darkly timbered voice that elicited a curious desire to follow it and discover the man to whom it belonged.

Kalinda Brady walked hesitantly through the small, empty shop, her gray-eyed glance roving absently over the eclectic collection of watercolors of local scenes from the Colorado Rockies, wood carvings, and some woven wall hangings. The name of the little store was The Mountain Gallery and Kalinda had made three trips to it this morning before finding it open.

It was almost noon now and, not having much else to do in the tiny, Colorado mountain resort town, Kalinda had made one last trip down the short street of rustic boutiques and crafts stores. Sure enough, this time the owner had seen fit to finally open his doors to potential customers.

But while the door stood invitingly open, there was no one inside. A voice called to her, though, as Kalinda tripped the shop bell.

"I'm out in the back! Yell if there's anything you want!"

The masculine voice came through the door on the far side of the small room and Kalinda walked toward it, her curiosity getting the better of her.

She moved across the sunlit floor with an easy, confident stride that said a great deal about her personality. At twenty-nine and with the recent success she'd had of taking over the reins of her father's firm in Denver, Kalinda didn't normally lack confidence. One couldn't and still retain leadership of a major business. Still, her natural self-honesty forced her to admit that thoughts of what she was going to do this weekend here in the picturesque, lakeside village sapped even her healthy store of assurance.

But her outward demeanor remained unruffled and coolly controlled. The chic, casual cotton tuxedo shirt she wore was open at the neck to reveal a thin strand of gold around her throat. The shirt was paired with khaki trousers done with a designer's touch. The sophisticated tailoring revealed a slender, supple body. The high breasts were small but firm and gently rounded. The feminine hips flared with a fullness Kalinda had always wished was a little less so but which fairly screamed her femininity from within the confines of the narrow-legged trousers. The short, wooden-heeled sandals which arched her well-shaped feet came from Italy.

As she walked the sunlight filtering through the trees and into the window danced briefly on the wealth of brown-blond hair which had been neatly twisted into a knot behind one ear. The strict style revealed a strong, composed face, the features of which were less than beautiful. Instead of flagrant beauty, the intelligent gray eyes, straight, proud nose and readily curving mouth combined into a subtly attractive countenance which drew the attention of the more perceptive.

Kalinda wore both the expensive clothes and the inner assurance with a naturalness that spelled success. She had worked hard for that success and it annoyed her for some reason when others didn't work hard as well. Others such as the owner of The Mountain Gallery who didn't bother to keep regular hours. There was a look of mild disapproval in her eyes as she came to a halt on the threshold of the back door and took in the sight before her.

"I'll be with you in a minute. See anything you like?"

The owner of the heavily shaded voice glanced up from the body of a rainbow trout lying on a wooden bench. There was a stack of such unfortunate fish at the far end of the bench. A hose trickled water over the silvery scales as each awaited its turn under the knife. Kalinda unconsciously curled her lip in disgust.

"You're supposed to compliment me on the nice catch," the shop's owner informed her politely, hazel eyes laughing at her expression. "Not look at me as if I were an ax murderer!"

In spite of herself, Kalinda grinned in response. "Those poor fish are, I presume, the reason you're three hours' late opening the shop?"

"If I'd known I had such an eager customer waiting I would have hurried," he drawled, the knife in his hand going to work efficiently on the fish in front of him. Kalinda looked away.

Her curious gaze rested on the bent head of the man in front of her, noting the dark fire in the thick, chestnut hair which was carelessly combed and a little long for her taste. The man stood naked from the waist up in the bright sunlight, his lean, smoothly muscled body well-bronzed. When she found her glance lingering on the curling red-brown hair which covered his chest and tapered down to disappear beneath the waistband of a faded pair of snug-fitting jeans, she looked away from the sight, also.

Which brought her gaze back to his profile. She found herself studying it with the same curiosity that had made her want to follow the sound of his voice.

It was an angular face, sharply etched and tanned like the rest of him. The hazel eyes were deep-set and flickered with intelligence when he glanced up and caught her watching him. Tiny lines crinkled the corners beneath heavy brows. An arrogant nose paired well with high cheekbones and a mouth which seemed hard in repose.

But the mouth smiled easily, she saw, and the deep lines at the edges bespoke a wealth of experience. She found herself wondering just what sort of experience, however. There was nothing polished or sophisticated about this man. And he definitely wasn't the sort she had expected to encounter running an art gallery, even if that gallery was in an isolated mountain town which catered to tourists. Her curiosity grew.

He must have been around thirty-seven or thirty-eight, she reflected absently. She sensed a latent male power in him and wondered how he could have been content to waste his life running a part-time gallery and fishing when the urge took him. In her world, given a little business experience, such a man could have built an empire. She knew it instinctively.

Well, hers was not to judge, Kalinda told herself firmly, knowing she was doing it anyway. He was probably a leftover from the antimaterialistic, anti-establishment era of a few years back. A man who lacked the basic drive and competitive inclination it took to make it to the top.

"I wanted to ask about that watercolor of the lake hanging in the window," she told him politely.

"You like it?" he inquired interestedly, pausing in his work to eye her.

"I know someone who will," she temporized.

"You *don't* like it," he stated, nodding. He went back to cleaning the trout.

"I'm not buying it for myself."

"What's this friend like? The one you're buying it for?"

"Does it matter?" she asked dryly. "Are you worried the painting won't be going to a good home?"

"I'm not worried about it, but Mary Beth will be," he explained with seeming patience.

"Mary Beth being the artist, I presume?" Kalinda hazarded.

"Umm. She's very particular about who gets her paintings."

"I see. I didn't think artists could afford that sort

of luxury. Tell Mary Beth that I'm buying it to give to a kindly, distinguished, older couple who grew up in Colorado and treasure scenes such as that one."

"I guess that sounds safe enough. Okay, you can have it."

"I can't tell you how thrilled I am that you're willing to part with it," she muttered, thinking if she hadn't been stuck in town anyway, she would never have made three trips to the gallery in order to buy the painting.

He laughed, a rich, full-bodied laughter that filled the yard in which he was standing. "Give me a chance to wash the evidence off my hands and I'll come inside and take your money. My name's Rand Alastair, by the way. What's yours?"

Kalinda blinked, surprised at the straightforward question from a stranger she never intended to see again. "Kalinda. Kalinda Brady."

He nodded. "On vacation?" He turned away to wash his hands under the hose, his body moving with a litheness Kalinda found unexpectedly pleasing.

"Not exactly," she replied unthinkingly and then wished she'd held her tongue. The last thing she wanted was a drawn-out discussion of her reasons for being in town!

"Business?" Rand pursued, coming toward her with a rather persistent expression.

"It's a personal matter," she replied, letting her annoyance show.

It didn't seem to faze him. "I see. Are you here by yourself?"

"I don't think that's any of your business," she told him gently, knowing any one of her employees would have immediately backed off after hearing that tone of voice.

To her surprise, Rand had the grace to wince. "Sorry, I still do that once in a while."

"Still do what?" Kalinda looked at him blankly, not understanding the remark. He led her back into the gallery.

"Never mind. Want a cold beer? It's going to get warm this afternoon."

She started to decline but Rand was already opening a small refrigerator against the back wall and rummaging around inside. He straightened with two chilled cans in his hand and popped the tops on both before Kalinda could think of a polite excuse. "Here you go."

She peered down at the can skeptically as it was thrust into her hand, then tried an experimental sip. It wasn't chilled, dry Chenin Blanc, but it wasn't bad on a warm afternoon in the mountains. She took another sip and glanced up to find her host grinning at her.

"Think of it as getting back to basics," he murmured and took a long, satisfying swallow. "Now let's see, I've got that price list around here somewhere...."

Beer in hand, Rand rummaged around in the drawer behind the counter, eventually producing a scrap of paper with a triumphant air. "I knew it was here!"

"Congratulations," Kalinda couldn't resist saying a little tartly. What a way to run a business! Any business!

He ignored the comment as if accustomed to the rudeness of visitors and gave her the price of the painting.

It was a bit higher than Kalinda had expected and automatically she glanced around to take another look at the watercolor landscape. As she did a charming pottery bowl caught her eye.

"Oh, I like that!" she exclaimed with genuine enthusiasm, walking across the room to lift the well-molded object. It fit nicely in her hand and the earthen colors were perfect for her dining room. "I can see this now filled with a lovely curry and rice dish or maybe a huge green salad."

She raised her head and found Rand watching her intently. "I'll take this, too," she said easily, carrying it back to the counter. "And you needn't worry about it. It's going to a good home."

"Yours?" he smiled.

"Mine," she confirmed, digging out her checkbook.

She hid a small frown as Rand calmly accepted her check without bothering to check her identification and then told herself it was his business. If he chose to take such risks who was she to tell him different?

"I'll wrap those in paper for you before you leave," he announced cheerfully, coming around from behind the counter.

"As a matter of fact," Kalinda said pointedly, "I was just about to go. Perhaps you could put the paper around them now?"

"Finish your beer first. Unless someone's waiting for you?" he added innocently.

"Well, no, but…" Too late she realized she'd just answered his earlier question about whether or not she was in town alone. Half-irritated and half-amused over the small trap, she met his laughing eyes.

"Believe me," he soothed, "there's not much else to do in town once you've been through the shops. Unless, of course, you're into fishing…."

"Not particularly," she sighed.

"I thought not. Come on outside and sit under a tree while I finish cleaning the fish. You might as well relax while you finish the beer…."

"Mr. Alastair," Kalinda began firmly, still unable to decide if she should laugh or treat him to one of her more repressive tones. But she was finding his unabashed persistence almost entertaining. And heaven knew she needed a bit of entertainment to take her mind off her own plans!

"Be nice," he pleaded with a beguiling smile that weakened her further. "Everyone likes to show off his catch. And I can tell by looking at you that you're bored and restless."

"Is it that obvious?" she groaned, following him back out into the yard.

"Let's just say you look a little out of your element," he said softly, waving her to a redwood chair under a tree. "But don't fret, I'm relatively harmless. I can produce any number of local references." He picked up a fish and threw her a quick leer.

Kalinda took a long sip of beer and silently lifted one faintly quelling eyebrow. Rand didn't appear to notice. Instead he chatted amiably, his knife moving expertly on the trout.

Afterward, Kalinda had to admit she wasn't quite sure how it had happened, but she wound up sitting under a tree with a can of beer and watching a man clean fish until nearly one o'clock in the afternoon. No one who knew her back in Denver would have believed it. But then no one back in Denver would have believed it. But then no one back in Denver could possibly know how desperately she was trying to kill the rest of this day and the next.

The light, easy conversation proved a tonic for her, succeeding in taking her mind off her inner, churning thoughts and giving her a temporary respite from the case of nerves she was in danger of contracting.

"What do you do in Denver?" Rand demanded casually at one point after giving her a humorous description of the life he led running a gallery in a tourist town.

"I run a company called Brady Data Processing," she admitted mildly, her cool confidence implicit in her voice. It was, after all, something she did very well.

"I've heard of it," he astonished her by admitting calmly. "You're in charge?" There was a speculative gleam in the quick glance he tossed over at her.

"I was elected chief executive officer a couple of years ago after my father was killed in a plane crash. I sort of inherited the reins. The board of directors was used to having a Brady at the helm," she shrugged. "I'm surprised you've heard of the company."

"We're not totally isolated up here," he informed her dryly.

"Could have fooled me," Kalinda laughed.

He swung around. "You are bored, aren't you? What are you doing here in our little burg, Kalinda Brady?"

"I think you already asked me that," she retorted blandly, feeling as if he'd almost caught her off guard with the question.

"And you didn't answer. Don't you know you're making me curious?"

"It will liven up your rather placid lifestyle."

He laughed, clearly enjoying the day and her. Kalinda felt herself relax and put her problem temporarily aside. More time slipped past until, conscious of having missed lunch, she finally stood up reluctantly and tossed the beer can into a nearby container.

"Well, thanks for the beer, Rand. I think it's time I was on my way. If you'll wrap the painting and the pottery, I'll…"

"I'll have them ready this evening," he drawled smoothly as he finished with the fish.

"This evening!"

"When you help me eat the evidence of my murder spree."

"Rand, I don't think…"

"Fresh trout? Grilled corn? How can you resist?

And you've already admitted you're bored," he coaxed, hazel eyes fastening on her with determination.

"Kalinda mentally ran through all the reasons she co⸱ldn't have dinner with him and found it a very short list. Why shouldn't she accept? She had a long evening to get through by herself if she refused and that thought wasn't very appealing. Alone with her plans and worries...

He met her eyes and smiled. Kalinda drew in her breath, aware that he'd seen the hesitation in her. Once again it struck her that this man might have been a formidable figure in the business world if he'd chosen that path in life. He knew how to manipulate others. Or was it just that she was willing to be manipulated that afternoon?

"All right," she agreed gently. "Thank you."

"I'll pick you up at six. My home is down by the lake," he said.

It wasn't until she had left the shop to return to her motel that Kalinda wondered which of them was intent on fighting off a boring evening. Could it be that Rand Alastair was a little restless, too? But that didn't make any sense. He had obviously chosen to live in this out-of-the-way town of his own accord. And he clearly enjoyed his fishing. Well, it wasn't her problem. She had her own!

· She chose the perfect little summer dress she had brought with her, a wrapped and ruffled silk crepe de chine print. It was bare, breezy and, combined with strappy little sandals, even flirty in a sophisticated way. She left her hair in the sleek twist behind her ear and added a gold wire of a bracelet to her bare arm. She wasn't going out of her way to dress for Rand Alastair. Kalinda liked clothes and she dressed to please herself.

She was prepared to find Rand in a clean pair of jeans and a shirt when she opened the door to him a little before six, but the subtle, pin-striped shirt and dark slacks looked expensive and well-tailored. The thick, chestnut hair was combed back in a broad wave and there was a clean, masculine scent of aftershave clinging tantalizingly around him. Still, it was the white Lotus behind him in the parking lot which took Kalinda aback.

"Yours?" she murmured unnecessarily as he guided her toward it with a casually possessive hand at the small of her back.

"It was either this or the motorcycle." He grinned engagingly. "And somehow I had a hunch you'd object to the bike." His eyes ran approvingly over the little flirty dress. "Although it might have been interesting…"

"The Lotus is fine," she told him dryly as he slipped her into the cockpit of the low-slung car. Her eyes narrowed slightly as she watched him walk around the hood. The gallery must be doing better than it looked, she decided. But that didn't make any sense….

"Why do I have this feeling that I'm turning out to be a source of amusement for you?" Rand asked sometime later as he pan-fried the fresh trout over the

open flame of a barbecue pit. The corn he was grill-
ing alongside gave off an enticing aroma.

"Don't you want me to enjoy myself?" she retorted, crossing her slender ankles as she reclined on
the outdoor lounger. The shaded patio was situated to
take full advantage of the tree-rimmed lake and privately Kalinda knew the glass-walled house with its
elegant, rustic lines had been another surprise to her.

It went with the Lotus, however. The wood-and-
glass structure was obviously designed just for the
particular, wooded, hillside lot on which it had been
placed. The walk through the entryway and living
room out to the patio had revealed a plush, cream
carpet, low, sleekly styled caramel and brown furniture and a scattering of beautiful, earth-toned pottery
pieces. Rand had merely smiled when she'd commented on them.

"Don't get me wrong," he said in response to her
flippant question. "I'm delighted to have you enjoy
yourself. It's just that I'd prefer the amusement to be
a shared experience!"

Kalinda gave him a slow, teasing smile as she
sipped at the tartly delicious concoction of apricot
brandy, lemon and orange juice he'd prepared for
them. "Are you artistic types always so sensitive?"

"Are you vacationing business executives always
so condescending to the local peasantry?"

There was an edge on the darkly timbered voice
that made Kalinda wonder if her new acquaintance
might not appreciate knowing he was merely a means
of getting through a difficult evening.

"You seem to eat rather well for a peasant," she murmured, glancing pointedly at the sizzling trout. "Off the land, as it were."

He grinned, a slashing, faintly predatory expression which sent a trickle of unease through her. Kalinda deliberately banished the unwelcome sensation. Rand Alastair was no threat to her and certainly not her chief concern.

"The trout may be free, but how do you know I didn't spend my last cent on the wine in a desperate effort to impress you?"

"Did you?"

"Not quite," he admitted, casting a rueful look at the bottle of Chardonnay chilling nearby.

"I didn't think so. That little gallery you run in town appears to be bringing in enough to keep you from starving to death," Kalinda commented.

"You sound as if you don't understand how that's possible," he retorted, examining the trout with a critical eye and giving the pan a gentle shake.

"Well, your hours do seem a bit erratic. And even if they were regular there doesn't seem to be a lot of potential customers up here."

"During the winter we get a very well-to-do ski crowd."

"Ah. I understand. It's a seasonal business."

"The gallery? A bit. Not that I let it affect my erratic business practices unduly. I get in my share of skiing!"

Kalinda shook her head. "Well, each to his own. You seem to live a very relaxed sort of lifestyle."

"Exactly. Just as you're supposed to do when you come up here. But you're not, are you?"

"Relaxed? At the moment I'm very comfortable," she countered firmly, taking another sip of the icy highball and preparing to parry his probing questions.

"Oh, you look the part, all right. Very cool and elegantly casual. But there's something about you that doesn't seem really relaxed. You're not nervous of me, by any chance?" he demanded interestedly.

"Of course not!" Her light laughter was genuine.

"You don't have to be so emphatic about it!" he growled wryly.

"Sorry," she mocked contritely. 'I forgot about the ever-present male ego."

Rand shot her a quick, perusing glance as he hefted the pepper mill. "Tell me the truth," he grumbled humorously, "did you accept my offer of dinner because I represent a change of pace from your usual run of admirers?"

"Isn't that what a vacation is for? A change of pace?" she chuckled, enjoying the banter.

"I knew it," he groaned dramatically. "I'm fated to be a vacation fling!"

"Don't worry," Kalinda smiled. "Giving me dinner doesn't exactly put you into the category of a fling!"

"Good," he said smoothly. "Because we artistic types prefer to think in terms of *affairs,* not flings!"

Kalinda's gray eyes went a little cold. "I'm afraid having diner is not a prelude to an affair, either," she informed him quite firmly.

He watched her curiously for a moment, raising

his own golden drink for a sip. "You don't like the idea of being the mistress of an artist-fisherman?"

"Not particularly!" The haughty tone was cool and definite.

"But all artists have mistresses. It's part of the mystique," he explained helpfully.

She let her budding annoyance show in her voice as Rand turned back to the trout. "Perhaps you can consider our association as a change of pace for yourself, then," she suggested deliberately.

"Yes, ma'am," he agreed humbly. Once again Kalinda felt a moment of unease. She had been quite certain since meeting Rand Alastair that she knew exactly what she was dealing with. But little things kept taking her by surprise. It was unsettling.

"Think of it as a case of two ships passing in the night," she advised blandly.

"A pity. I've been weaving artistic fantasies since I looked up and saw you scowling at me in the door of the shop," he grinned, reaching for plates on which to dish up the fish.

"Are you an artist?" she questioned, deciding it was time to switch conversational topics. "Or do you just run the gallery?"

"I dabble," he admitted, setting the food on the redwood table and lifting the wine out of the chiller.

"In what?" she asked, getting out of the lounger and coming across to join him at the table. The combination of crisp salad, fresh trout, and grilled corn was whetting her appetite as no restaurant meal could have done.

"Pottery," he replied succinctly, taking his seat. "I did the piece you bought this afternoon."

"You did! Why didn't you say something? It's lovely! I adore art that serves a purpose," she confided. "I know that's not a proper approach, but I was born with this depressingly practical streak. I like things to be both functional and beautiful. I'm going to get a lot of use out of that bowl."

"Good," he said cheerfully. "I feel exactly the same way. Perhaps I'm more properly described as a craftsperson than an artist?"

"A meaningless distinction," Kalinda declared regally, going to work delicately on the trout. "Why should useful art be downgraded to a 'craft'?"

"My sentiments exactly," he smiled, looking quite pleased with himself. "I'll show you some of the other pieces I've done after dinner. That is, if you'd like to see them?"

She met his encouraging glance and smiled warmly. "Of course, I would."

A short, potent silence hung between them for an instant as they looked at each other. Kalinda found herself swallowing with a new twinge of uncertainty. What was wrong with her? She wasn't interested in this man except as a casual dinner date. Why this new restlessness which had begun to temporarily replace the nervousness she'd been experiencing? This new sensation had nothing at all to do with her plans for the coming weekend. The confrontation with David Hutton still awaited her. It should be the uppermost concern in her mind. Yet here she was being subtly overtaken by an altogether different mood.

Irritably she gave a mental shrug and made a deliberate effort to pull back from the spell she sensed her host was trying to weave. They were exactly what she'd described a few minutes earlier, two strangers who happened to encounter each other briefly but who shared nothing lasting or binding. A casual dinner engagement.

"I'll bet you're telling yourself I'm not your type," Rand murmured easily, taking a bite off the corn cob. He didn't appear concerned by his accurate guess.

"Why not?" she countered breezily. "If you're honest with yourself, you'd be saying the same thing. We are two very different kinds of people, aren't we, Rand?" Firmly she tried to make him acknowledge that basic fact.

"Who can say? We've hardly gotten to know each other. Even if that were so, would it matter?"

"Oh, yes, it matters," she nodded.

"Meaning that you're much too practical to risk getting involved with a man who doesn't fit readily into your lifestyle?"

Kalinda decided it was time to take charge of the situation. Taking charge was something she did instinctively and well. "How long have you worked with pottery, Rand?"

He hesitated, as if trying to decide whether or not to let her change the topic. And then he lifted one smoothly muscled shoulder as if it wasn't all that important, after all.

"Nearly two years. I have a kiln in my workshop over there." He indicated a small building behind the house. "Are you sure you wouldn't rather talk about us?"

"Very sure," she smiled coolly.

"What can a host do except defer to the wishes of his guest?" he whispered gallantly.

"Thank you," Kalinda retorted with the self-possession that comes from regularly having her wishes deferred to by others. "The trout is delicious."

They lingered over dinner as the waning summer sun settled behind the mountain, casting the lake and its environs into shadows. The tall pine and fir among which the house nestled rustled lightly in the faint breeze and the bottle of Chardonnay slowly emptied. It was turning into a very pleasant evening, Kalinda decided, wondering how that could be when she had so much on her mind. But tonight Rand Alastair was making it possible for her to put her doubts and worries about the weekend aside for a while. She was grateful to him for it.

He displayed his pottery with an unaffected pleasure later after Kalinda had helped him clear the table and carry the dishes into the modern, compact kitchen. She went from piece to piece, genuinely admiring the warm colors, rich glazes, and original design.

"You're very talented," she remarked, carefully setting down the small pot she was holding and wondering privately how he could possibly make a living off the pottery and the gallery. She knew a lot about business, even if she didn't know a great deal about the specific business of running a small art and craft store.

"It's a hobby," he murmured as she turned around to face him. He was standing very close behind her, much closer than she had realized and Kalinda found herself swinging softly against his chest. His arms were around her even as she opened her lips to apologize. The impact sent a small shock through her and her gray eyes widened.

"I'm sorry," she managed, suddenly, fiercely aware of the warmth and strength in his lean, hard body. "I didn't realize you were standing so near…"

"My fault entirely," he assured her, his arms tightening around her, pulling her closer with a forcefulness she would have said earlier wasn't in character. "I've been looking for an excuse to kiss you all evening…."

Kalinda saw the lambent flame beginning to flare in the clear hazel gaze above her and wondered at her own reaction. It was curiosity, she decided, which was going to hold her still for his kiss. The same curiosity that had made her follow the sound of his voice that morning. There was something different about this man.

Before she had time to analyze the difference, Rand's mouth was covering her own.

Kalinda sensed the power in the arms which held her and knew with a rush of realism that, even if she hadn't been curious, she would still be standing in his embrace, awaiting his kiss. She knew in that moment that she couldn't have broken Rand's hold.

CHAPTER TWO

KALINDA WASN'T CERTAIN exactly what she was expecting from Rand's kiss, but it definitely wasn't the gentle, persuasive aggression she got. His kiss was a contradiction, she thought vaguely as her fingertips automatically came up to brace against the broad shoulders. Or was it? Could a man be both gentle and aggressive at the same time?

The warm, probing caress grew around her, enveloping her senses even as she tried to retain some control over herself and him. It was like stepping into an inviting pool of water only to discover silvery quicksand beneath one's feet.

"There's cool silk on the surface," he husked against her lips. "But I have a hunger to find out what's underneath…"

"Rand, please, I…" Kalinda's small effort to halt the soft invasion collapsed as his tongue parted her lips.

She heard him groan, felt his hands slide down the bare silk dress to her waist and was unable to repress the little shiver of excitement that coursed through her.

Her mouth yielded to the heated challenge with a

will of its own. Rand's tongue explored the sweet, intimate interior as a jungle cat seeks out a forest den. His lips moved on hers, forcing a dampening, electric contact that denied any attempt at retreat on her part.

Kalinda grew a little shocked at her own response. This wasn't like her, as any of her recent escorts could have testified! Even with David it hadn't been this sudden, this overwhelming....

Rand's fingers dipped lower, shaping the curve of her waist, pressing with growing urgency into the flare of her lips. He pulled her abruptly closer, nestling her into the cradle of his thighs and Kalinda sucked in her breath on a low moan of surprise mingled with dismay.

"Don't be afraid of me," he growled coaxingly. "I won't hurt you." His hands moved on her, sliding along the thin silk and leaving a trail of warmth on hips and thighs and waist. He felt her tremble and she heard his sigh of pleasure.

"We've been building toward this from the moment we met," he whispered, seeking the edge of her mouth with his lips and then beginning to track the line of her cheek to the corner of her closed eyes. "I spent all afternoon thinking about taking you in my arms."

"I...I hope you didn't shut the gallery again on my account!" she managed a little shakily. She wasn't surprised to hear him admit he'd wanted to kiss her from the start. She was old enough to know men often reacted quickly to a woman who caught their fancy. It was her own appallingly swift reaction that alarmed her. The moment she'd felt his arms go around her she'd known a strange kind of longing. And that was definitely not normal for her!

"Had to," he muttered on a laughing groan. "How could I work when all I could think about was feeding you and plying you with liquor?"

"Oh, Rand, this is ridiculous!"

"No," he countered thickly, the tip of his tongue dancing lightly in and around her ear, "this is desire. I told you I needed a mistress…"

"Then you'll have to keep interviewing bored lady tourists," she flung back with a trace of acid in her voice. "The trout was delicious but it was only worth a good-night kiss, not a night in bed!"

"Ah, well," he murmured philosophically, "I shall have to be satisfied with what I can get."

He lifted one hand and slipped off the small, gold earring she wore in her left ear. He dropped the earring into his pocket as his teeth closed teasingly, temptingly where the piece of jewelry had been.

It was a small, seemingly insignificant action, yet when he repeated it with the other ear, Kalinda began to feel as if he were stripping her of her very clothing.

She made an attempt to pull away from the growing spell of seduction, easing her head back out of reach and pushing firmly against him. But he only took advantage of the position to bury his lips against her throat. The next shiver that shook Kalinda was almost frightening in its intensity.

His hands stroked up her waist with slow, caressing movements until they rested just under the weight of her breasts. When she twisted slightly to escape the intimate touch she knew would come next, Kalinda somehow found her nipple caught under the palm of his hand. Through the material of the silk and the scrap of lacy bra her body reacted without her volition, the nipple hardening.

In spite of her resolve to keep the embrace from going any further, Kalinda's nails bit convulsively into the fabric of the pin-striped shirt, seeking the feel of the muscled flesh underneath.

"Silk and flame," he muttered, his voice deepening as he felt her response. "Where have you been hiding yourself, honey? Think of all the nights we've missed!"

"Just as we're going to miss this one," she retorted a little grimly, conscious of the catch in her words. "I'm not going to bed with you, Rand."

"Tell me that again in a few minutes," he advised and moved, sweeping her up into his arms before she realized his intention.

Her arm circled his neck in an instinctive gesture against falling although he held her with a rocklike security.

"I won't be carried off to bed, Rand," Kalinda snapped arrogantly, unaccustomed to having her dinner dates proceed against her declared wishes. She still didn't believe herself to be in trouble but there was no doubt matters were in danger of getting out of hand.

"The couch?" he suggested hopefully, the laughing gleam in his eyes somehow adding to, rather than subtracting from the desire she saw there.

He strode across the cream carpet to the long caramel couch and settled her gently down on it. When Kalinda opened her eyes after the ensuing moment of vertigo, she found him descending on top of her and her words of determined protest were muffled in her throat as she caught her breath against his weight.

"Damn it, I will not let you…"

"Just let me kiss you," he begged huskily, dropping tiny, featherlight caresses on her cheeks, her eyelids, her ears. When his mouth returned to hers his hand simultaneously moved once more to cover her small breast. The twin assault shocked her senses, causing her to writhe beneath him.

Instantly he responded by crushing her hips intimately with his own, forcing her into the deep cushions until she cried out in growing passion.

"Flame for me, Lady Silk," he growled urgently, nipping her bare shoulder with his teeth and then soothing the scented area with his tongue. "I want to see you go up in flames for me tonight!"

The soft material of the dress began to fall away from her and Kalinda realized dimly he had found the delicate fastenings. She knew she ought to stop him but she couldn't seem to say the words. A passionate curiosity was driving her now and when she felt him undo the front clasp of the small bra she wound her fingers deeply into the chestnut hair with a breathless moan.

"Oh, please! Please…"

"I will," he promised hoarsely, "I will!"

Rand bent his head to find the tips of her breasts with undisguised male need, his tongue curling around the taut nipples as his fingers traced patterns down her bare stomach.

Ahead of his questing hand, the silk dress continued to give away until Kalinda knew the touch of his fingers just inside the edge of her satiny briefs.

She gasped violently and her own hands worked their way inside the collar of his shirt. He moved under her touch the way a cat moves under stroking fingers. She found his uninhibited response deeply, incredibly arousing and without further thought she sought the buttons of the shirt.

A moment later they both lay naked from the waist up, the curling cloud of chestnut hair on Rand's chest exciting and sensual on Kalinda's softness.

Her breath was coming more quickly now and common sense was a rapidly deteriorating commodity. She arched beneath him and he used his strength to tease her by crushing her gently until she couldn't move. Somehow the restraint only served to excite her all the more and Kalinda felt the driving need surge through her body.

It wasn't until she felt him part her legs with his own and knew the hardening maleness of him even through the fabric of the trousers he still wore that some semblance of rational thought returned.

"Rand...Rand, please. That's enough! I never meant..."

"It's all right," he soothed, holding her still as she

began to struggle beneath him. "Just let it happen. It's going to be so good, honey. I want you so badly tonight."

Kalinda moved her head restlessly on the cushion, the sleek knot of her hair long since undone and floating around her. She heard the inevitable words, *I want you,* and they reinforced her efforts to regain control of herself and the situation.

"I'm sorry," she whispered, conscious of her own part in the matter. "I didn't mean for things to go this far!" Carefully she began to push against his bare shoulders, her nails digging into the bronzed skin.

"Kalinda!" His desire-deepened voice cracked slightly as he lifted his head to stare down at her. "What's wrong? Stop fighting it, sweetheart. You want this as much as I do!"

She shook her head in denial, well aware of the want in him. She had to deal with this very cautiously. She had allowed him to become thoroughly aroused and she knew so little about him! How did she know what to expect when he finally realized she meant to call everything to a halt?

For all she knew he might turn violent. God! How had she managed to get herself into this?

"Rand, please," she begged gently, straining away from his hardness, "I want to stop. I never intended for things to go this far. Please let me go...."

For an instant the hazel eyes flashed almost green and she knew a momentary fear. And then the frustrated, angry male glitter was gone to be replaced by a cold, masculine restraint. It was only when that, too, disappeared to reveal rueful dismay that Kalinda knew she could relax.

"You're serious, aren't you?" Rand muttered dryly.

"Yes, I…I never intended for this to happen tonight. Believe me!"

"I believe you! But you see, I fully intended for it to happen!"

"Rand, that's idiotic," Kalinda scolded bracingly, aware of her nakedness and the weight of his body. "You hardly know me!"

"I wanted you the minute I saw you," he told her succinctly, his hands framing her face between rough palms. "I'm more than happy to be a vacation fling for you, Kalinda Brady," he murmured enticingly.

"Thanks a lot! Very generous of you. But it so happens, I'm not interested in that sort of relationship!"

"How about the affair we discussed earlier?" he whispered seductively, his thumbs making probing circles at the corners of her mouth.

"Out of the question!" she snapped, beginning to grow angry. "Let me up, Rand, it's time I went back to the motel."

"Calm down, I'll take you back if that's what you really want…."

"It is!"

"On one condition," he concluded a little too gently.

She glared up at him. "What condition?"

"That I can see you tomorrow."

Kalinda grabbed a deep breath. "I don't see why

you should want that. I can guarantee I won't feel any differently tomorrow!"

"How can you be sure of that? I'll have all day to convince you," he reminded her, his mouth quirking in amused promise. "Who knows how you'll feel by this time tomorrow night?"

"I know what I want and what I don't want."

He hesitated and then said with unexpected coolness, "Yes, I've gathered that. Which brings up a very interesting point."

"What are you talking about?"

"You do seem like the sort of woman who makes up her own mind and does what she wishes most of the time."

Kalinda eyes him narrowly, wondering where this was leading. "I am."

"Then what are you doing here?" he countered swiftly.

"Here? I told you. I had nothing else to do this evening and the trout sounded good...."

"That's not what I mean and you know it. I find myself curious as to what you're doing here in our little mountain retreat. It's obvious you're bored and you're not the sort who likes to head for a rustic environment when you feel like getting away from it all."

"How do you know that?" she retorted, alarmed. "As I've already pointed out, you barely know me!"

"I happen to be a very good judge of character," he drawled. "And, honey, as delightful as you look at this moment, I have to say you did seem a little out of place today wandering around town in your hundred-dollar shirt and those designer slacks!"

Kalinda felt herself go red under his mocking gaze and tried to free her hands in order to cover her naked breasts. But he ignored the effort and waited for a reply!

"My reasons for being here are personal," she muttered with all the arrogance she could command under the circumstances.

He smiled dangerously. "I deduced that much. How personal?"

"I do not intend to discuss that."

"You really are used to giving orders, aren't you?" he observed wonderingly.

"I am, but you don't appear to be very good at taking them," she shot back grittily. "Will you please let me up?"

He didn't move for a moment and Kalinda found herself holding her breath as he studied her.

"If you'll grant my condition," he finally agreed with a short nod.

She sighed. "I'll have lunch with you tomorrow if you're sure you want to see me again." At least he was off the other topic!

He sat up almost at once and Kalinda could almost hear the belated *click* as her brain finally found the right gear. She sat absorbing the impact of his hard profile as he buttoned his shirt and then she moved her head in a wry gesture of self-disgust.

"You did that deliberately, didn't you?" There was a trace of unwilling admiration in her voice. Kalinda was businesswoman enough to recognize innate manipulative talent when she came across it. This man really had wasted his life out here in the wilderness!

"Did what?" he asked innocently, adjusting the collar of his shirt as he slanted her an intriguing glance.

She waved a hand. "You know. First you bring up your real goal, which is to see me tomorrow. When I don't leap at that, you bring up another matter about which I feel very strongly."

"The little issue of what you're doing here in the mountains in the first place?" he clarified helpfully.

She nodded. "And then, when you have me thoroughly ruffled on that subject, you reintroduce the main goal. By that time it seems easier to agree to it so that I can get you to leave me alone on the second topic!"

"You're very perceptive," he grinned engagingly.

"And you're very good at manipulating people," she grumbled dryly. "Now it's my turn to ask some questions."

"Go ahead," he invited cheerfully, sinking back into a corner of the caramel-colored couch and regarding her with lazy invitation.

"Why are you so set on seeing me tomorrow? You're not going to find yourself in bed with me tomorrow night, I can guarantee!"

"Can you?"

"Definitely! I have no interest in a fling with you or anyone else, Rand," she retorted steadily.

"I understand," he astonished her by saying softly.

"Then why…?"

"I still want to see you, Kalinda. I'm attracted to you. I was the moment I saw you. It sometimes happens like that, you know."

"For a man."

He said nothing, not denying the small accusation. There was a waiting silence and then Kalinda went on carefully, "Could it be you're a little bored, yourself?"

He blinked, the coppery lashes brushing the rugged cheekbones for an instant and then he regarded her with his clear gaze. "Why should I be bored? I have the gallery, the pottery, my fishing and I'm living in the heart of God's county. And there are a few women around, you know," he added placidly. "I mean, besides yourself!"

She flushed, looking away. "I'm sure there are!"

"So what makes you think I'm pursuing you out of sheer boredom?"

"Forget it." She got to her feet. "I was just making an observation. You're obviously content with your niche in life or you wouldn't be here, would you?"

"No."

She forced a smile. "So I was wrong in my observation, just as you're wrong if you think you're going to talk me into a fling or a short-term affair. Now it's time you took me back to the motel. The dinner was delightful."

He ranged easily to his feet, his gleaming eyes never leaving her still-flushed features. "About your personal reasons for being in my mountains…"

She smiled brilliantly. "I'm ready to leave, Rand."

He gave her a mocking bow. "I'm at my Lady's command. The Lotus awaits."

But she should have known he wouldn't give up that easily, Kalinda told herself the next day as she lounged beside him on a picnic blanket by the lake. Rand Alastair wasn't the sort of man to surrender so simply and easily. She knew that much about him even though he still confused her in many ways.

Added to her own growing restlessness and nervousness, his delicate probing was going to send her over the edge, she decided midway through the delicious lunch he had packed.

"How long will you be staying here, Kalinda?"

She munched the cheddar sandwich in her hand with relish. "A couple more days," she said cautiously.

He was stretched out beside her, wearing his jeans again and an open-necked sport shirt which revealed the tanned, sinewy length of his arms. The chestnut hair was lightly tousled by the breeze off the lake and his eyes were half-closed against the dancing sunlight. Kalinda was suddenly forced to acknowledge to herself that he seemed very attractive to her.

She directed her attention toward the opposite shore of the lake, feeling his hooded gaze on her. She had pushed up the sleeves of her button-necked tunic top which she wore over a pair of white pants and kicked off her sandals. Kalinda felt relaxed on one level, but wary on another. The lunch had been enjoyable but it hadn't taken her long to realize Rand was hot on the trail he had scented last night. His curiosity was aroused, she supposed. Just as hers was about him.

"You're not sure exactly how many days you'll be here?"

"I expect I'll be leaving the day after tomorrow."

"Why so soon?" he pressed.

"I have a business to run, remember?"

"Isn't the boss entitled to a vacation?" he smiled knowingly.

"Of course. This isn't it, though." As he'd already clearly guessed. There was not much point in pretending she was here for her annual holiday, Kalinda had decided early in the game. Damn the man's persistence! But she had only herself to blame, she admitted grimly. She had wanted to see him again today, even knowing what to expect.

"Ah, yes. The personal business which brings you to our neck of the woods. It will all be over within a couple of days?"

"Yes. Now, if you don't mind, I'd rather talk about something else."

"Fishing?"

She laughed. "Hardly!"

"My plans for us tomorrow night?" he suggested hopefully.

Her laughter died at once. "I'm afraid that's out of the question, Rand. I won't be seeing you tomorrow night."

He went very still beside her and she bit her lip in vexation. But it was the truth and there was no sense letting him think she would be free tomorrow night.

"Tonight's our last evening together?" he asked quietly.

"Yes."

"But you'll be here in town tomorrow night?"

She said nothing. Why was she letting him push her like this? It couldn't be that subconsciously she *wanted* to tell him the truth, could it? That she needed to talk to someone? She had always been so self-possessed, so confident. But she had doubts about what was going to happen tomorrow night when she confronted David. She'd had doubts all along. And that wasn't like her.

"So that's it," he growled softly.

"What?" She swung her neat head around to look at him, saw the cool fire in his eyes and wished she hadn't taken her gaze off the lake. She felt abruptly trapped by the power in him.

"You're here to meet a man." The words dropped like stones out on the lake.

Kalinda didn't move. "It's business," she finally said coldly, struggling to break the bonds he'd placed on her. "Personal, private business."

"You're not looking for a fling with me because you're here to have an affair with another man."

"Rand! Stop it! You know nothing about the matter!" Dear Lord! What was wrong with her to have let him guess so close to the mark? She must be crazy! Or secretly desperate to talk it over with someone, she added grimly to herself.

"Don't you think it might be just a tad dangerous to amuse yourself with me while you wait for

Mr. Wonderful to arrive? What if he hits town early and finds you've spent the time flirting with a local shopkeeper?"

"Of all the ridiculous things to say! I am not flirting with you!"

"I'd call it flirting if I arrived at a rendezvous and found my woman had spent a couple of evenings with another man while waiting for me to show up!" he rasped bitterly. "And what happened on my couch last night definitely does not come under the category of casual acquaintance!"

She realized he was angry, furiously so.

"That's the only category it could come under," she grated feelingly. "All we have is a casual acquaintance!"

"If that's how you treat your fleeting relationships, I'd like to see what happens after you've known a man a couple of weeks!"

She flinched, pulling her eyes away from his condemning glare. He still hadn't shifted from the sprawled position he'd taken, one jeaned leg drawn up as he rested on his elbow. Nevertheless, she had the distinct impression he was sorely tempted to wrap his fingers around her throat. Could she blame him?

"I'm not here to have an affair with anyone," she muttered, setting down the remains of her sandwich as her appetite vanished. She couldn't meet his eyes at all now.

"But you're meeting a man tomorrow night?" he prodded tightly.

Kalinda said nothing, letting her own silence tell the tale.

"Want to tell me about it?"

That brought her head back around with a snap to stare in astonishment. The wholly new tone in his dark voice took her completely by surprise. She had been prepared for belligerence; male outrage at her callous treatment of him, perhaps. But she certainly hadn't been expecting this sudden, soothing, calming offer! Where was the anger he'd been holding in check?

"You can, you know," he went on, mouth twisted beguilingly. "You can tell me the whole story."

"How do you know there's a story to tell?" she challenged carefully, uncertain of her own weakening reaction.

"Instinct. I know it sounds ridiculous, but I really do have fairly sound instincts about people and what makes them tick."

"I know," she whispered. "You're also good at using that knowledge to manipulate people!"

The edge of his mouth hardened. "You don't seem to lack much in the way of perception, yourself!"

"I've learned to recognize a few things," she half-smiled dismissingly. "But I've had on-the-job training in the business world. With you I think it must be instinctive, just as you said. Something you were born with!"

"Are you going to tell me about tomorrow night?"

"I'm not sure. The fact that I've let you push me this close to the subject makes me think I might," she said quite honestly. "But if I do, I shall probably be killing my chance at another trout dinner tonight!" She managed the last with an almost sad flippancy.

"It's steak this evening, not trout," he quipped. "And I promise I won't rescind the offer."

"Even if I admit I'm here to meet a man?" she dared softly.

"I already know that much."

She waited before saying very coolly, very remotely, "You're not going to talk me out of it, you know. I've come this far, I'm going to go through with it."

"That remains to be seen."

Kalinda rested her arms on her drawn-up knees and shook her head with grave determination. "No one could talk me out of it at this stage. A woman seldom gets this kind of opportunity. I'd be a fool to throw it away."

"Exactly what sort of opportunity are we talking about, Kalinda?" he demanded in a low voice that betrayed nothing of his feelings.

"Revenge," she said simply.

"Revenge!"

He sat up, reaching out to catch her chin and force her around to face him. "My God! You really mean it, don't you?" he breathed, searching her intent, determined features. "Who is this man you're going to have your revenge on, Kalinda Brady?"

"My ex-fiancé." The words sounded stark, even to her own ears. "He dropped me two years ago when my father was killed and it was discovered the firm was in bad shape. David Hutton, it turned out, was marrying me because he wanted my father's company."

"And now he wants you back?"

Kalinda smiled grimly. "I've let him think I'm interested. I've agreed to meet him up here for the sake of what we once had, as they say."

"Why did you agree to rendezvous here? Why not Denver?"

"Oh, we couldn't do that," she explained acidly. "David's married now, you see."

"You little fool," he breathed. "You crazy little fool. Exactly what are you going to do tomorrow night when he shows up expecting you to throw yourself into is arms?"

"I'm going to throw his offer in his face, naturally. I'm going to let David Hutton beg me for another chance, listen to him offer to divorce his wife, and then I'm going to laugh and tell him exactly what I think of him! The one thing David can't stand is to be laughed at."

CHAPTER THREE

RAND STARED AT her for a long, taut moment, his expression hard and unreadable.

"You can't go through with it," he finally said flatly. "It's too damn dangerous."

"Dangerous!" Kalinda almost smiled at that. "David's not the physical type. He wouldn't…"

"Rape you? Don't be a fool. Any man could be dangerous in a situation such as you're planning! And you've already misjudged him once, haven't you?"

She winced at his pointed comment. "That was two years ago. I've learned a lot since then. I know him for what he is."

He shook his head. "What makes you think that?"

"I learned everything I needed to know about the man when he came to me after my father's funeral and said he was breaking off the engagement!"

"All you learned at that point was that he'd wanted to marry you in order to gain control of what he'd assumed was a successful company. You discovered he was no longer interested in you or the company when its financial status had been revealed. But you didn't learn anything about what he'd be likely to do in a confrontation such as the one you're planning!"

Rand's voice was chilling. "Face it, he might very well turn vicious. But that's not the only risk you're running!"

She frowned, wishing on the one hand she'd never let him discover her real reasons for being in town and knowing on the other that some part of her had wanted to talk to another human being about the reckless plan. Why had that convenient human being turned out to be this unsympathetic male?

"What other risk could there be?" she snapped, goaded by his glowering disapproval.

"Are you sure revenge is the real reason you're planning this?" he growled. "Two years ago you were in love with the man. Maybe you're really here to see if you can pick up the pieces...."

"No!" The idea was ludicrous! "After what he did to me?"

"He hurt you. People hurt other people all the time but that doesn't always kill the love they have for each other."

"I assure you a healthy dose of reality killed any feeling I might have had for David Hutton two years ago," she blazed.

"You still feel strongly enough about the man to want revenge," he reminded her coolly. "They say hate is akin to love."

"That's absurd and you know it," she scoffed with great certainty. Whatever else she felt for David Hutton after two years, Kalinda knew love had nothing to do with her emotions.

"Exactly what did happen two years ago after

David took back his ring?" Rand regarded her probingly, sounding as if he were trying to get to the bottom of a serious mystery.

Kalinda lifted one shoulder casually. "I had my hands full trying to salvage the business. I didn't spend a lot of time brooding over my tragic romance, if that's what you're thinking."

"Brady Data Processing, I take it, is no longer on the skids?" he murmured dryly.

"No, it's not." That remark brought an unconscious smile of pride and satisfaction to Kalinda's lips. "We're on the way back. We've shown profits for the last three quarters, in fact."

One chestnut eyebrow lifted in acknowledgment of the accomplishment. "You must have worked hard during the past two years."

"I did," she admitted simply. It was the truth. She had literally buried herself in her work. And now, finally, it had all begun to pay off. She could afford to relax and enjoy her well-earned success.

"Why?" he asked evenly.

She hesitated. "I had to."

"In order to forget Hutton?" he demanded, sounding thoroughly irritated at that possibility.

She shook her head, her mouth quirking upward. "It had nothing to do with David. I had to try to salvage the company because so many people were depending on me. You don't know what it was like."

"An old, established family firm with employees and members of the board who'd started out with your father while still in their teens?" he hazarded dryly. "People who'd spent their whole working lives there?"

She looked at him in astonishment. "How did you know?"

"I told you, we aren't totally isolated up here," he retorted cryptically. "I've heard of companies like your father's. So bound by traditional ways of doing things that they gently begin to sink beneath the waves of progress. Is that what was happening at the time your father was killed?"

"I'm afraid so. After I got my degree in business administration I went to work for another company. I knew I wouldn't fit in at my father's firm. Then he was killed and the board of directors asked me to consider taking over the day-to-day management. After all, I'd inherited it and them along with all those long-time employees. It was almost feudal!"

"And you didn't have the heart to liquidate or sell out?"

"How could I do that to all those people? But after a few months I realized there was more to it than just a sense of responsibility...."

"It became a challenge?" he murmured.

"As I've said before, you're very perceptive." Kalinda smiled.

"So now, two years later, you've got the company back on its feet and David Hutton is trying to slip back into your life. Doesn't that strike you as something of a coincidence?"

Kalinda stared at him, shocked at that line of reasoning and then shook her head firmly. "David is thoroughly involved with his own firm; the manufacturing business where he was vice-president at the time of my father's death has moved him up to president. Why should he be interested in Brady Data Processing now?"

There was a lengthy silence from Rand's side of the picnic blanket.

"Simple greed?" he finally suggested caustically.

She thought about that, wryly admitting that finding out David's renewed interest in her was once again based on Brady Data Processing would be a blow to her ego.

"He married well. Very well. He's running a successful business."

"All of which might make him more greedy than ever."

"Where did you gain all this vast insight into the motivations of other people?" she grumbled. "You must meet quite a wide variety of tourists up here!"

"I do."

"Well, what you've just suggested only makes me more determined than ever to go through with my plan. If I'm right I'll have the satisfaction of denying him me. If you're right, I'll have the satisfaction of denying him the firm!"

"Neither of which is an adequate reason for taking the risk of seeing him again, dammit! You could get hurt in more ways than one, can't you get that through your head? What's the matter? Hasn't there been any other man in the past two years who could take your mind off him?"

Kalinda gave him a startled, too-revealing glance and he nodded in grim satisfaction. "So that's it. He's the last man you were serious about. You've spent the past two years devoting your energies to your firm and you haven't had time for a proper, flaming romance which might have dimmed the memory of your ex-fiancé!"

"That's a crazy line of logic! And here I was thinking you so perceptive!" she hissed, infuriated with him suddenly.

"What you need is someone to replace the memories with a much more interesting reality." Rand reached for her as Kalinda, seeing the flicker of intent in his eyes, started to edge away. But she wasn't quick enough.

"Rand, don't…"

"Give me one night, Kalinda," he grated, his hands on her shoulders. "Just one night…"

"Why, you egotistical fool! What makes you think one night with a vacation *fling* would be enough to wipe out the memories of another man? How dare you even suggest…"

Her words were choked off as she was pressed back onto the blanket. Rand moved swiftly, anchoring her twisting legs with his thigh and catching her wrists in one of his callus-roughened hands. Memories poured through her at his determined touch, but the memories were of the previous evening, not two years ago.

"You weren't thinking of Hutton last night, were you?" he challenged, holding her still beneath him, his hazel eyes gleaming with purpose and the beginnings of desire. "And somehow, I get the feeling you're not thinking of his kisses right now either!"

"Rand, listen to me," Kalinda pleaded, knowing she was not exactly in a position to goad him further. She would have to use reason and the truth if she wanted to calm him. "I'm not carrying a torch for David Hutton. I'm angry at him for what he did to me two years ago, but I'm not still in love with him! Believe me! I just want a chance to pay him back for treating me so shabbily. It's called poetic justice!"

"It's called being stupid," he retorted, leaning his weight across her chest and gently crushing her breasts beneath the thin covering of the tunic top. With his free hand he lightly stroked the line of her throat. Kalinda felt the slight tremor of response in her body and knew he'd felt it, too.

"I can assure you that calling me stupid is not a good method of seducing me!"

His fingers trailed to the unbuttoned collar of the tunic and he smiled crookedly. "Who knows? Perhaps lady executives respond to the more unusual methods!"

"Let me go, Rand," she ordered forcefully, her eyes narrowed as she looked up at him from the vulnerable position.

His face softened and she heard the new, coaxing note in his voice. "Honey, can't you see you're on the verge of making a gigantic mistake? You've said I'm perceptive. Why don't you pay more attention to that perception? Regardless of your motivations, the risks are too great. In addition to being perceptive, I'm also a man. Give me some credit for being able to predict how another man might react in the situation you're trying to set up?"

"How would you react?" she whispered, eyes widening with the question. She didn't know what had made her ask it. Overhead the pines swayed, breaking the path of sunlight so that it dappled their bodies. Kalinda was violently aware of the warm strength of Rand and the way his maleness seemed a part of their wild surroundings. The clean, musky scent of him reached her nostrils with a tantalizing tang that elicited a response from her body.

"That's not easy to answer," he confessed a little roughly, "because I can't conceive of ever letting you go in the first place."

"Of course you can," she scoffed bitterly. "I'll bet you're an old hand at managing the short-term affair!"

"If I did find myself in Hutton's shoes for whatever reason," he went on deliberately, ignoring her provocation, "I doubt I'd meekly sit back and let you have your revenge. If I'd arrived at an isolated mountain resort expecting to rekindle an old romance, I'd make damn sure something did, indeed, get ignited. You'd wind up in my bed, Kalinda, regardless of your intentions."

"But you're not David!" she shot back warily.

"No, I'm not Hutton," he agreed deeply and lowered his head to take her lips with a passion that Kalinda forced herself to admit she'd wanted to taste again. Ever since he'd first exposed her to it last night.

His mouth moved on hers with mounting desire as his hand slid down the buttons of the tunic, unfastening each in turn. When his fingers found her unconfined breasts, Kalinda gasped, the soft, broken moan in her throat stifled by his probing tongue.

Her own tongue moved instinctively to engage in the small, intimate duel with his and her arms circled him. She raked her nails almost tenderly down the back of his neck and under his collar, delighting once more in the reflexive arching of his body against her.

"Kalinda, Kalinda," he groaned as he slid his leg between hers. "Give me one night. Just one night. I swear you'll forget all about him by morning!"

He reached down to push her legs farther apart, letting his hand trace an erotic pattern against the material of her white pants. She sucked in her breath as he wove the pattern steadily upward along her inner thigh. His mouth began to explore the line of her throat, moving slowly, inevitably toward the hardening peak of her breast.

"Oh, Rand, Rand," she cried softly, "I shouldn't let you do this to me. I know I shouldn't. It's crazy…"

"Stop worrying about it and just accept the way things are between us," he murmured against the warmth of her skin. "There's nothing wrong with two people getting very lucky unexpectedly."

Before she could summon her thoughts for a rational protest, his teeth had closed carefully on one nipple, sending electric waves through her. The seductive hand traveling along her thigh reached the warm juncture of her legs and she closed her eyes tightly, knowing he must be aware of the heat he was generating in her.

"Honey, you're practically melting in my hands," he breathed with beguiling satisfaction as his fingers closed briefly over the feminine heart of her desire. "Don't you realize I must have all of you? I have to know what it's like to lose myself completely in your body. I've never ached so badly for a woman in my life!"

Kalinda writhed, arching herself against his hand and felt the instant response of his own body. Trembling, she began a sensitive, questing path down his side until she reached the barrier of his jeans. Restlessly, deliciously, she slipped her fingers just inside and heard his hoarse reaction.

"Please touch me," Rand begged, even as he began to fumble with the clasp of her white trousers. "I need to feel your hands on me. So soft, so exciting."

Unable to resist the urgent demand in him, Kalinda slowly undid the fastening of his jeans. She felt the trembling in him and knew a womanly power she had never before known. It was somehow very important and wholly satisfying to know she could make this one particular man respond. As her senses whirled dizzily some vague instinct told her that this was the only man in the world whose response counted.

With delicate, tender caresses she explored the hard, fully aroused male frame. He reacted to the buttery touches as if they were glowing lasers. When she sank her fingers into the muscular buttock, she heard him call out her name with a fierceness that excited her beyond reason.

But even as she sought to inflame him further, Kalinda was slipping rapidly under the spell Rand was working on her own body. She felt the possessive spread of his fingers on her stomach and turned her head into his shoulder with a sigh of need when his hand went lower.

"You can't respond like this to me and still be thinking of that other man," Rand groaned huskily, his mouth on the silky skin of her stomach. "You can't! I won't let you!"

"No," she whispered brokenly. "I'm only thinking of you. I can barely think at all!"

"That's the way it should be. Lose yourself in me, sweetheart, just as I'm losing myself in you."

Kalinda felt the waves of desire wash over her, knew a surging excitement she'd never experienced and slowly common sense fell aside.

With a deep sound of pleasure and anticipation, Rand moved, rolling onto his back and pulling Kalinda down across his chest. She blinked as her equilibrium swam momentarily and then reacted to the hot invitation in his eyes.

Dropping passionate little kisses along his shoulder, Kalinda pushed aside the sport shirt Rand wore. Recklessly she wound her fingers in the hair on his chest, tugging gently.

"Vixen," he muttered enticingly and tightened his grasp on her hip until she gasped from the curious pleasure-pain.

"You're a menace to the male of the species, do you realize that?" he charged on a husky note of impassioned laughter.

"No," she denied vehemently, her light-colored hair falling loose to swirl across his chest as she dipped her tongue into the pit of his firm stomach. "I'm not normally like this," she added uncomprehendingly. "I've never felt quite like this. You do something crazy to me, Rand Alastair."

His hold on her became at once soothing and even more demanding as he heard the honest bewilderment in her words.

"The feeling," he growled, "is mutual. My God, woman! To think we could have gone for the rest of our lives not knowing this sensation! If nothing else, I shall have to be grateful to Hutton for luring you up here!"

Kalinda froze. David's name was like a dash of cold water in her face. Slowly, with a gathering sense of amazed confusion, she lifted her head. What was she doing? This was utterly insane! She hardly knew this man and here she was making love to him as if he were a lover of long standing!

Mutely she met his eyes, knowing he was at once aware of the self-disgust in her own bleak gaze.

"Kalinda?" he whispered pleadingly. "What's wrong, sweetheart?" His hands encircled her waist, holding her in place above him. "Stop looking at me like that. I'm not going to hurt you."

"I…know," she managed, struggling to bring her reeling sense back under control. "But I never meant… I didn't mean to get involved like this again today. I don't understand what you do to me, but it's all wrong! We're all wrong. We…we don't belong together…."

Painfully, she tried to separate herself from him, thrusting a hand through her hair to sweep it back from her face. She sat up with the greatest care, as if the movement was incredibly difficult. His eyes never left hers and she saw dismay and a growing coolness begin to wipe out the passion that had looked out at her from the hazel depths.

"Damn it to hell," he muttered, his hands still on her waist. "It was Hutton's name that did it, wasn't it? What a fool I am. You'd think a man would know when to keep his mouth shut!"

In spite of the charged atmosphere, Kalinda knew a rueful spark of humor as she listened to him condemn his own stupidity. "I'm sorry, Rand. I should never have let things go this far. I honestly don't know what got into me."

He regarded her with a narrowed, seething glance. "You've been a chief executive officer for so long you automatically accept the responsibility for whatever happens around you or to you, right? I've got news for you, darling, I was involved in this, too! In fact, I started it!"

He sat up, releasing her to rake his hand impatiently through his thick, tousled hair. "And it's all my fault it's ground to a premature halt!"

"For which I'm very grateful," she flung back,

stung by his scathing tone. "I have no intention of being a one-night stand for you, dammit!"

"And I have no intention of letting you be a one-night stand for your ex-fiancé!"

"How many times do I have to tell you, that's not the way it's going to be? I'll be in charge tomorrow night and I know exactly what I'm doing!"

"The hell you do! You're so blinded by your memories of that bastard you can't see the stupidity of your own plans! If you ran Brady Data Processing with that degree of insanity, you would have lost it to bankruptcy long ago!"

"What do you know about running a company into insolvency?" she gritted tersely. "Don't talk to me about how to run my life or my business. We live in two separate worlds and you aren't in any position to give me advice!" She leaped to her feet, madly straightening her clothing and frantically trying not to cry. Why the threat of tears? She wished desperately she could figure out why this man had such an incredible affect on her. It made no sense at all!

He stood up beside her with a quick glance and caught her wrist.

"Kalinda, I'm sorry," he muttered. "Please believe me. I never meant to shout at you like that. But it's so damn frustrating...."

"A man your age must know how to handle a little masculine frustration by now!"

"I'm not talking about the way you just frustrated me physically," he rasped, giving her a small shake. "I'm talking about how frustrating it is to try to make you see reason. You can't go through with your plans for tomorrow night. It's too dangerous." His voice lowered gruffly, persuasively. "Please give me a chance to make you change your mind. I meant what I said a little while ago. Give me one night and I can make you forget him."

"Your ego is as vast as David's!"

The moment the words left her mouth Kalinda could have bitten her tongue. Red stained the tanned heights of his cheekbones as he reacted to the comparison of himself with the other man. His fingers on her wrist tightened bruisingly.

Impulsively, without stopping to think, Kalinda lifted her hand to touch the side of his face with a placating gesture, her eyes soft and apologetic.

"I'm sorry I said that," she whispered huskily. "I didn't mean to imply you were anything like him. I know you're not, believe me."

She waited in an agony of suspense, watching the play of emotions across his features. She hadn't meant to hurt him, hadn't really stopped to think that he could be hurt. Not by her. He hardly knew her!

"That," he finally said evenly, "was a rather low blow!"

She winced, unconsciously sinking her teeth into her lower lip as she met his hard, accusing stare.

"I know. I'm sorry." She didn't know what else to say.

He searched her face a moment longer and then appeared to relax slightly. "But maybe you weren't so far off the mark," he sighed. "I suppose it must sound like sheer male ego talking when I tell you all I need is one night to put that man out of your head forever."

Kalinda said nothing, but she didn't deny his statement. His mouth twisted wryly. He raised his free hand and wrapped it around her neck under the fall of brown-blond hair. She felt him lightly massaging her nape and against her will her knees seemed to weaken. She didn't understand his effect on her but she knew it was dangerous. Far more dangerous than any risks she might be running in her plot to avenge herself on David.

"All I can say, sweetheart, is that it isn't my ego talking, it's that 'perception' you keep crediting me with," he half-smiled. "Won't you listen to it?"

"Rand, we aren't meant for each other. Not even for a night," Kalinda said sadly. "Can't you understand that? We're two entirely different people. You need an easy-going, outdoorsy sort of woman. Perhaps someone who is also an artist."

"And you're a high-powered, competitive female executive who likes the good things in life, right?" he finished for her with a knowing look. "A woman who knows what she wants in a relationship and doesn't think she's going to find it in me. After all, I'm a lazy, good-for-nothing, ski-bum-fisherman who sells a few artsy-craftsy things on the side to keep the wolf from the door. Completely lacking in the good old American work ethic."

Kalinda thought about the white Lotus and the expensively furnished home by the lake and refrained from inquiring as to the source of those things. She might not like the answer. The thought that she had met up with a professional gigolo and had almost let him make love to her was totally unnerving. She didn't want to know which rich lady tourist had paid for the Lotus last winter!

But even as she thought the worst of him, Kalinda knew she didn't have all the facts. She barely knew him. She would try to refrain from judging him. He had his own life to live just as she had hers.

"Rand, please, don't put words in my mouth. Let's just say we come from two different walks of life, okay? We should never have let ourselves get carried away like this on the basis of a simple physical attraction."

"Well, at least you're admitting we have got that much going for us!"

She smiled weakly, shaking her head in exasperation. "I can't very well deny that, can I? But it's not enough. I'm not in the market for a weekend affair and that's final. I think I'd better be getting back to the motel."

"What about dinner tonight?" he countered coolly. "I've already bought the steaks and the wine."

She looked at him helplessly. "And changed the sheets on the bed, too, I expect?"

He stared at her for a second and then grinned that engaging, slightly feral grin which was so unbelievably attractive on him. "How did you guess?"

"I have this strange feeling you've got the routine down pat!"

"No," he denied at once, sobering. "This time it's

special. There's nothing routine about it. Please, Kalinda. Have dinner with me tonight."

"So you can spend the evening trying to talk me out of my plans?" she sighed.

"Yes."

"No thanks!"

"I swear I won't drag you off to bed." There was a meaningful pause. "Unless, of course, you decide that's where you belong, after all. Just promise to have dinner with me. I swear I won't muscle you into the bedroom."

"We'll only spend the time arguing over what I'm going to do tomorrow night," she protested, knowing she was weakening before the persuasiveness in him.

"Have you got anything better to do than argue with me?" he murmured, his fingers on her nape moving lightly, seductively. "Think of it as an opportunity to convince me you know what you're doing!"

"How can I refuse such a charming invitation!" she muttered dryly, wretchedly aware that spending the evening with him was exactly what she wanted to do, regardless of the complications involved.

"You high-powered female executives are all alike," he taunted on a soft rumble of laughter as he bent to brush his lips against hers. "Can't resist a challenge!"

CHAPTER FOUR

Rand was a man of his word, Kalinda decided much later that night as she grimly closed her motel room door and went to the window to watch the Lotus disappear into the night. Never had she spent an evening like the one he had just put her through!

She turned away from the window, letting the drape fall into place and morosely surveyed her room. It had been one line of reasoning after another, one argument after another, one persuasive attack on her logic after another. She felt utterly exhausted, she thought with a rueful grimace.

He had amazed her with his strategy, leaping nimbly from one point to the next in his efforts to convince her she was making a mistake in trying to take revenge on David Hutton.

And, in spite of his hints to the contrary, Rand had not resorted again to seduction. Kalinda shook her head wryly. Instead, he had fed her well, spent several hours intently "discussing" the matter at hand, and then he'd left her on her doorstep with the most singly devastating comment of the evening.

"Ask yourself," he'd ordered softly as he'd opened her door for her, "why you're even bothering to listen to me in the first place. Face it, Kalinda, you want to be talked out of this fiasco. That's the reason you told me the truth this afternoon, isn't it? So that I could have a chance to play devil's advocate?"

He hadn't waited for her crushing retort. Instead, he'd vaulted easily down the steps, slid into the Lotus and disappeared. Leaving Kalinda behind to face a serious attack of self-honesty.

The depressing part about the evening, she thought as she slipped into the satin and lace nightgown and climbed into bed, was that all of his arguments were reasonable. It was a foolish and potentially dangerous scheme she had concocted. But even Rand hadn't hit on the one factor which was really troubling her about her own plans.

It was a factor which Kalinda had kept pushing into the background but which had become stronger than ever as Rand's arguments had weakened the rest of her logic. That factor was David Hutton's wife.

As Friday night approached, the unknown wife loomed larger and larger in Kalinda's mind. It was one of the reasons she'd arrived early at the rendezvous point. She'd wanted time to think about what she was doing. Time away from the pressures of work, from planning the party scheduled for the following week to entertain business associates, time away from her current and casual escorts of the moment.

She'd retreated to the mountains to convince herself she was doing the justifiable thing and here she'd met a man who probably should have been a prosecuting attorney instead of a part-time arts and crafts dealer!

Kalinda had never met Arleen Hutton but she knew a certain amount about her. At the time David had broken off the engagement there had been no lack of "friends" to tell Kalinda who'd taken her place.

Arleen was the daughter of a wealthy Colorado rancher. She'd brought money to the marriage, according the Kalinda's acquaintances, and she was reputed to be a very beautiful woman. She was also a few years younger than Kalinda.

It had been easy not to think about her, especially since Kalinda had no intention of actually trying to steal her husband away. But more and more frequently during the past week an insistent image had come to mind. The image of an innocent wife discovering her husband was meeting a woman at a remote mountain retreat.

Kalinda, blessed with an empathy she could have done well without in the business world, couldn't help wondering how she'd feel if she were that wife. And now Rand had systematically demolished all the reasons for revenge, leaving only the face of the unknown wife to haunt Kalinda's conscience.

Damn the man! She turned furiously over in bed, pounding the pillow with a disgusted fist. His talents truly had been wasted in life! With that sort of single-minded strength of purpose, he could have done just about anything he wanted in the world! But, she supposed thoughtfully, perhaps that's exactly what he *had* done. Perhaps he was quite content to fish and ski and make lovely pieces of pottery. And date rich tourists!

She lay staring at the ceiling for a long time after that, trying to recall the hurt and humiliation she'd felt two years ago. A hurt and humiliation that had come in the wake of the tragedy of her father's death and had, therefore, been all the more devastating. Kalinda's parents had been divorced several years previously and her mother had moved to Europe with her new husband the year Kalinda had gone off to college. Kalinda had faced both the tragedy and the humiliation quite alone.

But it was difficult tonight to resurrect those old feelings. The habit of wanting revenge was still there in her mind, but the emotions driving those feelings were gone. If she were completely honest with herself, Kalinda thought wonderingly, she'd realized they had been missing for some time. Two years of hard work and success had killed them rather effectively.

It had been only the habit that had made her jump at the opportunity of paying back David Hutton. Now, a combination of her conscience and the relentless arguments of a man she had only known for two days seemed to have succeeded in killing even the habit of wanting revenge. Kalinda thought once again of the unknown wife and of her own stupidity in wanting revenge on a man who wasn't worth the time of day. She made up her mind about what to do in the morning and went very soundly to sleep.

She dialed the private line number of David Hutton's office promptly at eight o'clock the next morning. He was there, just as she had expected him to be. Whatever else could be said of the man, he was a hard worker. It was one of the things she had admired about him in the beginning....

"David, this is Kalinda..." she began firmly, coolly.

"Getting impatient, darling?" he chuckled knowingly. "It won't be much longer now. I'm taking off around twelve. I'll be in the mountains by the middle of the afternoon. Enjoying yourself? Your office said you'd taken a couple of extra days."

"I left that message in case you tried to get in touch with me," she affirmed. "But, David..."

"I can't wait to see you again, Kali. God, it's been a long time! I keep wondering what happened to us two years ago. We had so much going for us," he murmured deeply into the phone.

Kalinda gritted her teeth. He knew very well what had happened to them two years ago! He'd caused it to happen! But the momentary anger died quickly, leaving once again her newfound determination.

"David," she said calmly, "it's no good. I'm not going to meet you up here. I'm calling so you won't make the drive for nothing."

There was a fragment of stunned silence on the other end of the line and then David's voice came soothingly.

"This is hardly the time to get cold feet, Kali. We've got everything planned. Don't panic, darling. Just sit tight for a few more hours until I get there. We'll talk everything out. You'll see!"

Mentally Kalinda pictured him sitting behind his

desk in the downtown highrise where his company had its headquarters. It was a handsome image in many respects. David Hutton was a good-looking man with dark brown hair and eyes. He would be thirty-six now and, unless he'd changed a lot in the past couple of years, still lean and dynamic. He dressed well, and admired those who did likewise. Two years ago Kalinda thought they would have made a good couple. It was with a small start that she realized this morning they would have made a disastrous couple. It would probably have been her David was planning to cheat today instead of the unknown woman who was his wife.

"I'm not getting cold feet, David. I've simply changed my mind." She'd decided earlier on the approach she would use. If she told David she'd only been plotting to make a fool of him, he would be infuriated and she didn't feel like putting up with that sort of scene. She would leave him with a sop for his ego, annoying as that course of action might be for her.

"Why, Kalinda?" he demanded with the first touch of a chill in his voice.

"It's wrong, David, and we both know it. There's your wife to consider, for one thing and there's the little matter of both our reputations. What if someone were to discover what's going on?"

"That's hardly likely," he growled forcefully. "And you didn't have to concern yourself with my wife. I've never really talked to you about my marriage, darling. It's one of the things I wanted to discuss with you this weekend. It's…it's been something of a business arrangement," he hinted delicately as if casting out a lure.

Kalinda lifted one brow sardonically but said calmly into the phone, "I'm afraid that's your problem, David. All I know is I don't want to be involved in a triangle...."

"Kali, honey, stop talking like that," he coaxed, sounding a little desperate and very determined. "This is just between you and I. Now you stay put. I'll be up there in a few hours. I can get away earlier than planned. We'll talk this out in person."

"Go ahead and drive up here, David, if you like. But I won't be here. I mean it, I'm not seeing you again." Kalinda felt her patience and reasonableness slipping away. The firmness in her words was unmistakable. "Let's just agree we were on the verge of doing something we both would have regretted and let it go at that."

"No! Kali, listen to me. You would never have agreed to see me again if you weren't still interested. You know that. We can recapture what we once had if we only give it a chance..."

"Oh, go to hell, David!" she finally snapped, disgusted with him and with herself for having gotten into the mess. "Do you want to know the real reason I agreed to meet you up here? I was going to let you drive all the way up with notions of starting an affair and then I was going to encourage you to think I was equally interested. I was going to let you wine and dine me, make you think you were on the point of seducing me and then I was going to laugh in your face! I never had any intention of rekindling our old romance, you idiot! How could I after what you did two years ago? You destroyed whatever we might have had together and I have no interest in raking through the ashes. Goodbye, David. Don't call me again!"

She set the receiver firmly back into the cradle and surged irritably to her feet. Dammit! She hadn't meant to wind up the phone call that way, but he'd asked for it. She wanted out of the awkward situation and she'd offered him a reasonable way of calling it quits. He had only himself to blame for having annoyed her to the point where she'd told him the truth.

She glanced around the small hotel room, impatient to escape now that the decision had been made and action taken. She wanted away from these mountains, away from the scene of the canceled fiasco.

She went to the closet and began packing the chocolate leather luggage. She wore the white cotton tuxedo shirt she'd had on the first day with the khaki trousers and her hair was in the neat twist behind one ear. She felt as cool and self-confident as she looked. She had made the right decision.

Or had it made for her, she reflected ruefully, thinking of Rand Alastair as she swung the soft leather case into her silver Mercedes.

By the time she checked out of the motel it was nearly nine o'clock. She climbed behind the wheel of the car and wondered what Rand was doing. Was he thinking about her? Concerned about what her final decision would be?

Kalinda sat quietly in the seat before starting the engine, staring straight ahead through the windshield and thinking about Rand. She would never see him again and that seemed rather strange, considering the effect he'd had on her during the past two days.

But it was for the best, of course. There was no chance for anything solid and lasting between them. He was obviously content to live the undemanding life here in the mountains and she was born to thrive in the city. There would be other lady tourists to amuse him and with the coming of ski season he'd probably have to close up the shop completely in order to handle both his skiing and his dates, she told herself grimly.

With a decisive gesture she started the engine and backed the car out of its slot. No, Rand wasn't her sort of man by a long shot. She needed someone altogether more like herself. And she didn't need an affair that came to life only on weekends she managed to drive up into the mountains.

But somehow Kalinda wasn't altogether surprised to find herself guiding the silver car along the narrow lakeside road toward Rand's home. She would only stop long enough to say goodbye, she told herself. He deserved to know his arguments had been effective. She really believed he'd been genuinely concerned for her in this matter.

She was still justifying her reasons for stopping to say farewell several minutes later as she parked the Mercedes next to the Lotus and opened the door. The sight of the sleek, white sports car brought up the depressing image of a professional gigolo again and Kalinda told herself she was absolutely right in her decision not to see Rand again after this morning. Two ships passing in the night.

The morning sunlight was coming cheerfully through the swaying pines as she knocked tentatively on the door. She really didn't know that much about his habits, Kalinda thought as she waited for a response. Perhaps he'd gone fishing. Or perhaps he was still asleep. Maybe today he would rouse himself sufficiently to open the gallery.

She was running through the list of possibilities for not finding him at home when the door was abruptly flung open.

Whatever Kalinda had planned to say was squelched before she could form the words by the sight of him standing on the threshold staring at her. He looked terrible! The chestnut hair was ruffled as if he'd been combing his hand through it. The hazel eyes were dark and strained and there was a desperately tired, haggard look about him which caught at her heart. He was wearing the faded jeans and an unbuttoned white shirt with the sleeves rolled up. He held a cup of coffee in one hand.

In the instant of silent regard that passed between them, Kalinda felt the taut emotion vibrating in the atmosphere. She met his eyes and began a frantic search for something reasonable to say. He didn't look at all reasonable, however.

"Rand, I…I only stopped to tell…" she began.

His hand fell away from the door and the cup of

coffee was set down on a nearby stand. The hazel eyes flared to life with a deep, hungry gleam as he reached for her.

"You came to tell me you've changed your mind about meeting Hutton tonight at the motel," he stated evenly, his fingers sliding around her neck while his thumbs went under her jaw to hold her face so that she could not look away.

"Yes," she said simply, feeling the currents of physical awareness passing through her. He looked awful, she told herself again, and somehow he made her want to take him in her arms and comfort him. How could that be?

"It's about time you got here," he whispered thickly, pulling her gently, inexorably toward him. "I've spent most of the night walking the floor over you, Kalinda Brady. Thank God you've finally decided to put me out of my misery!"

His mouth came heavily down on hers before she could think of a way to respond to his words. And as soon as she felt his warm, aggressive passion flood her senses, Kalinda realized this was the real reason she'd talked herself into saying goodbye to him.

"I was sure I could get you to make the right decision," he said huskily against her lips. "So sure. But there was always the possibility I'd guessed wrong."

"Are you often wrong about people?" she asked softly, her hands sliding up his chest, pushing aside the loosely hanging shirt.

"Very seldom," he replied equally soft. "But it's never been quite this important to be right before!"

Then his mouth closed fiercely over hers once more, the tip of his probing tongue flicking across her lips and ultimately claiming the inner warmth of her mouth.

Kalinda shivered beneath the onslaught, thrusting aside her common sense and knowing as she felt his hands move on her that this morning she was going to surrender to the pull of an intense passion she'd never known before.

He heard the soft sigh with which she accepted the reality of their desire and Rand folded her tightly, tenderly against him, an answering groan of need deep in his chest.

His fingers found the line of her spine and tracked upward, sending out little eddies of sensuous current at every point along the way. Kalinda felt him arch her against his lower body and she moaned her aching response.

"I've wanted you from the moment I saw you," he breathed, stringing slow, damp little kisses along her cheek to the nape of her neck. With one strong hand he held her face buried in his shoulder while his teeth nipped erotically at the vulnerable neck he was baring.

The tuxedo-styled shirt and lacy bra seemed to float free of her body, leaving her nude from the waist up. The morning sunlight danced along the silky skin of her shoulders and she heard Rand's indrawn breath. Gently he freed her hair.

"I'm exhausted from pacing my floor; I've had so much coffee it's a wonder I'm able to think at all.

Never in my life have I had so many doubts about my own judgment, but suddenly I feel fantastic," Rand growled as she played her fingers across the muscles of his back, her hands moving under the white shirt.

"Oh, Rand," she breathed helplessly, finding his tanned throat with her questing lips. "I shouldn't be here…"

"But you are and that's all that counts," he interrupted in a passion-roughened voice. He trembled beneath the touch of her lips and Kalinda was thrilled to be able to arouse him as he aroused her. It was crazy and it could only happen between them once but she was twenty-nine years old and she was suddenly determined to sample the depths of true desire. All the arguments against one-time encounters with virtual strangers could be dragged out later when she was back in the reality of Denver. This was a stolen moment out of time that would never come her way again. How could she pass it by?

"Kalinda, Kalinda, I want you so much I was so afraid at times during the night that you wouldn't come to me…."

She shook her head wordlessly, her lashes dusting her cheeks as she lowered her eyes from the flaming want in his gaze. She hadn't known herself that she would come to him like this. Nor did she want to think about her own actions in that moment. Instead she clung to him with an intensity that amazed her. She felt the lean strength in his hips as her hands searched out the feel of him beneath the tight jeans.

"Why are we standing here? I have the perfect

place for us," he rasped and swung her high into his arms. Kalinda pressed her lips to his now-naked shoulder and closed her eyes once more as he strode down the cream-carpeted hall to a bedroom full of caramels and browns.

He settled her gently on the sun-dappled bed, her light-colored hair fanning out across the rich golden brown bedspread. For a moment he stood gazing down at her and then he sat beside her, his hands going to the long tendrils of hair.

"It's almost the same color as my bedspread," he half-smiled, stroking luxuriously. "Your skin looks like cream in the morning light." His eyes roamed warmly over her as he slowly unbuckled the web belt of her khaki trousers and finished undressing her.

He performed the task with infinite care, pausing to caress each inch of skin revealed until she lay naked beneath his hands. He stroked his fingers in languid, delicious little circles along the length of her leg from ankle to thigh. By the time he reached her hip Kalinda was trembling with desire.

Apparently satisfied with his efforts, Rand pulled away for a moment, sliding quickly, impatiently out of his jeans and returning to her welcoming arms with a hoarsely whispered exclamation of need.

"I was going to head straight back to Denver after calling David this morning," she whispered as he gathered her close. "But somehow I couldn't leave without seeing you…."

"I would have gone mad if you hadn't."

He buried his lips at the curve of her shoulder,

nipping gently at her skin while his hand closed possessively over her breast. The firming nipple beneath his palm seemed to arouse him further and Kalinda reached down to touch him with intimate wonder.

"Did you really spend the night pacing the floor?" she asked breathlessly, as his body stirred ardently against hers.

"What does it look like?" he growled ruefully. "But it was worth it to open the door this morning and find you standing there. I took one look at you and knew I didn't have to worry any longer!"

He raked a trail of pleasure across the taut nipple, down her sensitive stomach and along her thigh, following his hand with his lips. Her fingers twisted passionately in his hair as he slid lower on her body and when his exciting kisses found her secret core of desire she cried out.

"Oh, my God, Rand! You're driving me wild. I've never known this kind of...of *aching!*"

He turned his head and kissed the inside of her thigh. Her leg shifted reflexively, her knee lifting alongside his body.

"I know exactly what you're talking about," he murmured thickly, his fingers squeezing into the softness of her curving bottom. "After I took you back to the motel last night I told myself I was a fool, that I should have kept you here and taken you to bed regardless of what you thought you wanted at the time. But I knew it would be better if it happened this way...."

"You seem to have known me better than I knew

myself for a while," she admitted, twisting restlessly against him. Her breathing came in short, broken little pants as she felt the raging hunger take control of her.

"And now I'm going to know you even more thoroughly," he vowed. "I'm going to make you mine this morning, Kalinda Brady. I have to!"

She saw the smoldering fire in his eyes as he raised himself with sudden intention and her own whirling senses spun chaotically out of control.

Rand trapped her ankle with his leg and an instant later he settled along the length of her, covering her soft, curving body with his hard, thrilling strength.

But even as she reached up to cling to him and draw him down to her, Kalinda was aware that he was determined to hold off the ultimate union a little longer.

"Please," she whimpered, becoming incredibly aroused as he stoked the fire in her even higher. "Please, Rand I…I *need* you!"

His response was to move against her with a teasing, provoking movement that nearly drove her out of her mind when he failed to complete it.

"Tell me," he commanded, a yearning tone lacing the fierce order. "Tell me how much you need me; how much you want me…."

"More than I've ever wanted any man," she confessed raggedly, her head thrown back against the pillow, her body arching with consummate pleading into his. "I've never even known how…how *necessary* it could be!" That was nothing less than the shattering truth. Never had she felt like this, wanted a man so desperately.

"That's how I need you," he swore deeply. "I had to hear you say it. I had to *know!*"

His hands gripped her shoulders and his body surged passionately against hers, claiming it utterly and completely. Kalinda's breath caught in her throat and she could only cling and cling and cling to the powerful masculine body. Instinctively she sought to envelope his strength, make him a part of her.

Rand held her so tightly they seemed to merge into one being. He licked at the sheen of perspiration that shimmered on the slope of her breast as he set the rhythm of their desire.

"My God, sweetheart," he groaned. "You're flaming like a torch for me!"

Kalinda could only gasp her wonder and desire. No man had ever beckoned to her deepest needs with the irresistible lure of such honest and overwhelming male hunger. It was primitive and it was real yet it was astonishingly tender at times. It cut through all the layers of civilization and sophistication.

She cried out as the threshold was reached, her body shivering with a sudden convulsive energy she'd never known before. It arched her throat, tautened every muscle in her and brought a mind-spinning sense of release.

Above her she heard the harsh, muffled shout of satisfaction and male triumph as Rand followed her over the magic threshold, wrapping her tightly to him in preparation for the long, languid descent on the other side.

"Kalinda, my sweet Kalinda," he breathed over and over again as the sunlight played across their damp, naked bodies. The fragrance of the mountains drifted through the open window, combining with the earthy, honest scent of their passion and Kalinda inhaled it deeply.

"Tell me the truth," Rand grated urgently. "Do you have any regrets about not seeing that other man? Any at all?"

She turned against him, lifting her eyes to meet the surprisingly vulnerable expression in his own.

"None," she smiled softly.

He closed his coppery lashes for a long moment and she felt the gratitude in him.

"You had me so damn scared," he admitted wryly, leaning back against the pillows to stare intently at the ceiling. 'So damn scared!"

"Somehow I can't envision you scared of anything," she retorted lightly.

"You should have seen me at four this morning!"

"Were you really so concerned about me?"

"If you hadn't shown up here or at the shop by this afternoon, I would have taken matters in my own hands. I couldn't let you meet him, Kalinda. It would have been so dangerous!" He shook his head once on the pillow as if awed by the near miss.

"I appreciate your interest," she murmured gently, "but it really wasn't that big a risk! He's simply not the violent sort!"

"You're a little naive, sweetheart, but that's okay," he half-grinned, lifting a hand to ruffle her already tangled hair as he turned to look at her. "Even if you were right about his degree of potential violence, there was my other, equally strong fear!"

"That I'd fall back under his spell? That was never a possibility, Rand. Believe me."

"But you still felt so strongly about him," he persisted.

"No, talking to you made me realize all I felt was the *habit* of hating him. The feeling that he ought to be punished. But it was a hollow sort of emotion. It was a relief to call the whole thing off. Then, too, I kept thinking about his poor wife. In the end, I just thanked my lucky stars I wasn't in her shoes as I so easily could have been."

"How did he take it when you phoned him this morning?"

Kalinda lifted one bare shoulder dismissingly. "He wasn't very pleased. I gave him all the logical reasons why we shouldn't meet. His wife, our reputations. I tried to make it sound as if two reasonable people should agree to call the whole thing off before it got started."

"Did he buy it?" There was a wary look in the hazel eyes as they narrowed slightly.

"He kept trying to talk me into staying here until he could arrive and talk me around," she confessed. "I finally got fed up and told him the truth, that I had agreed to the weekend in the first place because I wanted a little revenge for the way he'd treated me two years ago. Then I told him not to call me again and hung up the phone."

"Hmmm."

"What's that supposed to mean?" she demanded, mouth curving at his skeptical tone.

"Forget it, honey. We'll talk about it later." He yawned extravagantly. "Hell, I'm exhausted! You wore me out," he chuckled affectionately.

"You wore yourself out pacing a floor for no reason at all!"

"Oh, I had my reasons," he retorted sleepily. "But my reasons are all tucked safely into my bed for the moment. Will you think I'm a callous brute if I grab a nap, honey?" He slanted her a pleading glance.

He looked so sleepy that Kalinda found herself smiling with a tenderness she'd never felt toward a man. Almost lovingly she stroked the angled plane of his cheek.

"No."

"We've got a lot to discuss," he murmured, already half-asleep.

Kalinda felt the moisture behind her lashes and blinked it away determinedly. She waited until she felt his hold on her loosen and knew for certain he was making up for the sleep he'd missed the previous night.

Then, aware there could be only one ending for this kind of passionate interlude, she slowly rose from the caramel bedspread and began to dress.

CHAPTER FIVE

KALINDA STOOD AT the window of her office in downtown Denver and looked out across the Mile-High City with remote eyes. Situated on the plains with the mountains nearby to the west, Denver had become the lively, thriving headquarters of the business empire of the Rocky Mountain states.

The swirl of new money from the energy boom which had so affected the city had, in turn, stimulated other businesses. Gleaming highrise buildings in the downtown area gave evidence of the investment capital pouring into the area.

Oil, coal and uranium had beckoned the modern prospectors and speculators. In the last century it had been the lure of gold. But Denver's residents, while they may have been lured to the gateway city by the promise of new opportunities, soon became a fiercely loyal lot for other reasons.

Not the least of those reasons was the city's proximity to the fabulous vacation areas of the Rockies. During the winter the mountains offered some of the finest powder snow for skiing that could be found in the world. Many claimed the Colorado mountains were the United States' equivalent of Europe's Alps.

During the summer those same mountains were a breathtaking wonderland of craggy peaks and green valleys.

And that, Kalinda thought with disgust as she turned away from the window, was all she seemed to be able to think about for the past two days. The mountains. Was she doomed to remember the man she had met there every time she looked out her window?

How long did it take to recover from a weekend fling? she asked herself for the thousandth time as she poured a cup of tea and moodily surveyed her office. It was an attractive office with gold carpet and a heavy mahogany desk she had inherited when she took over her father's role. The colors weren't hers, but there had been more important uses for the company's funds during the past two years than redecorating the president's quarters!

She sipped her tea, staring at the report in front of her and told herself she was going to have to put Rand Alastair out of her head once and for all. And the most efficient way of doing that was by throwing herself back into her work. She should be worrying about the cocktail party she was giving that evening, not dwelling on the exhausted features of the man she had left sleeping in the house by the lake. Determinedly Kalinda brought her well-developed powers of concentration to bear on the company's recent audit report. She wanted the numbers clear in her head when she met with the members of the board later that week.

She was well into the matter at hand when the intercom chimed softly on her desk.

"Yes, George?" she said absently into the speaker, her eyes still on the figures in front of her.

"There's a call from Mr. David Hutton, Miss Brady. Will you take it?" George Barrett's calm, efficient manner was laced with just a hint of his own feelings on the subject. George, to the astonishment of almost everyone, had turned out to be the perfect secretary. He saw himself as breaking the sexual discrimination barriers in reverse and strove tirelessly for professionalism and competency. He never allowed a hint of his personal thoughts to interfere in the conduct of business unless he sensed something crucial was at stake.

Over the past few months, ever since Kalinda had hired him for the permanent position after he'd been sent as a temporary by an agency, Kalinda had come to respect George's instincts. He knew she was routinely refusing calls from David Hutton. He must have a reason for bothering to check with her now to see if she had suddenly changed her mind.

"What's wrong, George?" she asked quietly, switching her attention completely to the little intercom. "You know I have no wish to accept his calls."

George hesitated. She could visualize him in the outer office wearing his three-piece suit and dominating the entrance to the inner sanctum. He was a young man, about twenty-five, pleasant looking and serenely competent. The other office workers had eyed him skeptically from the start but he was now a well-accepted figure in their day-to-day world. In fact, Kalinda knew, he had recently had to set down some very strict rules. Not for Kalinda's sake, but for his own. George had become quite popular with the women on the staff.

"I don't believe this call is of a personal nature, Miss Brady," he finally announced formally. "He won't explain the reason but there's something else involved. I can tell."

Kalinda gritted her teeth and then sighed in resignation. "Okay, put him through. If you're wrong about this, George…"

"I know," George interrupted, unbending slightly at the mild threat in her words. "I'll be the one who has to explain why you hung up on him."

Kalinda grinned and took the call.

"What is it, David?" she asked without preamble, her voice turning cold and crisp.

"It's about time you took my call," he drawled. "That damn secretary of yours has been putting me off for two days!"

"On my instructions. Now that you're through, will you please state your business and get off the line? We really don't have anything to say to each other." Kalinda realized vaguely that her only feeling toward David Hutton now was one of impatience. The thirst for revenge that had driven her into the mountains last weekend had been well and truly eradicated. Another reason why it would be difficult to stop thinking about Rand Alastair.

"Business is exactly why I'm calling, darling," he

murmured, and something in his tone chilled her. "You should have met me at that motel, Kalinda. Things could have been handled a lot more pleasantly if you had."

"What in the world are you talking about?"

"A merger, Kalinda. You've done some astonishing things with Brady Data Processing. Two years ago everyone said it had no choice but to go under. You've created a total turnaround situation and your company, my love, has become one very enticing little pigeon. I want it."

Kalinda swallowed in shock and outrage. It was several seconds before she could control her anger into an icy refusal. "Out of the question. Brady Data Processing is not interested in merging with anyone, David, and quite definitely not your firm!"

"You aren't going to have any choice. I'm filing forms with the Securities and Exchange Commission this week."

"What!" Kalinda stared at the phone. Filing forms with the SEC? There could be only one reason for that...

"That's right, love," he taunted with pleased satisfaction. "I'm going to force the merger on you since you weren't willing to discuss it under more amicable conditions."

"You mean since I wasn't willing to give you an opportunity of trying to seduce me into surrendering the company without a fight!"

"Precisely," he agreed smoothly. "I would have preferred a 'friendly' sort of takeover but since you've proven obstinate, you may as well know I don't mind a fight. It will cost more this way, of course, because I shall have to offer a premium price for your stock, but it will be worth it in the end."

"How much of the outstanding stock have you picked up already?" Kalinda forced herself to ask bravely.

"Just under the five percent limit," he acknowledged easily.

She winced. Anyone going after more than five percent of a publicly held stock had to register that intention with the SEC. Hence the papers David claimed to be filing. He could now start hunting down vast quantities of the shares on the open market. All he needed were enough to give him control of the firm. Kalinda felt the panic begin to rise in her. After all her work in getting Brady Data Processing back on its feet! She couldn't bear the thought of having it forcibly taken from her. What about all the people who worked for her? Company morale would go to hell when word of this leaked out. Nothing sent shivers of fear through a firm faster than rumors of an intended hostile takeover move. And there were so few defenses for a company in Brady's position.

"Why are you doing this, David?" she asked coldly, trying desperately to think of defense tactics. She knew so little of this sort of thing. She'd never faced it before.

"The usual reasons," he retorted bluntly. "My firm is heavy in cash right now and we need some acquisitions. I've seen your balance sheet, darling, and you are ripe."

"You're telling me there's nothing personal in this, right? Just business?" she scoffed angrily.

"Oh, no, I wouldn't say that," he chuckled arrogantly. "It will give me great personal satisfaction to take Brady Data Processing. It should have been mine two years ago."

"You didn't want it two years ago!" she flung back.

"I've changed my mind. Thanks to you, Kalinda. No one thought you could pull it off, you know. Everyone was sure that firm was headed for the bottom. But now that you've done all the hard work…"

"You think you can just step in and help yourself? I've got news for you, David. We'll fight."

"They all say that in the beginning. Go ahead, love. It will only make the process that much more interesting. Perhaps somewhere along the line you'll even consider that little mountain rendezvous we planned. Now *that* would be amusing, wouldn't it? I wonder how many chief executive officers of firms facing a hostile merger have tried to buy off the raiding company with their bodies? Interesting thought, isn't it…?"

Kalinda slammed the phone down, his confident, knowing laughter ringing in her ears.

She sat in stunned silence for several minutes, gazing with unseeing eyes at the framed mirror on the opposite wall. It reflected her well-tailored white business suit with its narrow skirt and close-fitting jacket. Her hair was up, as usual, and the yellow silk blouse she wore was open at the neck with a rakish air.

My God, she thought dazedly. What did she do now? Handling hostile mergers wasn't one of those subjects stressed when she had been in business management school. It was something one learned on the streets, a true urban guerrilla warfare. She knew all about building a company up from within, obtaining capital, promoting research, making the firm's stock appear attractive to the analysts of brokerage houses so that they would, in turn, encourage investors to buy it; she knew about those things. She'd learned some the hard way and some she'd studied in school.

But this was a different kind of game. Unfriendly mergers were something that happened to other companies, not to one's own! She closed her eyes briefly in self-reprisal. She had made a bad error in not planning ahead for such an eventuality. But she had been so swamped just trying to save the business it had never occurred to her that someone would come along and take the salvage prize right out of her hands.

Not to mention the hands of the loyal management. Breaking the news to them would be the hardest part. It was their jobs, after all, which were most likely to be destroyed by such an action. The rank and file were probably the safest. They would be needed to keep things running. But all those in management positions who had worked their way up during the years would find themselves in real jeopardy. They could be replaced and most likely would be by aggressive young movers from the acquiring firm.

Everything she had worked for during the past two years would be gone. Kalinda, of course, would be the first to go...

But that was negative thinking, she told herself furiously, getting restlessly to her feet and walking back to the window. She was going to fight. She had to. She owed it to her company to try to save its independence. Tomorrow morning she would call in the company officers for an emergency strategy meeting. She shook her head sadly. It was going to be a shock for all of them.

But in spite of the crisis and the need for planning, there was nothing she could realistically do that evening. She couldn't very well call off the party and it wouldn't do her any good even if she could. Grimly she paced back to her desk.

Several hours later Kalinda paused in her duties as hostess to take stock of the cocktail party's success. There were several important business associates here this evening, many of them male and that meant she had to be especially nice to their wives. The last thing she wanted was to risk a case of wifely jealousy. She had walked a fine line for two years and thought she'd done a good job of reassuring suspicious wives and still maintaining the solid business contacts she needed.

She glanced around the room, taking in the well-dressed, affluent crowd in their expensive suits and gowns, wondering who among them she might go to for advice and professional consultation. She needed to talk to someone, she thought. Someone who knew about the dirty in-fighting that went on in a hostile merger situation. It was a cinch she wouldn't get much constructive help from her own staff. They'd never encountered such a maneuver.

Before she could decide if there was someone in the crowd who could be potentially helpful, Kalinda was interrupted by the effusive thanks of a charming, older woman who glided up to her in a cloud of perfume and wispy chiffon.

"Kalinda, my dear! Thank you so much for the lovely picture you gave Harold and I! So nice of you to think of us while you were on vacation! But your dear father was like that, too. Always so thoughtful of others."

"I'm glad you like it," Kalinda smiled, thinking of the price she'd paid for the watercolor she'd purchased in Rand's gallery. A weekend affair...

"It looks perfect in Harold's den! And you look quite perfect yourself tonight," Mrs. Sebastian added with a warm smile, surveying her hostess's printed beet-red silk jacquard sheath with its touches of peacock blue. A fine gold braid edged the neckline and wrists. It was a sumptuous, almost oriental effect which Kalinda wore well. The buttery material slid fluidly over her small breasts and rounded hips.

"Thank you," Kalinda said, hastening to return the compliment. She stood talking for several minutes to the wife of one of her top managers and then edged away with the excuse of checking the buffet table.

Around her the crowd swirled happily amid the lush green and ripe apricot décor of the town house.

The green in the plush rug gave the apricot print-covered furniture a dramatic background. The color scheme emphasized the focal point of the room which was a huge sun parlor that formed one entire wall.

Brilliant patches of white had been used sparingly against the rich colors in the form of an occasional lamp and glass-topped coffee table. The dining table was also a stark white and stood in front of a mirrored wall which reflected the colorful buffet food set out on it.

As usual, Kalinda spared no expense when she entertained, deeming it a business necessity. But even she had to smile at that justification. The truth was, she enjoyed entertaining. Tonight was an exception. But, then, who could take pleasure in such things with a sword hanging over one's head?

Only a few people knew that she, herself, prepared the elegant little canapés and hors d'oeuvres served at her parties. Others just seemed to assume she used a caterer and she let them think that. Only she knew that such gourmet cooking was a source of relaxation for her. She had discovered it during the past year and was continually amazed at how she could escape her business concerns for a few hours in a kitchen.

Across the room she caught Colin Wayne's eye and smiled at him as he advanced. She had gone out with him on a couple of occasions recently and found his easy charm made for pleasant evenings. He was in his early thirties, with carefully styled blond hair and laughing blue eyes. He was also, she had discovered, a brilliant player on the lively Denver Stock Exchange.

"Another great party, Kalinda," he grinned approvingly, reaching behind her to help himself to a little cracker covered with rich, dark caviar. "Beats me how you throw these affairs together so easily when you work so hard! You'd have made a great corporate wife, you know!"

"You've got a lot of nerve eating my food and insulting me at the same time!" she grumbled in response to his teasing.

"I know, I know, you'd rather be a great corporate manager than a great corporate wife. But that's only because you haven't met the right man. Someday..."

"Have some more caviar," she advised dryly. "We both know I'd be bored to tears as a housewife!"

"How can I argue with that? I'd feel the same," he laughed.

"It is rather difficult to picture you as a housewife," she agreed.

"Still," he went on jokingly, "if I can find myself a woman who can keep me in the style to which I would like to become accustomed..." He glanced meaningfully around the elegant town house and back at Kalinda who narrowed her eyes at him in mock warning.

"Don't look at me," she said hastily.

"How about a business marriage?" he suggested brightly, munching more caviar. "I can keep track of your company's stock movements for you and you can do things that make it move. Preferably upward. Which it seemed to be doing this past week," he added slyly.

She glanced at him quickly and then deliberately forced a smile. "You noticed."

"That volume was picking up? Yes. And the price went up a bit, too. Something I should know, love? Always happy to help spread the good word if it will raise a stock's price. Got something new coming out on the market?"

"It's nice to know you love me for myself and not for business reasons," she mocked, hiding a wince as she realized the activity in her company's stock was undoubtedly from David's move to start buying shares.

"No reason the two can't be combined," he observed cheerfully.

"Well, I hate to disappoint you, but there's no smashing new product about to hit the market. I guess the stock activity is just a matter of people knowing a good investment when they see it," she tried to say lightly. She didn't want to discuss the merger with Colin or anyone else until she knew what she was going to do, how she was going to react. Dammit! She needed professional advice. There were law firms and investment bankers who specialized in this sort of thing. If she just knew someone who could point her in the right direction! The sense of panic had to be forcefully fought back down.

"No hot tips, huh?" he asked sadly.

"Not tonight," she retorted firmly, wondering why she had hardly even given Colin a passing thought since she'd returned from the mountains. But she knew the answer to that, she told herself honestly.

It was going to be a long time before she thought of him in a romantic context again. How long was the image of Rand Alastair going to dominate her? She supposed that, even with a full-fledged business crisis facing her, he would be the last thing she thought of before she went to sleep tonight. Just as he had been last night and the night before that.

"Well, how about a hot date, instead?" Colin countered with a laughing leer. "That new French place sounding interesting."

Kalinda's mouth curved ruefully. "Can I let you know, Colin? I'm going to be very busy this week and I really don't know my schedule yet." It was the only way she could think of to phrase the excuse.

His good-looking features contrived to appear disappointed and philosophical at the same time. "Ah, well. Perhaps next week?"

"I'll check my calendar," she promised apologetically.

"The perils of dating a lady executive," he groaned and glanced automatically toward the door as a knock sounded. "Looks like you've got a late arrival."

Kalinda frowned, unable to think of anyone still unaccounted for. "Excuse me. I'll see who it is."

She crossed the lush green carpet, skirting a chatting cluster of guests and reached for the doorknob, an automatic smile on her face as she opened it.

The polite words of welcome died in her throat as the light spilled over the figure in her doorway. Chestnut hair gleamed from a recent shower, chestnut hair that had been trimmed and carefully combed since she'd seen it last. The light-colored suit looked hand-tailored and was complimented by a satin bow tie. The crisp white shirt was understated and elegant.

"Rand," she whispered finally. "What are you doing here?"

"That's obvious, isn't it?" he murmured, hazel eyes regarding her with an intent, considering expression. "I'm here to rescue you."

"Rescue me!" she squeaked, still trying to recover from the initial shock of seeing him on her doorstep. She stared up at him, dumbfounded, unable to comprehend his meaning. Why had he come like this? It was going to be hard enough getting over him without seeing him again. But if he tried to prolong the hopeless affair it would be impossible.

He lifted his hand and she saw for the first time he was carrying an orchid; one very perfect, very exotic, very brilliant golden orchid. He smiled as she instinctively put out her hand to accept the proffered gift.

"Honey," he murmured softly, putting both hands lightly on her shoulders and pulling her close long enough to drop a warm, hungry kiss on her astonished, parted lips, "if you don't even know yet that you need rescuing, you're in worse trouble than I thought!"

"Oh, Rand, you shouldn't have come," she heard herself whisper brokenly. "This is crazy. It's going to make everything so much harder…" She lifted misty-gray eyes to his.

"Hadn't you better let me in?" he drawled invitingly. "Your guests are beginning to wonder if I'm a traveling salesman you're trying to get rid of!"

Unwillingly, Kalinda smiled. "I don't get many salesmen dressed like that!" That much was the truth, she thought vaguely. Rand could hold his own with anyone else in the room tonight. She wondered why he had invested in such a wardrobe for the mountains. But, then, it rather went with the Lotus. She shook her head in confusion.

"I don't know what you're doing here," she began firmly, feeling a new kind of panic. "But it's all wrong. Can't you see? You shouldn't have come after me. I won't…I won't have an affair with you, Rand. We're totally unsuited. I should never have gone to your house that morning…" she broke off helplessly under the impact of the memory that flamed warmly in his eyes.

"Personally, I happen to think that was the only smart thing you did last weekend! Now move out of the doorway, sweetheart, and let your rescuer inside."

Unable to think of anything else to do, Kalinda did as instructed.

"Got anything to eat?" Rand went on easily, taking in the crowded room with a single, sweeping glance. "I'm starved."

"Over there," she admitted, gesturing toward the long white table in front of the mirrored wall. "Help yourself," she added wryly. She still held the golden orchid clutched in her hand.

He put a proprietary hand on her lower back and urged her forward. "Stop looking like a cornered kitten. I'm friendly, remember? Although why I should be after waking up and finding you'd run off..."

"I'd rather we didn't discuss that," she began stiffly.

"You want to discuss the rescue operation instead?" he invited, bringing her to a halt beside the buffet and perusing it with keen interest.

"What are you talking about? What rescue?" she finally managed a little blankly. He was throwing one curve after another tonight.

"The rescue of Brady Data Processing from the grasping talons of a corporate raider, naturally." Rand reached for a salmon and cucumber canapé. Several of them.

Kalinda stared at him, openmouthed. "How in the world did you know about that?" she breathed.

"There had to be a reason Hutton wanted to try his hand at seducing you after all this time. When you told me a little about the history of your firm and Hutton's newly aroused interest in you, I got suspicious. I asked you to consider the fact that it might be the business he was after, if you'll recall."

"Well, yes, I know, but I never dreamed..." Kalinda sighed. "You have no idea how shocked I was when he called today!"

"Sure I do," he contradicted calmly, slanting a glance at her. "It always hits the unsuspecting ones like a ton of bricks."

"But how did you know what was going on?"

"Monday I did some checking. There's always someone in a company who will talk. I got hold of one of Hutton's vice-presidents."

"Just like that?" she demanded.

"Just like that."

"You'll excuse me if I seem to be having a hard time taking all this in!" she snapped, growing a little irritated over his complacency. The shock of finding him on her doorstep was wearing off to be replaced by confusion. She thought she understood this man. How was it he was surprising her like this? What did he know of the high-powered business world?

"Take your time." He reached for another morsel from the table.

"Thanks!" she muttered and then took a short rein on her temper in favor of an attempt at reason. "Rand, what do you know about all this? What do you mean by 'rescuing me'?"

"If there's anything that can be done, I'll do it," he promised simply, munching contentedly.

"But how is it you know what to do?" she almost wailed.

He stopped munching for a moment and eyed her thoughtfully. Then he swallowed politely and a slow smile shaped his mouth.

"All it takes is total ruthlessness, an instinct for making war, and a willingness to stop at nothing."

Kalinda's eyes widened as she momentarily sensed a menace in him she hadn't dreamed existed. An instant later she shook her head, telling herself she was mistaken.

"But you don't have any of those awful qualifications, Rand," she smiled wanly, thinking of his leisurely, undemanding lifestyle. If he'd had any of those qualities he would have been making his living in a far different manner than the one he'd chosen.

"Want to bet? Watch this."

Something flickered in the hazel eyes, hardening, turning unbelievably cold. The smile he wore became far more dangerous than Kalinda would have believed possible. "What would Brady management think if the members discovered that their president had arranged to spend the weekend at a secluded motel with the head of the firm which is trying to force a merger? They might be forgiven for believing they'd been sold down the river, don't you agree? I'd say there's a good chance they might turn on their little lady chief executive officer, lose all confidence in her, and make it utterly impossible for her to rally the firm for the coming battle. The company would fall into Hutton's lap with only a whimper."

"Rand!" Kalinda couldn't believe what she was hearing. No! The problem was she *could* believe it. There was something in him that proclaimed him capable of such an action and the knowledge shook her deeply. "You…you wouldn't do anything like that…"

"I might," he countered lazily. "If you don't agree to continue the affair we started last weekend!"

CHAPTER SIX

THE CHATTERING, HAPPY crowd seemed to recede into the distance as Kalinda forgot about everyone else in the room and stared, appalled at her uninvited guest.

"Are you saying you'd blackmail me into an affair?" she finally whispered.

He continued to regard her with that incredibly ruthless expression, everything about him hard, unyielding, and determined. Rand said nothing. He didn't need to say anything. The message was plain.

Shakily Kalinda reached out to steady herself with a hand on the edge of the white table. "I…I would never have thought you capable of doing anything like this."

"Perhaps in the short time we spent together you didn't get a chance to know me as well as you might have," he suggested coolly.

"No," she got out, her words barely a thread of sound as she tried to think what to do, how to handle him. "No, perhaps I didn't."

"Now you're seeing another side of me. Do you believe this side is capable of a certain ruthlessness?" he persisted.

"Yes." It was the truth and he must have seen it in her eyes.

"Good," he nodded, the hardness in him fading away on the instant as he turned to reach for another interesting tidbit. "I think I've still got the old shark instincts and talents."

Kalinda heard the wry satisfaction in his words and blinked, confused more than ever. "What's going on here, Rand? Are you telling me you were teasing me just then? That you were faking that...that threat?"

She put a hand on the sleeve of his jacket, urgently demanding his attention. His head swung back to her, the white teeth flashing in a reassuring grin that made her want to kick him.

"You believed me, didn't you?" he countered pointedly. "For a minute or two you thought me fully capable of blackmailing you into an affair."

"You sound proud of it!" she accused, cheeks staining with annoyance and growing embarrassment at her obvious gullibility.

The grin faded into a self-mocking grimace. "No, I'm not proud of it. But it is a useful business skill, I'm sorry to say."

"What's a useful business skill? Blackmail?" she raged heatedly, having difficulty keeping her voice down.

"The skill of being able to make people think I'll stop at nothing when it comes to getting what I want," he explained kindly, soothingly. "I just wanted you to have a small demonstration so you can introduce me to your..."

"Introduce you as what?" she gritted.

"The outside consultant you've hired to direct the defenses of Brady Data Processing," he retorted easily. He appeared about to add to that when his glance went suddenly to a point beyond her head. The hazel eyes gleamed warmly. "Hey, you really did like the pot, huh?"

"Your conversation is getting more and more difficult to follow," Kalinda muttered and turned to follow his gaze. The lovely, wide-mouthed bowl she had bought the first day in his gallery sat in a prominent position at the far end of the table. It held long loaves of sliced French bread which guests had used to build small sandwiches.

He glanced down at her, looking enormously pleased. "I'm glad you didn't try to forget me completely. I've still got a token of your short visit, too."

"What token?" she asked warily.

"The earrings I took off you that first night."

"Oh." She'd forgotten about those.

"You shouldn't have run away that morning after we made love, sweetheart," he went on, dark voice turning slightly husky as he regarded her a little hungrily. "Although I understand why you did."

Kalinda flicked an uneasy glance up through her lashes. "You do?"

"Of course. You thought there was no future for us, didn't you? You thought I wasn't the kind of man you should be giving yourself to so completely. And it was completely, honey. You came to my bed without any reservations, didn't you? For a little while you stopped thinking about the fact that I was an unmotivated, unambitious, undynamic wastrel who had no further goal in life except to fish and seduce bored tourists!"

Kalinda felt her blush deepening and she could no longer meet his eyes, even through the partial veil of her lashes. She remembered her unwise surrender only too well. What really worried her now was the flash of pure happiness when she'd opened her door a few minutes ago and found him standing there.

"You have to admit we do come from two different worlds, Rand," she managed a little grimly.

"Which is a polite way of saying you don't admire my lifestyle," he retorted dryly. "I'm here to change all that. I'm going to prove myself to you, sweetheart. And your ex-fiancé has put the tool I need right into my hands. You admire successful, dynamic, aggressive businessmen? Okay, I'll show you I can wheel and deal in your world with the best of them. Don't worry, Kalinda, you don't have to be ashamed of our affair. You'll be giving yourself to a man who can out-shark anyone on the business street!"

"Rand! This is crazy! I don't know what you're talking about, but I certainly have no intention of… of continuing what should never have been started up there in the mountains. I do not routinely indulge in affairs for heaven's sake! I haven't been even remotely serious about any man since my engagement with David ended."

"Except me," he pointed out, smiling. "Or are you

going to stand there and tell mc you weren't perfectly serious that morning in the mountains?"

Kalinda glared at him, aware that he was deliberately goading her and still too confused and upset by the combination of the day's events to think clearly enough to flatten him verbally.

She was desperately trying to concoct a suitable response when Harold Sebastian and his wife emerged from the crowd with pleasantly expectant expressions.

"Kalinda, my dear, you must introduce us to your new guest." Tall, stately, and silver-haired, Harold beamed complacently down at her. While she was his superior at Brady Data Processing, his long association with her father had given him a decidedly paternalistic air toward the new president of the firm. It was an attitude Kalinda encountered from many of the longtime employees of the firm. They gave her their loyalty and even admired her ability, but they never quite let her forget they all considered themselves honorary uncles and aunts.

"I'm afraid my arrival was something of a surprise for Kalinda," Rand said smoothly, thrusting out a polite hand. "I'm Rand Alastair."

"Harold Sebastian. This is my wife, Edna," Harold said genially. "Alastair," he repeated with a thoughtful look. "That name sounds familiar. Have we met?"

"No, I don't believe so. But I can assure you the name is going to sound a lot more familiar in the future. I'm going to bc working for Kalinda."

Kalinda froze as Harold's inquiring, interested gaze switched to her. "I see. In what capacity?"

"I'll, uh, be explaining Mr. Alastair's role to everyone tomorrow morning," she got out weakly, feeling trapped. "He will be with us in a very limited, short-term capacity," she added spitefully as Rand shot her an amused look.

"Well, well, I'll look forward to having you with us, Rand. You won't find a nicer boss in town!" Harold assured him with a vast chuckle.

"Like father, like daughter," Edna Sebastian added warmly. "Everyone at the company is delighted that she took over the reins two years ago. Just ask anyone in the room!" Edna waved gaily at the crowd behind them.

"I'm sure I shall thoroughly enjoy my association with her, also," Rand said glibly, his eyes still on Kalinda's studiously composed face.

He grinned down at her as the Sebastians faded back into the crowd. "You seemed to be well-liked by your staff," he drawled.

"It's positively feudal at times," she sighed, acknowledging the truth. "We're a publicly owned company but somehow everyone still thinks of it as a family firm."

"How long ago did you go public with your stock?" he asked, suddenly serious.

"Almost as soon as I took over. We needed capital and we needed it badly. I had to convince everyone that it was a clear turnaround situation, make investors think that they could get in on the ground floor of a company that was about to make a big comeback. I've never worked so hard in all my life!"

"I'll bet," he nodded assessingly. "The stock is now widely held?"

"Yes, I'm afraid so." She winced. "Not so long ago I was glad of that!"

"Now you realize that it just makes it easier for Hutton to buy up shares. You don't have any large controlling blocks sitting in friendly hands."

"You needn't look so superior. I had no choice at the time! I couldn't get the loans I needed from the banks. There was no choice but to raise capital by selling shares in the firm!"

"You don't have to defend your actions to me, sweetheart," he murmured caressingly. "I understand completely."

She fixed him with a narrow glance. "Just how much do you understand? Who are you, Rand? Why does Harold think he remembers your name? How do you come to have contacts high enough in the business world to find out what Hutton's doing even before I do?"

"It's a long story, honey. Remind me to tell it to you later. For now, though, I think we'd better circulate. People are beginning to notice that I'm getting your undivided attention!"

He put a hand firmly under her elbow and waded into the crowd. Kalinda felt herself helplessly swept along, her thoughts in a turmoil, her heart beating a little too fast and her nerves singing a tune on the ragged edge of an emotion she didn't want to admit to feeling.

But she knew how to deal with a crowd of business-oriented people. By the time the last of the guests had regretfully taken his leave, Kalinda would have been willing to wager that none of them had guessed at her inner uncertainty and confusion. She *was* aware, however, that more than one knowing glance had absorbed the fact that Rand seldom left her side during the evening. She saw the assessing look in Colin Wayne's eyes although he was cordial when he was introduced. Rand paid him no particular attention, apparently oblivious to the querying glance in the other man's gaze.

Kalinda was also conscious of the pleased speculation from the members of her own staff in the crowd and the curious, smiling looks from others. And some, like Harold, looked as if they could almost place Rand.

It seemed like forever before she gratefully closed the door on the last guest and turned to see Rand pouring himself a snifter of cognac. He had drunk very little during the course of the evening and he looked as if he were anticipating the nightcap with relish.

She watched grimly as he lowered himself into an apricot chair and put up his feet. He saluted her briefly with the glass in his hand.

"I must thank you for an interesting evening, honey. I trust I didn't embarrass you with my unsophisticated mountain manners?"

She started forward, not certain yet how she was going to deal with him but knowing she must handle matters firmly. "You know very well you fit in as if you'd been in the business world all your adult life!"

He took a tentative sip of cognac as she came to a halt in front of him, his green-and-gold eyes laughing up at her.

"To the manner born," he intoned. "Except for the past year and a half."

She fit her hands to her hips, the silk dress soft beneath her fingers. "I would like an explanation, Rand. Is that too much to ask?"

"I would like to go to bed with you. Is that too much to ask?"

The sudden lazy desire in his words stopped her for an instant. It also sidetracked her from her initial intent. Something far more immediately crucial was vibrating in the atmosphere between them.

She gathered her courage. "You're not staying here tonight. I meant what I said. Last weekend was a mistake and I don't intend to repeat it."

He surveyed her with a probing expression. "A mistake? Do you really think of it that way?"

"Yes, dammit! I do!" The protest was a little too vehement and Kalinda was aware of it.

"Come here and let me change your mind," he offered deeply, extending invitingly upward to draw her down onto his lap.

Kalinda stepped away, trying vainly to cover her nervousness by scooping up a stack of glasses and heading for the kitchen. She knew he was following her, his footfalls soft on the thick green carpet.

She couldn't retreat any further than the sink. Just

as she set the glasses down with a clink Rand came up behind her, his hands gliding possessively, longingly around her waist.

"I want you, sweetheart," he murmured, his breath warm on her hair. "More than I wanted you that morning in the mountains and at the time I didn't think anything could be stronger than that need."

"Oh, Rand, please don't do this to me! I don't want an affair. I don't want to be one of your weekend women...."

"There won't be any other women, Kalinda," he promised with absolute conviction, his fingers sliding up to cup her breasts. "You are the only one I want. Why do you think I followed you back to Denver? What we found together was very special, sweetheart. Can't you at least admit that much?"

She trembled as his lips touched the back of her neck. He kissed her nape and the curve of her shoulder as his fingertips gently circled the tips of her breasts through the material of the silk. She felt the need and want in him and it was like a drug, stirring her own responses even while she desperately tried to talk herself into a rational course of action.

"We...we had something very short and meaningless...."

"Meaningless!" He swung her around to face him, a raw, demanding look on his face. "I'll grant it was a little *short*," he said tightly, "but it sure as hell wasn't meaningless! At least," he went on accusingly, "not to me. Are you trying to tell me you were using me,

Kalinda? That you only came by my house on your way out of town to conclude a weekend fling with a man who amused you?"

"Don't put words in my mouth! You know it wasn't like that!"

Anxiously she frowned up at him, her fingers splayed across the finely woven material of his suit jacket. "I...I felt I had to see you again to tell you that you had succeeded in making me see reason where David was concerned. You were so worried about me."

"With good reason, as it turned out. The man's trying to destroy you!"

"But I never intended to go to bed with you!"

"Then why did you?" he countered with the trace of a smile.

"Because...because..." She broke off, floundering for an explanation of the unexplainable.

"Because you wanted me as much as I wanted you," he finished for her, all sure, masculine triumph as he pulled her close. "And I'm going to see if I can't make you want me even more in the days to come. Starting tonight."

"No! All you want from me is sex. I won't fall into that trap," she cried as he lowered his head to take her lips.

"You're wrong, honey," he whispered seductively against her mouth. "I want something much more important from you. I want a commitment."

Kalinda struggled. Struggled to ask him what he

meant by a commitment, struggled to free herself from his embrace. Both efforts failed abysmally as his kiss swamped her senses.

Just as it had that morning in his home by the lake, the potent desire in him reached out to trap her senses and send them reeling. It fed the desire in herself until Kalinda could barely sustain the futile struggle to control it.

He seemed oblivious of her hands pushing on his shoulders, his hold on her a warm, confining, unshakable thing that kept her gently, securely in his grasp. It lured her, seduced her, promised the stars to her and her traitorous body believed everything.

He groaned with relief and longing as he coaxed apart her lips, feeling them soften and yield beneath his own. His hands slid down her back, urging her body more firmly against tautening thighs.

Kalinda felt herself sinking against him, responding to his passion with a desperate craving of her own. A craving she had never known before she had met this man who mystified her. Reality spun away, leaving only the knowledge that he was here with her again. The emptiness she had experienced as she drove away from him that morning in the mountains was at last being filled.

His tongue, moving with hot aggression in her mouth, slowly withdrew as Rand gently, reluctantly broke the kiss.

"Take me into your bed, Kalinda. I swear I'll be as loyal as any of your faithful band of employees.

I'll keep the marauding sharks away from your door for you."

She turned her head into his shoulder, felt his damp, arousing kisses on the vulnerable, sensitized skin behind her ear and then on her throat.

"I thought it was yourself you called a shark," she reminded him shakily, trying to think straight and knowing it was hopeless.

"It takes one to fight one, sweetheart." He trembled against her, eliciting that seductive feeling of female power that she had known before with him. It was power combined with the illogical desire to satisfy. It made no sense to Kalinda but it seemed to make perfect sense to her body.

"Are you really a shark?" she whispered, tipping her head back to meet his eyes searchingly.

He sucked in his breath, his hands tightening around her waist.

"Yes," he said with heavy honesty. "But you can control me, darling. I'll only work for you, never against you. Please believe me!"

She shook her head, dazed. "But I don't understand, Rand. If you know all about the ruthless side of the business world, if you have those abilities, what were you doing for the past year and a half in the mountains?"

He hesitated, as if uncertain how to explain himself. "I was running away from what those abilities had made me. I was running away from the shark I had become. A year and a half ago I took a good look at myself, sweetheart, and decided I didn't like what I saw. I needed time to think, time to discover another side of life. So I went to the mountains."

Kalinda saw the naked, vulnerable look in his eyes and knew in that moment that he'd never told another soul what he'd just told her. Before she could stop to think, she lifted her palms to either side of his harshly carved face.

"And now you think you want to come back to the life you left behind? What makes you believe it will be any different this time, Rand?"

"This time I have you. This time I have something more important than building an empire."

In spite of the tension of the moment, Kalinda's lips twitched. "I'm supposed to be a civilizing influence on a shark?"

"I seem," he observed, sweeping her up into his arms with an easy movement, "to be fated to serve as a source of amusement for you!"

"I wasn't laughing at you," she protested, clinging automatically as he began striding out of the kitchen.

"Yes, you were," he said beguilingly. "But I know how to wipe that smile out of your lovely eyes!"

When he turned unerringly down the hall to her bedroom, Kalinda's head fell back against his shoulder, her lashes drooping softly to flicker on her cheeks.

Her implicit surrender made itself felt. Rand held her with fierce passion as he walked into the bedroom at the end of the hall. With a glance around the room, he made his way to the bed and settled her gently down on it.

The green and apricot color scheme had been reversed in this room; the apricot in the carpet, the verdant green in the bedspread and chair. In her red and gold and peacock blue silk, Kalinda was a splash of vibrant color as she lay on the green spread.

"You look like some exotic creature from a harem lying there waiting for me." Rand stood beside the bed, pulling free the satin bow tie and dropping it onto the carpet.

"Your harem?" she asked throatily, her gaze trapped by his.

"Definitely," he smiled, his fingers on the buttons of his white shirt. "But it's a harem of one."

Kalinda felt herself melting beneath the heat of his gaze and when he had finished undressing himself and reached for her, she shivered violently with the emotion his touch aroused.

"Kalinda, my gentle, passionate Kalinda," he rasped, pulling her into his arms and finding the fastenings of her dress with fingers that shook ever so slightly. "I couldn't believe you had left me when I awoke that morning. I couldn't believe you hadn't found in my arms what I had found in yours. You credited me with good perception but you were wrong. I would never have guessed you would have left like that...."

"I saw so little future for us." She stirred as the coolness in the room bathed her skin. He removed her dress with deftness and a sensual touch that was a caress in itself. She lifted appealing eyes to his intent face. "And I'm not sure there's any more of a future now than there was before. Why *did* you follow me, Rand?"

"Hush, darling," he whispered, bending to kiss the nipple of her breast as it hardened beneath his hand. "Stop trying to put obstacles in our path. We need each other tonight. Let that be enough for the time being."

Under his possessive, exploring touch, Kalinda had no choice but to put the doubts and fears aside. What he offered at that moment was too important, too wonderful to turn down. And he knew it. He was using that fact to seduce her as surely as he used his lips and fingers and the strength of his hard, lean body.

Cradling her against him, Rand rested on one elbow, his free hand trailing exciting patterns down the length of her side to her thighs. He felt her response and slowly built the tempo of the random patterns until she moaned and turned her mouth into his chest.

Finding the male nipples with her quick, gentle teeth, Kalinda returned the mounting excitement, glorifying in his reaction. She felt him shift his legs, inserting one foot between her own. Then his circling, feathering hand went to the inside of her thighs.

"Oh!" The sob of desire was muffled against his skin but he heard it and growled her name against her shoulder.

"My God, Kalinda, you make me wonder how I ever got along without you in my bed!"

She raked her nails convulsively but lightly along

his back, down to the sensitive point at the base of his spine and beyond. He arched into her, his hand moving exquisitely at the point where her thighs joined her body.

She felt the arousing, passionate sensations take her beyond the edge of reasoning thought. All that mattered was Rand. She wondered how she could ever have survived without knowing this powerful emotion again. In the back of her mind, Kalinda acknowledged the truth. She would have eventually gone back to the mountains looking for him.

"I would have come back, Rand," she confessed huskily. "I told myself I had to get over you, that there was no future for us. But I know now I would have come back."

Gently he turned her on her back, his leg thrown heavily across hers. "I couldn't wait, sweetheart. I had to follow you. I had to know if I could make you need me as badly as I needed you!"

He strung fiery little kisses all down her throat, across her soft breasts and along the curve of her stomach. She surged beneath his questing hands, unable to hide her desire.

"Do you have any idea what it does to me when you ignite like this in my arms? I couldn't stand the thought of you coming back to Denver and finding someone else! You're mine, Kalinda. I made you mine last weekend. I swear you'll find me worthy of your sweet surrender."

Kalinda gasped at his progressively intimate demands, her eyes tightly shut as her head fell back over his outstretched arm. "Such a risk, it's such a risk…."

"No," he whispered forcefully. "I'll take care of everything. You don't have to worry about getting pregnant!"

And Kalinda, who had been too far gone in the dazzling world of sensation he had created to even think about that particular risk, gave up trying to tell him her real fears.

He soothed her body with his hands and lips, finding the secret places he had discovered once before and reforging the bond he'd created then. Even as he made love to her, tuning her body to his, Kalinda realized the strength of the link he had bound her with that morning in the mountains.

He knew her so well, she thought wonderingly. She had called him perceptive, but even she hadn't realized the depths of that perception. He had known he could show up on her doorstep tonight and reweave the magic they had found once before.

Her own instincts had been more confused on the issue but under the impact of his desire they homed in on the truth.

When she thought she could stand no more of the teasing, exhilarating lovemaking, when she thought it must surely drive her insane if he didn't stake the final claim, Rand came to her with a fierce and gentle power that left her no option but to respond in kind.

In the darkness she clung to him as she had that morning by the lake, knowing an almost violent satisfaction at the knowledge that this time she couldn't run away when it was over.

The driving force of his need took them both into a timeless world of sensuality that left no room for the unbidden questions a portion of Kalinda's mind still asked.

CHAPTER SEVEN

KALINDA AWOKE THE next morning with a curious sense of expectancy. She sensed the missing weight beside her in the bed and turned her tousled head on the pillow. At the same moment that she registered the empty place where Rand had been she realized the shower was going full blast.

She lay perfectly still for a moment, letting the memories of last night's passion and intimacy wash over her. Again and again in the darkness Rand had reached for her, pulling her close, telling her of his need.

And she had gone to him, refusing to think of the future, allowing only her woman's need to satisfy and be satisfied to guide her.

In the morning light, Kalinda lay gazing across the expanse of apricot carpet and asked herself the question she hadn't wanted to ask during the night.

Why had Rand followed her back to Denver? It was hard to believe that he wanted an affair so badly he felt obliged to "prove" himself worthy of her regard. He didn't strike her as the sort of man who had ever felt it necessary to prove himself to anyone.

He must have met and probably seduced any num-

ber of tourists, she thought wretchedly, flinging back
the covers. But how many had he followed back to
Denver, seeking an affair?

But if it was routine for him, it was not routine
for her. Kalinda had not been seriously interested in
anyone after David Hutton had taken back his ring.
There had been two reasons for maintaining the most
casual of relationships. One had been the necessity for
almost complete attention to Brady Data Processing.
She had always been a hard worker, but the effort to
save the company had required a ceaseless effort for
the first couple of years. And memories of the fool
she had been for trusting in David had constituted
the second reason for extreme caution in her asso-
ciations with men.

Yet within two days of knowing Rand Alastair she
had gone to bed with him, and when he had shown up
on her doorstep last night, she had known the probable result. Known it and put up very little argument
against it.

Kalinda got to her feet and winced at the unexpected soreness in her muscles. The evidence of the
intensity of Rand's lovemaking was going to be undeniable for a day or two, she thought dryly, reaching for a soft velour robe and belting it firmly around
her waist.

She took a deep, steadying breath and headed for
the bathroom where it sounded as if Rand was going
through her hot water in record time. It was as she
tentatively opened the door, the steam hitting her full

in the face, that she realized she didn't know exactly what she was going to say.

But something had to be said, she told herself resolutely. Last night had been only the beginning of an affair as far as Rand was concerned, but for her it had brought the blinding realization that she was in love with the man.

She didn't want to be. Kalinda had no real desire to be in love with anyone. The last time she had allowed her emotions to become vulnerable she had been made to look a fool. Yet two years later she found herself swept into a far more passionate situation than she had ever known with David and with a man she barely knew.

How even as she stood there in the bathroom doorway letting the steam escape Kalinda recognized the depths of her feelings for the man standing complacently under her shower. She had let him in last night because she had taken one look at him and realized the strength of the bonds he had forged that morning in the mountains. She had gone to bed with him last night and let him strengthen those intimate bonds until by morning she had no alternative but to acknowledge them.

"Come on in and close the door, you're letting all the heat out!" Rand called from behind the shower curtain. "About time you got up. I was just about to come in and wake you!" He stuck his head around the curtain, water plastering the chestnut hair to his head, the hazel eyes gleaming with remembered satisfaction as he took in her robe-covered figure.

Kalinda found herself responding to his obvious good mood in spite of her newfound resolution to have a serious talk. "Were you going to wait until you'd used up all the hot water before you called me?"

"I've been saving some for you," he retorted imperturbably. "Come on in."

"I'll wait," she declared firmly. "Rand, I want to talk to you..."

"Come a little closer, it's hard to hear over the noise of the water," he remarked innocently, ducking back behind the shower.

Uncertainly Kalinda moved forward. "I suppose it can wait until you're finished," she began and then belatedly tried to step backward as a long, wet arm darted out to snag her waist. An instant later he reappeared from behind the curtain, a teasing grin slashing his tanned face.

"Come on in, honey. The water's fine."

"Rand, this is serious," she began earnestly and then had to stop her argument in order to push away his fingers as they reached for the belt on the robe. "I need to talk to you."

"I'm listening." He pulled her closer, slipping the robe off her shoulders and, still holding her, plunking the green shower cap down on her head. "You look cute this morning," he murmured, surveying her with a satisfied nod. "Rather like a grumpy cat."

"Are you always in such a lively mood at this hour of the day?" she demanded caustically as he tugged her into the stall beside him. The full force of the water struck her and she found it pleasantly reviving in spite of her mood.

"You'll have a chance to do a statistical analysis on the subject and find out, won't you?" Rand reached for the soap and, cradling her with one arm against his slippery side, began to lather her back.

"That's…that's what I wanted to talk to you about," she said breathlessly, violently aware of the uncompromising maleness of him. It was entirely disconcerting to have him taking over her bathroom and her life and Kalinda fought for a means of self-defense.

"First my good-morning kiss," he intoned, bending his head to find her lips as his hand slid possessively down her back and over the curve of her hip.

"Rand, please listen to me. This is very serious…."

"Ummm," he growled against her mouth, tasting her with evident enjoyment. "Just what a man needs to get the day started properly!"

Beneath the warm water streaming over them his mouth moved even more warmly over hers, probing deeply, lazily, possessively. Kalinda found herself clutching his glistening shoulders, aware of just how much he was telling her with this proprietary good-morning kiss. It was very clear that as far as Rand Alastair was concerned, she was now his. Kalinda wasn't sure how to argue with that overwhelming assumption, especially since her whole being longed to agree.

The hand on her hip began gliding upward, fingers spreading briefly across her stomach before continuing the journey to her breasts. He caressed her with slick, sensuous motions that made her tremble against him.

But when she unconsciously moaned a throaty response and moved her own hand down to his waist and beyond, it was Rand who lifted his head and turned her firmly around to break the contact.

"Enough of that wantonness, Miss Brady. You and I have work to do today," he chided bracingly. "None of which is going to get done if you seduce me here in the shower!"

"I wasn't seducing you," she began wrathfully, feeling the laughter in him. "I was the innocent victim!"

"It's all in one's point of view, I suppose." He shrugged philosophically. "Now, what was it you had to tell me?" Briskly he finished soaping her body.

"I'll...I'll tell you during breakfast," she sighed. Then she realized there had been no scrape of morning beard when he had kissed her. "How did you manage a shave?"

"I had my things downstairs in the car. I threw on my slacks and went down to get them before you awoke."

"You really came prepared, didn't you?" she muttered.

"A man has to look his best first day on a new job."

"You meant what you said last night? You're really going to help my company fight off David's takeover bid?" she asked uncertainly.

"Don't worry, honey. One way or another I'll see to it Hutton doesn't get the firm."

It was only later over the breakfast of scrambled eggs and toast she prepared that Kalinda finally found the courage to bring up the subject which had been on her mind since she awoke.

"Where did you plan on staying while you're in Denver, Rand?" She didn't meet his eyes as she set the plates down on the table.

There was a heavy pause from the other side of the table. Unwillingly Kalinda finally looked up from her eggs. Rand was regarding her with a rather enigmatic speculation.

"Is this the opening volley in your small war to make sure I don't stay here with you?"

She held onto her determination. "I think that as long as you're intent on working for Brady we ought to maintain a…a more businesslike association."

"I'm supposed to prove myself worthy of the affair before you'll continue with it?" he murmured mildly.

"I'm not asking you to prove anything, Rand. You're the one who showed up unannounced on my doorstep last night in the middle of a party and said you were coming to work for me!" she flared.

"I didn't come back to Denver only to work for you."

Kalinda felt herself go warm under the caressing glance he poured over her. "Do you always follow your latest female interest in order to pursue an affair?" she whispered.

"I haven't been out of those mountains for eighteen months," he said evenly.

"Then why have you come after me?" she managed tightly.

His face gentled. "I thought I made that obvious last night."

She shook her head. "Rand, we knew each other for only a couple of days...."

The edge of his mouth turned upward and he said carelessly, "As you are soon going to learn, I am nothing if not a first-rate strategist and decision-maker. I know what I want, Kalinda."

"And you think you want me?"

"I know I want you. I also want to show you I'm fully capable of the business skills you seem to admire so greatly. I saw the disapproval in your eyes when you commented on my rather easygoing way of life in the mountains. You admire men from your own world. So I'm going to show you I can handle myself in that world."

"There's no need..."

"There's every need. But if it will make you less fretful this morning I'll tell you I have a place to stay. You don't have to worry about giving me room and board." He dug into his eggs with gusto.

"Where?" she asked, wishing it didn't seem so right having him here sitting across from her at breakfast. But she had to know more about him, more about his motives. She simply could not believe he had followed her just to take her to bed again.

"An apartment here in town," he smiled. "Now eat your breakfast, sweetheart, we have a lot to do today."

It wasn't until later that morning when Kalinda

convened an emergency meeting of the highest-ranking members of her staff that she realized she wasn't the only one with a profound wariness of Rand Alastair's motives.

But the hard chill in the air that greeted her as she walked into the conference room with Rand at her side took Kalinda by surprise. She was accustomed to an easy, comfortable, respectful familiarity from the circle of mostly middle-aged faces. The shock of the cold nervousness she saw in even Harold Sebastian's eyes left her momentarily unnerved.

Rand seemed totally unaffected by it, taking a seat with a casual nod to the ring of eyes that focused on him. Then he politely turned his attention to Kalinda and she automatically took control.

"What I have to say will be a shock for all of you," she began grimly, glancing around the table. "But perhaps that's my fault. I should have anticipated such an event, given the current merger fever in this country. To put it bluntly, Brady Data Processing has become the target company of a hostile bid…"

The rumble of stunned, accusing voices interrupted her. Before Kalinda could recall the meeting to order, she realized that Rand was the focus of the grim glances and angry murmurs. He sat unheeding, his eyes on Kalinda.

"If I may have your attention," she said dryly, still not fully comprehending the reaction of her staff. Why were they staring at Rand like that?

"You'll have to understand, Miss Brady," Palmer Greyson said finally, his portly body rigid with indignation. "We're all a little stunned by this. When Harold told us this morning that you'd been seen on friendly terms with Rand Alastair, well, we just couldn't believe it. How could you? Your father would never have done such a thing. I'm sure he would be as shocked as the rest of us to know you…"

"I assure you, Palmer," Kalinda said, appalled, "the takeover attempt is not my idea. I believe I mentioned the bid being made is a hostile one!"

"But Harold said you were more than a little friendly with Alastair last night and others saw you…"

Kalinda, realizing the drawbacks to running business in a more or less democratic way, tightened her mouth and regarded her accusers coolly.

"I'm sorry to have to admit it, but, frankly, I don't have the skills necessary to combat the bid. And neither, if you're honest with yourselves, do any of you! We have gone our own way here at Brady, staying out of the conglomeration movement and concentrating on building our firm from within. As a result, we've allowed ourselves to be taken by surprise.…"

"You can't just turn the company over to him without a fight!" Harold Sebastian interrupted forcefully, bringing his hand down flatly on the table. He swung his head around to stare at Rand who merely arched an eyebrow in response. "I knew your name was familiar last night but it took me until this morning to place it. How did you talk Kalinda into this? She's always been as concerned with Brady as her father was.…"

"That's enough, Harold," Kalinda said quietly, the

authority in her voice bringing all eyes back to her. "There seems to be some misunderstanding here. If you know something I don't know then perhaps you should tell me about it. In the meantime, hear me out. We will then throw the subject open for discussion. Is that agreeable?"

With muttered remarks and a few resentful glances at Rand Kalinda's staff settled back into their seats, clearly expecting to hear nothing hopeful from her.

"We need an expert. Mr. Alastair claims competence in the specialized area of business we need at this moment. With your approval I intend to hire him to advise us during the next few weeks."

"Hire him!" The startled exclamation was repeated around the table as everyone turned to stare uncomprehendingly at everyone else. Only Rand remained aloof, looking half-amused.

"Yes, unless, as I noted earlier, you have some serious objection or a better suggestion," Kalinda finished forcefully.

"Miss Brady," Margaret Vannon said very slowly, her graying blond hair still an attractive frame for her pleasant features. "Who, exactly, is proposing to take over Brady?"

She told them the name of David Hutton's firm and saw the astonishment in their faces.

"Hutton is trying to force a merger on us?" Harold asked a little blankly, staring at Rand again. "Not Alastair?"

It was Kalinda's turn to look blank. "That's correct."

"And you're proposing to hire Rand Alastair? To have him on our side?" Palmer Greyson said in wondering disbelief.

"Yes. Now I'm prepared to throw this discussion onto the table, although it already appears to be there," she noted dryly. "I'm quite willing to have your input since this affects all of us. Hutton, by the way, has already filed with the SEC. We're running out of time. May I have your comments, please? Perhaps you would like to question Rand on his qualifications."

"His qualifications!" Margaret Vannon echoed wryly. "They could hardly be any better, as I'm sure you know." She looked frankly at Rand. "Have you really agreed to help Brady in this matter?"

Rand inclined his head in silent agreement.

"You'll be working for us?"

"Yes," he smiled politely.

There was a thoughtful silence while everyone absorbed this. Kalinda was still trying to figure out what her staff knew about Rand that she didn't when the vice-president in charge of marketing said half-humorously, "How's it going to feel being on the other side of the action, Mr. Alastair?"

"Interesting," Rand replied, a small, anticipatory grin on his lips.

As if the single word had removed a barrier, the questions started coming fast and furiously. But this time they were asked with a growing excitement and confidence that told Kalinda the turning point had been reached.

Rand had gone from being the villain at the table to the hero. She didn't understand it but she was too good a businesswoman to question her luck. Her staff's obvious confidence in Rand's abilities reinforced her own decision to believe in him. She sat musingly and watched him handle the questions and comments with easy skill. He really did know what he was doing. And he appeared familiar with the respect he was receiving. Yes, she thought privately, she had a lot of questions for Rand Alastair.

But it was Harold Sebastian who answered many of them for her. He approached her as the meeting broke up sometime later, an apologetic smile on his now-pleased face.

"You've really pulled off a coup, Kalinda. Your father would have been proud of you. Alastair may have been maintaining a low profile for the past couple of years but there's no doubt he's still got the ability! I'll admit when I finally remembered who he was this morning and realized just how friendly the two of you seemed last night, I had a few bad moments. So did everyone else. That man's reputation alone might be enough to spike David Hutton's guns! How did you ever persuade Alastair to come back into battle? Word had it he'd retired a couple of years ago."

"Just what is his reputation, Harold?" Kalinda asked ruefully. "I mean, he's admitted he knows something about the conglomeration business, but…"

"Knows something about it! My God, Kalinda, that man was the terror of every firm in the rockies up until about two years ago. He had a reputation as a corporate raider that made Genghis Khan look tame! He had a piece of the action wherever he wanted it. Sometimes he would force a takeover, sometimes he only wanted a seat on the board of a particular firm. He manipulated stock, added any firm that took his eye to his own conglomerate, and generally seemed unstoppable. It got to the point where the mere mention that he was interested in a company was enough to send the management into panic."

"How is it I never heard of him?"

"The timing, I suppose. You were working at that firm in Houston until about three months before your father was killed. You got engaged, as I recall, shortly after you moved up here from Texas. Alastair was going into retirement about the time you were going through the shock of your father's death. When I saw you walk in with Alastair this morning I knew we were headed for disaster. And then when you said we were a target company…"

"You saw Rand sitting there and assumed I'd just handed over the reins to a shark?" Kalinda mused with a wry smile.

"I should have known you'd never do anything like that. I guess I panicked, too, just the way everyone used to do when they heard Alastair was coming!" Harold grinned. "But to have him actually working for us…!"

"You don't mind having a shark around as long as he's on your side?"

"Business is business," Harold chuckled and then excused himself to hurry off to his office. Rand had already begun dispatching people for the various reports and records he wanted to see.

The management offices of Brady Data Processing took on the atmosphere of an armed camp preparing for battle. Word went like wildfire through the company of the takeover bid, but word of Rand's presence spread equally as fast. Instead of the sudden depression in morale, Kalinda was amazed to find everyone invigorated with a purposefulness that told its own story. Brady management had a battlefield general and they were prepared to follow him into the fray, no questions asked. There was nothing like having a shark on your side, Kalinda thought idly at one point when George Barrett appeared with coffee and sandwiches.

"Thanks, George," Kalinda smiled gratefully, looking up from the pile of papers on her desk. Rand, sitting across from her, glanced up almost curiously and then looked appreciatively at the sandwiches.

"I didn't know an order for food had gone out," he grinned, helping himself to a thick pastrami on rye.

George lifted an eyebrow. "Miss Brady would never think to send me out for sandwiches," he murmured. "She respects my professionalism far too much, even in a crisis, to do such a thing. But I have eyes and it was clear neither of you had remembered lunch today!"

He left the room with a stack of rough drafts that needed typing, all business. Rand watched him go, one brow cocked bemusedly.

"Things seem to have changed in the business

world during the past couple of years," was his only comment.

"George is the perfect secretary," Kalinda said calmly, watching his expression.

"Bosses," Rand drawled, "are known for falling in love with their secretaries."

"George would never allow such an improper situation to develop," Kalinda said blandly. "Here's that breakdown on Brady's line of credit you requested."

Most of the management staff stayed late that day, but not as late as Kalinda and Rand. The ultimate responsibility was on their shoulders and Kalinda found her new employee seemed avid to accept his share. It was, she decided, as if the shark had swum back into his element. An impressive sight.

The dinner hour came and went, sandwiches and coffee once again the only fare. After the brief break during which Rand asked a series of probing questions concerning the material he'd been going through they both plunged back into the task of planning the defense strategy. Rand was intent on immersing himself in a thorough understanding of Brady's resources, weaknesses, and possible options.

Finally, shortly after ten o'clock he closed the manila folder in front of him and got to his feet. "Come on, honey, let's go home. We're not going to be worth a damn tomorrow if we don't get some sleep tonight."

"Where is your apartment, Rand?" Kalinda asked bravely, rising to her feet and stretching as a yawn threatened. She must be firm.

"I'm going to show you," he smiled benignly.

"I meant what I said this morning," she began determinedly. "I think we ought to maintain a business relationship until we have a chance to know each other better."

"I said I'd show you the apartment, I didn't promise to seduce you, too." He gathered up a stack of papers and shoved them into a leather case. "I'm not even sure I could at this stage," he reflected seriously. "It's been awhile since I worked like this. I'm a little out of shape!"

She smiled at that. "You don't look it. You look like an eager warhorse getting back into harness!"

He took her arm and walked her toward the door. "Nevertheless, the stamina requirements are a trifle different than those of fishing and pottery-making!"

The white Lotus sped through the night toward an elegant apartment building near the downtown area. It was not far from her own town house, she thought ruefully.

"Come on up for a nightcap. We deserve it," Rand instructed, giving her little option as he took her arm once again and assisted her out of the car.

"How do you happen to have an apartment, Rand?" she murmured, trying not to think of the decision which lay ahead of her tonight. How could she refuse him if he made love to her? His touch was like magic on her skin and the warmth in him was almost irresistible. She loved the man. But she had to have the answers to her questions about him. No amount of logic could convince her he had followed her out of the mountains merely for an affair. And he'd said nothing of love....

"I own the building," he confessed.

"Own it!"

"It was one of the few things I hung onto when I opted out a year and a half ago," he explained, watching her face as he pushed the elevator button. "It was something that didn't have to be managed in person and provided a nice income."

She shook her head. "You're proving to be one surprise after another."

"Good surprises, I trust," he smiled.

"Are you so very concerned about my opinion?" she breathed, stepping into the elevator.

"I prefer seeing respect in your eyes rather than disapproval. Is that so strange?" he asked wistfully.

Kalinda could think of nothing to say to that. But some instinct warned her that a man like Rand Alastair didn't worry much about other people's opinions.

A moment later the elevator opened and they emerged into a thickly carpeted hallway. Rand fished a key out of his pocket and paused before the only door in sight.

"I phoned ahead and had the place put in order," he began as he opened the door. "I hope it's decent."

He flipped on the light, revealing a clean, uncluttered room furnished in an utterly masculine style. It was similar to the décor in his house by the lake, Kalinda thought, walking inside curiously. Browns and caramels were the predominant colors of the low-slung, modern furniture. Wide, sweeping vistas of the Denver night were provided by an expanse of windows.

Automatically Kalinda walked toward the view, knowing he was watching her. "It's lovely," she smiled, looking out into the darkness and picking out familiar buildings. They were on the twentieth floor.

"I prefer your place," he said dryly.

She swung around to see him going over to a liquor cabinet and begin hunting through the collection of bottles.

She accepted the snifter he held out to her a moment later, meeting his eyes silently over the rim as they each lifted their glasses. For an instant as she met the glittering promise in the hazel eyes, Kalinda forgot all about her promise to herself. And when he took her wrist and led her silently across the tan carpet to the sofa, she couldn't find the words of protest.

He sank down onto the leather cushions, tugging her gently down beside him. Then, wrapping the arm holding his drink around her shoulders so that she was forced to curl into his side, Rand reached for the leather case he brought with him.

He put his feet up on a hassock and fumbled briefly in the case. "Now, I've got a couple more questions about your relationship with the banks," he said calmly.

Kalinda turned her head quickly to stare at him and saw that he was quite serious. He didn't appear to have any intention of trying to seduce her tonight.

She honestly didn't know whether to be glad or feel insulted.

The amusement lit her eyes and quirked her mouth as she dutifully answered his precise questions.

Half an hour later she was still answering the occasional question as Rand continued reading beside her. With a strange feeling of contentment she settled more closely against him, finding his obvious interest in the work at hand somehow endearing. He was enjoying this, she thought sleepily.

Her eyes were closing when the impact of that statement finally made itself felt.

He *was* enjoying himself! He was thriving on the opportunity to get back into the dangerous game he knew so well. Belatedly Kalinda remembered the occasional feeling she'd had in the mountains that he'd latched onto her because he had been as bored as she was up there.

She was almost asleep when the plausible answer to all her questions popped into her head.

Had Rand followed her back out of the mountains because she had made him realize he was bored with the easy life? Was he using her to find his way back to the high-powered business world he'd once dominated?

The thought of serving as an accidental catalyst for a man who once again was seeking a change of lifestyle was not a pleasant one. What happened to the catalyst after it had served its purpose?

CHAPTER EIGHT

KALINDA AWOKE HOURS later to find dawn pearling the sky outside the massive windows. She blinked, stirred warmly and finally opened her eyes to find herself wedged between the back of the sofa and Rand's lean frame.

They were still wearing their business suits, she realized, minus the jackets. Her camel shirt and white, bow-tie blouse would never be the same. Sometime during the night Rand had located a blanket and pulled it over both of them before going to sleep himself. Kalinda shifted position carefully and found herself snugly cradled, Rand's arm firmly wrapped around her.

She managed to prop herself on one elbow, desperate to stretch cramped muscles. Her hair was hanging loosely around her shoulders and she felt terribly mussed and sleep-tousled.

In the pale morning light Rand's firmly etched features appeared more relaxed. There was an unmistakable contentment in the eased lines around his mouth and eyes. His shirt had been undone at the collar, tie removed.

For a long moment Kalinda stared down at him,

absorbing each detail along with the fact that she loved him. That look of contentment, she now realized, wasn't because he'd spent the night by her side. It was because he'd spent the night by her side. It was because Rand Alastair was finally back where he wanted to be. He had emerged from his year and a half of retirement to resume the fast-paced, perilous life he had known before opting out of the business world.

For how long would he see Kalinda as his means of getting back into the high-powered atmosphere he'd once dominated? Helping Brady Data Processing fight off a hostile merger attempt could only be a stepping-stone for such a man. Kalinda might have been the one to galvanize him into realizing he was bored with retirement, but how long would she hold his interest once the transition back to the business world had been made?

If her time with Rand was fated to be short-lived, why was she telling herself that she must control the passion in the relationship? Why shouldn't she be taking advantage of the precious, stolen moments? With luck she might have weeks, perhaps even a few months before he got swept up completely in the world he'd left behind. But it was already going to be incredibly difficult to say goodbye. How much worse would it be if the affair went on for months? The thought of watching Rand grow bored with her was frightening.

She was staring at him, wondering unhappily how she would explain her feelings to Rand when the chestnut lashes flickered against his cheekbones and lifted. The hazel gaze gleamed at her with sleepy contentment.

"Good morning, Miss Brady," he growled lazily, moving the hand that cradled her up to snag luxuriously in her hair. "You have an interesting way of conducting late-night business conferences. Do you always go to sleep in the middle of them?"

"I don't appear to be the only one who dozed off at this particular conference," she replied, warming under the possessiveness in his gaze. "Perhaps you should serve coffee instead of cognac when you conduct your late meetings."

"My only regret," he murmured, his mouth quirking with an intimate, teasing expression, "is the unfinished business we failed to get through."

Kalinda knew her cheeks were reddening under the complacent, very male look in his eyes. But before she could frame a properly light retort, the hand in her hair was moving to urge her head down to his.

With a muffled sigh Kalinda let herself be pulled across Rand's chest, her hair tumbling over his shoulders as he kissed her with slow satisfaction.

"I think we've got time to tie up a few loose ends," he whispered against her mouth.

Kalinda tried to take a firm grip on her new resolutions. "I agree," she said lightly and saw the pleased look on his face. "And I think an early-morning walk would be just the way to do it."

"A walk!"

"Ummm. A little exercise to get us revitalized for the new day."

"If it's exercise you're after, I have a better suggestion," he began determinedly, sliding his fingers up her throat and encircling the nape of her neck.

Kalinda resisted the temptation and the want in him with every atom of restraint she possessed. She had to start drawing the line. She had to ease out of this relationship before it became impossible to do so.

"Consider this little suggestion of mine as an order from your boss," she said, easing herself to a sitting position beside him.

He regarded her with a measure of fascination. "I'm not accustomed to taking orders," he finally pointed out.

"As you said yesterday, things have changed a bit in the business world since you opted out a year and a half ago!"

"Some things are basic. They never change." He reached for her.

"I'm serious, Rand," she said quietly, evading his arm. "I want to go for a walk. We…we need to talk."

He hesitated, as if testing the determination in her and then he shrugged eloquently. "Okay, boss, if that's really what you want."

They must have made a rather strange sight, Kalinda decided later as they walked briskly along the path of a nearby park. It was one of many such islands strung throughout the city. There were more than one hundred and fifty parks in Denver and Kalinda would have been willing to bet that few of them were being used at this hour of the morning by a couple dressed in business suits that had recently been slept in.

But it was invigorating. The beginning of a Colorado summer day shone down on them and to the west the mountains seemed to hold out the same promise they had for generations.

"Do you do this a lot?" Rand grinned wryly, clasping her hand as they walked.

"Of course not. I'd be afraid of getting mugged!"

"You think I can protect you?" he asked, slanting her an interested glance.

"If anyone dares menace us we'll just tell him who you are and use your reputation to scare him off!"

He winced. "That took you by surprise yesterday, didn't it?"

"Your reputation? Frankly, yes," Kalinda said simply, inhaling the morning air. "I'm told you really were the shark you joked about being that night at the party."

"Does that worry you?" he asked with surprising hesitation, not looking at her.

"Should it?"

"No. It's supposed to convince you I'm the sort of man you admire," he said softly.

"Which brings us to the subject I wanted to discuss," Kalinda said, amazed at the calm in her voice.

"I had a feeling it might," he sighed. "What's wrong, Kalinda?" His fingers tightened around hers, as if he were preparing for a physical struggle.

"There's nothing wrong, Rand. I just want to make it clear that I meant what I said yesterday morning about maintaining…a businesslike relationship for a while. There's a lot we have to learn about each other.…"

"You were upset about finding out about my past, weren't you?" he interrupted harshly. "But, honey, it's that past which is going to help your company. Don't you see?"

"I see. And I'm grateful. But that's not the point." She tried to speak rationally, keeping her emotions under control. But it was difficult with him looking at her like that, as if she really were more important to him than business.

He drew her to a halt on the path, turning her so that she had to face him. "Then what is the point, Kalinda? What are you trying to say?"

She faced him bravely. "Rand, I'm grateful for your help in this crisis. But, please, don't confuse your feelings about coming back to the business world with…with any feelings you might have for me!"

"What the hell are you talking about?" he rasped, his hands tightening forcefully around her upper arms, his face darkening.

"Please," she begged earnestly, gray eyes wide with concern for him, "don't be angry. I'm just pointing out the obvious. You're finding it exciting to get your feet wet again in the world in which you were once so successful. It was very clear yesterday that you were enjoying yourself. And if it's what you want, then I don't mind having been the catalyst that drew you out of the mountains, really I don't…"

"Catalyst!"

"Yes! Remember how I asked you a couple of times if you were bored with your trout fishing and the little gallery? You denied it, but I think the truth is that you were getting restless. After a year and a half, you felt the urge to compete and win getting the better of you. When I came along representing a portion of the world you'd left behind, something clicked, didn't it? I became an excuse, a reason, for coming back to Denver and picking up the reins of business."

He stared at her. "You've got it all worked out, haven't you?"

"Is my conclusion so very far from the truth?" she whispered sadly. "Are you going to deny that you're enjoying yourself as you begin to wheel and deal again?"

"That's a very neat trap you've worked out, Kalinda Brady," he muttered icily, hazel eyes hardening as he surveyed her face. "I can't very well deny the fact that there is something in the business world which challenges and interests me. You saw me at work yesterday. I never stayed up half the night working on a piece of pottery!"

She nodded in mute understanding, trying to hide her unhappiness.

"And I'm not going to deny that I might have been growing bored with my lifestyle in the mountains. A year and a half of fishing and part-time employment can be a bit more than relaxing. It can make a man restless...."

"I knew it," she murmured, lowering her eyes as she listened to the confirmation of her fears.

"But you're caught in the trap with me," he went on relentlessly, lifting her chin with thumb and forefinger. "You made it very clear in a lot of little ways that you weren't interested in an affair with a lazy trout fisherman and pottery-maker! You wanted a man from your own world. Okay, you've got him. I not only understand and function very well in your world, Kalinda, I can dominate it if I wish. I'm giving you what you asked for in a man. Don't you dare try to back out of our deal now!"

Kalinda froze at the cold, hard edge in his voice. "We didn't have any sort of 'deal,' Rand!"

"We do now," he countered and crushed her lips beneath his own as if to seal it.

It was a harsh, ruthless, dominating kiss, with none of the warm, seductive persuasiveness she'd known in the past. It was as if he was intent on letting her know that he could dominate not only the world in which she made her living, but Kalinda, herself.

His mouth moved aggressively on her lips, forcing them apart and giving her no option but to accept the invasion of his tongue. Desperately Kalinda tried to pull away, break the ruthlessness of the kiss, but he only wrapped his arms around her and forced her closer. In the chill morning air he molded her body to his own, letting his inner heat trap her.

When she tried to free her lips, he used his teeth to nip warningly and she crumpled against him at the first threat. He accepted the surrender as if it were his due, not taking his mouth from hers until she had stopped fighting him completely.

When at last he lifted his head to gaze forbiddingly down at her helpless face, Kalinda sagged in his arms. He let her bury her face against his shoulder, holding her with bonds of steel.

For a long moment they stood silently. Kalinda knew she was trembling with reaction. Not just to the kiss, itself, but to all the male implacability that lay behind it. He did want her. Regardless of his other reasons for following her out of the mountains, he wanted her. Would that ever be enough?

"Don't fight me, Kalinda," he finally got out on a hoarse thread of sound. "Please don't fight me!" He turned his lips into her hair, kissing her gently now, almost apologetically. She felt a tremor go through him and knew he was shaken by the moment.

"Is that a warning, Rand?" she managed, her words muffled by the fabric of his jacket. "Are you saying I'll get hurt if I don't go along with what you want?"

His grasp on her tautened. "I would never hurt you, honey. But I can't let you go, either. I need you too much!"

"Rand…"

She wasn't sure just what she was going to say under the tension of the moment, but whatever it might have been died in her throat as he gently set her a little ways from him and forced a quirking smile.

"Don't say anything more this morning, sweetheart. For both our sakes, I think we'd better get back to business. Come on, let's go find ourselves some breakfast."

Without waiting for a response, he tugged her gently down the path.

The rest of the day passed much as the preceding one. Rand was constantly on the phone to banks, old acquaintances who owed him favors, and people who knew an astonishing amount about the inside workings of David Hutton's fledgling empire. When he wasn't using her telephone, he was going through the endless paperwork generated by a thriving enterprise such as Brady Data Processing.

"You know, this whole thing is turning out to be quite an education," Kalinda observed truthfully at one point as they munched sandwiches and prepared once more to stay late at the office. "I'm going to be a much more aware businesswoman when this is all over!"

He smiled, a genuine flash of humor. "That's one thing that can be said about a company that gets caught up in a merger battle. Management is never quite the same thereafter."

"A matter of facing reality, I suppose," she nodded seriously.

He took her home that night around ten o'clock and he didn't try to invite himself inside. Kalinda thought he looked rather preoccupied, in fact, and wondered at his almost casual good-night kiss. But she didn't argue with it. She knew she needed the time to herself.

But she came to no revealing conclusions as she lay alone in her bed. Instead, she found herself dreaming that Rand was beside her. When she went into work the next morning, she didn't try to deny her own eagerness to see him again.

He was there ahead of her, already on his second cup of coffee apparently and he looked up inquiringly as she stood in her doorway.

"I give up," he smiled. "Why the frown?"

"You're drinking too much coffee," she said with automatic concern as she walked into the room and seated herself behind the mahogany desk.

He glanced down at his cup in surprise. "An old habit, I guess."

"A little caffeine goes a long way. I think you should switch to tea."

He studied her determined expression for a long moment and then pushed aside his half-finished cup. "Whatever you say, boss."

That made her grin. "There's nothing quite like a truly deferential, obedient employee!"

"I'll make a bargain with you. I'll be deferential and obedient on the job if you'll be deferential and obedient after hours!"

"Facetiousness and flippancy in employees, however, is not condoned in the offices of Brady Data Processing!"

"I'll try to remember that. Now, suppose you pour me a cup of tea?" he suggested smoothly, eyes gleaming.

She thought about that. "If I do you're liable to get the notion you can manipulate the boss."

"The only time I intend to manipulate the boss is

in bed," he growled, leaning forward with just enough menace to make her sit back in her chair.

"You *have* been up in those mountains too long," Kalinda complained, jumping to her feet and striding quickly over to where a pot of hot water simmered on a hot plate alongside a pot of coffee. "You've forgotten your office manners!"

"I'll rely on you to keep me in line," he chuckled as she returned with a mug of tea. He accepted it with a smile but there was something in his eyes that told her he'd meant what he just said. He'd rely on her to keep him in line? That didn't make any sense.

"What's the battle plan for today?" she questioned in a decidedly business voice, eyeing him pointedly.

"Today we plan dinner," he announced, sipping the hot tea and watching her interestedly over the rim.

"Dinner!"

"Dinner at the restaurant where David Hutton will be dining tonight," he amended casually.

She stared at him. "But why?"

"Financial maneuvering is only half this battle," he explained calmly. "Psychology is a critical aspect, too."

"You want him to see you out with me?" she hazarded as his line of reasoning clicked in her brain.

"By now he knows I'm involved with Brady. Tonight he'll find out just how much."

"But why?"

"So he'll see that there's no point in trying to subvert me," Rand told her carelessly.

"Subvert you! Good lord! Rand, are you telling me he might try buying you off?"

"He already has. I got the call last night after I'd taken you home." Rand appeared totally unconcerned. "It's a logical step. I didn't talk to Hutton directly, of course, I just received a feeler from one of his high-ranking employees."

"My God!" Kalinda shook her head, unable to believe it. "What…what did you tell the person who called you?" Somehow she had never envisioned such a ploy on Hutton's part. She knew such tactics were used but they had never impinged on her world. Kalinda found herself wondering for the first time if sharks could be bribed.

"What do you think I said?" Rand muttered gruffly.

She stared at him, assessing, remembering, analyzing and finally came up with the only possible conclusion. "You told him no, of course."

"Why 'of course'?" he demanded interestedly, watching her intently.

"You would never break your word to us," she replied positively, relaxing slightly as she realized it was the simple truth.

There was a tension-filled moment as they sat regarding each other in silent understanding and then Rand smiled gently.

"Thank you, Kalinda."

She shrugged. She trusted him. There was nothing more to say on that subject. "So why are we having dinner in the same restaurant tonight?"

"Because he'll try upping the offer again and

again, thinking he only has to find the right price. I want to squash that notion flat. I want to start closing doors on him as rapidly and as solidly as possible so that he begins to panic." Rand spoke intently, a frown of concentration creasing his forehead. "If we can turn the tables on him quickly enough, I think we can get him to withdraw the offer. He has to know we've got a whole series of options and we'll use every damn one of them until he's out in the cold."

"Have we really got a whole series of options?"

"Yes, but most of them are expensive. It would be nice if we can kill his interest before we have to resort to them."

"What's the worst possible case?" Kalinda asked bluntly.

"A friendly merger with another company," he told her, not shielding the truth.

She groaned. "I was afraid of that. A white knight?"

He nodded, tossing down the stack of papers he had been reading. "That's what the 'friendly' company is usually called in cases like this. It can be done, Kalinda. I have contacts. We can find a friendly suitor for Brady Data Processing who will agree to merge with us on our terms. It's better than turning everything over to Hutton!"

'I know. But even in the friendliest of situations, Brady Data Processing will lose some of its autonomy."

"If it comes to that, we'll negotiate very carefully. But there's another option, I think. You have surprisingly good credit for a company this size. Your assets are solid and generally rather understated. I think, with a little fast talking, we might be able to get that line of credit expanded."

"For what purpose?"

"So that Brady can better Hutton's offer for its own shares," he said quietly.

"A tender offer for our own shares? That would be expensive," she whispered thoughtfully. "Credit costs a fortune these days. Interest rates are high…."

"I notice from your records that you've been shy of using bank credit in the past, Kalinda."

"I have an instinctive dislike of being in debt, I suppose," she admitted dryly. "A holdover from Dad."

"But borrowed money is the way big businesses are run these days. Brady is going to have to recognize that if it wants to stay competitive and autonomous." Rand spread out a financial report and began talking in detail.

Kalinda listened, fascinated with the expertise she was witnessing. Where would Rand Alastair have been today if he hadn't dropped out a year and a half ago? The thought crossed her mind that he might be the one trying to take over Brady Data Processing. She wouldn't have stood a chance!

Properly appreciative of the importance of fighting David Hutton on all levels, Kalinda dressed with care for the important evening. She chose a dinner suit of rich, printed velvet. The small, shaped jacket fit over a softer velvet skirt and a silk blouse complimented the chic combination. Over it she flung a dashing sequined and fringed shawl. Hair sleek and held with a glittering comb, she looked sophisticated and elegantly sure of herself. Which was exactly the note she wanted to set in front of David, she told herself.

As she dressed she thought again of how close she had come to confronting him in the little mountain town. Even if Rand Alastair failed to save Brady Data Processing, she would always be grateful for his having put a stop to the ill-advised attempt at revenge. She didn't even want to think of all the disastrous complications that might have ensued. Somehow, she knew, David would have used the confrontation against her, perhaps to compromise her in front of her own staff. There was no doubt about it, she'd had a close call. What if Hutton had gotten word to Brady management that the company's president was secretly meeting its biggest enemy?

Her gray eyes were sparkling with inner excitement when she opened the door to Rand that evening. And as she took in the sight of him in a hand-tailored evening jacket and dark trousers, she acknowledged that the excitement she was feeling wasn't just for the adventure of combating David Hutton.

"We both look dressed to kill this evening, don't we?" she laughed as they stood admiring each other.

"Very appropriate," he murmured, taking her arm. "That's exactly what we're going to try to accomplish. A little killing."

"How did you know where David would be dining tonight?" she remembered to ask fifteen minutes later as Rand turned the Lotus over to a valet parking attendant and started her toward the expensive restaurant.

"I'm afraid I made use of your secretary," he admitted.

"George?"

"I can see why you hired him. George is a very competent person. He managed to get the information out of Hutton's secretary without even giving her a clue about what was going on behind the scenes."

Kalinda had a mental image of George smoothly extracting the information he wanted and grinned. She was still smiling as they were shown graciously to an intimate table for two.

Rand saw Kalinda idly taking in the candlelit scene of white linen, shining silver and fresh flowers and grimaced.

"Please don't tell me Hutton used to bring you here a lot," he ordered gruffly, reaching for the wine list.

"He didn't. The place wasn't open back then." She smiled obligingly. She thought fleetingly of the whirlwind courtship David had given her and realized with a start that the memory no longer had any power. She felt neither the flash of anger or the hurt she'd once known.

"Good," he stated evenly. "I wouldn't want any misty memories coming forth to mar the image we're trying to establish tonight!"

"There aren't any," she replied easily, smiling at him across the flickering flame of the candle. She met his eyes with total honesty and he nodded, apparently satisfied.

"But I could use a little guidance on how to play the coming scene," she went on determinedly. "Are we supposed to create the impression of boss and consultant holding a dinner conference? Or should I let him think you're an old friend of the family who stepped in to give me a hand because of a friendship you once had with Dad? Or..."

"I never met your father," he reminded her with an enigmatic smile.

"But it would lend a nice touch to the 'image,' wouldn't it?" she suggested seriously, struck with the brilliance of her own idea.

"Just follow my lead, all right?" he said repressively.

"But what, exactly, is your lead?"

"You'll see... Ah! Here he comes now. Looks just like his picture."

Kalinda stiffened, the sense of adventure going out of the evening as reality intruded. She looked at Rand, watching for some sort of signal, some indication of how to greet David.

And then the other couple was beside the table and Rand was getting politely to his feet as David came to a pointed halt.

"Good evening, Kalinda," the well-remembered voice said suavely. "I hadn't expected to see you here tonight. I don't believe you ever met my wife. Darling, this is Kalinda Brady. She and I are presently involved in some business negotiations."

Kalinda could have screamed at the harmless way in which he said that, but she looked beyond David's handsome features to the face of the woman she had used as one of the arguments for not going through with the confrontation with David.

It was a lovely, charming face, a face that said the other woman knew nothing about the darker side of her husband's nature and preferred it that way.

"Good evening, Mrs. Hutton," Kalinda said politely, holding out her hand. It was taken graciously as the other woman smiled and said something polite in return. And then Kalinda glanced at Rand, preparing to introduce him.

"I don't believe we've met," Rand was already saying smoothly, before Kalinda could get the proper words out of her mouth. He looked straight at David. "I'm Rand Alastair, Kalinda's fiancé."

CHAPTER NINE

ONLY DAVID HUTTON'S wife appeared to accept Rand's deceptively casual announcement at face value. Kalinda decided rather cynically that she and David both owed Mrs. Hutton a vote of thanks for giving them time to recover from the shock.

With polished charm the lovely woman at David's side extended her congratulations and made the proper remarks. Rand responded to her calmly, easily, until they were interrupted by David who had obviously managed to begin reasoning things out.

"I hadn't realized you were engaged, Kalinda." The dark gaze that Kalinda had once found so attractive pierced her, looking for the lie.

"It's a very recent development," she explained, astonished at her own coolness. She flicked a quick look at Rand who came to her rescue.

"Last weekend, in fact," he elaborated, smiling fondly at Kalinda who felt herself redden. "We haven't even had a chance to buy a ring. We were on vacation in the mountains," he went on, speaking apparently to David's wife. "Soon after we arrived back in town we discovered some rather urgent business had developed."

Kalinda felt David stiffen at the words, his narrow gaze going to Rand's hard profile.

"Kalinda and I will have to settle the business matters this week and then we'll have time for all the little niceties of an engagement." Rand turned his head with an amused gleam in his hazel eyes, catching David Hutton's assessing glance. "Nothing very complicated, so it shouldn't take too long."

"I had heard you'd gone to work for Brady Data Processing," David said coldly. "It must have taken the promise of a considerable financial reward to draw you out of retirement...."

"Money, I'm afraid, had nothing to do with it. Kalinda was the reason I decided to get involved in the business world again."

Kalinda felt a happy warmth flood her veins. Rand had just made it very clear his interest in going to war against David was entirely personal, not monetary. He could not be bought.

'I see," David said icily. "You don't appear to think this rather urgent business matter you mentioned will take long to settle?"

"Not at all." Rand smiled his shark's smile. "A quite simple bit of corporate game-playing. I've had a great deal of experience in this sort of thing, as you may know. In this instance, it's all a piece of cake. Kalinda's firm is surprisingly strong. Her credit flexibility would astound you. I rather think when the current matter is settled I may encourage her to do a little corporate hunting. Brady is in a very strong position to get involved with the merger craze as a buyer."

The meaning in his words hung in the air, unsaid, but clear. Brady Data Processing might soon be seriously looking at David Hutton's firm as a potential acquisition. The thought of turning the tables on David nearly made Kalinda laugh. It was all she could do to maintain only a polite, amused smile.

"That's enough business for tonight, David," Hutton's wife was saying cheerfully, a fine-boned hand on her husband's sleeve. "We really should leave these two by themselves. They're probably taking an evening to celebrate their engagement…?"

"How did you guess?" Rand said dryly.

"Yes, of course, my dear," David said absently, his angry gaze on Kalinda's amused expression.

Her smile broadened as she politely inclined her head in farewell. There was so much David wanted to say and so little he could say under the circumstances. She saw it all in those handsome dark eyes. He was calling her every name in the book, frustrated, angry, and beginning to perceive his own potential failure.

Without a word he turned and walked stiffly away with his wife. Rand sat down slowly, his thoughtful gaze on his opponent.

Kalinda didn't hesitate. Leaning forward, she hissed, "You might have warned me!"

"It was a spur-of-the-moment inspiration," he defended, his gaze swiveling back to her accusing features.

"The hell it was! You've been planning this all day. Why didn't you tell me you were going to let David think we were engaged?"

"Because I thought I'd only get a lot of static from you," he retorted imperturbably, reaching once more for the wine menu as the wine steward approached.

Kalinda sat impatiently, one toe tapping the carpet in irritation as Rand deliberated with the steward. When they were alone again she resumed the attack.

"Aren't you afraid you might talk yourself into a corner with lies like that one?" she grumbled, wishing with all her heart it hadn't been a lie; that Rand wanted to marry her, not just have an affair.

"I have never talked myself into a corner I didn't want to be in or couldn't get out of if I wished," he declared emphatically, beginning to study the list of delicate salads on the front page of the menu.

"Well, that's very nice for you, but what about me?" she protested feelingly, annoyed at his casual arrogance. "Word of this so-called engagement is going to go around like wildfire. I have no desire to go through the process of being jilted again! It's… it's humiliating!"

Even as she spoke, Kalinda thought ahead to just what Rand's announcement might mean. It was easy for him to use whatever tactics came to hand in this business battle, but she was the one who was going to be left to deal with the aftermath. And right now the aftermath of an affair seemed far more depressing than the aftermath of a merger action.

Rand set his menu down with care, eyes turning a little golden in the flickering candlelight as he caught her half-accusing, half-despairing look.

"Do you really believe I would deliberately humiliate you, Kalinda?" he asked softly.

The simple question stopped her in her tracks, effectively cutting off the flow of angry words she had been preparing to launch as the full realization of her new predicament registered. It struck her very forcibly that this was the second time that day Rand had asked her for a show of faith. The first had occurred that morning when he'd asked her if she thought he'd let Hutton buy him off.

She eyed him thoughtfully, wondering why he was pinning her down like this. But forced to consider the question in depth, rather than in irritation, she knew there could be only one answer.

"No," she sighed, sitting back in her chair and lifting her chin with a regal air. "I don't believe you would deliberately humiliate me, Rand."

There was a long, weighty pause while the implications of her confession hovered between them. Rand's eyes never left hers and she could have sworn there was the faintest of smiles playing at the edge of his mouth.

"So why," Kalinda went on steadily, needing to know the answer, "did you use that line on David?"

"Number one because it was effective...."

Kalinda said nothing, waiting for number two.

"And number two," he went on obligingly, "because I think the idea has a lot of intrinsic merit."

"Meaning?" she challenged bravely.

"You and I make a good team, Kalinda," he began

intently. "We work well together, we're attracted to each other, we're…"

"Is this a proposal?" she gasped, horrified.

"If you like…"

"If I like! I have never heard such an unromantic, unemotional suggestion in my life! You might as well be proposing a…a *merger!*" Kalinda felt like crying and heaving the crystal at him at the same time. How dare he sit there and calmly suggest a business arrangement?

"A *friendly* merger," he emphasized dryly, his eyes wary.

"Not so long ago you only wanted an affair!" she reminded him tightly.

"There are other factors involved now, don't you think?" he asked reasonably.

"Business factors!"

"May I take it from your seething expression that you're turning down my proposal?" he inquired politely, his eyes enigmatic.

"You may consider the proposal hurled back in your teeth!"

"Then I'm off the hook? There will be no future accusations that I've deliberately humiliated you?" he drawled.

She whitened, shocked by the twist in the argument. Desperately she grabbed at her pride and her strength of will. "You…you may consider yourself quite free," she muttered. "You have, after all, given me my chance, haven't you?"

He shrugged. "It wouldn't have been a bad arrangement, Kalinda."

"No wonder you call yourself a shark when it comes to business. You can be quite cold-blooded, can't you?" she snapped, desperately using anger to shore up her willpower. She was deeply shocked at her desire to say yes to his proposal; to accept him on any terms.

Something in him hardened perceptibly. "I would think that 'cold-blooded' is the one accusation you wouldn't make. You are, after all, in a position to judge the issue. Have I ever been cold toward you, Kalinda?"

She ground her teeth. "That's got nothing to do with this!"

Suddenly a slow grin began to replace the firmly marked line of his lips and the hazel eyes softened. "Does it strike you that you're on the verge of becoming slightly irrational in your arguments? It's a good sign, actually. It gives me hope."

Kalinda's hands knotted the white linen napkin in her lap but her voice was properly flippant. "A good businessman doesn't rely on hope. He relies on facts and figures."

"You're wrong, you know. Business people are essentially optimists. Who else but an optimist would wager such vast sums of money on anything as tricky as competing in the national economic marketplace?"

"Are you going to argue with me all evening?"

"No, honey, I'm not. I'm going to enjoy this evening and I'm going to do my damnedest to see that you enjoy it, too!"

"Of course. We have an image to maintain, don't we? As long as David and his wife are in the vicinity…"

"We shall do our best to appear the happily engaged couple," he concluded firmly.

And much to Kalinda's surprise, Rand proceeded to do exactly that. He was charming and attentive. He entertained her throughout the first course until she finally began to relax and respond to the intelligent, amusing conversation.

By the time the entreé arrived, she had firmly pushed the depressing business proposal into the background of her mind, telling herself that it had all arisen out of Rand's determination to help her defend Brady Data Processing. It wasn't his fault she had overreacted.

They were lingering over dessert, a fresh raspberry torte, when Kalinda glanced up to see David and his wife leaving. The other couple did not stop to say good-night to Rand and Kalinda.

"Are you beginning to find it amusing?" Rand inquired blandly.

"David's reaction to us? Yes, I am. I could almost see the little wheels going around in his head when he realized you were firmly on the side of Brady," she admitted, grinning.

"So I'm forgiven for my claim to being your fiancé?" he asked whimsically.

"I'm sorry I blew up," she apologized meekly.

"It's just that it took me by surprise. You should have warned me, Rand."

"I was afraid you wouldn't agree to it."

"So you sprung it on me just as you sprung it on David." She shook her head. "When I first met you in the mountains I kept telling myself your talents were being wasted. I was right."

"I'm not sure that's a compliment," he groaned. "But I'll let it go for now. Are you finished?"

"One last raspberry."

"Good. It's a shame to waste all these fine feathers we're wearing. I thought we'd go dancing at a nightclub I used to know near here."

Kalinda made no protest, knowing in her heart that she would do anything to prolong the evening. Anything to prolong her fragile, dangerous relationship with Rand Alastair.

A few moments later, the fringed, sequined stole glittering around her shoulders, Kalinda found herself gently stuffed into the front seat of the Lotus. When Rand slid in beside her, turning to smile, she became very aware of the dark intimacy of the small car. And of the proposal she had just turned down.

There was little conversation between them as Rand drove to the nightclub, a delicate, stirring, undeniably sensual feeling permeating the confined atmosphere. Kalinda didn't want to fight it even though she knew she should.

But the evening had made her realize how tenuous her relationship with Rand now was. He would help her stave off David Hutton's takeover bid, but after that there would be nothing to keep him by her side. She sensed he still desired her, but she couldn't shake the feeling his need was somehow connected with the fact that she had been his ticket back to the business world. He claimed he'd come back to prove himself to her, but she was far too aware of the satisfaction he was taking in the effort. Rand had wanted an excuse to come back to the thing he knew best and she had been that excuse.

Torn by the knowledge that she would have leaped at his proposal if it had been delivered with even a modicum of love, Kalinda sought to justify her response when Rand took her into his arms on the dance floor. If she wasn't going to marry the man, why was she clinging to him like this? There was no future, or at least not one which boded well. Why prolong the agony of a final goodbye?

His arms slid warmly around her waist as the soft, slow music drifted through the dark, romantic nightclub. Other couples moved nearby, each lost in a private world. Kalinda rested her head on Rand's shoulder, her arms moving with an aching intimacy around his neck.

Rand's fingers gently kneaded the curve of her hip as he pulled her close. "I think we make a very convincing engaged couple," he murmured in her hair. "No, don't you dare tense up on me. I was merely stating a fact. Did you forget how good we are together when you turned down my proposal this evening?"

"Mutual desire is not enough to justify marriage," she whispered into the fabric of his jacket.

"But it is enough to justify an affair, isn't it?" he whispered deeply, lips grazing the top of her ear. He pressed her closer, deliberately melding her body with his until she was keenly aware of the hard warmth and the beginnings of arousal in him.

"Rand, I don't think we ought…"

Her fumbling words were gently cut off as he turned her head with one hand and kissed her. It was an incredibly seductive experience, Kalinda discovered, to be kissed on a dance floor. The lazy, probing passion of it somehow combined with the flow of music and the gleaming shadows. She melted against him as she always seemed to do when he held her like this.

Sensing her surrender to the moment, Rand slowly, deliberately began to increase the physical tension already blossoming between them. His mouth moved moistly on hers, parting her lips, sipping her honey. He used his hands to fit her close to the cradle of his thighs, shifting his feet occasionally so that his leg somehow lodged suggestively between hers.

Kalinda knew the need and want in her was being coaxed into a smoldering fire but she told herself she was safe enough on the dance floor. And when he took her home later she would have the long ride in the Lotus during which to cool off.

He lifted his mouth from hers, finding the nape of her neck, the line of her jaw, the edge of her eyebrow with his lips. Kalinda shivered and she could feel his satisfaction at the obvious sign of her response.

"Why did you turn down my proposal tonight, sweetheart?" he asked gently.

"I came much too close to a…a business marriage once before," she breathed shakily, not meeting his eyes. She wished he would stop talking and just hold her.

"And you're afraid that's all it would be between us?" he pressed huskily.

"I think Brady Data Processing is only a first step for you on your road back to an empire. I don't want to be used…."

"Used!"

"I know you wouldn't do it deliberately," she placated urgently, feathering her fingertips on the back of his neck. "You really believe you're offering a fair deal."

"Aren't I?" he demanded roughly.

"I suppose. But it's not enough…" she trailed off helplessly at the glittering expression in his gaze.

"Then that leaves us with the affair, doesn't it?" he said coldly.

She drew in her breath, knowing the seductive moment was over and she now had to make her stand. The same stand she had tried to make during the early-morning walk in the park.

"I don't think that's very wise, Rand," she began steadily. "You need time to readjust to the business world. Your interest in me is bound to be fleeting once you've reestablished yourself."

"And you're afraid I'd be using you, just as you're

afraid I'd be using you if we were to marry," he broke in grimly.

"Wouldn't you?" she dared, lifting her lashes to meet his eyes.

"Use you? I don't care what you call it at this point," he bit out with impatient savagery. "Whatever it is, it's going to happen. Because I'm going to take you back to your apartment tonight and make love to you until you are no longer capable of finding reasons for it *not* to happen!"

"Rand!" His name was almost a cry. He meant it. She could see the intention in his eyes, knew he wouldn't be stopped now that he'd made up his mind.

"Come on, Kalinda," he ordered, his tone softening but becoming no less determined. "Let's go home."

The tension that tautened between them on the drive back to Kalinda's town house was palpable. It was also very silent. Kalinda didn't know what Rand was thinking, but she knew her own mind was whirling with arguments and counter-arguments. He intended to make love to her tonight and she knew of no practical way of stopping him because, deep down, it was what she wanted, too.

Rand said nothing as he guided her forcefully through the door of her home and locked it firmly behind them. And he said nothing as she tried to step nervously out of reach.

But his hand closed on her upper arm in an unshakable grip and she was hauled against his chest, the sequined shawl slipping unnoticed to the green carpet to lie in a sparkling heap.

Wordlessly they stared at each other and then whatever bits of protest Kalinda might have found were blocked as Rand began to renew the claim he had on her.

She should have known, Kalinda told herself as he rained aggressive, mastering kisses down her throat, that she could never withstand such a sensuous assault. The need in him was genuine even though at this moment it was combined with a desire to subdue. And her desire to match and satisfy that need was equally genuine, even though she told herself it was a dangerous path. She couldn't fight her own love for him.

"Kalinda, you can't deny this feeling between us. You can't possibly say it's based on business!" The words were grated roughly against her skin as he began to undo the velvet jacket.

"No, Rand," she acknowledged gently as the jacket fell to the floor beside the sequined shawl.

"Admit you want me, sweetheart," he commanded gruffly, sliding the silk blouse off her shoulders. "You must know I want you. Admit that you feel the same. Neither of us could walk away from an affair!"

It was the simple truth. With a moan of acceptance of her fate, Kalinda wound her arms around his neck, returning his kisses with passionate, yielding intensity. She had no choice but to acknowledge the effect he had on her and to admit her inability to walk away from him. He might not know it was based on love, but she knew it.

"I want you, Rand," she whispered against his

throat as his hands found her breasts and began bringing them to fullness. She wanted to say she loved him but knew he wouldn't want her love. He wanted an affair and, perhaps, a business-oriented marriage.

"I know that, darling," he husked. "You can't hide it. I see it every time I look in your eyes, every time your body comes alive under my hands. But it's so damn frustrating hearing you try to wriggle out of our affair!"

"I won't try anymore," she vowed thickly. With eager hands she went to work on the buttons of his shirt. "I should have known I couldn't out-reason a skilled manipulator like you," she added wistfully, her mouth lifting at the corners.

"Not when you're all wrong in your reasoning process!"

"Am I, Rand?" she whispered.

"Yes," he growled as the last of their clothes fell to the carpet. "All wrong…"

He ran his hands caressingly down her back, sinking his fingers into the curve of her bottom and letting her feel the hardening maleness of him against her thighs.

Kalinda spread her fingers across his chest, delighting in the roughness of the crisp hair even as his hair-roughened leg moved boldly between hers.

She closed her eyes in expectation as he bent to lift her into his arms. But instead of carrying her into the bedroom, he settled her on the thick green carpet beside the pile of clothes.

He came down beside her, sweeping his hand

across her breasts, pausing to draw teasing circles around each nipple before moving lower. She turned into his arms, the need in her shining in her eyes.

"Did you really think I'd let you try to talk me out of an affair?" he demanded hoarsely, pinning her gently to the carpet with his leg.

"Yes, no, I don't know. I haven't been thinking all that clearly lately." She reached up and pulled his head down to hers.

Committed now, she kissed him with all the longing in her heart, using the ancient, womanly wiles buried in every nerve ending. Letting her own need and desire take over she explored his mouth with a passion that clearly aroused him deeply. Once more, as she always seemed to do with this man, Kalinda put the future aside. It just didn't seem as important as expressing her love in the present. Even if that love must remain mute.

She felt his fingers on her thighs and then released his head as he groaned and began to kiss her breasts. Fingers locked in his chestnut hair, she held him to her and let her senses swirl.

"You're so perfect for me," he said throatily. "So exactly what I need. You must see I can't give you up, sweetheart."

She arched upward and felt his lips on her thigh. The tiny, stinging caress nearly drove her insane with desire. The shimmering, promising currents began gathering once again in her body, seeking the release they had learned to expect from this man.

He caught her arching hips with his hand, holding

her in delicious bondage as she struggled to complete the union. The sensation of being held back seemed to hone her need to an even higher peak. Kalinda twisted and curled, grateful for each new teasing, tormenting touch, but determined to have it all.

"Please, Rand, please," she begged, grasping at him, trying to pull him down on top of her.

He kissed her navel and then the slope of her small breasts, letting her writhe against him but not letting her take control of the lovemaking.

"Tell me again that you want me, sweetheart," he whispered beguilingly.

"I want you. Oh, God! How I want you!" Trapped in the depths of her own desire she would have told him the truth if he had asked it of her. She would have willingly told him of her love. But he didn't ask that question. Instead, incredibly, he asked another. One she wasn't prepared for at all.

"If you really want me so much," he grated heavily, "then there's no reason for us not to marry, is there? I could never tolerate letting you go to another man after what we've shared. Say you'll marry me, sweet Kalinda. Make the engagement real."

Stunned by the demand, Kalinda tried to think logically, tried to remember her fears. But it was impossible to do so while cradled so tightly against him. She loved him and he was asking her to marry him.

Weakened with longing and unable to argue with herself in that moment, Kalinda heard herself whisper the answer.

"Yes, Rand. I'll marry you. I'll do anything you want."

Nothing had changed. She knew the odds were that he was still caught up in a combination of desire and gratitude to her for providing him the excuse he'd needed to return to the business world. He had said nothing of love.

But she no longer had the strength to turn down that which her heart so desperately wanted. She loved him. Perhaps, in time, she could teach him to love her. If not, if the time ever came when he realized he no longer needed her, she would not regret the time she'd been his. Real love might eventually cause sadness, but not regret.

CHAPTER TEN

TWO DAYS LATER a somewhat tired-looking Rand appeared in Kalinda's office doorway. She had seen him only at work since the night he had seduced her into marrying him. He'd made compelling love to her on the plush carpet, whispering words of aching need. And when it was over he'd carried her tenderly to the bedroom, kissed her good-night, dressed, and left.

The next day at work he had been all business, never mentioning the traumatic events of the evening. He had devoted himself to his task at Brady with single-minded determination. She knew he'd talked to people high up in David Hutton's firm, spelling out exactly how Brady Data Processing was prepared to match the hostile merger offer to shareholders or to find a friendly corporate marriage partner. That night he'd taken Kalinda home late after work and left her politely on her doorstep.

She had just put down the receiver, a small smile on her face as she considered David Hutton's call when Rand appeared, leaning in the doorway with deceptive casualness. But she saw the flicker of excitement and satisfaction in his eyes.

"It's all over but the shouting, honey," he advised laconically. "You should be hearing something soon. I just talked to my contact at Hutton's firm. They're throwing in the towel. We're…I mean, you're going to get out of this relatively unscathed."

"Thanks to you." Her smile broadened as she absorbed the manner in which he was hiding his personal satisfaction. "I just got word from David, himself." She gestured at the telephone.

Rand lifted one chestnut brow inquiringly. "So soon?"

"He's withdrawing the offer." She decided there was no point mentioning what David had said prior to calling off the hostile merger attempt. "He wasn't particularly pleased, but you managed to leave him with very little option. He can't afford us. Not with the kind of credit we can command at the banks."

"He was counting on Brady's traditional dislike of using credit," Rand nodded as if to himself. "And sheer panic."

"Which didn't develop because we knew we had the best player on our team," Kalinda inserted warmly. There was something more than satisfaction in Rand's expression. A hint of anxiety? Perhaps even wariness? She didn't understand it, but if it was simply a matter of his ego needing a little stroking she had no objections. He deserved it.

"It's over, Rand, and you're the reason Brady is still an independent concern." Kalinda depressed the intercom button and leaned forward slightly. "George, would you please round everyone up in the main conference room as soon as possible?"

"Everyone, Miss Brady, or just management?" George asked carefully. He knew she'd just taken a call from David Hutton.

"Everyone, George. Including you."

There was a fractional hesitation and then George's curiosity got the better of him. "Good news, Miss Brady? Or bad?"

"The best, George. And as soon as you notify everyone about the meeting would you mind taking a minute to find us a place that can accommodate a celebration this afternoon?"

"A place that will accommodate *everyone?*" he stressed cautiously.

"The entire staff, George."

"Yes, Miss Brady."

She released the intercom button and stood up, meeting Rand's dryly amused gaze.

"What's the matter?" she grinned. "Not used to being on the side of the underdog?"

He winced, as if she'd stung him. "Frankly, I've never seen it from this side," he admitted.

"Well, I'll have to confess this is the first time we at Brady have had this particular excuse for celebrating. But we've had practice at the annual Christmas party!" She spoke lightly, trying to erase whatever it was she'd just said that had made him look so rueful.

"You'll be picking up the tab personally?" Rand asked.

"We don't run to office slush funds here at Brady," she affirmed with a grimace. "I'll be paying the bill. But it will be worth it."

Two hours later the jubilant Brady staff adjourned from work early to take an extended lunch hour which, Kalinda guessed with amusement, would last all afternoon.

George had succeeded in finding a colorful beer and pizza tavern that was willing to welcome so many people on such short notice. Foaming mugs of beer and pizzas with "everything" were being ordered unstintingly. Kalinda decided not to concern herself with the inevitable price tag. It was far cheaper than a merger would have been!

She glanced around the room as the staff began to break up into familiar groups. George sat at a corner table surrounded by the other secretaries, all female. The word processing group had claimed another table nearby. First-line supervisors were drifting cheerfully into their own territory and Brady's upper management occupied a long table with Kalinda and Rand in the center.

Kalinda smothered a grin as a toast went up, beer mugs on high. It was one of several and the subject this time was Rand. She could have sworn he was turning a dull red. Amused, she leaned close and under cover of the cheers, whispered, "One thing about being on the side of the good guys: We're big on heroes!"

In the dim light, Kalinda was positive Rand turned

an even darker shade of red as he slanted her a wry glance.

"It's not a role I'm accustomed to playing."

"Hero? But you're a natural for the part!"

He looked at her with sudden sharpness. "You think so?"

"Definitely," she laughed.

He continued looking at her levelly for a long moment. "Kalinda, I have to talk to you."

"Now?"

"As soon as possible."

She chilled, remembering the wariness in him earlier. What was wrong? Had he changed his mind about the marriage already? Realized he was now back in his natural milieu and no longer needed her? Beneath the rustically carved table, Kalinda's palms went strangely damp.

"All right, Rand. I don't think we'll be missed." She didn't look at him as she spoke.

There were several good-natured calls protesting their departure, but no one seemed unduly upset. In fact, Kalinda thought sardonically, everyone looked a little too understanding; a little too smugly pleased. It didn't take much insight to realize her slightly feudal staff had decided Rand would make an excellent consort for their president!

Rand drove back to his apartment without speaking, the white-knuckled grip of his hands on the wheel the chief evidence of the intensity of his thoughts. It made Kalinda even more nervous.

Perhaps…perhaps he would go back to the idea of continuing the affair. She could live without marriage, but she didn't even want to consider living without him altogether. Rand had bound them together on too many levels, made her too much a part of him. She would never be free again.

Kalinda's tension drove her to precipitate the confrontation. She must know what was happening. As soon as he opened the door of the apartment she stepped inside and turned proudly to face him.

"What is it, Rand? What's wrong?"

He shut the door and leaned back against it, his hands on the knob as if he needed to brace himself. There was hard determination in every line of his body.

"Kalinda, I've done a lot of thinking since the night you agreed to marry me."

"Have you?" What could she say? How could she stop him?

"I had to finish what I started at Brady. I had to stop Hutton's takeover.…"

She waited, not understanding.

His mouth hardened. "I realize that in so doing, in showing you I could operate effectively in your world, I've complicated matters between us."

"How?" It was almost a plea.

"It's obvious," he said grimly. "I've made you afraid of me."

He stepped away from the door, lifting a hand to stop the impulsive denial which leaped to her lips.

"No, it's true. I wanted you to be proud of me, to admire me. And instead, I've given you every reason to fear me. That's why you tried to call off the affair, isn't it? Why I had to trick and seduce you into agreeing to marry me. My brilliant plan has backfired. I realized that after I left you the other night. And I've seen the wariness in you for the past couple of days."

"But, Rand…!"

He shook his head, walking restlessly to stare out the window. "I honestly don't know how to reassure you, except with time. I thought about putting off the marriage, but I can't bring myself to make the sacrifice. Selfish, I know, but ask anyone: Selfishness is one of my prime character traits."

"Rand," Kalinda broke in a little breathlessly, hope and despair shredding her nerves. "What is it you think I'm afraid of?"

"That I'll take Brady away from you. Use it as the foundation of a new conglomerate controlled by me. In short, that I'll do to you what Hutton tried to do two years ago and again this week," he told her flatly, keeping his back to her.

She stared at the sleek, proud head, her heart almost too full for words.

"You idiot," she managed lovingly. "That thought never entered my mind."

The broad shoulders were held tautly. "You thought I was using you…"

"Not in that sense. I was only afraid that you were using me in your own mind as an excuse for coming back to Denver and your old life. I didn't want you confusing your emotions for me with those for your work. I certainly never thought you'd try to take Brady from me! Ask David Hutton," she concluded bluntly as he swung around almost violently.

"Hutton!"

"Oh, yes," she smiled, remembering the phone call that morning. "It was his last-ditch effort. He tried to tell me what you would do to me and the firm once you had salvaged it from his grasp. Tried to convince me I was much better off turning everything over to him."

"What did you tell him?" The question was low-voiced and vulnerable.

"The same thing I'm going to tell you. I trust you completely, Rand." She didn't move, but she knew her eyes would be reflecting her love and trust.

He watched her with a hunger that had nothing to do with physical desire.

"Do you realize," he said, each word deliberate and carved with dazed wonder, "you're probably the only human being in the Rocky Mountain Empire who has ever said that to me?" He came forward, pulling her into his arms as if he were afraid she might break.

"Oh, my darling, Kalinda, that's one of the reasons I need you so much. I need someone who believes in me. I know you haven't had time to fall in love with me but you want me, you can't hide that, and you trust me. Surely that's a start. Someday I'll make you love me as much as I love you. I swear it!"

Kalinda felt him tremble as she pressed her face into his shoulder. "And to think," she whispered shakily, "that I once credited you with an unusual degree of perception!"

"What's that supposed to mean?" he demanded.

"I love you, Rand. From the beginning, I think. I knew when I left you that morning in the mountains I'd never be completely free of you. I knew I'd never fully recover from my 'vacation fling.' When you showed up at my door the night of the party I was never so relieved to see anyone in my life. I realized that night I was in love with you."

"Kalinda, my love…" he breathed as if a great weight had been lifted from his shoulders. She felt the relief in him.

"Do you really love me?" She pulled back, lifting her hands to frame his face. He smiled at her, a heart-stopping look of love that told her everything.

"You do, don't you?" she said wonderingly.

"With all my heart." It was a solemn vow. "Didn't you realize that when I rigged the engagement? I did it more for my own sake than to ward off Hutton's bribery tactics. I figured once I'd gotten you past the shock of the idea I could talk you into it on reasonable grounds. Instead, I wound up seducing you into it," he ended with a groan of self-recrimination. "I should never have done that. It wasn't right. But I wanted you so much…."

"The sneaky seduction tactics were so successful because I wanted nothing more in the world than to marry you!" she assured him, eyes filled with fond laughter.

"I wonder if you have any idea how important you

are to me? You told me you were afraid I'd only followed you back to Denver because you'd made me realize I wanted to come back to this world. And I couldn't argue with your conclusion because it was true in a very real sense. But you didn't understand the whole truth, Kalinda. I wouldn't have wanted to come back without you. I would have found the business life just as empty, just as destructive for me as it had been before."

"Oh, Rand..."

"It's true, sweetheart. I do have the business instincts of a shark. I learned a lot about myself up there in the mountains, faced some important facts. I need that easy, contemplative side of life and I need the high-powered entrepreneurial side. But it wasn't until I met you that I realized I had a chance of having both."

"I don't understand." She looked up at him wistfully.

"Don't you see? You're more important to me than either of those two lifestyles. You're the most important thing in my life. And that puts things into perspective, making it possible to have it all. If I can have you."

"Every time I look at that beautiful piece of pottery you made I realize I love the man who made it just as much as the man who saved Brady Data Processing. And you're not the only greedy one, Rand," Kalinda smiled. "I want it all, too. I want you. I love you."

His hands moved yearningly along her back as he stared down at her. He looked as if he didn't fully trust his luck, Kalinda decided. But she was the lucky one. How could she have ever run away that morning in the mountains?

"I'll take care of you, Kalinda," he promised. "I love you so much. I *need* you so much. I need you to keep me from drinking too much coffee, to keep me from falling into the trap of becoming a business shark, to keep me from an empty, incomplete life."

"And I need you. A man I can trust, a man I can rely on for sound, rational advice, a man who wants me more than trout fishing or empire building." Her lips quirked invitingly, gently. "Love me, Rand. Please love me."

He folded her to him, a reverence and a deep desire forming opposite ends of the spectrum which constituted his love for her. Kalinda felt it and reveled in it, giving herself up eagerly to the urgent need to share the love they had.

"I think," he rasped close to her ear as he tugged at the comb that held her hair, "the president of Brady Data Processing should take a little time off now that the immediate crisis is past, don't you?"

She shivered as her hair tumbled down her shoulders, aware of his hands moving through the golden-brown stuff with masculine delight. "A vacation?"

"I was thinking more in terms of a honeymoon," he replied, slipping off the jacket of her suit. "It so happens I know of a delightful mountain retreat situated picturesquely on the bank of a scenic lake...."

"Indoor facilities, I trust?"

"Only the finest," he assured her simply, removing her small-collared blouse as she began fumbling with the buttons of his shirt. "Fresh trout in the morning, arts and crafts in the afternoon, daily picnics."

"It sounds charming."

As her lacy bra slid to the carpet, Rand groaned and crushed her to his naked chest. "It is charming. But to tell you the truth, the place has always lacked something."

"A woman's touch?" She nibbled suggestively at the curve of his throat.

"Not just any woman's touch," he murmured. "Your touch. Will you come back to the mountains for a honeymoon with me, Kalinda?" he begged, as they stepped out of the last of their clothes. "I promise you won't be bored."

"I wasn't bored last time, not after I met you," she confessed as he molded her body to his own. She trailed her nails sensuously down his back, feeling the instant response of his body. "But don't you think that tempting the president of the company with visions of a weekend in the mountains may constitute some sort of corporate bribery?"

"Haven't you learned anything at all about me?" he whispered thickly, lifting her and carrying her over to the sun-dappled couch. "Ask anyone in town, they'll all tell you I'm a man who will stop at nothing to get what I want!"

"As long as I'm what you want." She smiled up at him through her lashes, pulling his mouth down to hers.

"You're the only thing I really want. The only thing that counts."

And then he was demonstrating the wonder and depths of his love to the woman who had developed a passionate love for a shark.

* * * * *

LOVER IN PURSUIT

CHAPTER ONE

At first glance she thought it was only a trick of her senses—an illusion created by the soft, velvety light of dusk as it descended on the Hawaiian island of Maui. One of the old Hawaiian gods amusing himself perhaps.

Reyna Mackenzie stood ankle-deep in the retreating surf and watched the man who was striding toward her across the sand of the empty beach. Even in the fading light there was no mistaking him now, no convincing herself her eyes had been fooled by the evening shadows.

What on earth had possessed Trevor Langdon to walk back into her life?

And there could be absolutely no doubt about the identity of the man pacing purposefully in her direction. It had been six months since he'd coolly made it clear he no longer had any use for her, but Reyna knew a lifetime could have passed and her senses would still have responded with complete recognition.

She stood quite still, waiting in silence for the inevitable. Behind his approaching figure lights were beginning to wink on in the tastefully designed beach front condominiums which dotted this stretch of Maui coastline.

But even in the rapidly waning light the raven blackness of Trev Langdon's hair was easily detected. There was a shimmer of silver in the depths of that heavy, well-groomed mane, Reyna knew. Langdon was thirty-seven years old and he'd attained success the hard way. It showed.

It showed not only in the touches of silver in his hair, but in the lean, rangy hardness of a body which carried no trace of excess weight. For an instant the image of that smoothly muscled, uncompromisingly male figure, lying tanned and naked between white sheets, flashed through Reyna's mind. And just as quickly she forced the thought out of her head.

She'd know that face for all time, too, Reyna reflected wryly. Fifty years from now those deep amber eyes would still gleam with intelligence and cool appraisal. She doubted that time would be able to change the sheer aggression in that blade of a nose or the subtle sensuality of that seemingly hard mouth. The planes of his face were blunt, craggy lines which made a mockery of soft descriptions such as "handsome" or "good-looking." The high cheekbones, broad forehead and forceful chin reflected power and the utter masculinity of the man. He was six feet tall, perhaps a fraction over, and the clothes he wore fitted him as if they'd been hand-fashioned for his lean physique. Which, of course, they had.

Even if she hadn't recognized the man, Reyna thought with the beginnings of a rueful humor, she would have recognized the clothes, or at least the deceptively casual style with which he wore them!

No doubt about it, Trev Langdon was the only man of her acquaintance who, several hours after having landed in Hawaii, would still be wearing a crisp white shirt and tie together with an expensive jacket and slacks. The thought of the sand which must be pouring into those expensive Italian leather shoes made Reyna's mouth quirk in silent laughter.

She said nothing as he closed the remainder of the distance between them, but the smile stayed to play about her lips and she knew a tiny shaft of satisfaction as Trevor Langdon's amber eyes narrowed fractionally at the sight. He wouldn't expect her to be smiling at him, she realized belatedly.

"Hello, Reyna." The deep, gritty purr of his voice flashed with well-remembered intensity along her senses. He halted a pace or two from the water's edge.

"Hello, Trev. You are, quite literally, the last man on earth I ever expected to see here."

Her voice, Reyna was pleased to note, was light, carefree, pleasantly amused. With the crisp, professional attitude of a ship's captain requesting damage reports from various stations after an enemy assault, she ran down the list of her reactions. She was quietly satisfied with the results. Everything was under control.

"Am I? Perhaps you underestimate yourself, Reyna. Or me." He slanted her an appraising, assessing glance, the amber eyes moving over her figure with something approaching curiosity.

Reyna saw the look and her tiny smile widened. Deliberately she lifted her arms like a small child showing off a new dress and turned once in the splashing surf.

"I wouldn't think of underestimating either of us," she told him, facing him once again. "But you may be making that mistake. What's the matter, Trev? Don't I appear quite as you remembered?"

"Hardly," he retorted and Reyna chuckled.

Who should know better than herself just how much had changed since that fateful encounter six months ago? Gone was the expensive professional wardrobe of designer-styled business suits with their accompanying silk blouses and perfect leather pumps.

This evening she was wearing a pair of faded jeans rolled up to her knees for wading. A cotton pullover top was tucked into the waistband, its bright rainbow print a cheerful element in the gathering dark. No, she wasn't dressed as Trev had ever seen her before.

Her hair was different, too. It had grown a little in the six months which had just passed, falling below her shoulders now in a tawny, sunstreaked brown mass anchored with a wide clip at the nape of her neck. Very casual, very unstyled and not at all as she had once worn it. As a dynamic, successful, on-the-way-to-the-top career woman, Reyna had always kept her hair chicly upswept in a professional, businesslike style which had suited her manners and her clothes to perfection.

But more than her clothing and hairdo had changed, Reyna knew. Gone was the fashionably sleek slenderness which had been maintained by a driving work load and careful dieting. The high curve of her breasts was softer, fuller, as was the flare of hip and thigh. Her daily swimming, walking on the beach and other activities had given her a sensuous physical strength which made her feel healthy and kept her more rounded figure from looking at all plump.

The tawny hair, pulled straight back from her forehead, formed a casual frame for the wide gray-green eyes, slightly upturned nose and the softness of a mouth that smiled easily. Reyna was not a beautiful woman, but the animation of her features and the perceptive, intelligent light in the nearly green eyes lent an attraction all their own.

"I've been through some changes since you last saw me," she told Trevor Langdon and wondered if he could even begin to guess the extent of those changes.

"So I see," he murmured. The edge of his mouth twisted slightly in an expression of amusement. An expression Reyna remembered well.

"But I haven't turned completely stupid during the past six months," she continued dryly. "It's obvious that your presence on my beach isn't exactly a coincidence. What are you doing so far from Seattle, Trev?"

"I came to find you."

Even though she'd known that must be the case, the simple, straightforward words still sent a tiny jolt through Reyna's nervous system. "I see," she managed patiently. "That brings us to the next question, doesn't it? *Why* have you come to find me?"

Instead of answering immediately, he watched her

in a rather brooding silence for a long moment, his strong, square hands thrust into the front pockets of his slacks, his feet spaced slightly apart in a vaguely aggressive stance. Reyna sensed the determination in him and knew Trevor Langdon was prepared for battle. The knowledge struck a chord of humor somewhere deep within her.

"I have to talk to you, Reyna."

"So talk." She shrugged, turning to walk along the beach. She kept just within reach of the lapping little waves, enjoying the feel of the warm water and the wet, packed sand.

"You don't seem overly surprised to see me," he remarked, paralleling her course but keeping the expensive shoes well out of reach of the surf.

She sensed his slanting, searching glance and shook her head faintly. "Oh, I'm surprised, all right. I can't even begin to imagine why you've come all this way. How did you find me, anyway?"

"It took a little doing," he admitted quietly. "I asked a few of your friends, some of the people with whom you worked...."

"Of course," she nodded politely.

"And this evening when I arrived, the clerk at the front desk of the condo hotel told me you were down here taking a walk."

It hadn't been quite that simple, Reyna knew. For one thing, she hadn't kept in touch with very many friends back in Seattle. Trev must have asked quite a few people before he found someone who actually knew she'd moved to the Hawaiian Islands and he'd have had to dig even deeper to find an exact address. But, then, Trev Langdon could be quite resourceful. Who knew that better than she?

"My compliments on your detective work," she mocked lightly. "So you decided to take a vacation in the islands and look me up while you were here?"

"You know better than that," he growled.

"Yes, I suppose I do. You never do anything quite that casually, do you? Every move in your life is carefully planned, premeditated and designed to take you closer to a chosen goal, isn't it?"

Out of the corner of her eye she saw one black brow climb upward in a telltale movement that undoubtedly meant she was beginning to react as he had expected her to react.

"I understand your bitterness, Reyna," he said softly.

The laughter bubbled lightly to the surface and her eyes gleamed with it as she glanced at his profile. "Your usually brilliant analytical abilities have just failed you, Trev. I'm not bitter. I'll admit I'm surprised to see you, under the circumstances, but don't mistake that for bitterness. I am curious, however. Are you going to enlighten me as to the ultimate purpose of this visit?"

There was a certain pleasure in having put him even slightly off stride. The amber gaze slitted for an instant as he absorbed her amusement.

"It's a little difficult conducting a conversation while you're splashing about in the surf," he told her mildly. "Would you mind if we went back to your place?"

"Sorry. At the moment I feel like walking in the water. If you want to conduct your little discussion face to face, you can take off your shoes and join me. I'm willing to share my stretch of ocean with you."

"Very generous," he muttered, "but I'm not exactly dressed for wading."

"And you wouldn't dream of crushing the fabric of a two-hundred-dollar pair of slacks by rolling them up to your knees, would you?" she taunted lightly.

"There was a time when you wouldn't have had a pair of faded jeans like that in your closet," he shot back coolly.

"I know," Reyna agreed with a contented smugness. "I've changed."

"Have you, Reyna? Or are you just in hiding for a while?" The low, gritty voice was laced with a gentle sympathy.

"Did you think I'd spend six months licking my wounds, Trev?" she asked deliberately.

He drew in his breath and said carefully, "You went through a great deal six months ago. I didn't realize just how much until after it was all over."

"Thank you for your sympathy and understanding, but I assure you it's entirely unnecessary—"

"I didn't know, for example, that the whole mess was going to cost you your job," he interrupted grimly. "But you knew it, didn't you? You made every move with your eyes wide open."

"Yes." She gave the single-word admission without

any bitter inflection. It was the truth. She had known what she was doing. "But if you're feeling guilty because you think I got fired or was asked to resign, you're suffering for nothing," she went on easily. "I left of my own free will."

"Because you knew that the failure to conclude the deal for my brother-in-law's firm was going to ruin all your career plans. You never explained, Reyna. You never told me how much was riding on that business maneuver."

"Would it have made any difference if I had?" she whispered, knowing full well what his answer would be.

There was a long hesitation and then Trev said finally, "No."

"So it wouldn't have changed anything to explain all the gory details, would it?" she said consideringly. Privately she decided that was one small issue settled in her mind. She'd wondered at the time if knowing the full truth would have made Trev act any differently. After a couple of months of wondering, though, she'd recovered from the disaster sufficiently to realize that it wouldn't have mattered to him. She'd been right.

"I did what I had to do, Reyna," he said flatly.

"I know. As I said, I wasn't exactly fired," she reminded him dryly.

"I realize that. I also realize that once the momentum of the fast track to the executive suite is broken, there's no regaining it. Everyone headed for the top knows that. You could have stayed on with your company but the chance of another promotion was gone, wasn't it? You knew it was gone the moment you told me you would kill the negotiations for John's company. As far as your bosses were concerned, you'd blown the whole thing. They would never again have viewed you in quite the same light."

"There aren't any excuses for a failure of that magnitude," Reyna agreed, stifling the memories. "My management would have been right to turn their backs on me."

"And, knowing the inevitable outcome, you politely handed in your resignation," Trev concluded shortly. "Then you fled to Hawaii."

"'Fled' isn't exactly the word I would use." Reyna slanted him a look of mild protest. "I came for a vacation and decided to stay here on Maui. Are you here because, six months after the fact, you've become guilt-stricken?"

"It's not that! Damn it, I told you I did what I had to do, Reyna. When my sister begged me to come to the aid of her husband, there wasn't much I could do except agree to help. You were going to gobble up his computer firm for your company as if it were a light snack. He didn't stand a chance against you!"

She heard the buried explosion in his words and smiled again. "I was something of a female barracuda in those days, wasn't I?" she said reminiscently.

He frowned, obviously taken aback by her own self-analysis. "You were damn good at your job."

"But you were even better at yours, weren't you?

You found my vulnerable point and moved in with a brilliance I've admired ever since."

"You must hate my guts."

"No." She shook her head firmly.

"Yes, you do," Trev insisted stonily. "But I can deal with that. I'm going to put all the pieces back together again, sweetheart," he told her. "That's why I'm here."

The small shiver which coursed down her spine was gone almost before she noticed it. Reyna put it down to sheer shock, not to any genuine wariness. There was, after all, no need to be *wary* of this man who'd inadvertently changed her whole life. If anything, she was downright grateful. Emotionally, she was over him, she told herself. Six months in the Hawaiian Islands was a sure cure for even the most passionate heartbreak.

As those thoughts flickered through her mind, Reyna came to a sudden halt in the surf and stood peering at him in the darkness. He stopped also, facing her with that amber-eyed determination which was part of his very being. When Trevor Langdon set his mind on something, he went after it with the strength and certainty of an iron willpower which had never known defeat.

"Okay, Trev," she said quietly, "let's have it. Why have you come a couple of thousand miles to find me?"

He set his mouth in an even firmer line. "I've come to take you home with me, Reyna. I want you back."

Old habits, especially those learned the hard way, could survive for as long as six months, Reyna discovered with silent astonishment. When he looked at her like that, his whole body radiating his intent, he still had the power to shake her.

But only for a moment. The momentary twinge of emotional response was suppressed at once.

"No, Trev, you don't want me. I'm not the same woman you knew six months ago." Her chin lifted with mocking arrogance and the breeze off the ocean lightly tossed her hair.

"I understand, Reyna," he soothed. "You've every right to be bitter, but we can work that part out. You see, I didn't fully realize at the time just how deeply you felt about me. I knew you were attracted to me and I knew I could use that attraction to manipulate you. I didn't question the technique…"

"You had to use whatever tools came to hand," she agreed.

The gold eyes narrowed further. He was wondering why she sounded so gently perceptive, Reyna knew. If the situation had been reversed, there was no doubt about how *he* would have felt! But the situation probably never would or could be reversed. Trev Langdon knew about passion and desire and attraction. He did not know a whole lot about love. And until she'd met him, Reyna admitted silently, neither had she.

"Reyna, will you get the hell out of the water and let me take you someplace where we can talk?" He raked a hand through his dark hair in a gesture of annoyance. The interview didn't appear to be going precisely as planned. Trev didn't like matters to deviate from his plans.

"I'll come out." His frustration was amusing. "But I really haven't got time for an extended conversation. I'm meeting someone for dinner. Talk fast, Trev, and maybe you'll be able to get everything said on the way back to my apartment." She set off across the sand, heading toward one of the condominium complexes overlooking the ocean.

He fell into step beside her without a protest, but Reyna could feel the disapproval in him.

"Who?" he demanded starkly.

"I beg your pardon?" She cocked an eyebrow, knowing full well what he meant. He knew it, too, but he patiently rephrased the question.

"Who are you meeting for dinner?"

"A friend."

"A man?"

She sighed, her bare feet tramping easily through the sand while he labored along in the Italian leather shoes which had never been intended for such abuse. "I'm afraid I'm not pining, Trev. Yes, it's a man. A very nice one, in fact."

"Cancel the date, Reyna," he ordered softly.

"Poor Trev. What on earth made you think you could walk back into my life after six months and expect to find me waiting patiently?"

"I didn't expect to find you waiting patiently. I expected to find a woman who'd been through a painful ordeal. One who couldn't even bear to stay in the same city with me after what happened. I expected bitterness and anger and wariness. All the normal reactions of a woman who'd sacrificed a great deal for a man and then had him walk out of her life."

"My goodness! How dramatic!"

"It was," he returned simply.

"Yes, I suppose it was. But I knew what I was doing, Trev. That makes all the difference, you see. You don't have to start feeling guilty at this stage!"

"I'm not feeling guilty, damn it! But I do want you back." He halted, reaching out abruptly to catch hold of her wrist and pull her to a stop. In the lights of the condominium complex she could see the flare of amber flame in his eyes as he stared down into her face. "I want what you had to give six months ago, Reyna Mackenzie. I refuse to believe that what you felt for me has totally disappeared. I know this casual facade is a way of protecting yourself, but you don't have to put up barriers this time, honey. I'm going to make you mine again and this time there won't be any pretense or business maneuvers going on in the background. This time what happens will be just between you and me."

She stood very still, her eyes meeting his without any hesitation. "It's all over, Trev. I knew it was probably going to be all over the morning I told you I'd let your brother-in-law's firm escape my net. And you confirmed that fact after I'd formally ended the takeover bid for his company. Don't you remember?"

"I remember," he whispered heavily. "I remember you surrendering in my arms that last night, telling me of your love, giving yourself to me without any reservations. I remember how you looked the next morning when you told me you were going to give me what I wanted. Your eyes were filled with gentleness and love and I decided I must be reading you all wrong. I didn't believe you'd really fallen in love with me, not then. I thought the seduction had been successful and that you were willing to leave John's company alone for the sake of the attraction you felt for me."

"And later, after I'd assured you your brother-in-law's firm was safe, you calmly told me that was all you'd wanted from me," Reyna concluded.

"At that point I didn't understand exactly what had happened. I'd been so intent on using the one weapon I had, so intent on getting what I wanted from you, that I hadn't stopped to think about what was happening between us on another level. Reyna, you fell in love with me!"

"I know." She smiled up at him serenely. "But I wasn't under any misapprehension, Trev. I knew at the time that you probably didn't love me. I fully understood that you had an ulterior motive in seducing me. You didn't trick me, so you don't have to feel guilty."

"You gave me what I was after because you loved me," he breathed huskily, his fingers on her wrist tightening. "You sacrificed your whole career for my sake. It took me a while to comprehend that, Reyna. At first all I could think of was that I had won."

"Yes, you are very single-minded, Trev Langdon," Reyna drawled flippantly.

"That day you told me John's company was safe

I...I felt confused. I kept telling myself the game was over and I'd come out ahead. I felt some sort of need to reinforce that notion by making sure you knew it, too. I told myself you were a shrewd, tough businesswoman, an opponent I'd successfully outmaneuvered. I thought the fact that you'd surrendered in the bedroom instead of the boardroom only meant you were weak."

"I was. Love makes you vulnerable in some ways, Trev. It makes you do things which aren't strictly logical and rational."

"Like sacrifice a whole future for the sake of a man who hadn't offered anything more than an affair? A man who told you he'd willingly taken advantage of your vulnerability?"

"My God!" Reyna moved her head in vague disbelief. "You've really talked yourself into a guilt trip, haven't you?"

"It isn't guilt that's brought me here, Reyna," he snapped. She felt the growing frustration in him as he used the grip on her wrist to draw her closer. "I want you, can't you understand that?"

Once again a faint chill touched Reyna, but she shook it off. She was close to him now, too close. She could feel the heat and vitality of his body. It provoked old memories and brought back suppressed images.

"Why should you have changed your mind after six months, Trev?" she asked steadily.

He caught his breath and she sensed the urgency in him as his free hand reached out to touch the side of her cheek. "Reyna, Reyna, sweetheart, can't you see? I didn't realize what you were offering me. I've never had a woman love me, really *love* me before. I didn't recognize what I had..."

"And now you do?" She tipped her head to one side, her mouth turning up wryly.

"Yes, now I do!"

The hand on her cheek moved with a sensitive roughness, curling around the nape of her neck and holding her still as he slowly lowered his mouth to hers.

Reyna didn't struggle. She knew it would be useless. On a purely physical level his strength far outmatched hers and he would use it to hold her in place. And besides, perhaps this would be a good test, a way of assuring both of them the fires within her had died.

There was a kind of deliberate, persuasive passion in his kiss, as if he expected to find resistance and was determined to overcome it right from the start. Poor Trev, Reyna thought fleetingly. He was still using the only tactics he knew, the ones which had worked so well for him. He was approaching the task of seducing her a second time in the same manner he had approached it the first time: with single-minded, resolute, self-confident purposefulness.

His hard mouth roved over hers, the almost-hidden sensuality in his lips springing to life as it reacted to the softness in hers. Deliberately he deepened the contact, his fingers massaging the back of her neck with a lazy, erotic stroking action.

Reyna stood with her hands at her sides, aware of the degree of mastery he was exercising. No one had ever stirred her senses the way this man had six months ago. Tonight, she knew, he was intent on reasserting his power.

She waited passively, even a little curiously, as he slid the tip of his tongue gently along her closed lips. When she didn't voluntarily surrender her mouth to him, the coaxing movement became more demanding. The damp, warm insistence of his prowling assault was creating a compelling intimacy.

But any reaction she might feel this time around would be purely physical in nature, Reyna reminded herself. She no longer loved Trev Langdon. Knowing that fact with great certainty, she did not fight the marauding kiss as he strove to excite her.

When he grew tired of trying to persuade her to part her lips for him, Trev growled something low and impatient and then he was surging aggressively into the warm recesses of her mouth with a hunger that astonished Reyna. Her body shuddered a little beneath the sensual impact but she told herself that was only natural. It meant nothing.

Boldly he explored the tender flesh inside her lower lip, hunted out her carefully quiet tongue with his own and forced it into conflict. Although the kiss had begun with the masculine artistry Reyna remembered so well, she realized in surprise that it was rapidly escalating. Too rapidly. The knowledge confused her. Trev had always seemed in control, always a master of his passion. He had wielded it as if it were a sword and he a brilliant duelist.

Reyna caught her breath in a small gasp as, satisfied at last with conquering her mouth, he withdrew slightly to nibble suggestively on her lip. She felt the deep groan which emanated from somewhere in his chest and then his hands flattened on her back.

Instinctively she reacted as she began to mold her body to his own with a long, sliding caress. Her fingers lifted abruptly to splay across the front of the fine sport coat.

"No," he whispered thickly against the corner of her mouth. "Don't fight me, Reyna. Please don't fight me. It's been six months and I've spent too many nights lying awake thinking about you, longing for you!"

"It's all over, Trev." She was remotely pleased with the steadiness of her own words. But why shouldn't she feel steady and in command of herself? She'd told him the truth. It *was* all over.

But he refused to listen. Sealing her mouth shut once again with a heavy, drugging kiss, he slid his palms down the length of her back, crushing her close.

Reyna couldn't fight the strength in him. All she could do was remain quiet and unresponsive beneath his touch. But when the rough palms reached her hips, pressing hard to force her deep into the cradle of his thighs, she couldn't ignore the beginnings of a weakness in her limbs.

And there could be no doubt of his own arousal. The hard male power in him sought to overwhelm her, capture her response. His fingers sank erotically into the curve of her derriere and Reyna shivered in spite of her cool resolve.

Trev felt the response and sighed deeply as his mouth shifted to trace the line of her jaw. Reyna's eyes squeezed tightly shut as he found the sensitive skin of her throat. No, she thought grimly, I don't love him, but any woman would find it difficult to ignore his sexual expertise.

Her fingertips curved unconsciously, seeking the shape of the smoothly muscled chest beneath the hand-tailored clothing he wore.

"You see, Reyna?" he breathed as he felt the tell-tale movement. He lifted his head and she opened her eyes to find flickering satisfaction in his gaze. "It's going to be as good as it was before. Better this time because there won't be anything else at stake except our future together. I'm going to wipe out the memory of the past six months for both of us. Deep down you still love me, sweetheart, and I swear I'll make up for what you've been through…!"

"What I've been through?" Reyna echoed, recovering quickly from the chaos that she sensed still waited for her in his arms. "But, Trev, I don't want to recover from what you did to me!"

"You've been hurt…"

At that, Reyna's lips quirked with quiet laughter and the gray-green eyes gleamed with it as she lifted her hands to shape his face.

"I know this is going to be hard for you to understand, Trev, but running into you was the best thing that ever happened to me…."

"Sweetheart!" he began huskily, amber gaze softening.

"It was, I'll admit, a little like hitting a brick wall," she continued heartily. "I felt like a carefully targeted missile which had been blown off its trajectory. But I realize now it would have taken that kind of explosive force to deflect me from the path I was following and had been following since college. Without the impetus provided by my encounter with you I'd still be singlemindedly en route to the top of the corporate world."

"Don't you think I know that? Reyna, I'll make it up to you!" he vowed fiercely.

"Listen to me, Trev!" He still didn't understand, she thought wryly. He was as much a self-guided missile as she had ever been, and his guidance system was powered by a will that would never be deflected by anything as gentle as love. "I enjoy my new life! I wouldn't want to go back to that sixteen-hour-a-day grind on the corporate battlefield even if I could. When I realized I no longer had either a career or you I was forced to reassess my whole life. For the first time I had a chance to rethink everything. I came to Hawaii to do just that. And I've stayed here because what I found is what I want. I've discovered a whole new way of living and I love it!"

"Reyna, you don't have to pretend…"

She laughed, using her fingertips to smooth the lines of his answering frown.

"I'm not pretending. If you want to know the truth, I'm grateful to you. Without you I wouldn't have my wonderful new life-style. I'm happy, Trev. Happier than I've ever been in my entire thirty years. There's no need for you to feel any guilt over what happened. So go back to Seattle before the sand ruins the polish on those lovely shoes and before you're forced to take off that expensive silk tie. I'm sorry if you've been suffering from an uneasy conscience these past few months. There was no call for remorse."

She stood on tiptoe and brushed her mouth lightly against his. Then she stepped back. "This is my world, Trev," Reyna smiled, sweeping one hand out to indicate the balmy, tropical atmosphere. "You have my deepest thanks for being the catalyst which helped me discover it. But catalysts are no longer needed once the reaction has occurred. Good night, Trev. Enjoy your stay on Maui."

With a casual wave, Reyna turned and walked away from the man for whom she had once given up everything. The man she had once loved.

CHAPTER TWO

IT WASN'T UNTIL she'd reached the safety of her garden apartment that Reyna realized she'd been unconsciously holding her breath. She released it with a rueful chuckle as she stopped to rinse off her sandy feet under the garden faucet.

There was no denying that she was mildly amazed to have escaped so easily from Trev Langdon. No one knew better than she how coolly in charge of any situation he usually was. She wouldn't have been surprised if he'd resorted to force to hold her out there on the beach.

It was incredible that he'd come all this way to find her. Who'd have guessed a man like Langdon would have spent six months with a festering conscience? Or could it really be true that he'd begun to regret losing her?

She shook her head, a little dazed by either explanation. After fishing the key out of the back pocket of her jeans, Reyna turned it in the lock and opened the door of the beach-front apartment.

Everything in the light, airy room reflected the changes she had made in her life in the past six months. When she had made the decision to stay in

Hawaii on a permanent basis, she had also made a
decision to simplify her life.

The wicker and rattan furniture was upholstered in
cool, bright cotton. The floor was covered by a mat
of woven pond fronds which was cheerfully imper-
vious to damp feet. Overhead a lazy fan moved the
air about on humid evenings. Large tropical plants
and an expanse of windows with a sea view brought
the outdoors inside. In the bedroom a bamboo four-
poster bed was covered by an antique Hawaiian quilt.
The quilting techniques had been taught by American missionaries, but the stunning designs such as
the red-and-white one Reyna owned were uniquely
native.

All in all it was a far cry from the elegant town-
house apartment she'd maintained in Seattle, Reyna
thought as she made her way into the bedroom. Her
home was as different as her current choice in men!

As she stood in front of the wardrobe and selected
one of the bright floral print sheaths, she allowed
herself to assess her reactions to the appearance of
Trev Langdon.

She'd come through the unexpected test very well.
With an honest, analytical ability she hadn't left behind with her abandoned career, Reyna acknowledged
that there were still traces of a physical attraction, but
that was only natural, she assured herself.

After all, she'd once found the man totally irresistible. And it wasn't as if she hadn't made an effort
to resist him initially, she remembered wryly. She'd
known from the first that his goal was to protect his

brother-in-law's business. Trev Langdon had never lied to her. He'd never claimed he had fallen in love with her.

If his sister hadn't called him in to help in the crisis, Reyna would have made short work of the takeover bid. She'd had everything set up, all the corporate forces in place and ready. Her own management had no doubts about her ability to handle the situation because she'd already proven herself. Since the year she'd left college and joined the large conglomerate, her career had progressed in leaps and bounds toward the top. In her twenty-ninth year she had already achieved a large measure of power, and everyone who knew her realized it was only the beginning.

The battle plan for taking over the small, mismanaged computer firm had been hers, and it would have been successful if Trev Langdon hadn't been called to the rescue by his terrified sister.

President of Langdon & Associates, Trev was one of the powerful new breed of financial experts who specialized in securing venture capital for aggressive firms. In addition, his company helped provide the expertise for setting up new growth businesses. He could take one look at a firm's management and financial situation and know exactly where its strengths and weaknesses were. He'd done that with his brother-in-law's computer company and realized at once that there was no realistic business method of fending off Reyna's advance.

So he'd approached Reyna directly, sizing up the

opposition for potentially vulnerable areas. The attraction between them had been instant and electric, and he'd used it.

Trev had made no secret of his intentions. He wanted one thing and one thing only from her, and Reyna had known it from the beginning. But that hadn't prevented her from being swept off her feet. Even though she was aware that he would do anything to persuade her not to take over the computer firm, she had risked accepting his invitations.

In the years since college she'd dated many men, but none had ever been allowed to encroach on her life to the point where the relationship threatened to interfere with her career.

With Trev Langdon, however, everything had been different. She'd known the danger from the beginning, but it was as if fate had decided to take a hand. She'd begun falling in love with him from the moment he'd sauntered coolly into her office, planted both hands on top of her desk and announced himself and his purpose.

To her own shock, she'd actually agreed to his proposal that they discuss the business situation over dinner. During the first evening she realized he had all the qualities she demanded in an escort. He had an appreciation and knowledge of good food and wine, a natural sense of style, an intelligent humor that intrigued her and a well-mannered sensuality that was captivating. But there was something more, something which went far deeper and brought forth responses Reyna had never known in herself.

Over a period of two weeks Trev made certain they were continually in each other's company. She'd made no protest the first time he'd taken her in his arms, and, on that last night, when the inevitable occurred, she'd surrendered to his passion with love and longing.

The following morning she told him that she would give him what he wanted. That very afternoon she walked into her office and called off the attack on his brother-in-law's firm. She'd known as she did it that she was cutting her own throat as far as her career was concerned. She'd also known the odds were great that, having gotten what he wanted, Trev Langdon would lose all interest in her.

But deep down she'd prayed that what they had found together was important to him. She hadn't fooled herself into thinking he had fallen in love with her the way she had with him, but she wanted to believe he had shared the deep attraction. On that basis, Reyna had told herself, they could build something solid and lasting. In any event, as far as she was concerned, there was no real choice. She loved him. She would give him what he wanted, with no strings attached.

He'd been cool and remote when she'd told him his relative was safe from her. In fact, if she hadn't known him better, Reyna would almost have said there was a kind of wariness that day in Trev Langdon. Quietly he'd let her know he considered the battle won. He'd waited after he'd said the cold, devastating words. He'd been sitting behind the desk in his office, watching her as she sat across from him, and as soon as he had cut the bonds between them he had *waited*. To this day she didn't know what he had been expecting.

The logical, rational side of her had been anticipating his rejection, however, and having been somewhat prepared for it she had been able to handle the situation with an outward calm that amazed her. With a small, understanding smile, she'd gotten to her feet, said a polite good-bye and left. He'd made no move to stop her.

By the end of the week, she'd handed in her resignation and prepared for the trip to Hawaii. Since then she'd returned to the mainland only once, and then just long enough to break the lease on her Seattle town house and finalize preparations for her new way of life.

She'd made the right decision, she told herself now as she removed the clip in her sunsteaked hair and brushed it out so that it fell loosely around her shoulders. The flower-splashed sheath floated easily over her figure, its low, rounded neckline cool and casual. After she'd slipped into a pair of sandals, she was ready for the date with Kent Eaton.

And none too soon, she thought, turning from the mirror as the doorbell chimed. Kent, as usual, was right on time.

"Hi, I'm all set." She smiled up at the blond, darkly tanned man waiting on the other side of the door. "Just let me grab my bag."

"No rush." Kent grinned good-naturedly, lounging against the jamb. Kent lounged against just about anything that was handy. Good-looking with his blond, blue-eyed, surfer's appearance, he had a lazy, even-tempered attitude toward life that was appealing. At thirty-three he had put his love of the sea to practical use by opening a popular snorkel, surfboard and catamaran rental shop on the beach. His tanned, well-molded body reflected the hours he spent in the sun pursuing his main interests in life—sailing and skin diving.

"Where are we going? Down to Hank's?" Reyna inquired, sweeping up her light canvas shoulder bag.

"Yeah, Hank swears the mahimahi is fresh tonight, so I'm going to hold him to it." Kent chuckled, taking her arm in a casually affectionate grip as she came through the door.

The popular Hawaiian fish was in great demand with tourists, but it was difficult to find it well prepared now in the islands. The small restaurant run by Kent's friend Hank Morton was one of the few places locals could still count on for excellent mahimahi.

"How was business today?" Reyna asked conversationally as they walked down the attractively landscaped path toward the main lobby of the condominium-hotel.

"Too good. I only got to spend an hour in the water myself!"

"The price of success," Reyna teased, turning to slant him a smiling glance as they walked through the open-air lobby. The spacious area had been designed to take full advantage of the tropical climate. A wide, sweeping view of the sea was unblocked by walls and windows although there were shutters which could be pulled shut in the event of a severe storm. The tiled expanse of space was furnished much as Reyna's apartment, with exotic wicker and rattan. The front desk occupied one wall and Reyna automatically glanced at the clerk she knew would be on duty.

"Everything okay, Jim?" she asked.

"Sure." The middle-aged man behind the desk grinned, glancing up. "That guy in the suit find you earlier?"

"He found me," she affirmed.

"You don't look too thrilled with the fact." Jim chuckled knowingly.

"Well, he's not exactly my type," she retorted.

"Too bad. He's checked in for a ten-day stay."

"Checked in! Here?" Reyna's smile vanished.

"I'm afraid so. Don't worry, Rey. Just another tourist. They come and they go. If he gives you any trouble, one of the guys will take care of him."

"Or I will," Kent interrupted with easy confidence. "Who is he?"

"Just someone I used to know in Seattle," Reyna said quickly, recovering from the shock. She ought to have guessed Trev would be staying in her hotel. "No one important…"

"I'm crushed," Trev Langdon drawled from the open entrance behind them.

Reyna whirled to see him pace calmly forward. He looked as elegantly immaculate as he probably had when he'd gotten off the plane. Must have taken a few minutes to dump the sand out of his shoes, she decided with silent humor. Had he stayed out on the beach all during the time she was dressing for her date with Kent?

"Don't be offended, Trev," she said easily as he approached the front desk. "Sometimes we seem a bit cavalier toward tourists, but deep down we appreciate each and every one of you. After all, where would we be without you?"

"We?" he stressed inquiringly, but the amber gaze was roving over Kent Eaton assessingly. He took in the younger man's faded jeans, sporty pullover knit shirt and the sun-bronzed feet thrust into thongs. Kent returned the look with interest. It was obvious to Reyna that neither man was impressed by the other.

"Oh, definitely we," she murmured with a smiling glance at Jim. "I work here, so I have an interest in the economic mainstay of the islands. I'm well aware of the crucial importance of tourism!"

That brought the amber eyes back to her in a split second. "You work here?"

"I have the day shift behind the desk—right, Jim?"

"One of the best people we've got behind the front desk," Jim agreed cheerfully.

"Incredible," Trev growled. When Jim and Kent both stared at him uncomprehendingly, he added smoothly, "There was a time not too long ago when she could have been buying or selling this place. She wouldn't even have known your names. You would have just been part of the transaction." He leaned against the counter on one elbow with a deceptive casualness and shook his head with a kind of astounded amusement. "A *desk clerk,* Reyna?"

"How the mighty are fallen, hmmm?" She refused to let his mockery touch her. "I'm sorry to disappoint you, Trev, but I happen to like my new work. Now, if you'll excuse us?"

Kent needed no further prodding. He took her arm once again with a possessiveness that was new and started toward the front entrance. All the way out to the parking lot Reyna thought she could feel that flaming amber gaze on her.

"Who the hell is that?" Kent grumbled as they slipped into his small open jeep.

"That," she murmured, "was Wellington."

"Huh?"

"Did you spend your total high school career surfing? Didn't you ever hear of the battle of Waterloo?"

He glanced at her, forehead creasing in a small frown as he started the jeep. "I'm not sure I caught the class, but I did see the film. Who played Napoleon?" he added perceptively.

"I did," she said simply.

"An old flame." Kent nodded as he started the little jeep down the narrow two-lane road that led into Lahaina.

"Whoever said constant exposure to the sun addles the brains of a beachboy?" Reyna grinned. "You're quite right. It was short and bittersweet, as the saying goes, and it was also all over six months ago."

"So what's he doing here?"

"Beats me," she admitted thoughtfully. "Let's talk about something else, okay?"

He hesitated and then shrugged lightly. Kent was an accommodating soul. "Okay. How's the plan for the shop going?"

Reyna's gray-green eyes lit up enthusiastically. "Beautifully! I meant to tell you first thing, in fact. I've discovered the perfect location in that small complex of shops and restaurants on the water by the new hotel. Now I'll have to start negotiations with the bank and with the owner."

"You think there's really a market for a gourmet shop here?"

"Definitely. Kent, most of the people who come to stay in these condominiums are accustomed to entertaining and eating well. I know there's going to be a strong market for clever and interesting picnic lunches as well as specialties that they can buy and take back to their condos. I'll make it easy and carefree for them to entertain. They won't have to lift a finger during their vacations, yet they'll have all the gourmet conveniences of home."

Kent put up a hand to teasingly halt the flow of excited plans. "I'm a believer! You don't have to convince me, just the bank!"

"I'll start working on that little project this week," Reyna vowed.

There was a long pause from Kent's side of the jeep and then he asked interestedly, "Reyna? Could you really have bought and sold the condo-hotel you're working in now?"

She sent him a wry glance. "I worked for a large conglomerate that could have," she corrected calmly. "I was in charge of…acquiring various enterprises for them at one time. That's all."

"Did you like doing that sort of thing?" he prodded curiously.

"At the time I thought I did," she replied honestly. "I've since changed my mind."

"For good?"

"For good."

"And Wellington back there?"

"He's part of that past life, Kent. Not a part of my present one." Reyna felt a flash of satisfaction as she said the words. She meant them.

Hank's restaurant in the historic old whaling town of Lahaina was humming with its usual cheerful, friendly crowd. The mahimahi was, indeed, fresh and the mai-tai drinks were precisely what Reyna needed to take her mind off the farewell scene at the hotel.

At the end of the evening she went willingly enough into Kent's arms for one of his undemanding good-night kisses. It wasn't that Kent was an undemanding man by nature, but rather that Reyna had long since made it clear she was not ready for an affair. Kent, with his easygoing ways, had accepted that. In turn, neither made any attempt to tie the other down. Both felt free to date others and took full advantage of that freedom.

So Reyna bid her friend a casual good-night and crawled into her oversized bamboo bed with his kiss resting lightly on her lips.

But when she went to sleep it wasn't that affectionate embrace which shaped her dreams. It was the image of a pair of amber eyes that seemed to wait and warn.

THE NEXT MORNING Reyna plunged into her duties with alacrity. Inevitably, she knew, she was going to have to deal with Trev Langdon's presence in the hotel and the knowledge only made her more eager to become immersed in familiar routine. Perhaps if he saw her at work and realized she really was content, he would leave her alone. At any rate, she decided, surreptitiously looking at his check-in card, she only had nine more days to put up with him!

She was giving an elderly couple from Nebraska driving directions to Haleakala, the island's huge, dormant volcano when, out of the corner of her eye, she saw Trev approach.

"This is the only place on the island where you might want to take a sweater, or jacket," Reyna instructed the midwestern couple. "Remember, the summit of the volcano is about ten thousand feet high. It gets a little chilly two miles up!"

"It is fully extinct, isn't it?" the old gentleman asked, peering at the map. "We flew over Mount Saint Helens in Washington last summer and you could still see steam rising."

"Haleakala has been dormant for two centuries," Reyna assured them. "We don't use the word extinct," she added carefully. "The view from the summit is fantastic. On a clear day you can see some thirty thousand square miles of the Pacific, and the crater itself looks like a lunar landscape."

With a pleasant smile and a thank-you, the couple left to find their rental car in the parking lot. There was no longer any polite way of ignoring Trev Langdon's quiet presence, so Reyna took an aggressively cheerful tack.

"Good morning, Trev. I'm glad you brought along something besides a business suit!"

He was wearing a pair of camel corduroy pants and a glove-leather belt trimmed in solid brass. He'd managed to do without a tie, but the ecru button-down oxford-cloth shirt had an air of formality about it that survived even without the missing accessory. Everyone else in the lobby had on sandals or thongs. Trev was wearing a pair of supple calfskin casuals which had probably cost a couple of hundred dollars.

"Hello, Reyna," he murmured, taking in the picture of her at work. Her hair was clipped to the back of her head in a loose knot that was already beginning to straggle in charming disarray and her sundress was a garish splash of color guaranteed to make anyone from Seattle blink. "I was on my way to breakfast, but I wanted to see you in action behind the front desk. How long have you been, uh, clerking?"

"Since shortly after I arrived," she told him lightly, refusing to rise to the not-so-subtle goad. "I was lucky, you know," she added confidingly. "Good jobs like this one are hard to get here."

He smiled slowly, a thoroughly charming expression laced with a dash of wickedness. It was a smile which had once had the power to make Reyna respond in kind. "I know where you can get a better one."

She said nothing, merely arching a highly skeptical eyebrow as she busied herself with a stack of reservation slips.

"Have dinner with me tonight and I'll tell you about it," he continued invitingly.

"No thanks."

"Are you afraid to go out with me, Reyna?"

"Not afraid. Just not interested."

"I don't believe you," he retorted flatly, the taunting gone from his voice. "You're afraid I won't leave you on your doorstep with a polite little good-night kiss, aren't you?"

Reyna froze and then her head snapped up suspiciously. "Did you hide in the bushes and watch Kent bring me home last night?"

"Do I look like the type to sneak about in the bushes?" he protested.

"Trev…!"

"My room isn't far from your apartment and with the quiet evenings you have around here…" he began by way of explanation.

"You heard us come in," she finished disgustedly. "You may think I've sunk a bit low taking on this job, but offhand, I'd say you've fallen a lot farther if you're resorting to spying on ex-girlfriends!"

"Lover," he countered. "Not girlfriend. And I don't think there's anything 'ex' about it. I think you still love me, Reyna," he growled, the amber gaze going darkly golden.

"No, Trev."

"But you're right about one thing," he went on as if she hadn't offered a protest. "I have reached a low point in my life. So low, in fact, that I wanted to brain that overly tanned, blond beachboy last night and probably would have if he'd shown signs of planning to spend the night with you!"

She met his eyes with a level, assessing stare. At that moment she wasn't certain just how serious he was, but it was probably best not to take any chances.

"Cause any scenes while you're here, Trev, and I won't hesitate to call in reinforcements." Then she leaned forward and added with heavy melodrama and a thick stage accent, "We have ways of dealing with you off-islanders!"

"You're laughing at me," he said, looking surprisingly hurt.

"You've got it in one," she agreed cheerfully, straightening and returning to the stack of reservation slips.

Something burned for an instant in the golden gaze, something that might have been quite dangerous, but it disappeared almost at once.

"Reyna, I've come a long way to find you."

"That's hardly my fault. If you're asking me to reimburse you for travel expenses, you're out of luck. This job doesn't pay nearly as well as my last one did!"

"The least you could do is have dinner with me tonight without a fuss," he went on as if she hadn't interrupted.

"Why?"

"To prove you're not secretly afraid of the effect I might still have on you?"

"You used to be a little more subtle with the psychological manipulation," she complained mildly.

"So I'm getting a little desperate."

"You thought I'd fall into your arms the moment you reappeared in my life, didn't you?" She looked up wonderingly.

"Reyna, please." There was a curiously harsh wistfulness in the words.

She considered him, thinking that she'd never seen Trev Langdon in a wistful or pleading mood before. Was the man so desperate to make amends?

"I like that," she finally observed.

"What?"

"You playing the humble supplicant for my favors," she chuckled, vaguely astonished at the way she was beginning to enjoy teasing him.

"If I get down on my knees, will you agree to have dinner with me?"

She sighed, her humor fading. "Trev," she said gently, "can't you see that it's no good? I don't love you anymore. I don't want to go back to Seattle and I don't want any part of my old life."

"Then have dinner with me for old times' sake."

When she lifted her eyes helplessly toward heaven, he leaned forward, both strong hands flattened on the counter top in a gesture that reminded her vaguely of the way he had first approached her in her office.

"Is it too much to ask, Reyna? After I've come all

this way? I swear I won't make things awkward when the evening is over."

She looked at him, knowing with a sense of mild disgust that she was weakening. It was a novelty having Trev Langdon pleading for a dinner date. My God! she thought ruefully, I gave him a lot less argument than this the night I went to his bed!

But perhaps she could use the evening to make it clear to him that she harbored neither an undying bitterness nor the embers of an equally undying love.

There was, she reminded herself honestly, one other factor to be added to the equation. Trev Langdon could be excellent company and it had been a while since she'd dined with a man who could make an evening's conversation shimmer with interest the way Trev could.

Before she quite realized what she was doing, the words were out of her mouth.

"All right, Trev. I'll have dinner with you."

CHAPTER THREE

HE SHOWED UP at her door wearing a light-colored linen jacket, a chocolate-brown shirt and a beautifully striped silk tie. The crease in the dark, perfectly tailored trousers had somehow survived the humidity. The black pelt of his hair was still damp from the shower, and in the patio light there were traces of silver buried in the thick, carefully combed depths.

Reyna took in his appearance with a politely repressed smile. She was dressed in a gold-and-red print sheath that fell to her ankles. A long slit up the side provided ease of movement and revealed the little strap sandals on her feet. Her hair was down around her shoulders, trimmed with a brilliant red blossom. The sheath left her shoulders nearly bare, revealing the gold cast to her skin—a legacy of the Hawaiian sun. If it wasn't for the hint of deviltry in those amber eyes, she thought, she would have felt like an island girl going out on a date with a visiting missionary.

The thought lightened her mood, removing the small flickers of anxiety which had begun to annoy her during the day. It wasn't that she was nervous about any residual emotions she might still have for this man, Reyna had told herself several times during the afternoon; it was more a case of questioning her own judgment. Trev could be a little overpowering when he chose and she didn't want to wind up fending him off all evening.

"Don't look so nervous," he advised on a note of gentle, perhaps slightly satisfied, laughter. "You should know my manners are reasonably good. I like your hair down, by the way," he added, reaching out unexpectedly to touch the soft mass experimentally. "You never used to wear it that way."

"It didn't fit my old life-style," she pointed out, stepping delicately out of reach of the questing fingers. His hand fell back to his side. "And I'm not nervous—I'm just hoping you're not going to spend the whole evening making advances."

He moved, taking her arm in a firm grip as she shut the door behind her. "Worried about falling victim to my brilliant seduction techniques?"

"No." She smiled as he started her down the path. "I'm quite cured."

"You keep saying that. But I don't believe you, Reyna. Your kind of love doesn't die in six months' time."

"You speak as an authority on the subject?" she taunted as they walked through the lobby and out into the parking lot.

"Let's just say I've become one since you left. If I'd been an authority at the time, I never would have let you walk out of my office that day," he remarked. "It took me a while to realize what I'd lost."

"What were you expecting me to say that day,

Trev?" Reyna asked suddenly as he slipped her into the front seat of the car he had rented. She looked up to find him watching her intently as he held the door. "I had the strangest feeling you were…well…*waiting* for something."

His mouth hardened. "I was expecting a scene, I suppose. I was waiting for you to turn into an infuriated woman scorned. I had made it very clear I felt I'd won our little encounter and I thought your temper would explode when you realized you'd lost completely."

"I see," she whispered as he slid in beside her. "And what were you going to do after I'd tried to scratch your eyes out?"

"Offer an affair," he said easily, starting the engine. He cast her a sideways glance. "But I never got the chance. You simply accepted the situation and walked out the door. My first thought was to say the hell with it. I'd gotten what I wanted."

"And since then," she said quite pleasantly, "I've gotten what I wanted. I really do owe you a lot, Trev. I've always been curious about one thing, though."

"What's that?" he asked quickly as he piloted the car out onto the road.

"Whatever became of your brother-in-law's firm? No offense, but he'd managed to run that poor company nearly into the ground. I've always wondered if someone else came along after me and took it over anyway."

"Someone else would have if I hadn't spent the

better part of the last six months putting John back on his feet financially," Trev allowed grittily.

"So he had the sense to realize he needed expert help, hmmm?"

"Your nearly successful takeover bid scared the hell out of him," Trev agreed. "Afterward he was more than willing to listen to some advice."

"Well, that satisfies the last bits of curiosity I have about my old life. Where are we going?"

"I'm told there's an excellent place by the water in that little shopping complex a couple of miles up the road. Know it?"

"Yes, it's very good." Reyna nodded, thinking that he was taking her to the collection of boutiques and restaurants she had chosen for her new gourmet shop. She smiled with pleasure as she ran through all the statistics of the place she had picked. The square footage was adequate and there would be room for a small wine collection. She'd have to make arrangements for a freezer and a chilled-foods cabinet. Tomorrow she would see the bank about a loan for inventory....

"Am I boring you already?" Trev inquired blandly.

"Sorry, I was thinking of something else."

"So I gathered. You never used to drift off in the middle of a conversation!"

His barely shielded annoyance made her chuckle. "I know. I used to hang on your every word. Ah, sweet love!"

"It was," he retorted a little ruthlessly. "Very sweet. And tender and gentle and a lot of other things I didn't have the sense to recognize at the time. They were new to me, Reyna. I didn't know what to make of them. I didn't quite believe in them, I guess."

"But you do now?" she quipped, her disbelief plain in her words.

"Yes, damn it!"

"Then when you find the right woman you'll be ready to respond properly next time, won't you?"

"I think I could easily take to beating the new Reyna Mackenzie," he noted reflectively.

"I wouldn't advise it," she drawled.

"No?"

"Might get your nice clothes all mussed up." Reyna grinned at him as he slid her a dark glance and suddenly she felt very much on top of the situation. In charge, in control, serenely in command. She would relax and enjoy the evening.

It proved easy to do. Trev was clearly determined to play the perfect escort and, as Reyna had observed on more than one occasion, when he set his mind to a task, he performed it with dazzling ability.

The restaurant was a perfect setting for a sparkling evening. The casually lush decor took full advantage of the ocean view, and the normally attentive service was a little more attentive than usual since most of the staff recognized Reyna.

"Did you have an enjoyable day on the beach?" Reyna asked, opening her menu as two tall tropical drinks composed of rum, passion fruit and orange juice arrived at the table.

"Not particularly," Trev retorted. "I spent it worrying about this evening."

Reyna glanced up, gray-green eyes full of laughter. "That must have been a novel way to spend your time!"

"It was. I did manage to get into the water, though. I'm tempted to rent a mask and snorkel. I'd like to try getting a closer look at some of the fish near the reefs."

"No problem, my friend Kent runs a little shop—"

"I'll find my own source, thanks."

"Suit yourself," she returned airily. She glanced back at the menu. "As far as the food here goes, I can recommend the butterfish steamed in ti leaves or the Malaysian prawns. That cucumber and seaweed salad is excellent, also."

"And the papaya laced with port?"

"Makes a great starter," Reyna agreed readily.

They went through the menu, discussing it with the intelligent enthusiasm which had characterized their eating adventures six months ago. By the time they had settled on the coconut and macadamia-nut soufflé for dessert, Reyna found herself having to fight off a tendency to reminisce. She won the silent battle.

Trev, on the other hand, was not above using any weakness he sensed.

"Do you remember that great Japanese restaurant down by the waterfront in Seattle? They've put in a sushi bar. You'd love it."

"Really?" She kept her voice deliberately noncommittal. "There's a lot of fantastic Oriental cooking here in the islands, you know," she went on chattily.

"When I go to Honolulu I always make it a point to stop at—"

"Reyna! Good to see you. Who's your mainland friend?"

The handsome man in the Hawaiian-print aloha shirt and lei who had strolled over to the table Reyna was sharing with Trev smiled benignly down on them.

"Hello, Eddy," she smiled back. "Eddy, this is Trev Langdon. He's from Seattle. Trev, meet Eddy Cannon. He manages this restaurant."

Each man acknowledged the introduction, Eddy with the easy charm of the professional restaurateur and Trev with a distant politeness.

"Just hit the islands this afternoon?" Eddy asked, his friendly dark eyes on Trev's tie and jacket.

"No," Reyna answered before Trev could respond. "He got in yesterday. If you're wondering why he's still in a tie and jacket, it's because Trev is sometimes a little slow to see the light."

Across the table the golden eyes gleamed with promised vengeance. "But when I do finally get started in the right direction, I'm damn hard to stop."

"Don't worry, we'll have you into one of these aloha shirts in no time," Eddy said quickly, too astute not to sense the strong undercurrents between the two. "You'll love 'em the same way the ladies love muumuus. Very comfortable. Say, Reyna," he said quickly in an effort to change the subject, "what's this I hear about your leasing one of the shops here in the mall?"

Aware of Trev's immediate interest, Reyna

shrugged lightly. "I'm going to go ahead with plans for that gourmet-foods shop I mentioned to you a few weeks ago. I'll start checking out financing tomorrow, as a matter of fact."

Eddy nodded. "I think it's a great idea. I can see you making a fortune on gourmet picnic lunches. The L.A. and San Francisco crowd will really go for them!"

By the time Eddy had finished his polite conversation and taken his leave, Reyna knew Trev was waiting impatiently with questions.

"What shop?" he demanded immediately.

Stifling a certain wariness, Reyna told him of her plans and when she'd finished she found herself waiting with a strange expectancy. Whatever she thought of him on a personal level, there could be no denying that Trev Langdon was a very shrewd, very successful businessman. Not only that—he specialized in obtaining capital for new and growing firms and helped them acquire management expertise.

True, he worked with large-scale enterprises, not small businesses, but Reyna knew she would find herself paying attention to his opinions on her financial plans.

But instead of commenting on the business aspects of the project, Trev said gruffly, "Going into business here isn't quite the same as working the front desk of that condo, Reyna. You'll be committing yourself."

She shook her head in exasperation. "I keep trying to get it through your head that I already am committed to my new life."

He looked at her and she winced inwardly as she saw the undeniable glint of challenge in his eyes. "Then I'll just have to work very hard at changing your mind, won't I?"

"This conversation is heading for a dead end," she said sadly.

His expression tightened and she waited, wondering if he was going to lose his temper. It occurred to Reyna that she'd never had occasion to see Trev in a fury. The amber eyes narrowed slightly.

"Why are you looking so expectant?" he asked cautiously.

"I thought you might be on the edge of losing your patience," she murmured impishly.

"The prospect intrigues you?"

"I've never seen you in a flaming temper. You're always so cool and collected."

"Stick around, you may have a treat in store," he muttered. "But not tonight."

"No?"

"Tonight I'm intent on seduction," he explained in a matter-of-fact tone of voice.

Reyna felt the prickle of a warning chill. This man had a habit of achieving his objectives. She banished the uneasy sensation almost immediately, reminding herself that here they were on her turf.

"I never thought you were the type to waste time on a useless project," she murmured, her index finger tracing the rim of her glass.

"Look," he interrupted with sudden tension, "could we skip the flashy repartee? I don't particularly want to trade a lot of cutting banter with you this evening. I just want you. Period."

The abrupt and deliberate confrontation shook her.

"It would never work a second time, Trev." Reyna attempted a weak smile. "It's like a merger attempt. You have to strike while the iron is hot. Once everything's cooled down, there's no going back."

"How can you be so certain? Reyna, I want a second chance. I'll take care of your love this time."

"It doesn't exist anymore, Trev," she whispered. It was true, wasn't it? She'd left her love for him behind when she'd left her old life behind.

"It exists," he stated roughly. "You've buried it as a way of dealing with the pain of rejection. But I'm betting everything on the belief that deep down you couldn't have fallen out of love with me in six months."

"Why do you want that love now?" Reyna asked gently. It was becoming obvious that although he talked a lot about regaining her love, he hadn't said anything about being in love with her. What was driving him? Sheer desire or a mixture of desire and guilt?

"There's been no one else for six months, Reyna—"

"That's hardly my fault!" she managed flippantly, not caring for the urgency in him.

"I've spent more nights than I want to remember trying to tell myself that all I needed was another woman, but it didn't work," he plowed on. "I want to be loved. I've had a taste of the real thing and now I'm addicted. I know I've got a job ahead of me convincing you to come back to me but I'm going to do it!"

The blazing intensity in his gaze belied the outward calm of his voice. Reyna realized as she met that molten amber glance that something was happening to her nervous system. Her breath felt shallow and a little tight and there was a tingling awareness throughout her body. She'd experienced those sensations before around Trev and she knew they were dangerous in the extreme. *He* was dangerous.

"Keep talking along those lines and you're going to find yourself with a lot of spare time on your hands this evening," she forced herself to joke.

He ignored the attempt to divert him. "There's something I've got to know, sweetheart. Did you mean it last night when you said you understood?"

"Understood what?" But she knew what he meant.

"About my position six months ago, about the fact that my first objective had to be stopping you from ruining my brother-in-law?"

"Yes," she whispered. "I've never blamed you for what you did. If I hadn't fallen in love with you, I would have tied up your relative's computer firm in one very neat little package for my company. Nothing else would have stopped me. Nothing, at that time, was as important to me as my career and your brother-in-law was a stepping-stone in that career. I knew exactly what I was doing, Trev. I was well aware of the risks, believe me. Don't think I didn't give myself any number of lectures of the stupidity of falling in love with you!"

"But you fell in love with me, anyway," he concluded whimsically. "Reyna, listen to me. We have everything going for us this time. I know now we're absolutely right for each other." He reached across the table and lightly touched her wrist in a small, intimate gesture. "Sweetheart, I'll give you anything you want…."

She had to break the spell. She had to do something, anything!

"Would you," she murmured with a reckless little grin, "take off that tie for me? It's driving me crazy. You're the only one in the whole restaurant wearing a tie!"

He blinked and sat back a little, trying to assess her mood. Then he folded his arms on the tablecloth and smiled in open challenge. Instantly, Reyna felt the tension tighten unbearably, excitingly between them and she knew a moment of quickly suppressed anger that he could still do that to her.

"If you don't like the tie," he drawled, "you're welcome to remove it."

He meant after dinner, she knew. It was a blatantly sexual invitation to undress him and Reyna realized she couldn't let him get away with it.

Eyes shimmering very green in the soft light, she reached across the table without any warning and tugged at the precise knot of the striped tie.

His astonishment was almost palpable and Reyna knew a flash of victory at having taken him by surprise. He didn't give her the satisfaction of retreating, however. Instead he sat unmoving as she deftly yanked free the offending length of expensive silk.

"There," she exclaimed cheerfully, pulling the tie from around his neck and laying it on the table. "That's much better."

"You're laughing at me again," he complained a bit too gently.

"I thought you wanted me to enjoy myself this evening!"

"I do. Don't let me forget to ask the waiter for a doggy bag in which to take the tie home," he muttered wryly.

Having successfully regained control of the evening, Reyna relaxed. As the meal progressed she found herself chatting more and more freely. In a rush of enthusiasm she described her pleasure in the islands, her plans for the gourmet-foods shop and her present work.

Trev listened, encouraging her when she showed signs of running down and making appropriate comments at various points in the conversation. Reyna was aware her wine glass was never empty but his attentive refilling of it didn't bother her. She was riding the very pleasant high of being serenely on top of the situation. It wasn't a feeling she'd known very often six months ago around Trev Langdon.

By the time the meal drew to a close, Reyna was almost sorry to see the evening end. She found herself willing to listen when Trev quietly considered prolonging it.

"What about a drink in the bar at that little place

across the street?" he hazarded as he parked the car in the condominium parking lot.

She heard the lightness in his voice and told herself there was no harm in the idea. Then an impish thought struck.

"I have a better idea."

It seemed to her that he tensed a little in the dark silence of the car. "Which is?"

"How about a swim? Have you ever gone swimming in the ocean at night, Trev? It's marvelously exhilarating. This beach is safe..."

"You do this a lot?" he demanded with a clear skepticism which only made her more determined to talk him into it.

"Oh, yes."

He uttered something she didn't quite catch, his hand resting casually on the steering wheel and tapping gently. Then: "You're sure you wouldn't rather have a nice, quiet drink?"

"Come on, Trev. I'm going to swim whether you come with me or not." She opened the car door and swung her sandaled feet out onto the pavement.

Behind her his door slammed shut with a vaguely annoyed sound, but when Trev caught up with her, he was smiling gamely.

"Never let it be said that I can't keep up with your blond beachboy when it comes to spontaneity."

"That's the spirit," she approved. "I'll change and meet you at the gazebo in the garden." Reyna hurried off to her apartment before he could change his mind.

In her bedroom she slipped into a vivid orange and

green bikini, one that suited her new taste in clothing, and grabbed a huge striped beach towel. Draping
the towel around her neck she halted momentarily in
front of the wicker-framed mirror to tie her hair up
in a loose knot on top of her head.

It was as she secured the sunstreaked tendrils that
she caught herself smiling a very secret, very private
sort of smile. She knew the cause. The notion of having more or less forced Trev into the late-night swim
amused her enormously. There was no doubt in her
mind that he would have felt much more at home finishing off the evening with a gracious glass of cognac
in the intimate setting of a nice cocktail lounge. Or
the even more intimate setting of his room! It was
much more suited to his nicely polished sense of style.

But he was waiting obediently at the gazebo, a
wide towel slung over one shoulder and a pair of snug,
racing-style swim trunks hugging his lean hips.

The sight of the sinewy, tough length of him was
more of a shock than Reyna had expected. In the sub-
dued garden lighting she saw the tapering shadow
of crisp, curling hair on his chest and felt an errant
need to reach out and tangle her fingertips briefly in
it. She stifled the feeling at once, thinking she'd had
one too many glasses of wine at dinner. But the taut,
strong thighs, solid, hair-roughened legs, flat stomach and sweep of broad shoulders all called to her
senses tonight.

Firmly Reyna took a grip on herself, praying he
hadn't noticed the slight hesitation in her approach.
She stepped briskly forward, wrapping the striped

beach towel around her in a fashion she hoped didn't appear protective, only to find the amber eyes fastening on her as she emerged from the shadows. She tried to shake off the faint anticipatory frisson that seemed to emanate from the bottom of her stomach as his gaze roamed over her, seeking to see what lay beneath the towel.

"Ready?" she demanded with a false lightness, unconsciously clutching the towel just a little more tightly.

"I'm ready." The answer was something of a growl.

He came forward and she moved quickly ahead of him, pretending not to see his outstretched hand. Trev said nothing, but she felt the frustration in him as he silently followed her onto the sandy, moonlit beach.

"The sea here at night is fantastic, Trev. Nothing else like it on earth!" Reyna said softly as they reached the water's edge.

He didn't appear convinced. "You can't see the bottom."

"It's safe. This stretch is sandy for several yards out." Laughing at his lack of enthusiasm, she let the towel drop to the sand and stepped quickly into the water.

Almost at once the sensual pleasure of the gentle, warm sea reached out to captivate her senses. A streak of moonlight stretched out on its dark surface, almost to the horizon, and she moved into it. With a contented sigh, Reyna went in up to her waist and turned to watch as Trev walked slowly in behind her.

"Isn't it heavenly? Trev, this place really is paradise. Do you wonder that I couldn't care less about returning to Seattle?"

He didn't answer immediately, moving close to her in the water. As he stepped into the streak of moonlight, she could see the slight, sensual narrowing of his eyes as he drank his fill of her from the waist up. The amber gaze was almost a physical touch on her rounded breasts and the line of her throat. She knew at once he wanted to make the touch very physical.

"You appear to have been seduced by the islands, sweetheart," he finally murmured, "but I can offer something far more seductive."

The low, dragon's purr of his words carried the lacing of raw hunger she had sensed in him yesterday. He did want her, she realized with a twinge of nervousness. It might be guilt which had brought him all this way, but the desire was there, too. And he was right about one thing: His unshielded, masculine need *was* very seductive. No, she wasn't still in love with him, she told herself, but her body remembered his effect on her senses.

Gliding her hands in gentle arcs through the water, Reyna turned away, determined to ignore his quiet, urgent approach. With a small splash she struck out to swim parallel with the shore.

"Reyna!"

She had only taken three strokes when his arm closed around her bare waist.

"Damn it, Reyna! You have a right to be bitter, to hate me, to want revenge. I don't care if you want to claw me to shreds, but I can't let you just ignore me!"

She gasped as he hauled her upright in the water. But before she could find her footing or the words of protest needed to stop him, Trev was crushing her wet, slippery body close to his own.

She heard the low, fierce groan against her mouth as his lips took hers.

CHAPTER FOUR

SHE HAD BEEN a fool to prod him into the late-night swim. Here in the caressing sea there was no protection against the sensuality of their physical contact. The water surged around them as Trev stood with his feet planted solidly on the sandy bottom. He held Reyna so that she couldn't get her balance, lifting her just off her toes in the buoyant salt water. The lapping waves seemed to push her even more tightly against the lean length of him and she clutched automatically at his shoulders for support.

"I'm going to show you that you haven't forgotten what we can do to each other. You may have relegated it to the back of your mind because you no longer want to admit it, but it's still there, Reyna. I know it is!"

His mouth moved heavily, masterfully on hers. Deliberately, he worked to soften her lips and mold them to his own. With deep persuasion he invaded the damp warmth behind her teeth.

Last night Reyna had stood passively, almost curiously, certain that she would feel nothing more than a mild physical response. Tonight her instincts warned against taking that risk. She didn't love him, she insisted in silent rage, but the physical response was not going to be mild or harmless this evening.

He had spent the past few hours seducing her with his charm, allowing her to feel serenely in command of the situation. Recklessly she had told herself she could handle him and her own emotions, but she had not reckoned on the depth of the physical desire he could arouse.

Nor, she thought wildly, had she factored in the potent pull of his own unmasked need. The early charm of the evening had vanished in an instant as he had swept her up in the water. Now all the raw, honest hunger was vibrating through him, communicating itself to her in an earthy, impossible-to-ignore demand.

"Trev, no!"

She managed the gasp of protest as he momentarily lifted his mouth from hers in order to search out the line of her throat. His hands slid wetly down to her hips and he forced her intimately against his thighs as he took her lips and silenced the exclamation.

Reyna struggled for air as he made her overwhelmingly aware of his need. The male hardness was aggressive evidence of the state of his passion and he made certain she knew of it. He cupped her rounded bottom, his fingers slipping just under the elasticized leg opening of her bikini, and held her audaciously against his lower body.

"I want you so, Reyna," he rasped, raising his head once again to bury his mouth against the sensitive skin behind her ear. "It's been six long months, darling. Now that I have you back in my arms I can't let you go."

"Trev, please, I don't...I don't love you anymore. This isn't what I want!"

"I'll make it what you want. Trust me, Reyna. Give yourself to me again. I'll take care of your love. God knows, I need it so badly."

Her nails dug into his shoulder in what must have been a painful grip, but he didn't seem aware of it. "Trev, I can't just summon back a love that has died...!"

"Stop saying that," he breathed, his teeth sinking lightly into her earlobe in an exciting caress that made her shiver in spite of herself. "I can feel you trembling. You can't deny your own response. Don't fight me or it, sweetheart. Just let me show you that everything's going to be all right."

Reyna's lashes flickered and then shut tightly against the urgent persuasion. She could feel the beginnings of a tightly coiled tension in her lower body, a tension she hadn't known since she had lain in Trev Langdon's arms. The beginnings of her own desire both frightened and excited her.

The excitement she could understand, but, damn it! Why should she be afraid? Mentally she forced herself to deal with the almost instinctive wariness. So what if he still had the power to arouse her? Was that so wrong or even dangerous? She was no longer made vulnerable by the added emotion of love. And this man had the ability to affect her senses in a way no other male ever could. What was wrong with taking some passion from life…?

The insidious reasoning alarmed her. She had never been promiscuous, had never been the type to take pleasure where she found it. But that, she argued silently, was probably because up until now physical pleasure had been inseparable from a loving relationship. Six months ago the two factors had come together for her when she had fallen head over heels in love with Trev Langdon.

It had been the wildest, most intense emotion she had ever known, and the physical side of the relationship had been the totally inevitable expression of her deepest feelings. She had given the gift of her love freely to him and he had accepted it, giving only the physical side of himself in return.

Perhaps, even though her love had died, the physical responses her body had learned were still there, waiting to be unleashed once more. Just because the two aspects of her nature had come together in one stunning love affair six months ago didn't mean that the sexual side of her could not continue to exist without the loving emotion.

Would it be so very wrong if, after six months of dormancy, she once again allowed this man to release the wild spiral of physical sensation?

Her fingertips sank a little more deeply into the smoothly muscled shoulders and she experienced a curious sense of power as he trembled against her. The hardness of his chest was an inducement to her building need. It fed the feminine sense of power and stimulated the level of response beyond the safely controllable limits.

Holding her arched against him with one palm flattened on her lower back, Trev slowly, tantalizingly, traced the line of her spine with his other hand until he found the clasp of the bikini top.

The realization of what he intended brought a moment of rationality to the havoc racing through Reyna's system. She sipped air and pushed abruptly away from his chest. But even as she did so, the clasp came undone and the orange and green bikini fell away.

She heard his sharply indrawn breath as she tried to struggle free, and then his lips were on the wet, silky skin at the base of her throat.

Reyna knew she could have resisted. She could have forced herself free, knowing deep down that Trev Langdon would never resort to rape. But somehow it all became too overwhelming, too exhilarating. His lips burned on her skin and she thrilled to the feel of him.

The seduction was all the more intense because of Trev's obvious, pleading hunger. Reyna flinched as his thumb grazed a little roughly across her nipple. The shiver ricocheted throughout her body, leaving her weak and clinging.

"My God! I've dreamed so often about touching you again, feeling your passion…" His voice trailed off on a husky groan of desire as the nipple budded fiercely under his thumb. He circled the rosy tip once more and then he lowered his mouth to it.

"Trev!"

Her cry was soft, full of her need and her growing wish to succumb to the moment. He responded by using his tongue on the hardening nipple, stabbing, circling, caressing until she thought she would collapse with want.

Reyna's fingertips fluttered around his neck and then began to curl into the black and silver depths of his hair. In another instant she was clinging violently and he was reveling in the implied surrender.

"I knew," he whispered raggedly, his mouth dropping strings of hot, damp kisses from one breast to the other, "I knew if I could only get you back in my arms I could make you realize that what we had isn't something that can die in six months!"

"Trev…Trev…I don't know what I'm feeling," she tried vainly.

"It's all right, sweetheart. It's all right. Hush now, just let me take care of you…."

She closed her eyes and nestled her head close into the curve of his shoulder, her palm moving down the line of his throat to the expanse of his hair-roughened chest. Dreamily she explored the contoured skin, finding the flat nipple and toying with it until he muttered something dark and blatantly sexual into her ear. He followed the urgent words with the tip of his tongue, inserting it provocatively until she shivered.

Of its own accord her hand slid further down his chest, following the tapering line of wet, curling hair until it halted at the edge of the snug swimsuit.

"Touch me," he begged as her fingers hovered.

With a soft moan she obeyed, seeking him intimately. He murmured hoarsely against her throat, his hands tightening on her. Then Reyna's senses swirled abruptly as he lifted her high into his arms and strode out of the sea toward the beach.

He paused, near the spot where the beach towels had been left, setting her gently on her feet without a word and reaching down to scoop up the discarded items.

She stood watching him in the moonlight, the darkness of his hair reflecting the pale gleam. The hot amber of his eyes returned the searching look as he carefully draped one of the towels around her partial nudity. Then his hands slipped heavily to her shoulders.

"You won't be sorry, sweetheart. This time I'll take care of what I have." He kissed her slowly, with an incredible gallantry that seemed somehow out of place in that passionate moment.

And then he was sweeping her back up into his arms and she nestled against him, unprotesting, as he carried her away from the beach and back toward the garden-shrouded condominium-hotel.

She wanted him, Reyna acknowledged. She wanted him more than any other man she had ever known. Why should she deny herself the physical thrill of his lovemaking? He couldn't hurt her this time....

But as he carried her with silent strength through the quiet grounds it became impossible to think logically. The sea-wet furnace of his body was binding her senses, captivating her beyond reason.

She was dimly aware that he was taking her to her own apartment, not his room, and wondered briefly at that. As if he understood her unspoken question, Trev smiled tenderly down at her.

"I want to get to know the new Reyna Mackenzie," he growled softly. "I want to learn everything there is to know about her. I'm going to make love to her in her own bed, not some hotel room!"

Her eyes glittered a deep green as she looked up at him. "Do you really want the new Reyna, Trev? Have you come all this way just to find her and make love to her?"

"You said, yourself, that I can be very single-minded," he groaned, hesitating at her door to push it open.

He carried her inside, kicking the door shut with one sandy, bare foot, and stood for a moment with her in his arms, taking in the sight of the room.

She watched him draw all sorts of silent conclusions but he said nothing about the casual, airy decor. Instead, with unerring instinct, he made for the darkened bedroom.

Reyna had a last pang of uncertainty as he set her in the center of the huge bed, but there was no time to dwell on her private questions. He followed her down onto the cool sheets, reaching for her with that passionate hunger which was so compelling to her.

The shaft of moonlight which had streaked the water flowed now into her bedroom, illuminating the bed and Reyna's soft, rounded figure. She could feel the golden heat of Trev's eyes as they pored over her, and her body reacted to it as if it had been burned.

Compulsively she twisted, seeking him, her arms going around his neck. Her legs twined with his as if she would pull him down to her. The urgency she felt was hard to define. She wanted him desperately. But there was also a need to heighten the sexual tension as rapidly as possible so that she no longer had to think at all. She wanted only to take the passion of the moment. She had a right to that much, surely!

"Do you want me, sweetheart?" he muttered, his palm moving in a long, flat glide across her breasts to the small curve of her stomach.

"Yes, Trev," she admitted, finding some relief in the honesty. "I want you."

Her response affected him deeply and she gloried in it. Her own fingers began to wander over him in an increasingly sensual dance. She felt his legs deliberately trap hers and then he was sliding his rough thigh along her smooth one.

"You're so soft. Your skin is like velvet against mine...."

The hand on her stomach prowled lower and then he slipped his fingers just inside the waistband of the bikini.

"Oh!"

Reyna moaned, a half-stifled cry of passion as he slowly slipped the clinging fabric of the bikini down over her hips. She turned her head into his shoulder and nipped a little savagely.

"Let yourself go, honey," he urged, removing the

bikini bottom completely. "Just let yourself go tonight. I've been waiting so long to have you like this."

Under the coaxing of his words, his hands and his lips, Reyna seemed no longer to have any choice in the matter. She was committed to this night in his arms.

She shivered and whispered his name achingly as he slowly traced the line of her leg up to her hip. When his fingers dug thrillingly into the curve of her thigh, she arched against him, trying to pull him toward her.

"I've waited so long," he growled, slipping down the length of her body until he was sliding hot kisses into her navel. "So long. I'm not going to let you rush me tonight...."

Indeed, he seemed to be tasting her, enjoying her, reveling in her as if she were a long-denied luxury. She felt his tongue as it surged into the tiny depression in her stomach. Then, as her fingers clutched violently into his neck he trailed his kisses lower.

When his fingers began to move in unbelievably exciting patterns up the inside of her thigh, Reyna thought she would go out of her mind.

"Please, Trev. I want you so much!"

"Not half as much as I want you!" he corrected fiercely and put his teeth to her inner thigh with excruciating excitement.

She shivered again and again as he increased the fervor of his caresses. His roving hand teased and tantalized until suddenly it found its goal and closed over the dampening heat between her legs.

"God!" he breathed in tones of stark wonder. "You're on fire. All hot and welcoming for me. I don't know how I've managed without you!"

Reyna, herself more than a little astounded by the sudden depths of her passion, said nothing, merely clutched at him more tightly. Her hips twisted and arched against him, and when he pulled away for a moment she protested anxiously.

In the moonlight she saw that he was pushing off his swim trunks, and she welcomed him eagerly back into her arms when he returned to her, naked.

"My sweet, loving Reyna," he muttered, stroking tendrils of hair back from her head. He cupped her face in his hands and kissed her, his legs pushing a little roughly now between hers.

"Trev...Trev, I think I'm going out of my mind!"

"So am I, darling, so am I."

Then he was lowering his full weight on top of her, mastering her body slowly and completely. She shuddered as he surged against her, the impact of him a shock to her senses.

At once he stilled. "Have I hurt you, sweetheart? Please, I don't want to hurt you...!" His lips feathered soothingly across her cheek and the lashes which concealed the gray-green eyes.

"No, no!" She wrapped him closer as the heavy strength of him seemed to satisfy a deep ache in her body. It was an ache she hadn't even been consciously aware of until that moment.

Still he waited, allowing both of them time to adjust to the intimate feel of each other's bodies, and then, slowly, so slowly she couldn't have said when the movement began, Trev began to build a rhythm that would lead toward an ungovernable crescendo.

He crushed her heavily into the sheets, but his weight was a source of excitement in itself. From head to toe, Reyna felt deliriously as if she were one with him. The hardness of him seemed a perfect counterpoint to the softness of her own body. His gruff, masculine tenderness complemented her feminine gentleness, and when she arched wildly in his arms he took a very evident satisfaction in riding the frenzy of her excitement.

Reyna's nails raked across Trev's shoulders as her passion swept blindly out of control. Her cries were short, breathless sounds that gave him pleasure.

"Reyna!"

Her name was a husky, impeded growl on his lips as she surrendered completely, uninhibitedly in his embrace. She sensed his own lack of control now as they were both swept into the vortex of the storm they had created.

Ultimately the growing thread of spiraling passion snapped. Reyna shuddered convulsively as the bursting sensation took her. She felt teeth sinking into her lower lip and it took her a mindless instant to realize it was Trev as he locked her close.

He let the shivers of completion wash through her, holding back his own satisfaction in order to enjoy hers first. When at last she began to descend, he gave in to his driving need, and she heard the muffled, indecipherable exclamation on his lips as he found his own thorough satisfaction. Slowly, languidly, they came down together.

Long moments passed in the rumpled, moonlit bed. Reyna, her eyes still closed, was aware of the perspiration-damp warmth of Trev's body as he continued to sprawl across her. She was also vaguely aware of sand in the bed. Her toes found it as her foot moved idly across the sheet.

"Stop twitching," Trev murmured on a note of soft, indulgent humor as he cradled his dark head more comfortably against her breast.

"I'm not twitching."

"Yes, you are. I can feel your foot moving around down there."

"Sorry. There's sand in the bed," she explained, her fingers lifting to wander absently through his tousled hair.

"I'll buy you a new bed."

"That should take care of the problem, all right."

He raised his head suddenly to meet her languorous gaze. She saw the flash of amusement fade as something else took its place in the amber eyes.

"Ah, Reyna, my sweet. I feel like a new man tonight," he vowed a little thickly.

"Do you?" She smiled gently.

"After six months of trying to live with my own stupidity, I'm finally back where I want to be. In your arms. This time everything will be different," he added resolutely.

"Will it?"

"Reyna, I'll take care of your love this time. I swear it!"

She lowered her lashes before the intensity in him. All of a sudden his weight began to prove uncomfortable. She stirred beneath him.

"Reyna?"

"You're rather heavy, Trev," she tried to say lightly. He didn't move.

"Reyna," he said again, this time a little more deliberately. "It was good for you, wasn't it, sweetheart? You couldn't fake a response like the one you just gave me!"

She wondered whom he was trying to convince, her or himself. "It was good, Trev. You must know that. There's never been another man who could make me go out of my head the way you do."

He seemed to relax a little, his mouth curving at the corners as he lowered his head to drop a soft kiss on either edge of her lips.

"Has there been anyone else since you left Seattle?" he whispered. "I know I have no right to ask, but…"

"No, Trev," she returned with perfect honesty, "there's been no one else. Were you telling me the truth? That you haven't wanted anyone else since I left?"

"It was the truth? I haven't even wanted to take another woman to bed in six months, only you. When I saw you last night wading in the sea, it was all I could do not to pull you down onto the sand and take you then and there. Six months is a very long time, Reyna," he explained as if he were afraid she might not appreciate what he had been through.

"Poor Trev," she teased gently, touching the side of his cheek with questing fingertips. "It must have been rough on you."

"It was getting damn intolerable!" he gritted and then shook his head as if still a little dazed at having found her in his arms again. "But everything is all right now, isn't it?" His palms tightened slightly on her face and he trapped her gaze.

"What do you want from me now, Trev?" she whispered, a strange wariness crawling down her spine.

"The words," he muttered heavily. "The words you gave me last time. Reyna, tell me you love me."

She stiffened, her body reacting as if he had struck her. Her mind recoiled instantly. Very carefully she said, "But I don't, Trev."

At once she realized he didn't think he'd heard properly. And then the golden eyes slitted dangerously. "The hell you don't, Reyna Mackenzie! Don't lie to me, not now!"

Sensing the danger of the moment, Reyna wanted to retreat. She knew a surge of anger at him for making her feel that way and she rallied her defenses at once.

"I'm not lying to you, Trev," she managed steadily. "I've been telling you since the moment you arrived that I am no longer in love with you."

"I don't believe you! You wouldn't have surrendered again in my arms the way you just did if you weren't still in love with me!"

"Don't tell me you're one of those men who thinks a woman can't feel passionate without being in love," she mocked lightly, trying to soothe him with humor. It was a dismal failure.

"Damn you! I don't believe you!"

She saw the growing frustration and rage in him and began to panic. Had he really believed that everything could be put back the way it had been six months ago with one night in bed?

"Trev, please, I'm sorry if you misunderstood, but I never misled you. I never implied I was still in love with you!"

For a moment she wasn't certain what he was going to do and she wished desperately that she wasn't in such a vulnerable position. He pinned her to the bed with his weight, and the menacing glitter in the amber eyes was totally unnerving.

"Why?" His voice was raw. "Why did you let me seduce you if you don't love me?"

"You're the most physically exciting man I've ever known, Trev. And, it *has* been six months…." She let the explanation trail off, not knowing what else to say.

"You *used* me!" He looked thunderstruck at the realization.

"Trev, there's nothing wrong with two people finding a little pleasure in each other's arms," she began anxiously, feeling horribly disconcerted by the argument. Whatever she had been thinking when she'd allowed him to carry her off to bed, it wasn't that he would be infuriated afterward!

"You used me," he repeated as if he still couldn't believe it. "I came all this way to find a woman I thought loved me and she goes to bed with me because she happens to find me dynamite in the sack! Damn it to hell!"

He moved, heaving himself off her in barely controlled fury. At the edge of the bed he stood looking down at her, eyes flaming, expression taut and hawklike. Planting his hands on his hips, he towered over her, uncompromisingly male and thoroughly incensed.

"Trev, you have no right to be angry! You're the one who seduced me, remember?" Reyna fumbled for the edge of the sheet, pulling it up to her throat as she struggled to a sitting position. She sat coiled on the bed, her green eyes wary and defensive.

"What's going on in that sharp little brain of yours?" he gritted tightly. "Are you doing this out of revenge? Are you deliberately trying to punish me by refusing to admit you love me?"

"No!"

"What do you want from me?" he demanded ferociously. "Why did you go to bed with me?"

"I've told you!"

"You're going to sit there and tell me that you feel nothing more than a physical attraction now?" he hissed unbelievingly.

"There's nothing wrong with a physical attraction.

It's all you ever felt for me six months ago!" she retorted.

"So what happens next?" he shot back. "I'm here for another eight days, remember? Are you planning on having a torrid affair with me for the remainder of my stay and then casually waving goodbye when I get on the plane to go back to Seattle?"

"Not if you're going to behave like this after sex!" she snapped spiritedly. "I hate scenes and I have no intention of putting up with them for the next eight days and nights!"

"I could throttle you at the moment—do you realize that?"

"Yes, so I'd prefer that you leave as quickly as possible!"

"Why you little…!" Taking obvious hold of his raging temper, Trev paced to the foot of the bed, found his swim trunks and stepped back into them. Then he grabbed one of the beach towels which had fallen on the floor and turned for the bedroom door.

At the threshold he halted and glanced back at her over his shoulder. From across the room, Reyna could see that he had his anger under his control, but the golden eyes would have melted anything they touched.

"You want an eight-day affair? I'll give you an eight-day affair. We'll see which of us gets the most use out of the other!" He stepped through the door and then caught hold of the jamb, turning back for one parting shot.

"And we'll see just how good you are at casually

waving goodbye when I get on the damn plane for Seattle! Because you know something, Reyna Mackenzie? I don't believe you. I think you really do love me, and eight days from now you'll be getting on the plane with me!"

CHAPTER FIVE

REYNA SAT IN front of the open sliding glass doors, staring moodily out into her garden and the sea beyond. A ripe slice of papaya rested invitingly on the plate in front of her and she had already squeezed lime juice onto the fruit. But she was having a difficult time working up an appetite this morning.

Last night had left her unnerved and incredibly restless. She had stared at the doorway of her bedroom, listening as Trev had slammed his way out of the apartment, and her single, strongest urge had been to throw something after him. Preferably something that would shatter satisfyingly. The childish impulse had made her realize just how precarious the situation had become.

Why had she let Trev seduce her? She had asked herself that question—his question—over and over again as she had curled unhappily into the huge bed. What a fool she had been!

This morning she felt no closer to an explanation that was comfortable. The only one available was the one she had given Trev. It had been six months since she'd known the physical ecstasy of losing herself in his arms. She had no reason to blame herself for succumbing to the temptation again.

The important difference this time, she lectured herself sternly as she picked up the spoon, was that she was no longer in love with him. She knew what love was like. She'd learned that the hard way six months ago. No, last night was purely physical.

Reyna was reaching for the teapot when she sensed she was no longer alone. Her head snapped up, eyes widened, to find Trev moving quietly toward her across the expanse of the small garden. The sight of him in the morning sunlight made her swallow carefully and replace the teapot on its hot pad.

He was dressed in khaki, the slacks close-fitting and stylishly casual. The shirt had a vaguely bushjacket look, the sleeves buttoned crisply at his wrists, the collar worn with a rakish air. He should have looked like a parody of some fashion designer's image of the adventurer look. But he didn't, she thought with a sigh. He looked like the real thing. A very *stylish* adventurer, to be sure, but still, the real thing.

"You really must see about getting yourself one of those nice, roomy aloha shirts," Reyna said coolly, unwilling to let him see how his unexpected presence had startled her. "This isn't the African bush, you know. It's Hawaii."

The amber eyes scanned her short, slightly fitted yellow-and-white muumuu. Her hair was loose around her shoulders, catching the bright morning light, and her feet were in the barest of sandals. Then

Trev stepped through the open door, clearly not prepared to wait for an invitation.

"Believe it or not, I didn't come here this morning to discuss fashion with you." He ran an impatient hand through the carefully combed thickness of his dark hair and glanced at her small breakfast. "Do you think you could spare a cup of tea for a man as good in bed as I am?"

Reyna sucked in her breath, shaken by the degree of self-deprecating mockery in his gritty voice. "That all depends," she made herself say flippantly, getting to her feet. "Are you here to carry out your threat of throttling me?"

He shut his eyes briefly, the long, dark lashes moving for an instant along the high line of his cheeks. Then he looked at her directly, his whole face taut. "Reyna, I came here this morning to apologize. Please don't give me the benefit of your sharp little tongue. I'm feeling raw enough as it is."

"Sit down. Have you had any breakfast?" With a small sigh, Reyna turned toward the little kitchen.

"No."

When she returned to the living room a few minutes later carrying another slice of papaya, some toast and an additional cup, she found Trev stretched out in the cushioned wicker chair across from where she had been sitting. Without a word she set the dishes down on the glass-topped table in front of him.

"Thank you," he murmured, reaching at once for the teacup as she filled it. He drank deeply as she resumed the chair across from him. She tensed, aware of his tension. It communicated itself to her in a manner that was a little annoying. She didn't want to be that sensitive to his moods.

"Trev," she began almost formally, "there's no need to go through an apology. What happened last night was no one's fault—"

"Don't be ridiculous," he interrupted sharply. "It was my fault. And I got what I deserved."

She arched an eyebrow at that, scooping out another bite of papaya.

"My only excuse," he went on doggedly, "is that I've been thinking of no other woman except you for six long months. And I...I..." He broke off a little awkwardly.

"And you're not accustomed to going that long without sex," she finished for him, trying to sound placidly matter-of-fact. "Funny. My excuse runs along somewhat the same lines."

"You've been thinking of no one else but me for the past six months?"

"No," she admitted airily, "but it *has* been six months...."

"And I'm the most exciting man you've ever known." It was his turn to finish a sentence and he did so with a disgusted grimace. "It's a sign of the times, I suppose, that a man sits across from his lover the morning after and complains about being used!"

"Now you know what it's been like for women all these years!"

"My God! You are in a feisty mood this morning,

aren't you? Couldn't you try a little feminine compassion?"

"You might mistake it for the love you seem to think I still feel."

She thought she could almost hear his teeth snap together. What was it the sign on the cage at the zoo said? Warning: Don't Tease The Lion.

"Reyna," he began steadily, clearly opting for a reasonable approach, "no matter what you say, I can't believe you no longer feel anything for me except a physical attraction."

Her mouth tightened. "That's because you're not too sure of the difference between love and desire yourself, Trev. It's hard for you to distinguish between the two."

The golden gaze widened a little. "And you do know the difference?"

"Oh, yes," she whispered softly. "I know. I learned six months ago."

"I see." He waited a moment, apparently turning the words over in his mind. "Tell me something, Reyna. Why do you think I'm here? Why do you think I've come all this way to find you?"

She attempted a small, negligent shrug. "Some combination of desire, guilt and greed, I guess."

"Greed!" He looked startled.

"You've made it clear you've decided you liked what I was handing out six months ago. I can see where you might have convinced yourself that you wanted more of it. After all, an honest, open love with absolutely no strings attached could be a pleasant novelty for a man like you. Add to that the fact that you may or may not be feeling some form of guilt and that you do seem to still feel an attraction for me and I think we have the whole reason for your presence on my island."

He stared at her. "You've worked it all out, haven't you?"

She nodded firmly, determined to stick to her guns. She *had* worked it all out. It had taken her most of the night, but she was satisfied with her conclusions. "Trev, don't ask me to believe you've tracked me down because you've discovered an undying love for me."

"You don't think that's even a remote possibility?"

Her mouth lifted wryly. "You don't know what love is, Trev."

"And you do."

"Yes."

"So my motives in being here are condemned out of hand because you don't think I'm capable of loving you the way I want to be loved?" he muttered quietly.

"I know you fairly well, Trev," she reminded him gently.

"Well enough to say I'm not capable of love? That's a pretty sweeping assessment of another human being, Reyna."

"I won't say you're not capable of it; only that I'm not the one to inspire it in you. If it had been going to happen, it would have happened six months ago. Don't look so stricken, Trev," she went on, feeling more sure of herself as she spelled out the night's conclusions. "It's not your fault!"

"Thank you for your compassionate understanding," he growled sarcastically, gulping the last of his tea and handing out his cup for more. He glared at her as she poured obediently. "I'm not buying it, Reyna."

"My analysis of the situation?"

"Right. I think you're still in love with me, and we're going to start over."

She eyed him suspiciously. "What's that supposed to mean?"

"I rushed you. I'm aware of that," he told her with a generous arrogance that made her hackles rise. "It *had* been six long, lonely months and I'll admit that I thought once I had you back in bed everything would be fine."

"The usual male approach," she scoffed. "Well, you did get me back into bed and it was fine. I wasn't the one who left complaining. After all, you're—"

"If," he interrupted ruthlessly, jaw set in clear warning, "you tell me one more time that I'm good in bed, I really will throttle you!"

Reyna glared at him in mute resentment but she didn't push her luck.

"Now," he continued deliberately, sitting forward and cradling his cup between his knees, "as I was saying before you so rudely tried to put me in my place, I'm aware that I handled things badly last night. In fact," he gritted, "if I weren't such a mature, sophisticated man of the world, I would have gone back to my room and thrown things at the walls."

"A tantrum, Trev?" Reyna dared with the first real touch of amusement she had experienced that morning. She couldn't help it. She'd felt exactly the same impulse that he'd apparently felt! It *had* been a temptation to hurl something at the door. Something that would have shattered nicely.

"I was angry," he explained coolly.

"At me?"

"Mostly at myself. I don't usually do things so stupidly," he sighed. "Reyna, I meant what I said a few minutes ago. I want to start over. I want to get to know the new Reyna Mackenzie. Please, stop trying to analyze the reasons behind my actions and just let me spend some time with you, okay?"

"I don't want any more scenes, Trev," she said warily. It was the only thing she could think of to say. She was at a loss to know how to deal with the situation this morning. He seemed genuine in his attempt to apologize.

"Neither do I," he assured her. "I'll behave myself—I won't try to solve everything by taking you to bed."

"Trev," she said gently, "there's no point. I don't love you and you don't love me. The most we could have is an affair…!"

"No!" He surged to his feet, the teacup clattering loudly on the glass top of the table as he set it down abruptly. Striding over to the door window, he fixed his gaze on the sea. "I don't want an affair, Reyna. I want you to love me. There's a difference."

"I'm aware of that," she retorted stiffly. "But it's too late for us, Trev. Please accept that."

"No, damn it! I won't!" He swung around and caught her anxious gaze with his own fiercely determined one. "There's a hell of a lot more between us than a physical attraction now and I want a chance to show you."

"How?" Reyna watched him, feeling horribly uncertain. She didn't like the sensation.

"Just let me spend the remainder of my stay with you," he pressed. "I'm only asking for some time. I won't use it to try and seduce you, I swear it."

"Especially since you'd only blame me for using you afterward?" The gray-green eyes gleamed faintly with humor, and he pounced on it.

"You're laughing at me again, aren't you? You never used to laugh at me, Reyna." He gave her a reproachful glance that silently echoed some of her humor.

"I guess I just never realized how amusing you could be at times." She grinned, aware of a shaft of pleasure at sharing the joke with him.

"Then let me amuse you for the next week or so," he persisted in a slow drawl. But the gold in his gaze was liquid as he watched her.

Her fingers tightened on her cup. "It won't change anything, Trev."

"I'm willing to take the risk," he retorted steadily.

"You never take risks unless you expect to win," she pointed out.

He lifted a shoulder dismissingly. "I doubt that you do either, as a rule."

"Except on one occasion," she concluded in a dry whisper, glancing down at the remains of her tea. What was she doing even considering his suggestion? It could only lead to scenes and a variety of difficult situations. Trev Langdon was not a man to be casual in his pursuit.

"Honey," he growled, moving to step close and pull her lightly to her feet, "I'm here to show you that you didn't really lose six months ago. I know you're bitter, but I—"

"*Will* you please stop saying that! I am not bitter!" she suddenly stormed in open annoyance. "I'm just not at all certain I want to waste a lot of time with you now!"

Two patches of dull red stained the tanned line of his cheeks, but his voice was calm and steady. "It's only eight days, Reyna. And I promise I won't make things awkward for you. Please."

She trembled and hated herself for letting the emotion show. Especially since she couldn't begin to analyze the source of it. What was this man to her? She no longer loved him and she knew he didn't love her. He *couldn't* love her. She would recognize the symptoms in someone else after coming to know them so well in herself! But, like it or not, the physical attraction remained. And there was another aspect to the situation, Reyna realized, remembering how pleasant the previous evening had been up until the moment when he had stormed out of her room. They communicated well on some levels. She could talk to Trev in a way she hadn't enjoyed talking to any other man. As a dinner partner last evening he had been something of a relief from the men she had been dating casually for the past few months.

"What are you going to do if I refuse?" she demanded, tilting her head a little aggressively.

"Is that a challenge?" he asked with a half-smile.

"No, but I prefer to plan for the worst-possible-case contingency," she grumbled.

His smile died and she was a little sorry to see it go. "There's not much I can do if you refuse even to see me while I'm here, is there?"

She didn't trust the humble tone and narrowed her eyes skeptically. "Do you really think you'll enjoy hanging around with the new me?" she tried lightly. "I meant it, Trev. I'm not the same woman you knew in Seattle."

"I'm willing to take the risk," he repeated coolly.

Reyna came to a decision. For the life of her she wasn't certain what made her take the step; she didn't want to stop to analyze it. She only knew that if he wanted to see her while he was staying on Maui, she was willing to spend some time with a man who could be excellent company.

"All right, Trev," she agreed with a faint inclination of her head. "I suppose we could try dinner again this evening. *If* you're willing to behave yourself!"

"Don't worry," he murmured, his fingers beginning to massage her shoulders in a vaguely sensuous motion of which he didn't even appear aware. "I have no intention of winding up in the situation I found myself in last night!"

"Did you really feel used?" She smiled.

"Considering that I had anticipated an altogether different ending to the seduction scene, yes! I did."

"Ah, well. The experience was probably good for you," she told him roundly. "Now, if you don't mind, this is my day off and I have some business to attend to."

"I'll come with you," he said at once.

"Trev, I've agreed to have dinner with you. Surely that's enough? You can't possibly want to run around with me all day long!"

"Why not? It's either that or go sit on the sand and read a dull book."

"It's called relaxing. It's what you're supposed to do while you're on vacation in Hawaii!"

"But, then, I'm not really on vacation, am I?" he shot back easily. His hands fell away from her shoulders and he picked up the plates from the table. "What sort of business are we going to be handling today?"

"Real business, I'm afraid," she answered dryly. "I've got an appointment at the bank in Wailuku this morning."

He glanced back at her over his shoulder as he set the dishes in the sink. "About getting financing for opening the gourmet shop?"

"Yes. Still want to tag along? It's obvious you don't wholly approve of the idea." She chuckled, moving toward the bedroom.

"I'll have a look around the town while you're busy," he answered evasively. "Where are you going?"

"To change into something resembling a business suit, I'm afraid. Even here in Hawaii there is still a certain protocol to be followed when calling on a banker." A little smile curving her lips, Reyna shut her bedroom door. Trev had not looked particularly pleased.

Two hours later Reyna emerged from the bank wearing the white linen skirt and jacket she had chosen for the business trip. It had been months since she'd had on a pair of even moderate heels and already her feet hurt.

But the discomfort was crowded out of her awareness by the shock she had just received.

Waiting patiently at the curb behind the wheel of the rental car he had insisted on using for the drive, Trev sat reading a tourist guide. He glanced up expectantly as Reyna opened the passenger door and slid into the seat.

"Did you have an interesting tour of the town?" she asked with forced enthusiasm, not looking at him as she slipped her feet out of the heeled shoes and unbuttoned the white jacket. Her hair, which had been neatly wound in a businesslike knot, was next on the list. She already had unclipped the knot, letting the soft mass fall to her shoulders, by the time Trev had put down his guidebook.

"I went through the old Wailuku Female Seminary and stopped off for a brief look through the Historical Society Museum," he said neutrally, turning slightly in the seat to watch as she freed herself of some of the encumbrances of civilization.

"Good," she said briskly. "The Female Seminary dates back to 1834, you know. They completely restored the building in 1974. Lovely grounds, did you notice? And did you see the paintings of Maui done in the 1800s by the seminary instructor?"

"Reyna…"

"Wailuku is the seat of government for the county of Maui, did you realize that? Here in the islands, counties can be a bit unusual. Maui County, for example, takes in the islands of Molokai and Lanai," she continued, ignoring his attempt at interruption.

"Reyna, stop babbling and tell me how the meeting went," he commanded quietly.

"Oh, it was all business," she told him, glancing out at the street. "I doubt that it would interest you, given the fact that you're not exactly enthralled with the notion of my starting the shop."

"Precisely the reason I *am* interested in the outcome," he pointed out.

"I'd rather not talk about it, Trev. Are you hungry? I know a great little place where we can get lomilomi salmon and you can try some poi."

She could almost feel him gathering his patience. "What happened, Reyna?" he asked gently.

Her head swung around and she knew she wasn't doing a great job at hiding the disappointment and anger in her eyes. The knowledge that Trev would probably find her bad news gratifying bit deep. "If you don't want to eat, then let's go back to the hotel. I want to change out of these hot clothes."

"The answer was no?" he prodded, paying no attention to her attempt at controlling the situation.

"The answer," she said with deadly clarity, "was maybe."

He drew a deep breath. "And you're not accustomed to 'maybes,' are you?"

"The last time I dealt with a man like that, I could have walked into that bank and come out with anything I wanted!" she exploded, unable to contain her anger any longer. "I could probably even have had that fool of a banker's job! Doesn't he know who he's dealing with?"

"He's dealing with a hotel clerk who's been on the island only a few months," Trev observed mildly. "Tell me exactly what he said, Reyna."

She forced herself to relax. Trev was right. She'd been accustomed to dealing with men like the loan officer from a base of power, with the full clout of a strong conglomerate behind her. It was frustrating, to say the least, being treated as anything less than a VIP.

Reyna shot Trev a rueful, slanting glance. He might not want to see her succeed in her endeavor but she could talk to him about it. Trev knew about finance. He was the one person in her current group of acquaintances who would truly understand.

"I could use a drink," she managed lightly. "Take me to lunch and I'll tell you everything."

"It's a deal." He returned her weak smile with a

hooded, searching glance and then he started the engine.

She poured out the tale over a glass of chilled Chenin Blanc while they munched the salted salmon with tomato and onion called lomilomi. Trev listened in silence as she described the bank's reluctance to rush to her financial assistance. He sipped a cold beer and helped himself to a majority of the lomilomi while Reyna worked out her indignation.

"I think the problem was that I just wasn't prepared for the reaction I got," she groaned at the end of the story. "It took me by surprise."

"You're accustomed to having men like him rolling out the red carpet." Trev nodded with complete understanding. He wasn't being sarcastic; he was merely acknowledging the truth.

"True. This is my first venture back into the business world since I left the mainland." Reyna downed the last of her Chenin Blanc, one fingernail tapping with unsubtle impatience on the table. "If I'd thought about it, I would have realized the probable result. All I've been concerning myself with are the logistics of setting up the shop itself, not such things as collateral, credit ratings and other trivia! Well, I'll just have to get down to work."

Trev regarded her look of renewed determination with a remote expression of his own. It made Reyna wonder exactly what he was thinking. He'd listened to her tale with total comprehension but she could hardly expect him to be overly sympathetic.

"What are your plans?" he asked calmly.

"Right now it's back to the old drawing board." She stood up. "Let's go back to the hotel, Trev. I don't know why I'm telling you all my woes."

"You came out of that bank looking ready to consider murder. It was obvious you needed to talk to someone," he said quietly, rising.

"Perhaps," she agreed wryly, "but you're hardly the appropriate choice, are you? I mean, you do seem to feel you have a vested interest in the outcome." She turned and led the way toward the door.

"You are in a foul mood," he noted admiringly. "Are you going to take potshots at me all afternoon?"

Reyna wrinkled her nose at him as she slid into the car. "Potshots have never worked very well against you. It takes something a little more effective to stop you, doesn't it?"

"I'm glad you appreciate the extent of my persistence," he murmured. "What would you like to do for the rest of the day?"

"Work off my antagonism, I think. I'm going birding," she told him, making the decision on the spot.

That brought his head around in a startled fashion just as he was about to insert the key in the ignition. "Birding."

"Bird-watching," she explained with a small grin. "A new hobby of mine. I wasn't into it when we last met."

"I can't quite see you as a bird-watcher."

"Does that mean you won't be coming with me?" she challenged interestedly. "Giving up the attempt to get to know the new me already?"

His mouth firmed. "I'll go with you."

At once she repented. "Oh, Trev, I'm only teasing you. You'd hate it. Go ahead and spend the day on the beach. If you really want to get together for dinner this evening, I'll be back in plenty of time."

"I said I'll go with you and I will," he vowed.

Reyna lifted one brow in skeptical amusement but she said nothing more. Trev, it seemed, was intent on carrying out his new role. Far be it from her to try and stop him.

They drove back to the condo-hotel on the other side of the island where Reyna escaped with relief into her apartment and a change of clothing.

"Give me fifteen minutes," she instructed Trev before shutting her door neatly in his face. When he knocked precisely fifteen minutes later, she wondered if he'd spent the entire time standing just outside her door.

"No muumuu?" he drawled, taking in her snug-fitting jeans and tennis shoes. The short-sleeved blouse she wore was decorated with a colorful design of parrots.

She shoved a pair of field glasses into his hand. "No aloha shirt?" she retorted, thinking privately that he did look rather good in the khaki bush shirt.

"You may have succumbed totally to island living, but I'm still clinging to some vestige of style," he murmured, examining the field glasses with interest. "I see you're into this bird-watching bit in a first-class way. These are expensive."

"So don't drop them," she ordered, closing her door

and adjusting another pair of field glasses around her neck. Absently she patted her back pocket to make sure she had the notebook and field guide.

Trev grinned at her, slinging the glasses around his neck. "I'll be careful. Where are we going? Into deepest jungle?"

"Not today," she told him pertly. "You're new at this so I thought we'd take an easier route. We'll try the beach areas. Hawaii has some very interesting water birds. I know some quiet coves up the coast where we should be able to get in some good sightings."

"I can't believe this," Trev sighed, following her back out to the car. "If your friends could see you now. *Bird-watching!*"

"I keep telling you, I've changed." She smiled. It had surprised her that Trev had agreed to come along this afternoon. How long would his mood of accommodation last? Sooner or later he was bound to realize that the new Reyna was the real Reyna. She wasn't going back.

"You do keep telling me that," he agreed, unperturbed. "And I'm willing to grant that it may even be somewhat true. But I haven't."

She felt a prickle of wariness. "Haven't what?"

"Haven't changed," he elaborated pleasantly, golden eyes gleaming as he helped her back into the car. "I'm still the same old Trev Langdon who's accustomed to getting what he wants."

Her head came up quickly as she sensed the clear warning and then she smiled gamely. "Perhaps after you get to know the *real* me, you won't want me anymore! Have you thought about that?"

He slammed the car door and leaned down to look at her through the open window.

"Reyna," he said softly, "you're not going to scare me off with a little bird-watching."

"Don't be too sure about that. You haven't seen some of these birds!"

CHAPTER SIX

"I DON'T SEE how you can tell some of them apart!" Trev complained good-humoredly sometime later as he lowered the field glasses through which he had been peering.

They were lying on their stomachs on a cliff, looking seaward. Below them was a small rocky cove. They were well-concealed behind a lush patch of flowering vegetation.

"You have to learn to look for the tiniest details," Reyna explained softly, still focusing through the glasses. "The differences in the various petrels might be only a slight bit of color."

"When did you get into this?" he asked curiously.

"About three months ago. One of the tourists staying in the hotel got me started. It grows on you."

"Uh-huh. Everything about the islands seems to have grown on you!"

She grinned. "Who knows? If you stayed here long enough, you might become a willing victim, too!"

Instead of a sharp, negative rejoinder, Trev was silent. So silent, in fact, that Reyna lowered her field glasses to turn her head and look at him. He was concentrating on some object out at sea, holding his lenses with his elbows propped in front of him.

"Something interesting? Trev, if you're using my field glasses to stare at nude bathers, I'm going to take them away from you!"

"Spoilsport. Actually, I'm looking at a bird. A real bird. Large wings, dark, a sort of whitish throat..."

"Sounds like a female frigate bird. Known locally as an iwa. Let's see." Reyna lifted her glasses and followed his angle of sight. "Ummm. A beautiful one. They have wingspans of around seven feet."

"This tourist who got you interested in birding..." Trev murmured carefully.

"Ummmm?"

"Was it a sweet little old lady in tennis shoes?"

She felt the small, lapping waves of his potential jealousy and didn't know how to react to it. She ought to be impatient. After all, he had no right....

"No."

"A little old man in tennis shoes?" he tried, still watching the frigate bird.

"No."

"Someone you'll probably be seeing again?" he suggested with a deceptive blandness.

"Maybe."

"Reyna, please!"

Her mind went to the pleasant, forty-year-old, recently divorced man who had stayed for two weeks at the hotel. Tyler Bond had been an enjoyable diversion and his enthusiasm for birding had been contagious. But he had gone back to his law practice in

Phoenix and neither of them had missed the other sufficiently to even invest in a long-distance phone call. By mutual agreement the relationship had stayed light, friendly and very temporary.

"He's a forty-year-old lawyer from Phoenix," she explained equably.

"And did he try to take you home with him?"

"A little souvenir of the islands? Hardly. He was in the process of getting over a divorce and the last thing he wanted was a serious relationship." Reyna laughed. She could feel Trev relax.

"You don't sound as if you're eating your heart out over him," he observed cheerfully.

"I'm not."

"And your beachboy?"

"What is this? An inquisition? Look, Trev, if you're tired of bird-watching already, we can go back to the hotel…."

"I'll be good," he sighed. "Besides, I already have my answers. You gave them to me last night. It's just the territorial instinct in me that has to keep pressing. God! If you knew how many times I've tortured myself wondering if some *kind* male was letting you cry on his shoulder!"

"I haven't been crying on anyone's shoulder! And don't give me that line. If you'd really changed your mind after I left, you'd have been over here a lot sooner, Trev," she declared, using the field glasses to hide her unaccountably fierce expression. There were no birds in her line of sight at the moment, so she stared hard at the horizon instead.

"It took me over a month to find out where you'd gone," he said gently, continuing to stare at something through his own pair of glasses. "Before that I was swamped trying to rescue that dumb brother-in-law of mine. Not to mention all the time I took trying to talk myself out of coming after you at all."

"Poor Trev. You've had a difficult time, haven't you? You should use this trip to the islands to try and relax," she shot back with determined briskness. "Look!" she added in the next breath. "A white-tailed tropic bird. *Phaëthon lepturus,* to be technical about it. See the large, black wing patches and that beautiful, long white tail?"

"No."

"You're not trying," she accused, lowering the glasses to admonish him with a mischievous smile. Once again she felt in charge of the situation. It was pleasant being able to deal with Trev from her own turf. At bird-watching he was very much the novice, and that gave her a nice advantage.

"That's not fair," he smiled reproachfully. "Look at me. Grass stains on my shirt and slacks, mud on my shoes…" He set down his glasses and rolled onto his side, propping himself on one elbow. He took in the tousled, casual picture she made, and the corner of his mouth lifted.

For an instant their gazes locked and the familiar sexual tension flowed between them. Reyna shifted uncomfortably under it and knew she was waiting for him to make the next move.

"Don't fret," she tried brightly, hoping to dispel

the abruptly charged atmosphere. "A few grass stains won't hurt, Trev."

"They do look rather good on you," he admitted. His eyes moved leisurely over her scuffed clothing. "You couldn't wait to get out of that little business suit and back into your casual clothes, could you? Six months ago casual clothing for you meant tailored designer pants, a silk blouse and a suede blazer."

"Prefer the old me?" she taunted, unable to look away from his suddenly intent gaze.

"I'm not going to fall into the trap of saying I prefer one side of you over the other," he drawled. "But I do find myself wondering which life-style will ultimately make you the happiest."

She caught her breath. "It's kind of you to worry about my happiness, Trev." Her voice was very even.

"But I'm a little late in doing so?" he concluded for her dryly.

She tilted her chin. "Don't worry about me. I really am very happy. I keep telling you, there's no need for you to feel guilty!"

"Guilt, greed and desire," he murmured contemplatively. "You've got all my motives analyzed, haven't you?"

"I left a life-style behind, Trev, not my native intelligence!"

"Don't be afraid of me, Reyna," he pleaded wistfully.

"I'm not!" She felt herself tense under the admonition. But she wasn't afraid of him. He no longer had the power to hurt her. Something feminine and primitive coursed down her spine. He was still the one man who could set fire to her blood, she admitted to herself. If he attempted to seduce her again as he had last night, she wouldn't be able to put up much of a fight. And why should she? Surely in this modern age she had a right to sample that rare excitement occasionally?

"No," he growled in a low, grating whisper.

"No, what?" she breathed, aware of him with every inch of her body. She could feel the desire in Trev, saw it glowing golden in his gaze, sensed the force of it as a tangible bond reaching out to secure her.

"No, I'm not going to make love to you," he stated, just as if he had been reading her mind. Perhaps he had. After all, in this moment she could almost read his and that reading told her he wanted her very badly.

She felt the red stain on her cheeks and tore her gaze away from the mesmerizing amber one. Far out at sea a bird wheeled and plunged headfirst toward the waves, seeking its prey.

"Why?" she asked starkly, staring very hard at the diving bird. Unconsciously her fingers curled painfully around the bird-identification guide lying in front of her.

"Because," he said very steadily, "even though you claim you're not afraid of me, I'm discovering I'm a little afraid of you."

Her head snapped around as she turned to stare at him. "I don't believe you."

"Then you're giving me credit for a courage I don't

possess." He smiled almost tenderly. "Reyna, have I ever lied to you?"

Unwillingly, she considered the issue, knowing the answer was no. Rather than give him the satisfaction of hearing her admit it, however, she responded only with a dismissing shrug.

"Forget it," he groaned, turning back onto his stomach and lifting his glasses. "But rest assured you're quite safe from my...er...baser instincts."

She heard the return of the soft, bantering tone in his voice and knew a sense of relief. It was easier to deal with Trev when he was in this mood.

"Thanks," she muttered dryly, eyeing his profile as he stared through the lenses. The breeze off the ocean was playing lightly with the thick darkness of his hair, revealing and concealing some of the silver in it. The line of his body held the easy strength and grace of a relaxed cat, she thought. She wanted to reach out and touch him.

And before she could stop herself, she had done exactly that. Her fingertips touched his shoulder and she felt him tense.

"I said no." He didn't lower the glasses, but she could feel the coiled energy in him and she knew a curious sense of power at having been the cause of his instantaneous reaction.

Almost immediately, a little shocked at her own action, Reyna withdrew her hand. But along with the inner astonishment came a wave of sheer feminine pique. Who was he to set the rules of this relationship? He'd had no compunction about taking her to bed last night, and here he was today coolly telling her they weren't going to make love again.

"Are you really afraid of me now, Trev?" she taunted. "Just because you didn't get everything you wanted in bed last night?"

"I'm an excellent strategist under most conditions," he told her without any arrogance. It was the truth. "Doesn't it make sense that when I have a plan that backfires I'm going to be inclined to be a little more careful the next time?"

"Perhaps a failure now and then is good for you," she provoked languidly. The desire to prod him was growing. Was he genuinely determined not to wind up in bed with her again until he could be certain it would be on his terms?

"Very character building."

She summoned her courage, trying to sound amused. "You're so sure of yourself. You think everything's got to follow your plans or you'll change the plans."

He hesitated. "Things become dangerous when they get out of control," he finally stated quietly.

"Am I out of your control now, Trev? Is that why you're so tense?" Holding her breath she reached out again and trailed her fingers lightly through his dark hair.

"Perhaps," he allowed stiffly, still focusing on the horizon.

Her fingers tightened for a moment in his hair and then relaxed. But the tension in her body began to grow. This was the man to whom she had once given her heart completely, no strings attached. She had recovered from the rejection and in the recuperating process her love for him had died. She was certain of it. The physical attraction between them, though, seemed not to have diminished at all.

Slowly Reyna withdrew her hand again, aware of the tightening of his body as she did so. He wanted her, there could be no doubt. Trev, being Trev, however, wanted her on his own terms.

"Why don't you just relax, Trev?" she whispered invitingly. "Do as we say in the islands and 'hang loose.' Here in Hawaii a person learns that life is much easier if you don't take it too seriously."

"Is that the lesson you've learned?" he grated.

"I've made it a point to adapt." She half-smiled, still staring at his profile as he watched the sea through the field glasses.

"You haven't adapted to the point of sleeping with all your new, casual acquaintances," he reminded her grimly.

"I've never been interested in a string of casual affairs," she acknowledged mildly. "Something that fundamental in a person's makeup isn't likely to change. But you're hardly *casual* in bed."

"Damn you, Reyna!" he hissed, setting down the glasses with a vicious gesture and turning his head to glare at her. The amber eyes burned with masculine fury and frustration.

"You can't stand it when things aren't happening the way you want them to happen, can you?" she drawled, excitement roaring through her veins as she sensed the intense emotions of desire and anger in him. She wanted to show him that she could control a situation as well as he; that there were times when he was not in charge—not the one to whose tune she would dance.

"You're absolutely right," he bit out. "I don't like it when things don't go my way. But in this instance I have the power to see that they eventually will go my way. You may have changed, Reyna, but I haven't!"

"No?"

"No!" he exploded softly.

"Show me," she murmured, leaning close. The excitement in her was a torrent washing away inhibition, caution and rational thought. She would at least make him admit he couldn't dictate the boundaries of their physical relationship.

She touched the side of his lean, tanned cheek, half expecting him to pull away or slap her hand aside. But Trev remained where he was, still and tense, his eyes hooded and deep. Nor did he move when she lightly feathered her lips along his.

Achieving no response, Reyna's fingers slid down to curl gently around the back of his neck, moving tantalizingly in the black hair. Deliberately she softened her mouth against his in a coaxing, persuading movement that was not unlike his own seduction technique the previous evening.

Still he didn't move. His mouth remained obstinately hard, his eyes open, his body tight. Slowly, with tender urgency, Reyna began making tiny, intriguing circles on his shoulder. She leaned closer, letting a little of her own weight press against him.

When her breasts crushed lightly against him, Trev finally shifted, trying to lever himself up to a sitting position. Reyna felt the motion and leaned more heavily into him. With an aggressiveness that surprised her, she forced his lips apart with her tongue, only to run into the barrier of his firmly clamped teeth.

"Damn it, Reyna," he groaned, "I won't let you do this to me...."

She didn't argue. Already she could feel the need in him and knew he wouldn't be able to go on fighting her with passive resistance. Perhaps, she thought, he would be forced to push her away, to use his greater strength to put a distance between them.

The notion was strangely satisfying. If he found himself having to resort to force, it would be an admission that he couldn't resist her.

"Think of the moment, Trev," she urged sweetly against his mouth. "Don't fight it. Why should we deny ourselves?"

Her nails slid beneath the collar of his shirt, scraping along his skin with exquisite sensitivity. She heard his answering moan and felt the tremor in his body.

"Reyna!"

She opened her mouth on his, not trying to force her tongue between his teeth now but coaxing a response. Fingers trembling with excitement and a feeling of power, she opened the first button of the khaki shirt and then the next.

When she touched the crisp hair on his chest, Trev

once again tried to resist. He surged to a sitting position, reaching for her wrists.

"Don't be afraid of me, Trev..." Her green eyes mocked and challenged, and the passion in her flared as it sensed the barely contained desire in him.

"You're a witch," he breathed shakily.

"I'm a woman."

She pressed gently against his shoulders, stealing her way into his lap until she was lying across his hard thighs. His hands stayed on her wrists as she pushed, but he didn't seem able to use his superior strength to restrain her completely.

"I want you, Trev," she moaned daringly and felt his instant response.

"Reyna, Reyna, I should let you...." His words trailed off in a husky groan as at last he yielded to her tenderly persistent mouth.

As if the small victory were the first in a chain of falling dominoes, Trev fell back under her weight until she sprawled sensually across his chest. She heard his muttered exclamation of surrender, and her wrists were released.

Thrilled by the success of her feminine assault, Reyna felt her own passion spiraling upward, guiding her fingertips, her mouth, her twisting, sinuous body. He put his hands on her back as if he were touching superheated metal, caressing her body with ill-conccalcd longing.

Reyna explored the inside of his mouth with a hunger which she didn't stop to analyze. She found his

tongue with her own, twining, darting, and provoking until he responded in kind.

Delicately, she insinuated herself against his body,
her jeaned legs sliding between his until their hips
were pressed close. Then she arched against him,
glorying in the telltale surge of his body. He groaned
hoarsely, his knees flexing and rising alongside her
thighs so that she was cradled intimately.

"My God, Reyna! I can't fight this. Why am I even
bothering to try?"

"Let me make love to you, Trev," she murmured,
nibbling sexily on his earlobe.

"Yes," he rasped, "make love to me. Love me,
Reyna. *Love me.*"

She knew he was twisting the words, trying to
convince himself that she was, indeed, making love
to him in every sense. But she was too far gone along
the path of sensual need to correct him. It was a joy
to be able to provoke his surrender like this. A thrilling, challenging, incredibly exciting joy.

He gave in before her onslaught as if he were the
sea: strong, potentially dominant, invariably dangerous but irresistibly yielding to her touch.

She circled the interior of his ear and felt his hands
tighten and curve around the shape of her buttocks.
He pulled her close, arching her again and again into
him, making certain she knew of his rising manhood.

The buttons of the khaki shirt were all open now
and Reyna eagerly explored the line of his ribs down
to the waistband of his pants. Then she circled her fin-

gers lazily across the small depression in his stomach and felt him draw in his breath at the touch.

Boldly she worked her way down his chest, dropping strings of small, stinging kisses along his throat, across the male nipples and down to the navel. There she dipped her tongue tantalizingly, wetly, inside and held his hips while he arched upward in reaction.

"I want you," he admitted raggedly. "I want you so much…"

Her fingers shaking with the sexual excitement coursing through her body, Reyna began unclasping the brass belt buckle. Slowly she lowered the zipper, her nails straying with intentional carelessness just inside the fabric.

"My God, woman! I'm not made of stone." Reyna felt his fingers lift from her shoulders to tighten almost violently in her hair as she slid the khaki slacks aside. In a moment he lay nude on the grass.

For a fraction of a moment, Reyna knew a sense of shock at her own aggressiveness. Never had she been compelled to take the lead like this. Always with Trev she had been the one who yielded; the one who surrendered to the tide of passion he instigated. She lay alongside him now, running her hands over his well-muscled, lean body, and knew a kind of wonder.

For today he was the one surrendering. He was helpless to resist her caresses even though he had made up his mind to do so. She raised her head for an instant and saw him watching her beneath dark lashes, golden eyes glittering with arousal and masculine pleading.

"Trev?" she whispered, for the first time a hint of uncertainty entering her voice.

"Please, Reyna," he answered, taking her restlessly exploring hand and guiding it to the most intimate of embraces.

Slowly she bent her head, her sunlit hair flowing across his taut body, and kissed him. Her teeth sank tenderly, stirringly into the rough texture of his thigh and he gasped.

Then, drawing tiny circles on his hips and waist with one hand, she began unfastening her blouse. He watched her shrug out of it, his whole being radiating his passion. Her hand dropped to the fastening of her jeans.

In a few moments she was naked beside him, her hair in tousled disarray around her shoulders. Under the hot sun, lying on a secluded cliff overlooking an ocean, Reyna made love to the man she had once loved.

Deliberately she used on him techniques he had used on her, and he lay on his back, surrendering completely, willingly, to each new caress, each exploring touch. She covered his body with kisses from his ankle to his temple and he seemed to revel in the sensuous attack.

A little roughly he began to urge her with his hands, insistently trying to pull her down on top of him so that their union might be completed.

But Reyna refused to be rushed. In the golden sunlight she moved over him with deliberate, teasing caresses, taking pleasure in being the dispenser of

pleasure. Every muffled groan, every gasp or plea
for completion she managed to draw from him was
yet another small victory to be treasured and enjoyed.

Her own body seemed on fire with unbelievable
arousal. She could feel the flames licking through her
veins, spreading a tumultuous excitement.

Somewhere along the line she expected him to
take control. She was very certain that Trev Langdon
had never played such a gentle, yielding role before
in his life. In a sense, making fierce love to him was
a way of seeing how far she could push him before
he assumed the dominant male part.

But he didn't. And with every thrilling, dangerous step closer to the goal, Reyna became more and
more aware of the essence of his physical surrender.
It tempted her, goaded her, pleased her. She loved
watching him twist hungrily with his desire and she
loved the heat beneath her fingers when she touched
him.

At last, unable to contain her own need any longer,
she settled lightly on top of him, crushing her breasts
against his chest. His hands circled her waist at once
as he pulled her eagerly onto him.

The impact of their union sent a shudder through
both of them. Hair lying in curling tendrils across
his chest and shoulder, Reyna caught her breath and
slowly began to move against him.

"Reyna!"

Her name was an impeded sound buried deep in
his throat and her nails dug heavily into his shoulders as she clung to him. She set the pattern of their

lovemaking, acting out of an overwhelming desire to give him the satisfaction he craved in that moment.

Today he was not the gallant, sensitive, controlled man who had heretofore made certain of her satisfaction before taking his own. Today Trev was a man being taken by storm, and he was clearly giving himself up to the whirlwind of passion besieging them both. His hips moved with surging, driving power under her and, as he neared the heights, he held her with a strength which made it difficult for Reyna to breathe.

And then he was shouting his groaning, shuddering release into the silky skin of her breast. Reyna clung to him, gasping out his name as she found her own fulfillment a few seconds later. The hot sun beat down on their damp, exhausted bodies.

Reyna was a long time resurfacing. She lay limply nestled against Trev's chest, her head pillowed on his shoulder. Dimly she was aware of the slow, absent glide of his hands on her body as he stroked her. Eyes closed, she held herself still and quiet and tried to assess what she had done.

Would he be angry? she wondered. Would he be furious with himself or with her for having lost his self-control? Would he be disgusted with her aggressiveness? The questions began to sweep through her mind as she lay there, unwilling to open her eyes and face him.

"Are you going to fall asleep on me?" Trev's voice was an affectionate, lightly teasing sound that made her start.

Carefully she lifted her lashes, meeting his gaze warily. He didn't sound angry at either himself or her.

"It's the man who's supposed to fall asleep afterward," she said softly, searching his relaxed, tender expression and wondering at it.

"Only because he usually has to work so hard. This time it was you doing all the work." He smiled, eyes warm and gentle.

She felt the flush on her cheeks. "And you were the one..." She couldn't bring herself to say it aloud in case he really got angry.

"The one doing the surrendering?" he finished for her, his gaze steady. "Yes, I was. I want you to love me, Reyna, and having you *make* love to me is the closest I seem to be able to get right now. I told myself I wouldn't allow our physical attraction for each other to interfere with the direction in which I intended our relationship to go, but..." He broke off, shrugging philosophically.

"Trev...?" She looked at him, trying to understand her reaction to the usual lovemaking. What was it about this moment that was so unnervingly familiar?

He sat up, effectively breaking the delicate moment, and grabbed for his shirt as a suddenly crisp breeze began to play with it. "Wind's coming up, honey. We'd better get dressed or we'll spend the rest of the afternoon chasing after our clothes!"

He tossed her the parrot shirt and her jeans and she began to put them on, still trying to sort out the situation in her uneasy mind. But it was too late to try and find a way to talk about it. Trev was already on his feet, fastening his khaki slacks and reaching down to help her up.

"I had no idea bird-watching could be so enjoyable." He grinned devilishly as he slipped on his shirt.

Reyna caught the crisp retort on her lips, burying it forever. She had been about to make some flippant remark about keeping the tourists entertained, but the sudden, intuitive knowledge that he would be hurt at the thought of being a tourist romance for her made her reassess the comment. She didn't want to spoil the harmony that existed between them.

Instead, she put out her hand in an impulsive little gesture and stilled his fingers as he attempted to button the khaki shirt. when he looked up expectantly, she chuckled. Carefully she began to roll up his sleeves.

"It's okay, Trev. This is Hawaii. You don't have to be so formal."

He hesitated and then dropped his hands, taking hold of her wrist instead. Without a word he used his free hand to scoop up the field glasses and then they started back toward the car.

Out of the corner of her eye Reyna took in the newly casual sight he made, with his shirt unbuttoned halfway down his chest and the sleeves rolled up on his forearms. She suddenly felt more at ease with him than she had since the moment he had first appeared on her beach. He looked good—casual and relaxed in the aftermath of their lovemaking.

It wasn't until he had left her at her door after making arrangements to pick her up for dinner that Reyna finally realized what it was about Trev's response to her lovemaking that had elicited that strange sense of déjà vu.

He had surrendered to it in a way that reminded her of her own surrender six months ago.

The thought made her halt halfway through the living room on her way to a hot shower.

He hadn't intended to make love with her, but when the moment had come he had given himself completely.

And when it was over he had not been angry at this loss of self-control, nor had he berated her for "using" him.

CHAPTER SEVEN

THE FOLLOWING AFTERNOON Reyna stood examining a bolt of authentic Indonesian batik in one of the many fascinating shops in Lahaina. She had come here directly from work with every intention of buying a length or two to make up into a tablecloth. Now she found herself staring at the exotic printed cotton without being able to concentrate on the pattern.

Absently she touched the fabric and thought instead of the previous day and the evening which had ensued.

Trev had taken her to dinner, his manner warm and attentive. Still a little bemused by her own actions and his response to them that afternoon on the cliff overlooking the sea, Reyna had experienced an edge of wariness throughout the evening. Would Trev now assume he would be spending every night of his stay in her bed?

She couldn't blame him for coming to such a conclusion after the way she had boldly seduced him! Even before that fateful scene she had implied she was willing to become involved in an affair.

The thought made her shut her eyes in momentary

dismay and she dropped the length of fabric she had been examining.

"If that's not suitable, Reyna, I have some interesting tapa prints and a nice new selection of Malaysian batiks," the perky, dark-headed saleswoman offered cheerfully.

"Thanks, this is probably what I'll wind up choosing, but I'm going to think about it a bit longer, Carol. I've got a few other items to get in town. I'll probably pick this up on the way back."

"Fine. How are the plans for the gourmet-foods shop going?" Carol asked, smoothing a bolt of fabric another customer had been looking at.

Reyna winced. "Don't ask! A few glitches have developed."

"Couldn't you find a space?"

"I'm having a little work getting the loan, unfortunately," Reyna explained.

"Uh-oh. Maybe you ought to try some of the banks over in Honolulu."

"That's a possibility," Reyna sighed. "Well, I'd better be on my way. I'll see you later, Carol."

She quickly removed herself. Carol was a friend, but there was no one, not even a close friend, with whom Reyna wanted to discuss the real issue bothering her this afternoon.

Stepping out onto the tourist-crowded sidewalk, she turned toward the waterfront and the shops which occupied the restored buildings there. The old rough-and-ready whaling town was an inviting attraction today. Many of the historic buildings were being carefully refurbished, recreating the days during the last century when the missionaries and the visiting sailors had battled over Lahaina's future course of development.

The whalers had wanted to maintain a free and lusty port; the missionaries were concerned with creating a different sort of environment for the Hawaiians.

A cannery and a sugar mill provided nontourist-oriented work near town. Acres of sugar cane and pineapple stretched off into the distance toward the West Maui hills. Galleries, boutiques and restaurants abounded in the central district and the area was a shopper's delight.

Reyna wandered idly, going over and over in her mind the gentle fire in Trev's good-night kiss. She had been prepared for a major skirmish at her door, but he had meekly accepted her cool attempt to send him back to his own room.

She knew her actions had confused him. They'd certainly confused her! But she had known from the outset of the evening that there would be no repeat performance of the afternoon's unnerving behavior!

The chaos it had created in her emotions still raged. What was wrong with her? Why this strange, uneasy restlessness? There was only a physical attraction remaining between herself and Trev. She knew that. Trev Langdon knew nothing about real love, and she would never again be stupid enough to throw her heart away on a man who couldn't reciprocate.

When he had reappeared in her life, she'd been

forced to accept the fact that the sexual tension between them still held power. She had even accepted her own surrender to it—for a time. Trev was unique in her life. Why shouldn't she take a bit more of the physical ecstasy he offered?

But it had thrown her yesterday when he'd literally surrendered to her. Afterward she had found herself waiting for recriminations or mockery. Neither had resulted. The disquieting follow-up had been her own surge of inner chaos.

Perhaps she simply wasn't cut out to become involved in an affair that didn't contain the ingredient of love, Reyna decided with sudden understanding as she stood on the wharf and gazed across the protected Lahaina harbor. Her first attempt at such an involvement certainly wasn't proving very promising. She didn't need this feeling of unsettled restlessness.

And what about Trev's actions? His recent surrender was as unnerving as her own behavior! It didn't fit the image she had of the man.

By the time she returned to the hotel Reyna had reached a decision. It would be best to put some distance between herself and Trev for the remainder of his stay. Whatever the ultimate source of her confusion and wariness, it was evident she no longer could deceive herself into thinking she could handle a simple affair with him.

The decision firmly in mind, it was, nonetheless, something of an unexpected shock to encounter Trev in the lobby as she made her way back toward her apartment.

He was obviously returning from the beach and he was not alone. It wasn't merely the sight of the attractive, vivacious blonde wearing the tiniest of green bikinis which made Reyna blink—it was Trev's sandy feet and calves, his sea-tousled wet hair and the slapping thongs on his feet. He was wearing the racing swim trunks and had a towel slung around his neck. He seemed totally unconcerned about his appearance as he smiled down at the upturned face of the blonde.

It struck Reyna rather forcibly that there was a time when Trev Langdon wouldn't have been seen dead in a hotel lobby with sandy feet and that excuse of a bathing suit. He would have gone straight back to his room for a shower and proper attire before appearing in public again.

Whatever the blonde was saying seemed to amuse him. Reyna stood for a moment, unnoticed, watching Trev's mouth quirk slightly. The sight of him in his unexpectedly casual guise was almost as annoying as watching him charm the blonde. She didn't fully understand her reaction to either. With a briskly professional nod, she moved past the couple.

"Reyna!"

Trev looked up and called her name, more or less obliging Reyna to come to a halt and turn with a politely inquiring smile. She bestowed the smile on both Trev and the blonde with gracious impartiality. It was an effort.

"Yes, Trev?"

His dark brow arched in silent comment on her aloof tone, but he turned to his bikini-clad acquaintance. "Sorry, Lynn, but I've been waiting for Reyna. I'll see you around. Enjoy yourself."

The blonde took the dismissal prettily, shooting a slanting, considering glance at Reyna, who ignored it blandly. "Perhaps I'll see you later for a drink?" she suggested easily to Trev.

"Perhaps," he agreed noncommittally. Lynn swung off, already raising a hand to greet another male emerging into the lobby from the direction of the sea.

"I couldn't find you this morning," Trev began, sauntering toward Reyna while absently brushing sand off his feet with the beach towel. The grains clung to the crisp sprinkling of hairs on his legs, and Reyna distractedly found herself watching him. He glanced up, caught her look and grinned with familiar masculine assurance. "I thought you might have liked to join me for a swim."

"I had some errands to run in Lahaina. You don't look as if you lacked for company." Damn! What had made her say that?

"Jealous?" He chuckled, amber eyes hopeful.

"What do you think?" she retorted sweetly.

"I think I'd better not push the matter," he sighed. "It's not important, anyway. Lynn's only a casual acquaintance. I met her on the beach...."

"As you said, it's not important."

"I was afraid you'd agree," he groaned. "Well, let's forget that subject, shall we?" he went on with determined cheerfulness. "What time shall I pick you up for dinner?"

As if the near future were a movie, it flashed in

front of Reyna's eyes. She saw herself going out to dinner with him, saw the heightened excitement grow once more between them, heard the shared conversation, experienced the moment when he took her in his arms…

"I'm sorry, Trev," she made herself say as calmly as possible, "but I can't make it tonight. I have another date." She tensed for the explosion.

It didn't come.

What did appear, however, was a curiously vulnerable expression in his amber eyes. Unconsciously Reyna bit her lip and half-frowned for an uneasy moment. The thought of being able to hurt Trev Langdon was as laughable as the idea that he could actually fall in love. She might be in a position to do some damage to his pride, but that was about it.

"Your blond beachboy?" he hazarded.

"Well, yes," she lied, feeling a little desperate. But she was committed. The decision to put some distance between herself and Trev had been made, and she knew it was a wise one.

"I have an idea," he said enthusiastically. "Why don't we match him up with Lynn? They'd look great together. Both blond, blue-eyed and beachy."

Reyna realized she was having to hold back a sudden smile at Trev's look of ingenuousness. There were moments when this man could invite her to share a joke simply by catching her eye. It was part of the undeniable charm which had first captivated her.

"That might be a good idea, but not tonight," she agreed lightly.

"Tonight you need him to protect yourself against me?" he murmured shrewdly.

"Don't be ridiculous!" Her voice was all the more tart because Reyna had a horrid suspicion he'd hit the nail on the head.

"Nothing I can say will make you change your mind tonight, will it?"

"No."

"Have fun," he growled, and then, without another word, he turned on his heel and strode away.

Reyna was left to stare after him and wonder why she felt as if she'd just committed an act of cruelty. Trev's pride might have been touched but surely nothing deeper. But it wasn't like him to give up so easily. She had been prepared for a pitched battle over the issue of spending the evening with him.

With a wry grimace Reyna continued on to her apartment. The life she had so recently taken such pains to simplify was threatening to get complicated again.

The uncomplicated aspects of island life reasserted themselves easily enough, however, when she phoned Kent Eaton and asked him if he wanted to get together for a drink.

"Actually, I was about to call you," Kent told her cheerfully. "Tod, Sue and a few of the others are going into one of the Lahaina clubs this evening. There's a country-western band from the mainland playing. Sound like fun?"

"Nothing like dancing to country-western music

here in Hawaii. Do you think they'll refuse admittance to us if we don't wear boots?"

"If they do, we'll threaten to return with our ukuleles and drown out the guitars with a few choruses of the 'Hawaiian Wedding Song'!"

"Sounds terrific."

But Reyna's chief sensation when she hung up the phone was that of feeling a little flat. She wondered what Trev would do that evening. Probably look up his beachy blonde, she decided at once. Trev was not the sort to sit around pining. Why did she have to keep reminding herself of the man's basic characteristics?

The country-western band was fun, the atmosphere friendly, the company convivial. Nevertheless Reyna found herself glad later in the evening that she'd driven her own car into town. It made leaving earlier than she'd planned so much simpler.

"Feeling okay, honey?" Kent asked solicitously as she quietly explained her wish to leave. The din of a guitar made it difficult to communicate.

"A little headache. I had a rough day." Well, that last sentence was true at any rate. "You don't mind if I take off?"

Kent was casually sympathetic and even walked her out to the car. It was as she made her way home that Reyna finally admitted to herself that Trev would never have allowed her to return home alone from even the most casual of dates. Her mouth tightened in irritation. What was wrong with her mood? Trev's arrival on the island was definitely upsetting her.

Wide awake and not suffering in the least from

a headache, Reyna briefly considered a swim when she returned to her apartment. As she switched on the light, though, the stack of papers on top of her desk forcibly reminded her of more urgent business. If she was ever going to get her gourmet shop going, she'd better buckle down and learn how to get a loan without the full force of a huge organization behind her. Grimly she made a pot of tea and settled down at the desk.

The soft tapping on the sliding glass door a few minutes later brought her out of her mood of deep concentration with a start. She whirled around in her chair, staring at the darkened area behind the glass. Trev stood there, a small smile playing at the edge of his hard mouth.

Slowly Reyna put down her hand-held calculator and got to her feet. Honesty was forcing her to admit that she wasn't altogether surprised to find Trev at her door. Perhaps it was because at this late hour there seemed to be a certain inevitability about life, an inevitability one didn't sense in the full light of day.

She opened the sliding door and stood looking up at him. His dark head gleamed faintly in the moonlight and his long-lashed amber eyes reminded her of a cat in the night. He was wearing a white long-sleeved shirt which had probably cost a fortune, but tonight it was unbuttoned halfway down his chest instead of being worn with an equally expensive tie. It was tucked into dark trousers. He looked like the pirate he could be at times, and Reyna didn't hesitate to answer the unspoken question hovering in the suddenly taut atmosphere.

"No," she said quietly.

His smile widened slightly. "I know how you feel. I spent a great deal of energy saying the same thing yesterday afternoon."

He ignored her firm stance and pushed gently past her into the room, his eyes sliding over her gold-and purple-splashed muumuu and sandaled feet. Her hair was wrapped in a loose, straggling knot and she looked perfectly adapted to the perpetual summer of Hawaii.

"You're home early," Trev remarked, golden eyes a little too knowing.

"I had some work to do," she told him quite steadily. "I'd rather you didn't stay, Trev."

"Because you're afraid I'll turn your 'no' into a 'yes' just as you did mine yesterday?"

"Because I have some work to do!" she repeated stonily.

He glanced across the room and saw the papers and calculator on top of the bamboo desk. "Putting together a loan application?"

Reyna shrugged and moved forward. "Putting together a better loan application than the one I filled out the first time," she admitted, coming to a halt beside the desk and moodily flicking through the documents.

"You're determined to open that shop, aren't you?" he murmured softly.

"Yes."

"What makes you so sure it's what you want, Reyna?"

"I want to stay here in Hawaii," she said quietly, her eyes still on the paper work. "And in the long run I'd rather be my own boss." She glanced up a little defensively and was surprised by his small, understanding nod.

"So you're going to open your own place. Reyna, honey, I just can't see you clerking or selling gourmet foods over a counter. Eventually you're going to need more challenge than that."

"You think there's no challenge in running a small business?" she argued aggressively.

His mouth firmed. "For a time perhaps. What will you do when you've got everything running smoothly?"

"Open up branches on the other islands," she answered unhesitatingly.

He stared at her. "You've really got this all figured out, haven't you?"

"I'm afraid so, Trev," she smiled half apologetically. "There really is no point trying to talk me out of it. I love Hawaii and I'm looking forward to building up a business here. I'm never going back."

He continued watching her for another long moment and then he paced slowly forward, coming to a halt beside the desk. "What are you trying to do here?" he muttered, picking up a sheet on which she'd been scratching figures.

"Trying to make my assets look fabulously impressive, what else?" she joked awkwardly. "If I don't get any satisfaction out of the local bank, I'll try one of the banks over in Honolulu."

"How are you going to handle the logistics of importing and stocking?"

Reyna's gray-green eyes narrowed slightly as she tried to assess the reason behind his question. Was he genuinely interested or looking for points to attack in her plans? Finally she decided it didn't matter; he couldn't talk her out of her idea, anyway.

"I've established some contacts with a couple of important firms in Honolulu and I'm working on setting up a regular distribution schedule with some of the mainland sources. I'll also handle some local specialties like those great Hawaiian-style potato chips and some sushi hors d'oeuvres."

"You're going to have to show the bank you've got reliable sources of supply," he noted rather neutrally, scanning her figures.

"I will," she vowed sturdily.

He looked up, eyes deep and intense. "Tell me about it, Reyna."

"I already have," she reminded him, "the other night at dinner—"

"I mean about the financial side of the matter," he interrupted impatiently. "All the hard details."

"That's…that's personal business, Trev."

The corner of his mouth crooked upward. "Not as personal as some things we've…er…discussed."

"You'll just try and find all the flaws," she argued.

"Are there many?" he challenged.

"No! Damn it! There aren't!"

"So tell me about it."

Reyna eyed him resentfully for a moment and then surrendered. "Promise not to try and argue me out of my plans?"

"I promise."

She believed him. Besides, she admitted, she needed to talk out some of the details. She was accustomed to functioning with assistants and managers who acted as sounding boards or played devil's advocate. It wasn't as easy functioning in a vacuum.

Shooting him one last, suspicious glance, Reyna flung herself down onto the couch, crossed her bare legs and stretched her arms out along the back of the cushions. One foot swinging with nervous impatience, she began to go over the financial nuts and bolts of her plans.

Trev scooped up a sheaf of papers from her desk and assumed the seat across from her. He listened intelligently and intently, asking the important questions and verifying the facts she threw out. In a sense the discussion was more trying than the one Reyna had had with the banker. But that, she realized ruefully, was because Trev was better at his job than the banker was at his. She found the conversation stimulating and challenging but not a battle. True to his word, Trev didn't try to change her mind about the basic concept.

When she'd finished, he sat quietly for a while, scanning her work papers, and then he abruptly tossed them aside and got to his feet, heading for her kitchen.

"Got anything in here besides canned guava juice?" he demanded, opening a cupboard door.

"There's some cognac on the right-hand side," she admitted grudgingly.

"Thank God. I'm glad you haven't lost your sense of taste completely."

"Tell me the truth, Trev, are you really missing Seattle?" she heard herself ask with sudden interest.

She heard him pouring the cognac and waited expectantly for his answer. It was a while in coming. In fact, he looked as if he were still reflecting on his response a few moments later when he reappeared carrying two balloon glasses.

"If I went back to Seattle I'd be missing you," he finally said. "I'd rather miss the city than you." He handed her a glass and sat down beside her.

His arm brushed her bare one and his knee came into brief contact with hers as he sat down. Reyna drew a long sip on the cognac, fighting the prowling sensuality that now seemed to fill the room.

As suddenly as his decision to pour them a glass of cognac, the whole atmosphere had changed, becoming charged. Reyna knew what that meant. They were back to the moment when she'd opened the sliding glass door. She let the fire in the cognac burn down her throat and met Trev's eyes over the rim of her glass. She asked the question she'd been wondering about all evening and regretted the words even as they left her lips.

"What did you do tonight?"

There was a barely concealed flash of satisfaction in the golden gaze.

"I waited for you to come home. What else?"

"You wasted your time," she whispered.

"I don't think so." He swallowed appreciatively, inhaling the potent fumes trapped in the balloon of the glass.

Reyna gathered her courage. "Trev, there won't be any repeat of what happened yesterday."

"You're not going to rape me again?" he asked quizzically.

"Oh, for heaven's sake!" she muttered disgustedly.

"Sorry. Make that seduce instead of rape."

"This isn't a joke, damn it!"

"I know. What I really should be asking is, aren't you going to make love to me again?"

"Stop teasing me, Trev," she managed tightly. "I'm trying to tell you that I've decided I'm not prepared to become involved in an affair with you while you're here on Maui!"

He said nothing for a long moment, too long a moment. Then he took another sip of cognac and savored it.

"Trev?" She tried to prompt some sort of acknowledgment of her decision out of him.

"Ummm?"

"Don't sit there and pretend I didn't say anything! I meant it. I'm not going to...to go to bed with you again." She forced herself to meet his eyes unflinchingly.

He smiled slightly. "As I said earlier, I know how

you feel. I said the same thing yesterday. Take it from me, it's hopeless."

"What's hopeless?"

"Trying to resist each other," he explained easily.

"Mutual attraction," she declared forcibly, "is not enough!"

"I thought you said it was."

"I've changed my mind. Don't push me, Trev."

"What more do you want out of the relationship?" he prodded coolly.

"Love."

"Exactly what I want. Come give me some love, sweetheart...."

He had set down his glass and scooped her into his arms before she had quite realized what was happening. Reyna stiffened, prepared for the assault even as her blood began to take on the fire of the cognac.

"No, Trev! I said no...!"

He covered her lips with his fingers, stilling them as his gaze moved with tender hunger over her face. Slowly he slid his fingertips away from her protesting mouth, replacing them with his own warm lips.

With a kind of angry desperation she brought her hands up, pushing at his shoulders. He ignored the resistance, capturing her waist and holding her close. Reyna felt herself gently crushed back into the cushions and gasped for air as he settled on top of her.

Everything about his approach tonight was warm and enveloping. Reyna had the impression of being trapped in a huge, curling wave. She was caught up, tossed about and totally surrounded by the growing passion in Trev's hard, warm body.

His legs stretched along hers, the muscular thighs pinning her seductively against the couch as he searched the territory of her mouth with persuasive need.

Slowly, inevitably, Reyna began to succumb to the moment. Just as he had been unable to resist her yesterday, she was unable to resist him tonight. Perhaps she had known all along it would be like this. In any event, she did not want to consider the matter from an intellectual viewpoint. Not now, not tonight.

On a sigh of surrender she circled his neck with her arms.

"Sweet Reyna," he whispered thickly, lifting his head reluctantly for a moment to stare down into her passion-softened face. "You feel so perfect in my arms. How could you send me away tonight? I know I'm not the only one feeling as if there's fire in my blood. I can see the flames in your eyes, feel them in your body…!"

He buried his mouth in her throat and she arched her head back over his arm, sucking in her breath as her senses spun. Her breast seemed to swell as he touched her, finding the hardening nub of a nipple.

"Trev…" Her breathless moan aroused him further and he surged against her in a deeply intimate fashion. His legs slid between hers, the material of their clothing providing little protection.

For a few moments longer Reyna gave herself up to the gathering excitement. What happened to her in this man's arms had always been uncanny, a mystery she knew she would always be tempted to re-explore. When he circled the interior of her ear with his tongue and whispered the dark, enticing words, she was swept again into the storm of desire which flared so easily between them.

But something finally pierced the silken web he was spinning around them as his fingers roamed just inside the low oval neckline of the muumuu. Was this what she really wanted? Reyna wondered frantically.

Where were all her fine decisions of the afternoon? This way would lead to disaster—she knew it now, knew it with a certainty which hadn't been entirely clear until this morning.

The risk of succumbing to Trev's passion was far more dangerous than she had been willing to admit, even to herself.

She had told him she had decided she wanted a relationship based on love and he had pounced on the statement, agreeing. But they didn't mean the same thing by that overused word. Trev might want love but he didn't love.

And she no longer loved this man! Why was it becoming so important to repeat that over and over?

Panic flared. She couldn't resolve the conflict of her emotions under such circumstances. She needed to free herself of Trev's sensual, provocative, overwhelming presence. Even as she made the attempt, however, Reyna knew there was little hope of trying to stop him now. Her response had been too complete and Trev was not the kind of man to abandon his goal when victory was so clearly in sight.

"No, Trev. Please, no! I *can't…*."

He froze, and she wondered that he was willing to halt the rush of his desire for even a moment.

"I want you," he rasped, his fingers digging a little into the skin of her shoulders. His body was taut and heavy against her.

Reyna forced open her eyes only to find the flaming amber gaze far too close. She realized in that moment that she wouldn't be able to stop him if he chose to continue. He could and would kindle her own passion to the point where she would no longer even try to resist.

And there was the indisputable fact that Trev Langdon never ceased an attack of any kind once he'd begun. No, there would be no stopping him tonight.

"I don't want this…." Reyna's voice was small and breathlessly weak. Tense and trembling beneath him, she moved her head in a restless, negative motion on the cushion.

"You want me," he insisted deeply, cradling her face between rough palms. "I know you want me!"

She sensed an intense desperation in him, as if by forcing her to admit her desire her defenses would crumble.

"I know," she admitted shakily. "I know." She lifted her hands, spreading her fingertips across his chest. The color of her eyes was almost pure green. "But I've decided I don't want any more *encounters* like this."

She couldn't find the words to explain any further. She didn't fully comprehend her own decision.

"Reyna?"

The ragged sound of her name made her flinch. For a long moment they stared at each other, and then, with a fiercely muttered oath, Trev pulled himself away.

He sat for a few seconds on the edge of the couch, one hand possessively on her thigh below the hiked-up muumuu. He raked her startled face with eyes of searing gold and then he was on his feet.

"I could take you in my arms and have you clinging to me until morning," he grated as he stood looking down at her. His fingers clenched in silent frustration.

Reyna said nothing. They both knew he spoke the truth.

"Damn it to hell!" Trev scooped up one of the empty cognac snifters and sent it crashing against the wall.

Reyna caught her breath as the glass shattered. Never had she seen him vent such frustrated anger. Her astonished gaze went from the fragments of glass back to his taut face.

But he was already spinning around toward the door. Before she could assimilate Trev's surprising behavior, he was gone, slamming the glass slider behind him with a force that threatened to do damage similar to what had just been done to the snifter.

The silence which followed was a little frightening. For a long moment Reyna sat curled on the couch staring out into the darkness beyond the glass doors. One thought kept pounding through her bemused brain.

Trev Langdon had all the instincts of a buccaneer. He never gave an inch in any fight to which he committed himself. He was a winner.

Yet he had just accepted a defeat at her hands. A defeat they both knew he needn't have taken. He could have ignored her feeble protests and had her, as he'd threatened, clinging to him until morning.

His acquiescence to her wishes tonight was as astounding—given what she knew of the man—as his surrender on the cliff yesterday.

None of his actions lately seemed to fit the Trev Langdon she thought she knew.

CHAPTER EIGHT

REYNA CAUGHT THE wave exactly right. Planing on chest and stomach, she rode it in toward shore, body surfing almost all the way to the beach. It was a small wave, but the ride was perfect. She rose to her knees in the sand as the remains of her little roller coaster foamed around her, and she stroked the wet, streaming hair back off her face.

Eyes blinking against the salty water still pouring off of her, she opened them cautiously.

"I see you're picking up some new skills here in the islands," remarked an all-too-familiar voice a few feet away.

She swung her head around, lurching a little awkwardly to her feet. Her legs were coated with sand.

"Trev! What are you doing up? It's barely dawn!"

"I didn't sleep all that well last night," he told her laconically, coming closer. "How about you?"

Reyna muttered something under her breath, bending down to swish seawater against her sandy legs. It was an excuse not to meet his eyes and she knew it, but the memories of the previous evening were still too vivid. And she still didn't know how to interpret them.

"Will you teach me?" he asked quietly, halting a couple of feet away.

"Teach you what?" she asked, glancing up in surprise. He was wearing his swimming trunks. The water swirled around his feet as he stood at its edge.

"Body surfing." He gestured out at the small series of breakers rolling in toward shore.

"I'm not sure you'd like it," she offered hesitantly, eyeing him with a slanting green glance. "The ride's fun, but you get all sandy at the other end...."

He grinned sardonically. "So I see. I'll risk it. Look at the grass stains I got on my clothes the other day when you took me bird-watching. Did I complain about those?"

"Briefly, as I recall," she retorted, unable to resist the spark of laughter in his eyes. It was impossible to believe this was the same man who had stormed out of her apartment last night. But, then, she hadn't understood that man, either. What was happening to Trev Langdon?

"No complaints this morning about the sand, I promise." He held up his hand in the old scout's-honor sign.

Suddenly Reyna couldn't resist testing him. "Okay, mainlander. Come on out here with me."

She led the way out to where the small waves began the curling that would take them foaming in toward shore and demonstrated how to judge the merits of each. Trev listened intelligently and then disgusted her completely by catching his first one perfectly.

"You've done this before!" she accused laughingly,

wading up to him as he was deposited neatly on the beach.

"Never!" he swore, heaving himself to his feet and glancing ruefully down at the coating of sand on his chest and thighs. "Does this look like the sort of sport I'd actively engage in on a routine basis?"

"You've got a point there," she was forced to agree. Reyna cocked an eyebrow. "Going to complain?"

"Don't look so hopeful. I'm not going to complain—I'm going to do it again. It's fun!"

With his natural sense of timing and coordination, Trev managed to catch one good ride after another. The few times he underestimated a wave or misjudged it Reyna could hardly mock him. She made almost as many errors.

As if the sea provided the medium needed to reestablish an easy communication, they shared the special moments after an island dawn together, laughing and playing in the waves. Reyna accepted it with a kind of wonder. When had Trev ever let himself go like this? It was becoming difficult to imagine him now in a business suit!

"You don't start work for another hour or so," he remarked as they finally returned to the towels which had been left on the sand. "Have breakfast with me?"

"All right," Reyna replied with only a hint of returning wariness. They were out of the neutral territory of the sea again, back on dry land and back into the morass of conflicting emotions which awaited her there. He sensed her changing mood at once.

"Don't be afraid of me, sweetheart," he murmured, taking hold of her towel and briskly drying her hair.

"I'm not!"

"You shouldn't be," he agreed. "Didn't I leave on demand last night?"

"I was rather hoping you wouldn't mention last night!"

"Let's talk about tonight, then," he returned, finishing the drying process and taking her hand to start back toward the condo-hotel.

"Trev…" Floundering in a welter of confusion, Reyna experienced a shaft of pure self-disgust. It was bad enough trying to figure out what was happening to Trev: God help her if she was going to start finding herself a confusing issue, too!

"I thought we could have dinner down on the wharf in Lahaina," he continued as if she hadn't attempted to interrupt.

"I can't," she said quickly. It was the truth. "I'm involved in putting on a beach luau for the hotel guests tonight. I'm going to be busy all afternoon and evening."

He glanced assessingly down at her, his fingers tightening on her wrist. "Then I suppose I'll have to settle for seeing you there, won't I?" he noted evenly.

She blinked warily.

"I *am* one of the hotel guests," he reminded her.

"Oh. Yes, of course."

He sighed. "About breakfast…?"

"I have some papaya," she offered almost apologetically. Why the guilt feeling?

"Is that all you ever eat for breakfast?"

"Just about. I love it."

"I should be grateful, I suppose. It could have been worse."

"*What* could have been worse?" Reyna demanded, losing track of the conversation.

"You could have fallen in love with poi for breakfast. At least papaya tastes good."

"If I were offering poi, would you decline to share the meal with me?" She smiled.

"No, I'd find a way to wolf it down."

Reyna decided not to press for the reasons behind his implied adaptability. She wasn't sure she wanted to know the answers. Once again they shared fresh coffee, papaya and lime and a stack of rye toast in her apartment. The conversation stayed on reasonably safe subjects, and when it came time for Reyna to get ready for work, Trev rose politely and took his leave.

She didn't see him for the rest of the day. Behind the hotel desk she checked in a small tourist group and spent her spare moments going over the plans for the beach luau given once every two weeks by the management.

"Be sure and come," she cheerfully instructed everyone who stopped by the desk during the day. "This isn't one of those assembly-line luaus, the big hotels over in Honolulu put on, where they give you a bit of poi and a piece of pork and a fast-paced floor show. Ours are a lot of fun and there's plenty of food. The real thing!"

The guests needed no urging. Nearly everyone was making plans to attend.

"Everything under control?" Jim Darby asked as he prepared to take over the front desk late in the afternoon.

"I think so," she assured him with a frown of concentration as she went through her checklist. "Johnny assures me the pig he's roasting in the *imu* is on schedule. I've lined up an extra amount of poi since more people seem willing to try it lately...."

"I guess the mainlanders are getting a little more adventurous in their eating habits." Jim chuckled. "There was a time when a lot of folks wouldn't touch it!"

"It got bad press after Mark Twain labeled it library paste!"

"It is an acquired taste," Jim decided philosophically as he pulled out a booking schedule. The pounded root of the taro plant produced a tangy product which had been a mainstay of Hawaiian food for centuries. It was smooth and subtly sour, a complement to the more salty foods popular at luaus.

"So is caviar," Reyna noted. "Let's see, the lomilomi is accounted for and so is the poke," she added absently, naming the dish of raw yellowfin tuna, seaweed and candlenut mixed with hot peppers which served as an appetizer.

"You know, Walters was telling me just the other day how much simpler luau nights have become since you came to work here," Jim remarked, searching for a pencil. Phil Walters was the easygoing manager of the condominium-hotel. Since Reyna's arrival he had spent less and less time hovering around the front lobby. It was no secret he was more than happy to turn as many duties as possible over to her.

"Good," she said energetically. "I'm hoping he'll remember that when I quit to open my gourmet-foods shop. I want to provide the food for his biweekly luaus!"

"Anything that makes his life easier will be okay by him! Before you came along he had to fuss with all the different suppliers to get the luaus put together properly."

Dusk was beginning to settle over the array of long tables and benches which had been carried down to the beach by members of the hotel staff when Reyna again realized she hadn't seen any sign of Trev. The thought made her pause momentarily as she sampled the lomilomi, which had been made by a Hawaiian friend.

"It's terrific, Lani, as always," she said, quickly finishing the small spoonful of the salted salmon mixture.

"It's those good, sweet Maui onions." Lani chuckled, re-covering the pot. Her dark eyes smiled cheerfully.

"The guests are going to love it."

"How are you doing with the bank loan?" Lani asked.

"So-so," Reyna admitted, not upset about the spread of gossip concerning her personal business. It was a small island in some respects.

Lani hesitated, her attractive face suddenly serious. "You know, my father is vice-president at one of the big banks over in Honolulu. Perhaps he could help you."

"Even for the sake of friendship, a banker isn't going to hand over a wad of money unless he's got a fairly shrewd notion he'll be repaid," Reyna pointed out ruefully. "I'm working on convincing the bank I'm a good risk, though. One of these days…"

"Reyna! The rum isn't here yet!"

The immediate crisis broke off the conversation and Reyna hurried to correct matters.

Two hours later everything was moving smoothly. The foursome hired to provide the entertainment performed with rollicking humor and good harmony. Strumming ukuleles, they sang the lively songs of old Hawaii, and the guests, many on their third or fourth rum drink, had gotten to the point of joining in. Reyna knew what that meant. In a little while members of the audience would be volunteering to learn the hula in front of the others. It signaled the moment when she could fade quietly into the background and let the festivities go forward under their own steam.

Tonight it also gave her another opportunity to wonder what had become of Trev. Drifting to the edge of the good-natured crowd, Reyna realized that his failure to appear was beginning to get to her. That morning on the beach he had implied he would show up.

Not that it should matter to her, she told herself stoutly. After all, she ought to be grateful for anything which deflected him from his pursuit. Anything or anyone? A glance around the crowd did not reveal the blonde in the green bikini Trev had picked up on the beach the previous afternoon.

Damn it! What was the matter with her? She didn't need this kind of agitation in her life! Thank heaven there were only a few days left before Trev would be forced to return to Seattle.

The velvety Hawaiian night closed around the torchlit scene on the beach. The endless darkness of the ocean gleamed here and there with moonlight. The palm trees lining the edge of the beach in front of the hotel stirred gently in the evening breeze. Reyna sat quietly beneath one tree and tried not to wonder where Trev Langdon had decided to spend the evening.

She was creating lazy circles in the sand with her fingertips, knees drawn up to her chin, eyes gazing moodily out over the darkened sea, when she became aware of a quiet presence behind her.

There was no doubt about who it was. Reyna's fingers ceased their artistry in the sand. "Hello, Trev."

"Any food left?" he asked quietly, moving forward to stand beside her.

Reyna saw the expensive Italian shoes first. Slowly her eyes traveled up the length of the lightweight slacks of the refined suit. Mutely, she took in the silk tie, formal shirt and well-tailored jacket.

"I was wondering just a little while ago how you'd look back in a suit," she remarked dryly. "I'd almost forgotten."

His mouth lifted sardonically and he began to shrug out of the jacket. "So had I. What about the food?"

"There's some left." She hesitated in a moment of astonishment as he lowered himself to the sand beside her. "You're going to get sand all over those pants," she felt obliged to point out unnecessarily.

"I've had a hard day," he drawled, going to work on the knot of the tie. "Do you think you could get me a plate of something?"

"Where have you been? What have you been doing?"

"Believe me, you're going to hear all about it. A drink would be nice, too," he went on thoughtfully. "Something with a good shot of rum in it."

"Trev," she began in exasperation, "I'm not your servant."

"Please?"

"Where did you develop that look of humble appeal?" she complained, getting to her feet and dusting off her jeans.

"I've been working on it since you left Seattle. Don't forget the drink," he added quickly as she stalked off in the direction of the serving table.

Her curiosity, Reyna realized, was greater than her desire to argue with him. With a strange sense of foreboding she ladled out a variety of luau specialties and added a slice of coconut cake. Then she made a brief stop at the bar which had been set up under the palms.

"Something with a lot of rum in it, Ron," she instructed the bartender.

"Right. And maybe a little brandy and some coconut syrup and some cream," he suggested with a grin as he went to work.

Reyna added the well-laced, creamy concoction to her tray and headed slowly back along the beach toward the palm under which Trev reclined. The tie had been removed completely, she saw in the flickering light of a nearby torch, and the shirt had been unbuttoned, its sleeves rolled up. He had even, she saw in surprise, taken off the elegant calfskin shoes.

Carefully she sat down beside him, handing over the tray.

"What is this?" he demanded, reaching for the frothy drink. He looked at it askance.

"I don't know. One of Ron's specialties. It's got rum in it, don't worry. What have you been doing, Trev?"

He dug into the pork, which had been cooked all day long in an earth oven called an *imu*.

"I've been doing a little business," he announced quietly as he explored the other elements on his plate.

"Business!"

"Ummm. I took the noon plane over to Honolulu. I just got back an hour ago."

"Why on earth…?" She stared at him as she sat cross-legged in the darkness beside him.

"Time was running out," he explained cryptically, sipping experimentally on his rum drink. The amber eyes met hers, and for the life of her Reyna couldn't begin to interpret the expression she saw there.

"You had something important happening back in Seattle?" she hazarded quizzically.

"Something important," he echoed softly.

"You look exhausted," she whispered uncertainly. It was true. The lean planes of his face had a hard edge to them and the fine lines around his eyes seemed deeper in the dim light. The brackets which etched his mouth were firmly set tonight.

"Do I?" He appeared to consider that for a moment and then he took another sip of the drink. "I guess I am. But it's over."

"Satisfactorily?"

"Yes." He sounded quite certain of it. But, then, he would be. Trev always concluded matters to his own satisfaction.

"Why did you have to go over to the island of Oahu to do it?" she persisted, driven by her curiosity about the deepening mystery.

"There were some contacts there I needed to see."

Reyna's eyes widened. "Is that why you really came all the way over here to Hawaii?" she breathed, staggered. "Because you had business in the islands? Was locating me merely a convenient side matter?"

"Don't look so crushed," he mocked.

"I'm not crushed! But it would certainly explain a lot, if that's the case!" she bit out.

He managed to look a little more exhausted. "It's not the case. You're the only reason I came to Hawaii, Reyna," he stated flatly.

"So it was the business in Honolulu which became the convenient side trip?" Reyna couldn't explain the curious sense of relief she was experiencing.

"Not so convenient. But, yes, the matter came up after I'd already arrived on Maui," he confirmed tiredly.

She glanced at his plate, gnawing mildly on her lower lip. Why was she feeling sorry for him tonight? It was ridiculous. "Would you like another drink?"

"That would be great." He half-smiled. "But this time something without all the cream and ice, okay?"

"Ron will be hurt," she noted as she again climbed to her feet.

"Tell him the drink is for a tired businessman, not a fun-loving tourist. He'll understand."

When she returned a few minutes later with the tall, plain rum drink, Trev had almost finished the meal.

"Thanks, that's much better," he said gratefully, taking the glass from her hand. "Your luau appears to have been a success." He glanced meaningfully toward the cheerful crowd. The hula lessons had begun.

"They usually are."

"Did you organize it?"

"It's one of my duties here at the hotel," Reyna explained quietly.

"You have a flair for organization," he murmured.

She said nothing, sensing a new kind of tension creeping into the air between them. She felt the return of the old wariness. There was something different about Trev tonight and she couldn't quite put her finger on it.

Then he dropped the small bombshell into the thickened atmosphere.

"I'll be leaving in the morning, Reyna."

Her head snapped up and she found the bonds of his amber gaze waiting to trap her. "Leaving! But you're booked here for a few more days. Why...why have you changed your mind?" She scanned his intent face, shocked at her own reaction to his simple statement. She wanted him to go, didn't she? It was the best solution for both of them. She might not love him, but there was no doubt his presence was upsetting her. Yes, she would be much better off without him.

So why did she feel this heavy tug on her emotions?

He looked at her levelly. "You've convinced me you don't have any intention of leaving the islands, honey. There's not much point in my staying and trying to talk you into coming back with me, is there?"

"No," she got out carefully. She felt as if she had been thrown into a cold sea.

"No," he repeated laconically. "So I'm going back in the morning by myself."

"I see." She tore her eyes away from his and stared blindly down at the contours of the sand around the base of the palm tree.

She felt him gather himself to say something more and intuitively she tensed.

"Reyna, you said last night that you didn't want any more 'encounters' between us," he said gently. "I presume you meant casual encounters. But the times we've shared have never been *casual*."

Reyna met his eyes, her own wide and questioning. She could feel the desire in him reaching out to her and it sent familiar shivers along her nerves. Her sense of awareness focused on the man and the moment, building a strange kind of psychological high in her blood.

"Spend tonight with me," he pleaded harshly, his strong hand reaching out to take hold of one of hers. "Reyna, I need you tonight!"

She felt paralyzed, utterly torn between the promise of passion, her unidentified fear of another night in his arms and the need to respond to the urgent pleading in his eyes. *In the morning he would be gone. This time for good.*

"Trev, I don't think it would be wise," she ventured, horrified at the husky, uncertain note in her words. "I mean, I don't want—"

"Please," he whispered hoarsely, pulling her gently forward and brushing his mouth against her lips. "Please. I need you so much. You used to love me once. Love me again, Reyna. One last time."

"It's not love," she tried vainly to convince him, unable to bring herself to pull away from him while she still could.

"You keep saying that. Call it what you want but spend the night with me, darling."

His hand moved through her hair, twining itself in the sunstreaked, tawny mass. Reyna felt her senses begin the slow, spiraling swirl.

"One last night, sweetheart," he repeated with a fierce persuasion.

"Oh, Trev…" She was crumbling before the on-slaught of her unexpectedly strong need to satisfy the pleading, beseeching urgency in him.

"Reyna," he warned heavily, "if you say yes to-night, I won't be able to let you change your mind like you did last night. Do you understand? I couldn't walk out again. It took everything I had to do it last night. I'd never find the strength a second time."

"Are you really going back to Seattle in the morn-ing?" she whispered tightly.

"Yes. Please, Reyna. One last night together…"

"Trev, I shouldn't let you do this to me, I know I shouldn't—"

"Hush, darling. Don't think about it. Just let your-self go. I want you so much." His hand tightened in her hair. The amber gaze gleamed.

"Yes, Trev."

CHAPTER NINE

TOGETHER THEY SLIPPED away from the uncaring crowd on the beach, making their way across the sand and through the gardens back to Trev's room.

Reyna trembled slightly as she walked beside Trev and hoped he didn't sense it. She was wrapped closely against his side, his arm securely around her waist. The deep colors of the night helped provide some cover for the flush she knew would be in her cheeks.

"Cold?" he growled softly, his arm around her tightening.

It was a ridiculous question and he must have known it. The night was balmy and warm, as usual.

"No."

How could she explain the stirring, frightening sensation of inevitability? It wasn't just that she had committed herself to him for one more night. It went beyond that and Reyna didn't want to think about it. She was only spending a last night with a man who would always be unique for her. He wanted her and she wanted him. Why this foreboding sensation?

"It's not just another encounter, sweetheart," he murmured into her hair as he drew her to a halt in front of the hotel-room door. "It's always been special between us, hasn't it?"

She tried to parry the question. "If I disagree with you, I shall run the risk of admitting I'm capable of spending casual, meaningless nights with a man, and if I agree with you—"

"If you agree with me, you're only committing yourself for one night. One very special night. If you do agree with me, Reyna, take my hand and come inside with me. But if you disagree, if you're going to change your mind again like you did last night, please, for God's sake do it now. Not later when it will be beyond my power to let you go."

Something deep within her responded to the harsh plea. Whatever else Trev was, he was being sincere tonight. He wanted her, perhaps even needed her very badly. And in the morning he would be leaving forever....

There was really nothing else to say on the subject. Refusing to look into the future, Reyna lifted her hands to cradle his face. Standing on tiptoe, she gave him her answer with a feathery kiss.

A feathery kiss that escalated into a warm, throbbing commitment. But only for tonight, Reyna told herself fleetingly. Only for tonight.

"Reyna!" Burying his lips in the curve of her throat, Trev lifted her high in his arms and carried her inside the hotel room. In the darkened interior he kicked the door shut behind him and moved over to the bed.

She felt the taut strength in his arms and knew a

sense of satisfaction. Running her nails lightly along the line of his cheek, she smiled in an ancient and gentle invitation. This was what she wanted. For tonight.

He stood holding her above the bed, his gaze raking her softened features. There was a hunger in him that Reyna knew well by now. It had the power to reach out and capture her senses. It had always had that power. And perhaps, she thought dazedly, it worked both ways at times, as it had that afternoon on the cliff above the sea.

"You've become a creature of the sun," he whispered throatily, setting her down so that she lay in the middle of the bed. "You really aren't the same woman I knew in Seattle, are you?"

"No," she answered. "I told you the first night you arrived, Trev. I've changed." A sudden, irrationally painful thought gripped her. "Is that why you've decided to leave in the morning? You don't like what I've become?"

He sank down onto the bed beside her, reaching for her hand. Lifting it, he turned the palm upward and kissed the vulnerable inside of her wrist, grazing the sensitive skin with the tip of his tongue. "No," he denied huskily. "I want the new Reyna as badly as I ever wanted the old one. I would give anything to have had the sense to realize just how much I wanted you six months ago, though."

She met his look of self-chastisement and shivered. Compulsively, she touched his leg with her free hand, wanting to erase the past and the future, if only for a few hours.

"Don't talk about it, Trev. There's no point raking over the past."

His mouth tightened and she thought he wanted to argue but he swallowed the words. On a low groan of passion and need, he ran a hand down the length of her leg, snagging the ankle just below the hem of the blue jeans.

With an easy movement he slipped off first one sandal and then the other, letting them drop softly onto the floor. Then his hand moved upward again, fingers gliding along the inside of her leg to her thigh. Involuntarily, Reyna's toes curled into the material of the bedspread as a warm, twisting sensation began to invade her limbs.

"Trev," she whispered, pulling his head down to hers with a sigh of yielding abandon. "Oh, Trev. I have never wanted another man the way I want you...."

Slowly, with infinite care, he undressed her, his mouth clinging to her lips as if he drew strength there. Stretching out beside her, he cradled her head in the crook of one arm and moved his other hand in a flat arc up her stomach to the buttons of her brightly patterned shirt. He undid them one by one, lingering over each until Reyna began to twist with the beginnings of sensual impatience.

"Trev?"

"Don't ask me to hurry tonight, darling," he breathed into her hair. "I have to store the memories. The winters in Seattle are cold and rainy, remember?"

For a moment Reyna's throat tightened on a sudden urge to cry. What was wrong with her? Deliberately she banished the emotion, seizing only the moment. She would not think about Trev's potential for genuine loneliness and she would not think about her own future. Her new life was a good one.

But something within her began to understand his need for a long and tender night. She ran her fingers along the muscled length of his leg, probing through the fabric of his trousers to find the sensitive places. Then she touched the buckle of the belt.

His softly indrawn breath fed her own desire. As he opened the last button of her shirt, Reyna undid the fastening of his slacks. In another few languid moments they were both undressed, their nude bodies gleaming subtly in the pale moonlight filtering in through the curtain. Through the open window came the distant, ever-present roar of the sea, and bits and pieces of the ukulele music floated up from the beach.

Trev's hands seemed to drift across her body, the texture slightly, excitingly rough on her soft skin. Reyna sighed with a heated pleasure, letting herself think of nothing else except the joy of response. Her legs shifted delicately, and, as if that were a concealed challenge, Trev moved his thigh to pin her gently.

For some reason the chaining action sent tremors of excitement through her. Reyna's nails sank into the muscles of his shoulders and he gasped, arching toward her.

"Ah! Reyna, Reyna, my darling…"

He lowered his head to put his mouth to the pulse at the base of her throat and her head tipped back over his arm as she moaned a response. Instinctively she lifted herself toward him, begging him with her body to touch her breasts.

He found one budding nipple first with coaxing, stimulating fingers, and then he was trailing a string of kisses over her softness to the rosy tip.

She shivered as she felt his circling tongue and then the faintest hint of his teeth, and she groped blindly for the satisfying hardness of his buttock.

Working his way slowly, lingeringly down her body, Trev rained warm, damp kisses across her breasts, her stomach and beyond. Reyna was a trembling, twisting creature of aroused passion when he turned his lips to the inside of her thigh.

She felt him lift himself and prepared to take the glorious weight of him. But instead of lowering himself into her body, he used his strength to turn her gently onto her stomach.

"Trev?" she gasped, a little startled.

"I want to learn every inch of you one more time," he whispered hoarsely, tracing an erotic pattern down the length of her spine and back up to her neck. Then he bent and kissed the exquisitely sensitive place at the small of her back. Reyna's fingers clenched convulsively.

She lay drifting on a cloud of sensation as he wove patterns of desire from her ankles to her curving derriere. Everywhere his hands traveled, his lips followed, leaving every portion of her body sensitized. When his fingers closed a little roughly into the resilient flesh of her hip, Reyna writhed and turned on her side, reaching for him.

"I want you, Trev...."

She thought he hesitated, as if her words weren't quite what he had expected, but he lay beside her and met her gaze in the darkness.

"It's special, Reyna. It's always been special. I should have had the sense to realize what it meant—"

"No," she begged, sealing his lips with her fingers. "Don't talk about it. Not tonight."

Then it was her turn to make love to him. He shifted slowly onto his back, inviting her touch. Tremulous with her own desire, Reyna leaned across to weave her hands through the hair on his chest. Deliberately she nipped at the skin of his shoulders and delighted in his groan of response. Then she was seeking out the flat nipples, circling them with her tongue as he had done to her.

With growing urgency she strung wet little kisses down to the lean stomach, her palm gliding ahead of her lips to find the point where the tapering line of chest hair gave way to the bold maleness beyond.

His hips surged compellingly against her hand as she touched him intimately and her fingers closed around him.

"Darling!"

His hands wound thickly into her hair, urging her to deepen the intimacy. She felt the trembling in him and obediently touched her lips to his thigh, sinking her teeth into his skin with delicate violence.

"I wanted this to last forever," he hissed fiercely, hauling her abruptly up beside him and pushing her into the bedclothes. "But I can't wait any longer for you. You drive me wild, my darling Reyna. Wild."

"Yes, Trev, oh yes!"

He parted her legs with his own, gathering her close as he came down on top of her. The aggressive need in him was unbelievably thrilling, challenging and stimulating. Reyna reached for him with all of her strength.

He moved heavily, irresistibly against her, forcing a union that in that moment seemed utterly right, utterly unbreakable.

Reyna cried out with the shock of the impact and he closed his mouth over hers, swallowing the primitive little sound. Their mouths drank from each other, echoing the pattern of desire their bodies were finding. Trev's tongue surged boldly between her lips, summoning a response from her just as the hardness of his body urged another.

When she scored his back with her nails, he gasped aloud and muttered something darkly sensual. Reyna shivered beneath him, her body tightening in a promise of ultimate release.

Together they rode the storm, the mind-spinning energy flowing back and forth, becoming more and more charged. Reyna knew somewhere far back in her head that in that moment they were both giving completely to each other. And, with equal fierceness, they were both taking from each other.

It culminated in a staggering, totally satisfying release that wrung a stifled shout of elemental triumph from Trev and a panting, nearly soundless cry of ecstasy from Reyna.

Then, slowly, still clinging together, they fell through the unwinding layers of sensation, coming to a gentle rest on the reality of the bed on which they lay.

For long, precious moments Reyna held herself still, aware of Trev's steadying breath as his head rested on her breast. There were no words readily available to describe her emotions in that moment. It was over. The night itself would soon be over. A kind of sadness was threatening to well up and inundate the remains of her sensual satisfaction. Desperately she sought to halt the flood. She had no reason to feel sad!

"Reyna?"

Trev stirred, lifting himself a little so that he could look down into her face. She sensed the waiting in him, just as she had sensed it that first night he had arrived on the island. But it was different this time— not as if he expected a confession of love from her but as if he were preparing himself to say something vital.

Wordlessly she touched his face, searching his gaze. "What is it, Trev?"

He drew in his breath, and a small, fleeting smile edged his lips. "The reason I went to Honolulu, sweetheart…"

Reyna blinked uncertainly. Whatever she had expected him to say in the aftermath of their lovemaking, it certainly had nothing to do with his business trip to the island of Oahu!

He seemed to be having difficulty finding the words. He stopped and tried again, bending to drop a tiny kiss on the tip of her nose. "I went away this afternoon so that I could make arrangements to give you the one thing you seem to want."

"Trev, what are you talking about?"

He pushed the tangled hair back off her face and said gently, "The shop is yours, darling. Anytime you want it. All you have to do is walk into that bank over in Wailuku and ask for the loan. They'll be more than happy to give it to you."

"I don't...I don't understand." Eyes wide and questioning, Reyna tried to comprehend. "What have you done?"

"Arranged the loan. It's what I'm good at, remember?" he added whimsically. "Arranging capital for new businesses? I saw the people who count today at the main office of that bank where you're applying for the loan. The local branch won't give you any more trouble. Believe me."

"You—" Stunned, Reyna broke off her words, licked her dry lips and started again. "You guaranteed the loan?"

"Let's just say I convinced them you're a solid risk, sweetheart," he murmured. "There's nothing standing in your way now. You can build the gourmet-shop business to your heart's content. It's the only thing you seem to want and it was in my power to give it to you. So I did."

Reyna couldn't find any coherent words. She didn't know how to take the startling gift. She needed time to think about the ramifications. What was he doing to her?

Before she could pull herself together enough to figure out the subtle layers of meaning in his actions, he was stopping her thoughts once more with a kiss. Slowly, meltingly, he caressed and petted her, and, her mind in simmering chaos, Reyna somehow found it easier to give herself over once more to the world of sensation. It was much easier than trying to think about what had just happened.

The night was patient with them, allowing time for their desire to build and find satisfaction again and again before a deep exhaustion finally claimed them.

But tired as she was, Reyna couldn't fall asleep beside Trev. His slow, even breathing gave evidence that he was sleeping deeply. For her there was no such surcease.

What had he done to her? Over and over she asked herself the question. It tormented her because she knew Trev Langdon never did anything without a purpose. He had asked for this one last night together, made ardent love to her and then given her his incredible gift. *Why?*

Slowly, as the first rays of dawn crept into the room, a strange rage began to flicker through her body. At first the anger was turned inward on herself. How could she have been stupid enough to have allowed Trev to get so close after all that had happened between them? *Stupid!*

He was maneuvering her, playing some sort of dangerous game with her emotions.

No, that would be admitting she still felt emotions strong enough to be dangerous. And she didn't! She knew she didn't.

What was happening to her tonight? Why was she going through this torment, her anger spiraling into a reckless, inexplicable force that threatened to dominate her completely?

The rage was becoming as fierce as it was incomprehensible.

So what if Trev had given her the gift of the bank loan? If he wanted to be generous, why should she balk? Perhaps he was doing it to alleviate the guilt which had brought him after her in the first place.

Yes, that must be it. He had found a way to rid himself of the guilt she had once guessed he felt. He'd already satiated his desire, the other motive of which she had accused him. Now he would go back to Seattle.

He was going to walk out on her again. Again!

No! Damn it, she would not let him do this to her! Beginning to tremble with the flaring force of her anger, she turned it outward toward the man she had once loved. Slowly, painfully, she sat up beside him in bed, staring at his lean, hard body. The white sheet foamed at his waist, leaving an expanse of sinewy back naked. He sprawled in unconscious assurance, the silvered blackness of his hair against the snowy pillow.

Did he think she would let him humiliate her a second time? Did he think he could satisfy himself with her body, cleanse his mind of the remnants of guilt and then casually go back to Seattle? Her hand curled into a fist, the nails biting into the palm. How dare he? Who the hell did Trev Langdon think he was?

The six months of time stretching between their fiery encounters dissolved as if they had never existed. Reyna sat on the edge of the bed, clutching the sheet to her breast, and stared at the man who had hurled her love back in her face six months ago. In that moment she could easily have turned on him with her fists.

All the control she had used to handle the first rejection seemed nonexistent now that she needed to tap into it once more. Only anger—a deep, feminine bitterness—was available and it lent her a strength which amazed her.

She had squandered the gift of her love on this man and he had rejected it. He had taken everything he wanted from her and then declared himself the winner. Yes, she had known the risks she was taking at the time but six months ago it had all seemed worth it. Love was a blinding new force in her life, and she had been willing to sacrifice almost anything on its altar. Trev Langdon had taken advantage of that.

She had suppressed the rage six months ago, the rage of a woman scorned, because there had been no alternative. She had loved the man but she would not cling where she was not wanted. Her pride had come to her rescue—her pride and the necessity of putting her life back in order as her career was shattered around her.

There had been too many steps to take, steps that

she had known deep down meant the difference between despair and survival. By the time she'd redirected her life the time for anger had passed. She was safely in Hawaii.

Tonight she realized that the emotions she'd had to suppress six months ago had never really disappeared. They surged into life with a vengeance which meant they had never really died. And added to that old anger was the wave of new fury she was experiencing tonight.

Shaking like a leaf, Reyna slid from the bed, reaching for her clothing. She didn't know how to handle this twice-fueled fire burning in her. She longed for revenge—a powerful, physical revenge which seemed forever denied her because of the unalterable factor of Trev's superior strength. She could not beat him. She had no ready weapon with which to punish him for what he had done to her six months ago, just as she'd had no weapon then.

Or did she?

Her mind spun into gear, remembering his "gift." He was buying his way back out of her life, soothing his conscience with the gift of the bank loan. She whirled at the door of the hotel room, sandals clutched in one hand, and turned back to stare in narrow-eyed fury at Trev's sleeping form. She would not let him off the hook so easily.

She would take no favors or gifts from this man. The only revenge she could salvage was to refuse him the luxury of placating his conscience. Quietly, her nerves screaming for more violent activity, Reyna let herself out of the room.

She made her way back to her apartment, her mind growing clearer and more focused by the second. There was a fee for Trev's professional services. She would pay it.

Back in her living room she found her checkbook. Her fingers were trembling so badly as she picked up the pen that she wasn't certain she could write out the amount. But her will, fired with uncanny determination, overcame the weakness anger had brought to her nerves.

A fee. She searched her mind for the facts she had learned about Langdon & Associates six months ago. The standard fee for arranging financing was a percentage. She tried to figure what percentage of her loan it would amount to. A sizable sum.

But she wrote out the check with passion, heedless of the cost. Even this small revenge was worth any price. Trev could go back to Seattle, but he would not have had the satisfaction of wringing another confession of love from her, nor of salving his conscience by giving her a gift to compensate for the destruction of her former career.

She would put their second encounter entirely on a business footing.

Check in hand, Reyna once again made her way through the hotel gardens to Trev's room. En route she debated whether or not she hoped to find him awake, finally deciding it would be more satisfying to have him awake alone and find the check waiting for him on the dresser.

Outside his room she came to a halt, a portion of her courage briefly deserting her. But it returned in a rush as she pushed open the door and saw him still asleep. On bare feet she padded silently across the room and left the check on his dresser, where he could not fail to see it.

Then, with one last look at the man who had wrought new chaos in her life, Reyna fled.

Down to the beach she went, feeling an indescribable need to work off the seething tension boiling in her bloodstream. At the water's edge she began to run along the sand as if the sheer physical exertion would drain off the rage.

She ran without any thought of pacing herself, intent only on burning up the reckless energy. In only a few moments she was breathless, panting with the exertion.

But her remedy was working, she realized vaguely as she slowed to draw in oxygen. The red-hot rage was dying. She could feel it seeping out of her body at last. After six long months it was finally evaporating.

Had it really been festering inside all that time? she wondered as she paced now instead of running. Perhaps. Her love, her pain, her need to salvage her life had driven it deep. There had been no way to release it six months ago.

If Trev had never again shown up in her life, the rage would have eventually died a totally natural death. She had built a new world in his absence and she had been happy in it. Yes, the rage would have quietly disintegrated and she might never even have known of its existence.

But he had returned, and after only six months. The time was too short. Six months simply hadn't been long enough. The suppressed emotions had made their way to the surface and burst through when he had once again threatened to walk out of her life.

Perhaps it was all for the best, Reyna told herself bitterly. Perhaps last night and this morning would serve as a useful cathartic experience. Trev had been right that first night on the island when he had said he knew she must still be bitter.

She hadn't thought she was at the time. The layers of her happy new life had intervened and suppressed the underlying anger. Unwittingly, though, Trev, himself, had unleashed the buried emotion. She faced the fact bravely.

Yes, her rage was gone. The last of her strong feelings toward Trev had finally been vented. Perhaps a love as strong as hers had been six months ago needed some revenge. This morning she had finally taken it.

So why was she beginning to cry?

Horrified, Reyna brushed the back of her hand against her damp lashes. She *was* crying! She thought about Trev walking to find the check and the tears fell harder. Coming to a halt, she stared uncomprehendingly out to sea.

The brain she had thought was functioning so clearly under the impetus of fury was finally becoming clear, indeed. She stood on the sand and remembered that first night when Trev had found her here.

He had been the Trev Langdon she remembered right down to the polished Italian leather of his shoes.

Other scenes began to flash before her eyes: the grass stains on his clothing that afternoon on the cliff, the gradually developing casualness in his attitude as he adapted to island living.

Funny, she would never have thought Trev could adapt to such a life-style. But he had done so in a relatively short period of time. To please her?

That question reminded her of the way in which he had surrendered to her lovemaking that hot afternoon. He had wanted to control the situation, but when she'd done so instead, he'd accepted it.

Slowly the implications of his return began to coalesce into a potent, alternative point of view. What if she took everything he had said and done at face value?

Reyna swallowed painfully, the tears blocking her throat for an instant. Whatever else he may have done, Trev Langdon had never lied to her. If she gave him credit for that, what sort of interpretation did that put on his actions these past few days?

She realized she was frightened at the dawning implications. Terribly frightened. It meant she would have to view his gift of the financing arrangements in much the same light as her gift to him six months ago when she had said she would halt the takeover of his brother-in-law's firm.

A gift of love.

Had he given her the one thing he had that he knew she wanted? A gift of love in the hope that his love would be returned, but hers to keep, regardless?

For the first time in her life Reyna knew a strange fear. What if she had thrown away his love this morning? If what he had been trying to give this past week really was love, she had undoubtedly crushed it with that check left so cruelly on his dresser.

Fine, she tried to tell herself. The revenge would be all the more satisfying if that were the case.

But she no longer wanted revenge, she realized, terrified. The fury was gone. It was true, it had lain dormant for six long months, but another emotion had been lying dormant, too.

She still loved Trevor Langdon.

The realization swept to the surface with far greater force than the earlier rage, freed by the release of the darker emotion. She loved Trev just as she had loved him six months ago. Nothing had changed, except...

Except that now, just maybe, he loved her and had been trying to demonstrate that love for the past few days in the only way he could.

What had she done by leaving behind that check? Spinning around, Reyna stared back at the quiet hotel grounds and then she was running again, faster than when she had been trying to work off the rage, faster than she had ever run in her life.

She was too late. Reaching the hotel room, she

yanked open the door, a cry of protest against fate already on her lips as she took in the stark scene.

Trev stood in front of the dresser wearing only the khaki trousers. He was staring down at the check in his hand.

CHAPTER TEN

"YOU MUST HATE my guts." Trev looked stricken, a man who has just had his whole world collapse at his feet.

"I think I did," Reyna whispered bleakly. "For a while." She stood frozen in the doorway, unable to move, unable even to think clearly. The knowledge that she had destroyed everything with her rash action this morning was overwhelming.

He glanced down at the check in his hand and Reyna knew intuitively that he was searching for a way to handle the situation just as she had searched for one six months ago. If he chose the method she had chosen—that of cool withdrawal—they would lose everything again.

"I deserve it," he said quietly.

His words, his expression, perhaps the way she herself was reliving that morning six months ago from the opposite side of the fence—whatever it was—something finally broke through Reyna's paralysis. With a wrench, she tore free of the door and flung herself across the room.

"Trev, no! No! I came to take it back. I didn't realize…"

As she hurtled against him, Reyna grabbed at the

check in his hand, ripping it from his grasp and crumpling it in her fist.

His arms came around her automatically as he staggered backward a step under the impetus of her forceful rush.

"Didn't realize what, Reyna?" he rasped. But his arms had closed almost violently around her. She buried her face in his bare shoulder, holding him as tightly as he was holding her. "I didn't realize I wasn't the only one who knew about love," she managed in muffled tones. "I couldn't give you any credit for having learned to love because that would have meant…"

"Because that would have meant facing your true feelings for me again?" he suggested heavily. His head nestled alongside hers and his hands dug deeply.

"I'd buried them, Trev. I thought I'd dealt with them and gotten rid of them, but they were only buried. If you hadn't come back—" She broke off, unable to finish the sentence.

"If I hadn't come back, you would have soon forgotten all about me," he concluded roughly. "Don't you think I knew that? When I finally came to my senses, I was terrified it was already too late, that six months was quite long enough for your love to die. I kept countering that fear with the memory of how gentle and giving your love had been. I told myself a love like that couldn't be eclipsed in six months."

Reyna lifted her head slightly to meet the naked expression in his eyes. "When did you realize you loved me, Trev?"

He shook his head once in a dazed fashion. "I'm

not sure. As time went by I only knew I had to get you back. Life was becoming intolerable without you and things were getting worse, not better. When I finally realized that my only hope was to find you and convince you to come back to me, I didn't try to analyze my own feelings. I knew I needed you and that this time around I would have the sense to take care of your love. But I didn't think about the fact that I had fallen in love for the first time in my life until you began accusing me of not being able to love."

"I was protecting myself by saying that," she mused, her eyes turning very green. "I didn't want to admit you might know how to love because then I would have had to accept the fact that you could feel the same things I'd felt six months ago."

"Including the pain?" he murmured perceptively.

"Yes."

"It was easier on you to think I couldn't experience any deep emotions?" he hazarded.

"I told myself only your pride was at stake. And maybe a few twinges of your conscience."

He closed his eyes briefly. "That's why you left the check this morning? So that I wouldn't have the satisfaction of pacifying my conscience?"

"Yes. Oh, Trev, I was so angry this morning. It was out of all proportion. I couldn't think straight. By the time dawn came I wanted to lash out at you in the only way I could, by making your no-strings-attached gift into a business arrangement. If nothing else, I thought I could deny you your conscience appeaser. But you didn't arrange the loan for that purpose, did you?"

"No," he whispered. "I did it because it was the only thing you seemed to want that I could give you. God knows, it was little enough. I love you, Reyna. I honestly don't know when I fully realized it—perhaps that day you took me bird-watching...."

"That's when I first began to worry that what you were feeling toward me might involve more than your pride or your conscience or merely old-fashioned desire." She smiled wonderingly. "The Trev Langdon I knew would always be able to exert his own willpower under even the most tempting circumstances. And you barely put up a fight!"

"I had decided I wasn't about to let you use me again. That shook me, sweetheart, that night I carried you off the beach and back to your bed. When you calmly told me you didn't see why we couldn't have another affair, I was stunned."

He tugged her close again, his lips in her hair. His hands moved tremulously on her as if he still couldn't quite believe he held her.

"I was prepared to admit that we still shared a physical attraction," Reyna said. "I wasn't at all prepared to admit it could be anything more than that."

"Because you were afraid of being hurt again?"

"Maybe. To tell you the truth, I didn't want to analyze the situation too deeply. In any event, I soon realized that sex with you was still too dangerous to handle."

"So you tried sending me away the other night."

"And you went, which surprised the hell out of me when I thought about it later," Reyna concluded on the first thin note of humor. "Six months ago you wouldn't have halted a seduction attempt that showed every sign of being ultimately successful."

He shuddered. "Don't remind me."

"You could have pushed past my defenses that night, Trev."

He was still for an instant and Reyna wondered if he would attempt to deny it for her pride's sake. But honesty won out. "Perhaps. But I didn't want to give you another reason to hate me. And you'd already taught me the hard way that forcing sex on you wasn't the answer."

"You've changed since you arrived on Maui, Trev."

"I'm aware of that," he retorted a little dryly. His hands slid up to her shoulders and he held her a small distance away, scanning her face. "You took a certain malicious pleasure in trying to force me to adapt to island life, didn't you?"

"Guilty as charged," she admitted with a tiny grin. "At first it was a way of showing you how different we are now, how impossible it would be for me to ever come back to you. But somewhere along the line you began to look right in my island sun. Were you really going to go back to Seattle today?"

He hesitated.

"Trev?" she prodded curiously.

"I told myself yesterday that I would risk everything on an all-or-nothing play. If I could get you to come willingly to my bed once more and while you were there give you the one thing you seemed to want..."

"You thought it might break down the barriers?"

"I hoped it would," he sighed. "But if that didn't work, I was prepared to go on trying. I couldn't let you go again, Reyna. I couldn't bring myself to give up completely. You had loved me once and I had to believe I could make you love me again. But I also knew you must be harboring a fairly deep anger...."

She looked up at him curiously. "You said that first night that you knew I must be bitter. I didn't even realize it myself."

"I thought you must have had some genuine rage buried somewhere because all of your passions seemed to run deep. I had learned that much after I started analyzing what we'd had between us in Seattle. Any woman who would have walked away from everything she'd built for the sake of love knew a thing or two about passion! It stood to reason you'd experience the opposite emotions just as strongly. And I also knew how I would have felt under the circumstances," he added with a rueful movement of his head.

"Last night you pushed me into a corner when you tried to hand me that bank loan without any demands attached. All I could think of was the way I'd felt when I agreed not to take over your brother-in-law's firm. I knew my actions had been prompted by love and I was terrified of having to admit yours might have been prompted by the same. It uncorked something inside me, something I didn't want to face."

"So you told yourself it was a conscience gift, and that gave you the opening you needed to vent your anger?"

"Are all financiers such excellent amateur psychologists?" she teased shakily.

"The successful ones are," he joked tenderly. "It's a job requirement. But no amount of grounding in psychoanalysis could have prepared me for what you were offering six months ago. I was a fool not to recognize love when it was handed to me on a silver platter. My only excuse is that I'd never encountered anything quite like it before. I kept trying to equate it with physical attraction, with gamesmanship, with *business*. I don't suppose I fully understood it, even though I knew I wanted it, until I was trying to hand it back on that same silver platter."

"Yes," she whispered knowingly. "That's when you realize what you've got. When you're trying to give it."

His fingers worked at the nape of her neck as he studied her face with a familiar intentness. "Is all the anger gone, sweetheart? What happened to you this morning?"

"I wrote out that check and then I went down to the beach and admitted to myself just how much I hated you for what you'd done to me six months ago," she said starkly.

The pain came and hovered in his eyes, but he didn't release his gentle grip on her neck. "And then?"

"And then I cried." She touched his jaw with a sensitive fingertip. "I'd forgotten to do that six months ago, you see. There wasn't time then. Perhaps if I had, I would have worked the emotions out of my system for good. As it was…"

"They were buried," he finished for her.

"I think the love I felt would always have stayed buried. I'm not sure I could ever have worked that out of my system! Oh, Trev, it was after the tears came that I realized you might be feeling the same as I had felt six months ago. And if you did, I couldn't bear the thought of hurting you and myself both for the sake of revenge. I came running back here to destroy the check but it was too late—you'd already seen it."

"Seen it and understood it," he whispered reassuringly, folding her tightly to him. "I knew I deserved it."

"No…!"

"Yes," he contradicted on an uneven attempt at laughter. "Are you going to argue with an amateur psychologist? Honey, we could spend the rest of our lives rehashing how close we came to disaster. I think there are better ways of spending the time."

"Such as?"

"Such as furthering my adaptation to island life," he retorted blandly.

"What?" She had been prepared for a not-so-subtle comment about making love. His response confused her. "What do you mean, Trev?"

"I mean I like seeing you here in the sun. Furthermore, I like being here myself, much to my surprise. I've been seduced by you and by the islands. I'm going to stay."

She stared at him, astounded. "Are you out of your mind? You've got a business to run back in Seattle. The city is your natural element!"

"Not any longer. I can run a branch of Langdon & Associates here in the islands. Having the office in Seattle will give us an excuse to return to the mainland once in a while and put on business suits. What do you say, honey? Will you marry me and take me birding and body surfing and feed me papayas in the mornings?"

"Oh, yes, Trev. Oh, yes!" She tightened her arms around his neck and leaned into him for his kiss, her happiness a tangible force surrounding both of them. "And you don't have to think you're giving up everything you like about city life. That's the beauty of Hawaii. There's a way to have it all here."

"As long as I've got you, I've got it all," he said huskily.

"Wait and see," she promised, smiling.

ONE MONTH LATER Reyna parked her small compact beside Trev's BMW in the driveway of their Oahu Island home. Thick, lush tropical plants and flowers swarmed around the gracious beach home and a row of palms lined the edge of the beach beyond. The location was only a few miles outside the bustling city of Honolulu, but it might as well have been over in Maui, so serene and relaxed was the setting.

Reyna hurried toward the door, her fingers already undoing the buttons of the Paisley silk blouse she was wearing under a white tropical-weight blazer.

Her business heels clicked on the step and before she reached the door, it opened.

"It's about time you got home," Trev accused with good-natured impatience as he took in the sight of his wife trying to get out of her business clothes before she'd even gotten inside the house. He held out one of two rum punches he was holding in his hands, bending down obligingly for her hasty kiss.

Reyna grinned at the sight of him in his thongs, short-sleeved, open-necked shirt and casual slacks. Trev's hair had grown a bit longer and, while still neat, had a decidedly less-styled look these days. His tan had deepened, and the happiness in his eyes was a pleasant change from the cool calculation which had been a part of him back in Seattle.

"Not all of us get to set our own hours and take off early on Friday," she taunted, slipping by him to move on into the bedroom.

"How did things go?" he demanded, following her to lounge in the doorway as she changed into a pair of sandals and a flowered muumuu. He sipped at his punch and watched appreciatively.

"The location is perfect," Reyna enthused, taking down her hair and running a brush through it. "I've combed every street in Honolulu with that real estate broker, but I finally found the spot this afternoon. It's near the Waikiki beach area. Should be a good tourist location. I'll take you to see it tomorrow if you like." She set down the hairbrush and picked up her glass, turning to smile at her husband. "And

I have it on the best authority that I won't be having any trouble getting a loan."

Trev sauntered forward, his sexy grin sending a familiar thrill along Reyna's nerve endings. "Just remember that loan guarantors in my position expect to be repaid."

"You should have thought of that before you arranged everything so nicely for me," she teased. "Haven't you ever heard the old advice about not making loans to family and friends?"

"I'll find a way to recover any losses I may suffer," he promised, coming to a halt in front of her. The golden eyes gleamed with love and laughter.

Reyna slipped into his arms, her drink still in her hand as she wound her arms around his neck. Tipping back her head, she drawled, "I hate to tell you this, dear Trev, but you just don't have that old, dangerous, intimidating look any longer. Oh, I'll admit you can still pass muster when you're back in a business suit and on your way into downtown Honolulu in the mornings, but as soon as you get home…"

"I've succumbed to the lure of sunlight and sandals," he sighed.

"That's all right," she assured him cheerfully. "It's probably one of the reasons people in Hawaii live longer than they do on the mainland."

"They do?"

"Uh-huh. Average life expectancy here is higher than in most other places in the nation." She chuckled.

"Just think—all those extra years we'll have together," he noted wonderingly.

"Worried about getting bored?"

He grinned devilishly. "Not at all. I'm thinking about how nice it will be to still be making love to you on the beach sometime well into the next century."

"And think of all the birds we'll be able to watch together!" she tacked on ingenuously.

"How could I forget," he grated, his voice deepening as the familiar fire began to flicker in the depths of his eyes. "You know, I've been greatly attracted to bird-watching ever since you first introduced me to the hobby...."

Reyna vibrated to the sensual note in his words and arched against him. The laughter died out of her eyes, to be replaced by the unmasked longing and love which always hovered near the surface.

"My sweet, loving Reyna," he whispered, reaching up to remove the imperiled glass in her hand. He set her drink down beside his own on the dresser and slowly drew his hands down the length of her sides to her hips. His thumbs trailed teasingly across the tips of her unconfined breasts in the process and his gaze darkened. Beneath the flowered cotton, her nipples thrust with tingling urgency.

"I should go start dinner," she offered softly.

"We'll be eating a little late tonight." He massaged the base of her spine with slow, erotic little movements.

"Will we?"

"Ummm. There's something else I need more at the moment."

"But I'm hungry," she taunted throatily.

"I'll take your mind off food." He swooped, catching her up and tossing her lightly onto the huge bamboo bed they had moved over from her Maui apartment.

"I thought you didn't like having me think you were good in bed," she protested on a note of smothered laughter as he came down beside her.

"I just never wanted my excellent seduction techniques to be the only thing you admired," he explained, nuzzling hungrily at her throat while he stroked exploring fingers along her leg.

"You wanted me to love you for your brain?"

"I wanted you to love me. Period."

"I do, Trev," she vowed gently, the teasing light fading as she reached for him. "I'll always love you."

"You're the most important thing in my life, Reyna Langdon," he gritted as he put his mouth close to hers. "I was a little slow in realizing it, but once I've learned a lesson, I never forget it. I love you."

She parted her lips for the reverent, tender kiss. Trev Langdon had never lied to her.

The reverence in him quickly slipped over the boundary into the realm of passion as the kiss deepened and Reyna responded as she always did to the man she loved.

"If I'm good in bed," he grated roughly, his fingers at work edging the muumuu up over her head, "it's because you give me so damn much encouragement!"

"Is that a way of saying I'm good in bed, too?" she taunted, freed of her clothing. Her own fingers were fumbling with the few fastened buttons of his shirt.

"You're perfect," he groaned. His fingers closed excitingly over her naked hip as she undid the buckle of his belt. "I love you so much, sweetheart!"

She trembled as she knelt beside him, tugging off the remainder of his clothing. Her tawny hair danced invitingly around her shoulders, drawing the sunlight through the windows, and the firm, feminine lines of her face glowed with her emotion.

Trev lay back, letting her undress him, letting his hungry passion grow into an undeniable force. When she had finished, he startled her by sliding abruptly to the edge of the bed and getting to his feet.

"What's wrong?" Reyna knelt, staring up at him questioningly.

"Nothing at all," he murmured, bending over to sweep her into his arms.

"Where are we going, Trev?" She inhaled the scent of his bare skin, toying with the tip of his ear as he strode from the room with her in his arms.

"We're going to go play on the beach."

Down through the flowering garden and out onto the secluded beach he carried her. Reyna closed her eyes blissfully as he waded into the sea. A moment later he stood waist deep, letting her float in the warm water balanced on his outstretched hands.

Eyes still closed, Reyna smiled, luxuriating in the sensual warmth of the moment. When she finally raised her lashes, it was to find him regarding her through passion-narrowed eyes. In silence they watched each other, and then Reyna lifted a hand to push lightly against his chest.

He went backward in the water, pulling her on top of him. "When I think of what I've been missing all these years in Seattle," he muttered, using his hands to keep them both afloat. His mouth quirked upward as she lay along his chest, arms clasped behind his neck. "God! I feel fantastic!"

"So do I," she whispered, delighting in his exuberance. It was contagious. With a soft laugh, she entangled her legs with his, pushing him playfully beneath the surface.

He went with a quick gasp for air, pulling her with him and spinning her around so that she was underneath his descending body. Caught in her own trap, Reyna surrendered obligingly and went limp. In another instant she was swept to the surface by her laughing lover.

"Provoking wench," he growled, hauling her up beside him. Before she could make her retort, he was kissing her wetly, his hardening body thrusting against her with sudden fire.

Reyna knew the time for playfulness had just passed. She felt the urgency in him and her own desire rapidly unfurled throughout her body. The water surged around them as they lost themselves in each other's mouths, drinking deeply of the excitement they had always found in each other.

The taut peaks of her breasts pressed against his damp chest, and she moved slightly, teasing both of them. She heard his indrawn breath and felt the aggressive maleness in him, knew the force of his tensed thighs and bold virility. His hands slid slickly down her back, curving under her bottom and lifting her up into his lips.

"Oh!"

Her small cry was muffled as her head fell back and her lower body was arched arousingly against him. He bent his head and kissed each nipple, stabbing gently at the peaks with the tip of his tongue.

"Love me, my island woman," he commanded with heavy passion. "Love me for always."

"For always," she agreed, lacing her fingers behind his head and finding his mouth with hers.

He carried her back out of the sea to the water's edge and settled her lightly onto the wet sand. The waves lapped at her legs.

"Trev," she managed, feeling the hard graininess beneath her skin. "The sand…"

"Damn the sand," he muttered, stopping her mouth again with his own. He sprawled along her length, fitting himself to her body with a hunger which thrilled and captivated her senses.

Reyna forgot about the sand, forgot about the delayed dinner, forgot about the past. Only her present and her future with Trev seemed to have any real importance here on the beach under the setting Hawaiian sun.

Their lovemaking carried them out beyond the edge of the horizon, into the special world they created together. Bodies meshed in beautiful rhythm, they sought to give and receive pleasure, satisfaction and love.

Trev moved on Reyna with erotic power and she

responded in kind. Her small moans were a nectar he strove to draw forth again and again. In turn she gloried in his inarticulate words of love and desire.

As he slid his hands beneath her, bringing her hips even more tightly against his, she rubbed the soft skin of her legs along the outside of his calves. Simultaneously her nails dug of their own accord into the contoured muscles of his back, and his body surged violently against her.

Reyna shouted her satisfaction into his shoulder, her teeth bared in unconscious savagery.

He grunted huskily as he felt the stinging nip and then his own body tautened in mindless release. She clung to him wildly as the unwinding force of his passion flattened her deeply into the sand. United by a bond which would stretch between them all the years of their lives, they lay sprawled in a tangle of arms and legs, returning to the reality around them.

When Reyna raised her lashes, she found him studying the tip of her nose. As he bent to kiss it, she smiled up at him in languid amusement.

"About the sand problem…" she began delicately.

"What problem?"

"Well, for you, it probably isn't one," she allowed thoughtfully. "You're on top of me."

"A pleasant position."

"I am on top of the sand," she elaborated as if he weren't very bright.

"Are you trying to tell me something?" he asked helpfully.

"I'm trying to tell you my backside is going to be a little raw."

"One of the hazards of enjoying nature to the fullest extent, I suppose," he noted amiably.

"It's okay for you to wax philosophical," she complained. "You're using me for a cushion!"

"I thought you liked the idea of simplifying your life, getting away from all the needless trappings of civilization.... Hey!"

His yelp came as Reyna exerted her strength unexpectedly, urging him into a roll that carried him onto his back. In another moment she was lying comfortably on top.

"You were saying?" she prompted, resting her chin on her hands, which were folded on his chest. She fixed him with a bright, attentive gaze.

"You may have had a point about the sand," he murmured consideringly.

"It's okay in the throes of passion," she told him chattily. "A little extra tactile stimulation, as it were."

"I'll keep it in mind," he agreed, sitting up abruptly. Reyna tumbled laughingly off his lap as he got to his feet and reached down to pull her up beside him.

"That's all the appetizer you get, woman. Time for dinner."

"You're all sandy," she pointed out, grinning up at him.

"So are you." He took her hand and they started back toward the house.

She looked thoughtfully at the naked, sand-covered length of his body and chuckled. "There was a time, Trev Langdon, when you would have been appalled to find yourself in your present condition."

He turned to look at her, the love brimming in his amber eyes. "The man you married isn't the same man you met in Seattle, Reyna my love."

"Yes, he is," she whispered softly. "But lately he has revealed a few new aspects of his nature."

Trev tugged her closer, wrapping her nude body against his own and leaning down to drop a kiss into her tangled, sea-wet hair. "Aspects he didn't even know he had until you came into his life and turned it upside down."

She hesitated, looking up at him with a tinge of anxiety. "Trev, if you ever change your mind and decide you don't want to live in Hawaii, it would be all right with me, I mean," she added in a small rush, "I'd...I'd follow you anywhere."

"How dramatic and wifely," he chuckled. "But it's too late. I've already followed you, remember? Come on, sweetheart, let's eat."

* * * * *

A no-nonsense female cop reluctantly teams up with the one man who makes her lose control in a deliciously sensual new novel from *New York Times* bestselling author

LORI FOSTER

To bring down a sleazy abduction ring, Lieutenant Margaret "Margo" Peterson has set herself up as bait. But recruiting Dashiel Riske as her unofficial partner is a whole other kind of danger. Dash is 6'4" of laid-back masculine charm, a man who loves life—and women—to the limit. Until Margo is threatened, and he reveals a dark side that may just match her own….

Beneath Margo's tough facade is a slow-burning sexiness that drives Dash crazy. The only way to finish this case is to work together side by side…skin to skin. And as their mission takes a lethal turn, he'll have to prove he's all the man she needs—in all the ways that matter….

Be sure to connect with us at:

Harlequin.com/Newsletters
Facebook.com/HarlequinBooks
Twitter.com/HarlequinBooks

www.Harlequin.com

PHLF857

Two classic stories from the *New York Times* bestselling queen of romantic suspense

LISA JACKSON

Yesterday's Lies

It's been five years since Trask McFadden betrayed Tory's trust, landing her father behind bars. She'd hoped Trask was out of her life forever, but now he's returned to the Lazy W Ranch, claiming to have discovered a clue that might prove her father's innocence. For the sake of her family, Tory's trying to forgive, but she's finding it much harder to forget when Trask's presence begins to stir up feelings she'd thought were long gone....

Devil's Gambit

Tiffany Rhodes's horse farm was in trouble long before she met Zane Sheridan, a breeder with a shady reputation. Yet she can't help but feel relieved when Zane offers to buy her out. Though Tiffany doesn't trust him, she's drawn to him like a magnet. What does this mysterious man want from her...and can she contain her desire long enough to find out?

Available wherever books are sold!

Be sure to connect with us at:

Harlequin.com/Newsletters
Facebook.com/HarlequinBooks
Twitter.com/HarlequinBooks

HARLEQUIN® HQN™
™ www.Harlequin.com

Desire and loyalty collide in the riveting conclusion to *USA TODAY* bestselling author

KASEY MICHAELS's

series about the Redgraves—four siblings united by their legacy of scandal and seduction...

Punished for his father's crimes and scorned by society, fearless soldier Maximillien Redgrave fights to protect England. But his quest to restore his family's reputation is his own private battle. Trusting the irresistible young Zoe Charbonneau, whose betrayal destroyed his closest comrades and nearly unraveled his covert mission, is a mistake he intends never to repeat. So when the discovery of a smuggling ring compels him to embark on a voyage straight into danger, he's prepared for anything—except to find Zoe on his ship.

Believed to be a double agent for England and France, Zoe must clear her name in order to save her life. Convincing Max of her innocence seems impossible, until inescapable desire tempts them both to trust—and love—again. But a circle of enemies is closing in, and their time together might run out before they outrun danger....

Available wherever books are sold!

Be sure to connect with us at:

Harlequin.com/Newsletters

Facebook.com/HarlequinBooks

Twitter.com/HarlequinBooks

HARLEQUIN® HQN™

™ www.Harlequin.com

REQUEST YOUR FREE BOOKS!

2 FREE NOVELS
FROM THE ROMANCE COLLECTION
PLUS 2 FREE GIFTS!

YES! Please send me 2 FREE novels from the Romance Collection and my 2 FREE gifts (gifts are worth about $10). After receiving them, if I don't wish to receive any more books, I can return the shipping statement marked "cancel." If I don't cancel, I will receive 4 brand-new novels every month and be billed just $6.24 per book in the U.S. or $6.74 per book in Canada. That's a savings of at least 22% off the cover price. It's quite a bargain! Shipping and handling is just 50¢ per book in the U.S. and 75¢ per book in Canada.* I understand that accepting the 2 free books and gifts places me under no obligation to buy anything. I can always return a shipment and cancel at any time. Even if I never buy another book, the two free books and gifts are mine to keep forever.

194/394 MDN F4XY

Name	(PLEASE PRINT)	
Address		Apt. #
City	State/Prov.	Zip/Postal Code

Signature (if under 18, a parent or guardian must sign)

Mail to the **Harlequin®** Reader Service:
IN U.S.A.: P.O. Box 1867, Buffalo, NY 14240-1867
IN CANADA: P.O. Box 609, Fort Erie, Ontario L2A 5X3

Want to try two free books from another line?
Call 1-800-873-8635 or visit www.ReaderService.com.

* Terms and prices subject to change without notice. Prices do not include applicable taxes. Sales tax applicable in N.Y. Canadian residents will be charged applicable taxes. Offer not valid in Quebec. This offer is limited to one order per household. Not valid for current subscribers to the Romance Collection or the Romance/Suspense Collection. All orders subject to credit approval. Credit or debit balances in a customer's account(s) may be offset by any other outstanding balance owed by or to the customer. Please allow 4 to 6 weeks for delivery. Offer available while quantities last.

Your Privacy—The Harlequin® Reader Service is committed to protecting your privacy. Our Privacy Policy is available online at www.ReaderService.com or upon request from the Harlequin Reader Service.

We make a portion of our mailing list available to reputable third parties that offer products we believe may interest you. If you prefer that we not exchange your name with third parties, or if you wish to clarify or modify your communication preferences, please visit us at www.ReaderService.com/consumerschoice or write to us at Harlequin Reader Service Preference Service, P.O. Box 9062, Buffalo, NY 14269. Include your complete name and address.

From #1 *New York Times* bestselling author

NORA ROBERTS

come two classics about not letting your best-laid plans get in the way of life *or* love.

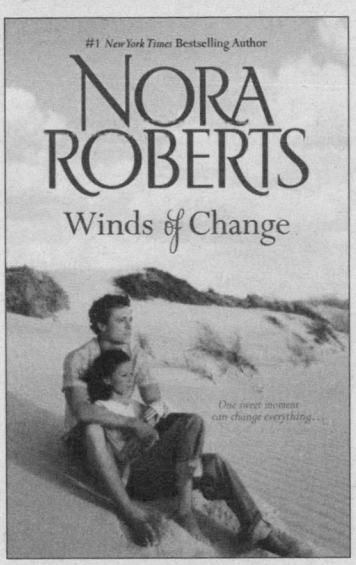

One sweet moment can change everything…

Be sure to connect with us at:

Harlequin.com/Newsletters

Facebook.com/HarlequinBooks

Twitter.com/HarlequinBooks

CINDY DEES

ON THE RUN AND UNDER FIRE...

Providing medical relief in a war-torn region helps Alex Peters forget his past and focus on the job—delivering babies. Less easy to overlook is his blonde comrade-in-arms, who knows nothing of the trouble he's running from. Katie McCloud makes the assignment bearable, although her perky innocence proves to be an arousing distraction. Then, as combat explodes around them, their only option is flight.

A kindergarten teacher seeking adventure, Katie hoped this humanitarian mission—and the mysterious, sexy doctor sharing it—would push her out of her comfort zone. With Alex, she starts taking tantalizing risks and becoming the survivor she knew she could be.

But back on U.S. soil, Alex and Katie face a new threat, and this time they're the target. Forced into close confines, neither can believe the other isn't the intended mark. With only each other to depend on—and suspect—Alex and Katie can't avoid the simmering attraction between them. But to stay alive, they'll have to trust more deeply than ever before....

Available wherever books are sold!

Be sure to connect with us at:

Harlequin.com/Newsletters
Facebook.com/HarlequinBooks
Twitter.com/HarlequinBooks